Twin River

Twin River

MICHAEL FIELDS

iUniverse, Inc.
Bloomington

TWIN RIVER

iUniverse books may be ordered through booksellers or by contacting:

iUniverse
1663 Liberty Drive
Bloomington, IN 47403
www.iuniverse.com
1-800-Authors (1-800-288-4677)

ISBN: 978-1-4759-8844-4 (sc)
ISBN: 978-1-4759-8846-8 (hc)
ISBN: 978-1-4759-8845-1 (e)

Library of Congress Control Number: 2013907654

Printed in the United States of America.

iUniverse rev. date: 5/10/2013

To Cliff
1933–2011

On every fishing trip, your lively banter was more entertaining than any hooked fish. On those many nights when nothing was biting, your conversation and good humor were priceless.

Chapter One

SHADOWS OF DEATH

1778

Two hundred miles west of Philadelphia, the town of Water Street on the Juniata River consisted of the three-story Water Street Inn and a single row of weathered log cabins. Standing on the steps of the most dilapidated cabin, Jacob Hare wore a luxurious fur coat over a silk-embroidered shirt. His face was smooth and thin, his blond hair long, reaching his shoulders. Large earlobes protruded from the carefully brushed flow of hair. His narrow eyes squinting, Jacob watched a rider race his horse down Pike Road. The rider, short and chunky in the saddle, was tightly clothed. Recognizing Jacob, he waved and guided the horse to the cabin steps. After shaking hands with Jacob, the rider took an envelope from the inside pocket of his leather coat.

"Your father sends his regards."

"Come inside," Jacob said, taking the letter. "You should rest before you start back."

"There's no time for talk, Jacob. There's rebellion up and down the river."

"Rumor has it that the British have marched into Philadelphia."

"George Washington's Patriot army of farmers is no match

against the best-trained soldiers in Europe. The British captured Philadelphia with no resistance."

"And my parents?"

"They prosper. Your father is a shrewd businessman and has always shown loyalty to the Crown. They worry about you alone in the wilderness."

"Assure them there is no need to worry. My future lies with our true king. Once the rebellion is crushed and the settlers are run out of this area, I'll purchase land at a cheap price and build a grand estate on the river. I'll import quality quarter horses from Virginia. On May Day we'll race down Penn Street in Stone Town. My parents will have a fine time when they visit."

"I'll inform them of your plans. I'm sure they'll be delighted." The messenger saluted, turned his horse east, and galloped down the pike. With the envelope clutched tightly in his hand, Jacob watched the rider disappear. Then he entered the cabin and sat at the table. Staring at the ornate style of writing on the envelope, Jacob laughed.

"You don't find such quality penmanship out here," he commented, carefully opening the envelope. The parchment inside was thin, the words transcribed in a flowery script.

Jacob was raising the letter to the light when the door slammed open and five men burst into the cabin. Two of the men grabbed Jacob and pinned him against the table. The leader of the group, Captain Simonton, was a tall man with a chiseled face. He had a muscular chest, wide shoulders, and large calloused hands. The captain ripped the letter from Jacob's hand and proceeded to read in a loud, overbearing voice.

Dear Beloved Son, Jacob,

On September 26th, your mother and I and prominent Tory merchants welcomed the British to our fair city. We were granted an audience with General Howe at Masters-Penn House on Market Street. When the general requested assistance in lodging, we agreed to board three of his officers. You will be pleased to know that the officers, all gentlemen, will bed in your room. General Howe guaranteed that the so-called Patriot army, now setting up camp in the wilderness at Valley Forge, would be defeated and the rebellion would be crushed soon. Once order is restored, all Tories and King's Men would be rewarded for their loyalty.

"You traitor!" Simonton shouted, throwing the letter on the table. He pulled out a razor and pointed at the exposed earlobe. "Let's mark the Tory!" And then he added with contempt, "This loyal subject of King George."

"I got it!" Leaping into position, a young, muscular man wearing dirt-spattered farm clothes grabbed Jacob's right ear at the fleshy apex and stretched the skin taut. Simonton steadied the razor, and with a swift motion, he sliced off the ear.

Jacob screamed in a shrill voice; blood spurted vertically toward the young farmer, who lurched clumsily out of range, dark circles spattering his shoes. An elderly, stout man dressed in a gray shirt and tight vest stepped forward. He had a light complexion, bright eyes, and thin lips. He spoke in a smug, authoritative tone.

"Went in at the one ear and out at the other. *Proverbs*," Reverend Dean annunciated in a loud manner. "While we're at it, let's rid the Tory of his remaining protuberance."

"What?"

"Just grab the other ear!"

"I got it," the young farmer said again. Annoyed, scraping at the blood on his shoe, he cleared away the strands of blond hair. Captain Simonton paused for a moment. Then he lowered the razor flat against Jacob's skull and sliced off the left ear. Blood streaming onto his silk collar, Jacob collapsed to the floor. Laughing, Captain Simonton placed both earlobes neatly in the center of the letter. Red smears soaked into the parchment, blurring the fine print.

"We Patriots ain't hung yet," Captain Simonton said, leaning close to Jacob's head. "Can you hear that clear enough now that we've unclogged them Tory ears?" His face white, Jacob pressed his fists into the stubby holes, stemming the flow of blood.

Two weeks after the incident at Water Street, Jacob Hare paddled a canoe down the Juniata River. The setting sun reflected in a glow over the water. Thin lines of smoke curled high into the air from the cabins on the bank. Looking past the smoke, Jacob saw Fort Standing Stone and angled the canoe toward the bank. After pulling the canoe onto the grass, he tucked his shoulder-length hair under his coonskin cap and walked up the bank to Stone Town. Muskets slung over their shoulders, two Rangers from the fort were walking down deeply gutted Penn Street.

You don't know nothin' about King George and the great court, Jacob thought, cursing silently. *And yet you want to be free. You and your kind will never be free!*

A horse and rider moved slowly past the Rangers. The horse was a sure-footed Narragansett Pacer; the leather saddle was polished smooth. The rider, a wealthy landowner with relatives in London, was middle-aged; his chubby face was full and cleanly shaven. John Weston dismounted, tied his horse, and motioned to Jacob. After a brief exchange, he and Jacob went inside the Stone Pub. Talking in gruff voices, farmers, woodsmen, and Rangers filled the wooden tables. Aged and bearded, the town tanner sat at a prominent position at the end of the center table. He coughed and raised his voice, silencing the chatter.

"Captain Jack came in the fort this morning all cut up. Four Indians jumped him at the Narrows. Jack killed all of them."

"It'll take more than four savages to put Jack in the ground," a Ranger commented. "Livin' in the wild so long, Captain Jack thinks like an Indian. After he lost his family to them, he started practicin' their ways. Ain't that why he's kinda crazy?"

"Yeah," the tanner confirmed. "When the captain returned home from huntin' last year, he found his wife and two children butchered. He's been killin' Indians ever since."

"Even the good Indians?" a farmer asked.

"Good or bad, it don't matter," the tanner said with conviction, staring at the blank expressions around the table. "I mean, it's like killin' them rattlesnakes when you clear rocks off the land. It's a good snake because it can't strike at you anymore. That's my reasonin'. Rattlesnakes and Indians—they're all good when they're dead." The men at the table roared with laughter. John Weston stepped back and whispered to Jacob.

"The Indians won't stop hunting Captain Jack. He'll be caught and scalped soon enough." Dropping some coins on the bar, John grabbed a bottle of whiskey and led Jacob through a blanketed door into a dark room. Two men, empty glasses in front of them, sat on benches around a table that tottered on the floor.

"Nathaniel." Weston nodded to a wiry man with a narrow face and protruding nose. "And my good friend Joseph," he said to a bearded, stocky man. After filling the empty glasses, Weston raised his over the table.

"To King George!" Weston said resolutely, his fleshy jowls lifting and falling flat against his neck. The Tories drank the toast with enthusiasm.

"Who you got with you?" Joseph asked, placing his empty glass on the table. "Who's this blond-haired gent?"

"Jacob Hare," John Weston answered. "He's one of us."

"You the one from Water Street?" Joseph asked. "You're the one they cut, ain't ya?"

"Yeah," Jacob muttered. He removed his coonskin cap and placed it on the table. Using both hands, he lifted the blond strands of hair out of the way.

"I'll be damned!" Joseph gasped. "It's true what they did."

"Let me see that," Nathaniel demanded. Moving closer, scrutinizing the scarred cavity, he had a puzzled, jocose expression on his face. "It's not as bad as I first thought."

"What are you talking about?" Jacob asked, replacing the coonskin cap.

"I bet you hear lots better now," Nathaniel declared in a laughing voice.

"Shut the hell up," John Weston said. Nathaniel's face reddened.

"Holy shee … it!" Nathaniel slurred, dropping his jaw. "I didn't mean nothin'. I've seen men scalped and gutted. But I've never seen anything like you got. How'd it happen?"

"A bunch of settlers ambushed me in my cabin. They said I was a Tory bastard and held me down. One pulled out a razor and sliced off my ears. It was that damn Captain Simonton and Reverend Dean. I plan to take care of them tomorrow."

"By yourself?"

"I hired me some Shawnee."

"Nathaniel and I will join ya'," Joseph said. "Dean has a big family. He's got a pretty daughter and those twin boys. It will be our pleasure watchin' 'em die."

"We can sleep at my place in Water Street tonight," Jacob said. "Then in the morning, we'll march to Hartslog and kill us some Patriots."

"I'll toast to that!" Joseph responded enthusiastically. Raising his glass, he laughed and pounded the wood with his fist, the table rattling with the impact.

That evening the members of the Dean family ate a dinner of turkey, corn, and potatoes. Reverend Dean and his wife, Mary, were drinking tea at the table when their daughter, Sally, began clearing the plates. Dean had fresh powder on his face and hair. Spending more time than usual in the washroom, he had vigorously rubbed powder into the dark spots on his vest.

Dressed in a white cap, a blue short gown with lace ruffles on the sleeves, and a dark blue petticoat, the reverend's wife had a cheerful, kind face. Her brown hair curling to her shoulders, Sally had her mother's soft facial features. Slender in build, she wore a yellow short gown over a white petticoat. After taking the last dishes to the water basin, Sally joined her parents at the table

The eighteen-year-old Dean twins, Will and Ben, sat on the porch steps. At five-foot-ten inches tall, they had identical lithe, muscular bodies. Will's black hair was cut short; Ben's was long, dropping low over his forehead. They had bright blue eyes and clear skin, tanned bronze by the sun. A scattering of crows dipped in and out of the cornfield in front of them. Will nudged his brother, who didn't react, a pensive expression on his face.

"You were late for dinner, Ben."

"I was busy nuturin' my relationship with Sarah."

"Why don't you just say courtin'? You're like Dad—always throwin' big words at people."

"Sarah treasures big words. And usin' them wisely but judiciously, I slid so close to her today that our bodies were touchin' before she knew it."

"Then you finally got to kiss her?"

"No," Ben said despairingly. "I put my hand on her knee and began leanin' toward her face, but she jumped out of reach. I'm gonna try again tomorrow. We're plannin' a picnic at the big pool where the Little Juniata and Juniata Rivers come together. Right where they're buildin' the new schoolhouse. They've got a wall up and part of the bell tower. Since Henry Dobb was donatin' the wood, he said it should be called Dobbs School."

"That's a foolish name. The Indians burned down Fort Dobbs. They should name it Twin River Schoolhouse because of the two rivers meetin' there." Then Will asked, a smile on his face, "What'd Mama say about you and Sarah picnickin' alone at the river?"

"She wasn't pleased by the news. She talked about the need for chaperones, so she and Sally are comin' to spy on us. Mama said that Captain Simonton and his son, Matthew, will be here tomorrow to help Dad at the spring. They're bringin' Beatrice. I'm thinkin' you should invite Beatrice to the picnic."

"Early this year, Beatrice and I went pickin' berries right there at Twin River. We sat on the river bank to rest. I was talkin' and lookin' at her blue eyes and the pretty freckles on her cheeks. We were just expectin' to cool off, but things got real serious."

"What do you mean, Will?"

"It was so hot that day. Without thinkin', I stood and began to undress. Beatrice smiled and looked away. Then she got to her feet and began to undress, too. When she lifted the shift over her head and dropped it in the sand, I felt my eyes would pop out of my head. Her body was all smooth. Her breasts were full and a beautiful pink. Right then I swore that I loved her. As soon as she heard the words, she motioned to me. We came together on the riverbank. But it was mighty poor judgment. Beatrice told me something secret today. Beatrice told me she's expectin'."

"A bun in the oven!" Ben exclaimed. "That's great!"

"You talk crazy, Ben. How can Beatrice havin' a baby be great?"

"You can have a wife you love, not one of those arranged women. No one will think ill of you and Beatrice, Will. Half the girls married last year in Hartslog and Stone Town had a baby within months. You can bet there'll be a big celebration. We'll roast a pig. Everyone will come to the weddin'." Ben laughed and slapped Will on the shoulder. "At Twin River tomorrow, I'm startin' a family with Sarah just like you did with Beatrice."

"How you gonna do that? Mama and Sally will be spyin'."

"I'll take Sarah berry pickin'. I'll tell her I love her. It worked for you."

"I'm thinkin' it worked too fast." Will lowered his head and was silent. The moon cast a bright glow over the barn and the cabin. The low howl of a wolf sounded from the distant mountain. Will heard hooves; looking past the cornfield, he saw the dark silhouettes of horses on Pike Road.

"Out kind of late, aren't they?" Ben asked.

"Probably damn Tories. Dad says the Indians and Tories are up to no good."

"I can't worry about no Tories now. I'm plannin' big things at Twin River with Sarah. Let's go to bed so I can rest up." Ben pulled Will to his feet, and they entered the cabin. There was a candle burning above the fireplace. The twins climbed to the loft, undressed to their long shirts, and settled into bed. The candle flickered brightly and went out. Crickets chirped in the yard; an owl hooted from the barn rafters.

Within walking distance of the Dean farm, Water Street echoed with shouts and laughter. A boisterous Jacob Hare swung a jug of whiskey in the air when he ushered Joseph and Nathaniel up the warped wooden steps into the dark shadows of his log cabin.

At the first light of dawn, clad in a knee-length white linen shirt, Jacob Hare heard noise in the yard, crawled out of bed, and pulled on his stockings. He quickly got into his trousers and tucked in the long shirt. After putting on his waistcoat and shoes, he went outside. Standing in a circle, their faces intricately painted in dark red-and-black hues, eight Indians turned and stared belligerently at him. Three of the Indians held muskets; the other five had bows and arrows. The Indian in the center of the circle had a scar on his forehead and was missing an eye. A short, stocky Indian with a deformed hand, two middle fingers stitched together, a rope tied around his waist, stood next to him. Pulling on their clothes, Joseph and Nathaniel sauntered through the doorway.

"How long they been waitin'?" Joseph asked.

"I don't know," Jacob answered. Glancing nervously at the blackened eye socket, he walked down the steps into the circle. "Chief One-Eye, you're welcome here."

"You promised me scalps. You promised me captives I can trade in Canada." The Indian stepped menacingly close to Jacob. "You look at my eye! Because you like?"

"Yeah, I like." Jacob swept his hair back, exposing a scarred ear. "You like?"

His mouth dropped open; Chief One-Eye glared at the black hole. Then, a look of glee spreading over his face, he grabbed the wrist of the Indian standing at his side.

"You No-Ear, me One-Eye, and this Two-Finger!" The chief rotated the deformed hand, swinging the stitched fingers in a grotesque warrior salute. Jacob laughed and returned to Joseph and Nathaniel.

"They're a happy lot," Joseph said. "Who the hell is the chief?"

"He's no chief," Jacob said. "He's an outcast. In a battle against the Delaware, he hid under a tree. Watchin' the butchery, he began to think clever, so he made a cut across his eye. When the Shawnee chief arrived and saw the dead warriors and one wounded survivor, he knew. Snappin' off a branch, the chief ordered the Indian bound. Then he stuck the sharpened end of the branch in the chief's eye socket."

"He's an ugly bastard with that eye missin'," Nathaniel observed. He glanced at Jacob's maimed ear. "I reckon you and One-Eye will work well together."

"What are you tryin' to tell me, Nathaniel?"

"You're missin' ears; the chief's missin' an eye," Nathaniel said, a wide grin contorting his face. "The way I figure it, you can see for him and he can hear for you."

"You ignorant half-wit," Joseph said, knocking Nathaniel on the side of the head.

"Don't mind him, Jacob. He's one of those come out of Dumb-Fifty."

"What the hell is Dumb-Fifty?"

"That village of them inbreeds on the other side of Burnt Cabins. It was named that because all the residents are half-witted, and not one of them born there can count past fifty. They're mostly all dead now. I think Nathaniel's the only survivor."

"Holy shee … it!" Nathaniel slurred slowly. "I visited some relatives there once, but I ain't never lived in Dumb-Fifty. And they ain't all so dumb. My cousin Witty—that's his nickname—dug his pit toilet right next to his well so he could drink cold water while usin' it. He informed me no one else done it that way. So I had to see for myself. I grabbed the ladle, excused myself, and went to the pit. And, you know, it was refreshin' on both ends just like Witty said it would be." Confident, rubbing his long nose, Nathaniel smiled to everyone.

Shaking his head, Jacob went inside the cabin and came out with his musket and two jugs of whiskey. He gave one jug to Nathaniel and the other to Chief One-Eye. The chief took a long drink. Pushing closer, the Indians began arguing and fighting.

"If we don't get started, we'll lose half your army," Joseph commented.

Jacob nodded and shouted at the Indians. They ignored him and continued to pull at the jug. Firing his musket over their heads, Jacob walked away. The Shawnee grumbled and followed him. When he reached the river, Jacob pulled a canoe from the thick bushes and slid it into the water.

"Get in," Jacob ordered, motioning to Joseph.

"We're separatin'?"

"Yeah," Jacob said. "You take the canoe down to where the two rivers meet. Wait there. You'll be in position if the Deans try to escape to Fort Standing Stone."

"Good thinkin'," Joseph said. He positioned himself in the middle of the canoe. Grabbing one of the wooden paddles, a thin Indian squeezed in front of him. A second Indian pushed off and jumped in the back. The canoe wobbled slightly, straightened, and knifed smoothly through the water.

"Let's go tender our greetings to the Dean family." Jacob started up the trail. Reaching Pike Road, the sun hot on their faces, the band of Tories and Indians broke into a fast trot. The jug of whiskey swinging from his waist, Nathaniel fell behind.

After finishing her chores, Sally Dean returned to the cabin and noticed her brother staring at his image in the oval mirror. His knife was on the table next to her bottle of perfume. Moving closer, she inhaled the sweet scent.

"Ben!" she shouted, blistering his ear. "What are you doing, using my lavender?"

"I'm sorry, Sally. I just finished my chores in the barn, and I can't smell like those cows today. I need to be sweet for Sarah."

"Sarah don't think that way. She's been farming since she was a girl. You should wash that sweet smell off before she notices."

"Maybe some of it." Ben went to the basin, splashed water over his face, and sniffed the air. "That's better. I don't smell much like flowers anymore. I smell like a man."

"When will you ever be a man?" Sally asked.

"Today," Ben said, a big smile on his face. He pounded his chest with his fist, and his smile widened. "Today, for sure."

"Lavender don't make anyone a man. And you'd best be careful today, Ben. Mama and I will be stoppin' any nonsense between you and Sarah."

There was noise outside, and sliding the knife under his belt, Ben went to the door. Captain Simonton and his son, Matthew, muskets slung over their shoulders, were getting down from a wagon. Beatrice Simonton and Sarah Bebalt sat on the back bench. At five-feet-seven inches, Beatrice was slightly taller than Sarah. She wore a straw hat covered with lace. Red curls spun loosely from under the hat. Her face was oval-shaped, and her cheeks were dappled with freckles. Will rushed over, and being very gentle, he helped Beatrice down from the wagon.

Watching this, Ben jumped down the steps and offered his hand to Sarah. She wore a yellow short gown that had a pattern of roses on the front. She had brown eyes, short brown hair, and a bright smile on her face. When Sarah accepted Ben's hand, she blushed slightly. Stepping next to him, she leaned closer and took a deep breath.

"Do you smell all those flowers?"

"It's the wind," Ben said quickly. "It's blowin' from Mama's garden."

"I got the food ready," Mrs. Dean announced, appearing with Sally in the doorway. She carried a basket down the steps and gave it to Ben. "Knowing how much you twins eat, I put in enough venison for ten people. And Sally found some apples that were almost ripe."

"I'm hungry already." Reaching into the basket, Ben selected a big yellow apple and gave it to Sarah. She took a bite. As she chewed, Ben noticed the movement of her cheeks and how silver drops of juice appeared on her lips.

"The morning's heating up fast," Mrs. Dean said to Captain Simonton. "With your permission, Matthew can join us. He'll have a good time swimming in the river."

Matthew wore frayed trousers and a blue shirt, sleeves rolled up to the elbows. His thick black hair brushed across his forehead and slid over his ears. He had brown eyes, a pointed, delicate nose, and a squared jaw. Matthew was tall, but standing straight as he was, he came only to his father's chest. He turned and listened to his dad's response.

"The reverend needs to repair the wooden sluice at the spring. That's hard work, and Matthew can help. And besides, Matthew will be fourteen in two days. He'll get his good time at the birthday party."

"I've been waitin' all month to celebrate. You bet I'll be ready for a good time."

"You have the cutest smile I've ever seen," Sarah said, kissing Matthew on the forehead. "Will you save a dance for me on your birthday?"

"I will," Matthew responded, smiling. "I'll almost be a man's age."

"You're already a man, working the way you do," Mrs. Dean complimented.

"Should we get started?" Will asked impatiently. He grabbed his musket and walked to Beatrice. Mrs. Dean and Sally joined them, and they started down the trail. Falling in behind them, Ben took Sarah's hand, squeezed it tightly, and began to whistle softly. Bird sounds resonated from the trees; a deer leaped across the trail in front of them.

It was noon when the group walked out of the woods onto a sandy beach. An eagle flapped its wings and glided across the deep pool where the Juniata Rivers came together. The water plunged out of the pool in swift torrents, forming rapids that raged white water against the protruding rocks. A steady roar echoed off the turbulent water. Immediately below the rapids, a narrow island lined with pine trees divided the river into two channels. The near channel boiled ominously and sprayed water against the cliffs; the far channel was deep and slow-moving.

Holy Pine Mountain towered above the river. A trail through dense woods led to the base of the mountain. Gazing upward, Will studied the sheer walls of the cliffs and the cluster of gigantic pine trees at the top. Clouds of mist from the rapids rose up the side of the mountain.

"Shadows of Death," Will said to his mother, pointing at the clouds. Black-winged birds swooped in and out of the mist. "There's a hot spring deep in the rocks. When it erupts, steam rises up and covers the mountain. The vultures here have fat bodies. They feast on all the dead stuff washed out of the rapids." Will watched a large branch float out of the pool and plummet down the rapids. He turned to his brother. "It's hot. Let's go swimmin'."

"I was waitin' on you," Ben said. When he pulled out his long shirt, his trousers dropped low over his hips. Ben tossed the shirt, sat next to Sarah, and unlaced his shoes. Stretching her hand beneath her petticoat, Sarah slid off her garters and unrolled her stockings. Her legs were pale and flawlessly smooth in the glare of the sun. Ben began to perspire; the lavender scent lingered in the heated air.

"Everything smells real sweet today," Sarah said. She removed her short gown and petticoat, and unlaced the tight-fitting stay.

"I don't smell nothin'," Ben commented. His eyes bulging shamefully, he watched her arrange the items of clothing neatly at his feet. When Sarah stood in front of him, the white folds of her shift hung loosely over her body. Ben gawked at the low neckline, the outline of her breasts against the cloth. A sudden rising heat reddened his face. Ben coughed and turned away, his glance now focusing on the bell tower and pile of cut logs.

"Twin River," Ben said, in a shrill voice, pointing to the bluff above the pool. "That's what Will and I decided to call the new school."

"Because you're twins?" Sarah asked, turning to Will.

"Because of the two rivers coming together," Will clarified, leaning his musket against a thick bush. When he took off his long shirt and placed it next to the musket, the bush began to shake. Two clawed feet appeared, and then a large, black shell slid out from under the bush.

"A snapper!" Ben exclaimed, jumping to his feet. "I never saw one this big!" Ben picked up a heavy branch and began tapping the shell. The turtle's beak-shaped jaws sprang open with a low hissing sound. Ben stepped closer.

"Leave it be," Mrs. Dean warned. "They can bite real hard."

"Snappers are too slow to bite me," Ben bragged, hitting the shell again. When the turtle lurched at his exposed foot, Ben dropped the branch and fell awkwardly to the ground. Flat in the sand, his legs were open in a wide V-shape. The turtle sped into the opening, lumbered past the knees, and stopped at Ben's crotch. When the turtle made a horrific hissing sound, Ben's face contorted, and he screamed silently; a hot liquid smeared his pants.

"Stay down!" Will shouted. In a quick motion, he grabbed the branch and swung it in the narrow space between Ben and the turtle. The snapper's head fired out; the jaws clamped onto the wood with a splintering noise.

"Holy—"

"Quit pissin' yourself, Ben, and grab the other end."

Getting to his feet, his knees shaking, Ben grasped the branch with both hands, and he and Will lifted the turtle out of the sand. Exchanging glances, they immediately took off running. With the guttural hissing sound growing louder, they hurried to the river and tossed the turtle into the rapids. Wiping perspiration from his forehead, Will nudged his brother in the side.

"You're lucky, Ben. If the snapper got hold of where it was aimin', you wouldn't need to worry about havin' a family with Sarah." Will rushed to Beatrice and grabbed her around the waist. They ran across the sand and splashed into the deep pool.

A blank expression on his face, Ben searched the rapids and saw the black shell hit a rock and spin downriver. Shrugging his shoulders, Ben walked to Sarah and reached for her hand. She gave him both hands, and he pulled her out of the sand. Laughing nervously, they waded into the water. Ben's trousers became saturated and slid even lower over his hip. He held them with one hand. With the other hand, he led Sarah into the deeper water, and they dove under the surface. Watching from the bank, momentarily alarmed, Mrs. Dean covered her eyes at the sun's reflection.

Sarah swam gracefully in the shimmering depths of the pool. The water loosened her shift, exposing silky-smooth skin that was remarkably pale next to her tanned shoulders and neck. Maintaining his position below her, Ben stiffened as she turned and glided toward him. When her swinging breasts approached his face, he excitedly pounded his chest, and a great quantity of air burst from his mouth. Sarah disappeared. Searching for her, Ben saw only the ascending bubbles and the bright glow of light at the river's surface.

The sun was blistering hot. Snapping an occasional twig and stumbling over hidden roots, the two Tories tramped through the woods. Jacob Hare heard voices and crouched behind a clump of bushes. Through the leaf cover, he saw the Reverend Dean, Captain Simonton, and the boy in the clearing. Two muskets were propped against the wooden bench next to the spring. Jacob motioned for Nathaniel to sit down, and twisting around, he searched the tall grass and low-hanging branches.

"Those damn Shawnee," Jacob whispered to Nathaniel. "After consumin' all that whiskey, how can they vanish out of sight like that?" Nathaniel shook his head. The tip of his nose was red and gleamed with oil and sweat. Suddenly, Chief One-Eye appeared at his side. The other Indians materialized from the shadows. After

Jacob and Chief One-Eye exchanged a series of hand signals, the Indians moved stealthily to their positions.

Yellow butterflies fluttered over the clearing; frogs croaked from the elevated, circular spring. Lush, green clusters of ferns grew in the moist earth. Blue violets embedded in the ferns swirled in the breeze. Reflecting sunlight, water gushed a silver stream from a large pipe. His chest and shoulders wet with perspiration, the boy stood next to the spring.

Young Matthew Simonton filled a tin cup with water and carried it to the captain. Returning to the spring, Matthew saw his image in the water. His brown eyes were bright and clear. When he smiled, the face in the spring smiled. Beads of perspiration dropped circles on the water. The ensuing ripples crested high in the still water, shattering the sparkling image of youth. Matthew frowned, and following a sudden impulse, he buried his head in the spring. There was darkness; an icy chill swept through his body. Matthew heard a steady ringing noise. Then there was a distant popping sound.

Holding the cup to his lips, relishing the cold water, Captain Simonton watched with amusement as Matthew lowered his head into the spring. There was movement in the clump of trees. A white man with a long, twisted nose stepped out, leveled his musket, and fired.

The explosion of noise echoed across the clearing. Dropping his shovel, the Reverend Dean watched the captain collapse. He turned to run toward the bench when an arrow zipped through the air with an irritating whirring noise. The noise grew louder, and the arrow ripped through the reverend's neck. When the Reverend Dean hit the ground, the slotted nock at the end of the arrow and a solitary turkey feather protruded from his throat.

Splashing his head out of the spring, Matthew Simonton saw his dad drop the cup, saw the gush of blood on his chest. Not hesitating, Matthew dashed to the bench and grabbed the musket. He cocked it and aimed at the red-faced Tory. As he pressed the trigger, he was struck in the head; the musket fired into the trees. Two-Finger bent down, unwound the rope from his waist, and looped the end around Matthew's neck.

Reverend Dean's body lay across the newly dug trench. Removing his knife, Chief One-Eye approached cautiously. Dropping to one knee, he positioned the head. Then, sliding the knife skillfully along the skin, he began to scalp the reverend. A steady flow of blood dripped dark circles in the springwater.

Two-Finger pulled Matthew to his feet. Stumbling forward, Matthew watched a man with a twisted nose approach the captain's body. The Tory took a knife from his belt and brandished it in the air.

"I ain't never tried this Indian scalpin'," Nathaniel announced in a robust, comical manner. "It looks to be fun." Grabbing a handful of hair and swinging the knife, Nathaniel lost his balance. When he fell over the body, he pushed the blade deeply into the captain's forehead. The handle snapped in pieces. Nathaniel struggled to his feet.

"It's a damn thick skull he's got!" he exclaimed, a frown forming on his face.

Matthew became dizzy, his feet a heavy weight. Protruding from the captain's forehead, reflecting flashes of sunlight, the silver blade blinded him with its glare. Tears filling his eyes, Matthew tripped and fell. The Indian dragged him to his feet and pulled him, sometimes on his hands and knees, to the cabin.

When Two-Finger reached the porch, he tied the rope to the railing, punched Matthew in the ribs, and went inside the cabin.

Through the blood and tears clouding his vision, Matthew saw the long-nosed man and the Indian walking toward him. The Tory grabbed the rope and pulled Matthew to face level.

"Maybe your scalp will come off easier," Nathaniel barked. He shoved the boy to the ground and climbed the steps to the cabin. There were sounds of furniture being smashed and glass breaking against the walls. Matthew sat motionless. Coughing at the pressure from the rope, he closed his eyes. Through the darkness, Matthew heard the captain's voice.

Matthew, this is a wild and uncivilized land, and bad things will surely happen. There are demons in the wilderness. These demons will bring you much sorrow, but by your actions to overcome them, you will become a stronger person. Remember always the words of Paul to Timothy: "You therefore must endure hardship as a good soldier of Jesus Christ." I remind you, Matthew, that as a soldier in God's army, you must remain strong. You must never cease in the struggle.

Matthew slid his hand over the knife the captain had sheathed securely around his calf muscle. Nathaniel, Two-Finger, and other Indians came out onto the porch. The Indians were eating venison. A succulent yellow apple protruded from Nathaniel's thin lips.

Like a stuck pig, Matthew thought.

Jacob Hare and Chief One-Eye walked through the door; black smoke billowed behind them. The Tories and the Indians moved quickly down the steps. Two-Finger grabbed the rope, tied it around his waist, and pulled Matthew to his feet. They began to run at a fast pace down the trail. Matthew glanced back and saw the front of the cabin engulfed in flames. The fire spread to the roof; dark clouds of smoke mushroomed in the air.

The Shadows of Death billowed up the side of the mountain. Directly overhead, the sun was bright in the cloudless sky. Mrs. Dean and Sally sat on the sandy beach. Sally grabbed an apple and threw it in a looping curve to Ben. His body suspended in the air, one hand clutching his loose trousers, he caught the apple and came crashing down on his chest. Surfacing, spitting water, he swam to Sarah, who was smiling.

"How'd you do that?" she asked, laughing. "You almost lost your trousers."

"I wouldn't mind losin' my trousers with you next to me," Ben said, and he gave the apple to Sarah. She took a small bite.

"It's sweet." Sarah held the apple for Ben, who bit out the whole side.

"It's sweeter now," he said, chewing slowly.

"How can it be sweeter?"

"I can taste your lips. I'll bet you can taste mine, too."

"Let me try," Sarah said, placing the apple in her mouth. Ben brushed against her body. Maneuvering his hand under the buoyant folds of the shift, he traced his fingers across her fleshy thigh and into the silky mound of hair. Sarah made a moaning sound; the apple dropped from her lips. Gleaming in the water, it bobbed and floated away.

"I did taste something sweet," Sarah admitted. A smile of contentment on her face, she slid her hand the length of his abdomen, gliding it through the loose gap in his trousers.

Ben's eyes opened wide, and he gasped for air. Looking over Sarah's shoulder, he saw Mother spying on him from the bank. She waved and said something to Sally; they both smiled and waved vigorously. Breathing deeply, Ben pressed his lips against Sarah's ear and said the words he had practiced all night.

"I love you."

"I love you, Ben," she whispered.

The ripple of waves grew suddenly hot and lapped over their bodies. The ambrosial scent of lavender drifted around them. Ben's legs trembled. In the boiling depths of the water, he was sliding inside her when there was a loud shout. Startled, he opened his eyes and saw Will's contorted face.

"Ben!" Will shouted again. He grabbed Ben by his shoulders, spun him around, and pointed to the canoe approaching the deep pool. A white man shouldered a musket; two Indians were swinging paddles through the water. Ben hastily pulled up his trousers and grabbed Sarah's hand.

Holding onto the women, Will and Ben splashed through the water. When Will reached the bank, he ran to the bush and grabbed the musket. As Beatrice and Sarah dressed, Will watched the canoe stop in the middle of the deep pool. The white man said something to the Indians and pointed upriver. Will looked in that direction and saw dark clouds of smoke rising in the sky.

"The cabin's burning!" Will shouted. Turning, lifting the musket, he aimed and fired. A shrill cry echoing across the pool, the Indian in the back of the canoe tumbled into the water. The canoe began drifting in a wide circle. Loud yelps emanated from the woods behind them.

"They're real close." Will took Beatrice by the hand and raced downriver. Ben, Sarah, Sally, and Mrs. Dean followed. The narrow path along the river began to angle upward; the roar of the rapids enveloped them. They entered a dense wooded area. When Will heard the shrill yelps again, he stopped and began reloading the musket. "We can't outrun them. I'll wait here and slow them down."

"No," Ben said. "There are too many. You'll get one shot off, and they'll kill you. Give me the musket. I'll stay."

"Why you?"

"Why me?" Ben asked incredulously. "Maybe you forgot, but I didn't. You have family now, Will."

"All the more reason to protect them." Will finished loading the musket. "I'll stay. I'm the better shot."

"You're not listening to me!" Ben shouted and lunged for the musket. Will did a quick sidestep, and Ben landed in the bushes. When Will helped him to his feet, he saw a thin flow of blood on Ben's forearm.

"I'm sorry, Ben. Are you hurt?"

"Nothin' but thorns," Ben said. After removing the slivers of wood, he took the knife from his pocket, cut some branches, and began to strip off the leaves. "You don't have to stay, Will. This will slow 'em down. You'll see. This will slow 'em down for sure."

Ben bent down, and slicing the knife through the dirt, he cut shallow grooves across the trail. He placed a branch in each groove and patted it down with dirt. Then he scattered leaves over the fresh earth; silver thorns slanted through the leafy patterns.

"That should fix them damn Tories and Indians," Ben said. He took Sarah's hand, and they began to run again. Reaching the base of Holy Pine Mountain, they stopped at the steep, sinuous trail.

"There's nothing but cliffs up there," Mrs. Dean said anxiously. "We'll be trapped."

"Spotters from the fort have seen the smoke by now," Will said. "Captain Jack will send the Rangers." There was a distant thrashing sound and loud screams. Ben pounded his chest and smiled at his brother; then they started up the mountain.

The afternoon sun scorched Holy Pine. Halfway up the trail, the women collapsed in the shade of a large boulder. A warm breeze blew down the slope. Perspiration dripping over his forehead, Ben sat next to Sarah and looked at the valley below. The surface of the river was a sparkling blue.

"I wish I had thought to bring water," he moaned.

"I wish I had kept that apple," Sarah whispered. There was shouting on the trail.

"We have to keep movin'," Will advised. Mrs. Dean got to her feet, but Beatrice, her hands cradling her stomach, didn't move. Will touched her shoulder. "I'll carry you."

"No, I can walk." Beatrice stood gingerly, and Will guided her up the trail. Ben walked slowly and started to fall behind. Soon he lost sight of the group. Pausing, shielding his eyes from the bright sunshine, Ben saw two man-sized boulders slanting high in the air.

Ben grabbed a broken branch and began to loosen the dirt at the base of the larger boulder. He heard the slight echo of voices, and when Ben looked down, he saw the first Indian step onto the trail. Moving cautiously, the Indian was chewing an apple.

Another Indian and then a white man came into view. They started shouting at the first Indian, who sat down on the trail and spat apple seeds in the air. The white man threw a rock at the Indian and pointed up the trail. The Indian sulked.

Ben buried the end of the branch deep under the boulder. Taking a breath, he threw his weight against the branch. The branch bent; the wood cut a groove into his shoulder. Perspiration blurring his vision, Ben gritted his teeth and pushed harder. His legs buckled; strong hands grabbed him.

"You're crazy thinkin' to do everything by yourself," Will said. "Give me that." He moved Ben out of the way and placed the branch on his shoulder.

"I'm wiped out," Ben said, holding his side.

"I'll do the liftin'. You push real hard. On three." Will counted quickly and leaned into the branch, which made a creaking noise. Bending low, Ben positioned both hands on the grainy surface and gave a tremendous heave. The boulder rose to the edge of the hole and tottered there. Will threw all his weight against the branch. It bent around the stone surface and snapped; the boulder jolted loose.

The boulder moved slowly at first, bouncing over a narrow gully. Its speed increasing, the boulder made a crunching sound that grew louder. As he turned to find the source of the noise, the Indian chewing the apple swayed drunkenly. The boulder smashed into his chest; pieces of apple spewed in the air.

Ben pounded his chest and cheered. An arrow whizzed over his shoulder. Will knocked Ben to the ground. Lying flat on his stomach, Ben watched the Indian slide another arrow into his bow. Suddenly, a small figure leapt out of the shadows and struck the Indian in the back. The arrow shot harmlessly in the sky.

"It's Matthew! He's alive!" Will grabbed onto Ben, and they ran up the trail.

Two-Finger dropped his bow, grabbed the noose around Matthew's neck, and punched the boy in the chest. Lowering his musket, the long-nosed Tory picked up a rock and swung it into Matthew's face. A large cut opened under Matthew's eye; Nathaniel smiled and readied the rock again.

"That's enough," Jacob said, knocking the rock out of Nathaniel's hand. "We need the boy for trade." Chief One-Eye nodded his head in agreement. Pulling the rope, Two-Finger threw Matthew on the ground and walked to Jacob and Chief One-Eye.

"Holy shee … it! Someone's got to teach the boy some manners." Nathaniel sat on a smooth rock on a steep ledge. He reached for his jug, took a long drink, and glared at the boy. Breathing hard, the overweight Joseph came into view and shouted at Jacob.

"What the hell's happenin' up here?" Joseph complained. "Rocks and all kinds of stuff come rollin' down at me."

Sitting upright, Matthew heard a slight clicking sound and saw the stump and the dark hole buried in its roots. Sliding his hand along the ground, he listened as the clicking sound turned to a rattle. Matthew studied the coiled shape in the shadows. When the noise of the rattle subsided, Matthew moved with blinding quickness.

Nathaniel was lowering the brown jug when he saw a smile appear on the boy's face. The boy's hand, which had been flat on the ground, suddenly disappeared under a stump. It reappeared holding a branch, which the boy flung viciously at him. Nathaniel watched in amazement as the branch became alive and began to twist in the air.

"Holy shee—" Nathaniel clamped his mouth shut when the dark shape hit him in the face. Fangs sank deeply into his nose and lower eye socket. He dropped the jug. It broke against the rocks, whiskey spilling over the trail. Nathaniel fell over the glistening shards.

Jacob turned and saw the snake slither away. Blood poured from Nathaniel's eye. The side of his face was purple; his arms and legs thrashed wildly. Two Indians limped up the trail. Their bloodied feet left wet prints on the rock. They both stopped and stared at Nathaniel. An amused look on his face, Jacob approached the body.

"You dumb-shee …it," Jacob mimicked and shoved Nathaniel over the ledge. He laughed uproariously, watching the body tumble out of sight. "If I'm countin' accurately, there goes the last of the Dumb-Fifty!"

Downriver at Fort Standing Stone, the alarm bells made a dull noise. Relayed by churches along the river, the ringing spread rapidly and soon resounded against the sheer stone cliffs of Holy Pine Mountain. Jacob moved quickly at the clamor.

"Hurry!" he shouted. Joseph and the Indians began to run up the trail. When Two-Finger pulled the rope, drawing it tighter around Matthew's neck, Matthew jumped to his feet. Blood flowing down his face into his mouth, he marveled at the clear clanging sound of the bells.

The trail at the summit ended in a flat clearing that was spotted with trees, brush, and odd-shaped boulders. One massive pine tree towered over the others. Under the tree, red-and-black ants streamed out of two large cone-shaped mounds. The ground was covered with pine needles. At the far end of the clearing, there were patches of grass and a slope of smooth rock that led to the cliff and the Shadows of Death. The pine needles there glistened with moisture.

"You'll be safe now." Will kissed Beatrice and lowered her under the shade of the pine tree. Clutching his musket, he ran back to the trail. Watching his brother disappear, Ben walked slowly across the clearing. When he neared the cliff, a cool mist swept across his face. The slope of rock was slippery; dark shadows rose in the air.

"Ben!" Sarah called.

The echo from the rapids thundered around him. Sliding forward cautiously, Ben peered over the edge at the sheer stone wall and the stunted trees that extended scraggly branches from dark crevices. The river far below was a cascading current of white water and massive rocks. There was movement in the sky, and Ben saw vultures descending in a circular pattern. As the vultures neared the cliff, one glided directly at him. Ben tripped backward, falling into Sarah.

"Ben," she said, steadying him, "I kept calling, but you didn't hear me. You were so close to the edge."

"I was looking for a way down. There's no trail." Ben took her hand, and they walked back to the pine tree. The crack of a musket, followed by a salvo of shots, echoed across the clearing. Mrs. Dean and Sally got to their feet as Will ran into view.

"I hit one of them," he said, reloading the musket. An arrow whizzed by his head, stuck in the pine tree, and quivered there. A second arrow pierced Will's shoulder. Shrill war yelps resonated from the woods. As the Indian cries grew louder, Mrs. Dean grabbed Sally's hand and led her toward the cliff.

Dark, naked forms ran from the trees. Ben lunged at one, grabbed onto his throat, and wrestled him to the ground. He had a death choke on the Indian when Chief One-Eye clubbed him with his tomahawk.

Bleeding from the shoulder, Will ran toward Beatrice and lifted her off the ground. As he turned, Beatrice screamed. A white man with long blond hair swung his musket and smashed Will in the back of the head. Will collapsed, his body falling over Beatrice.

Two-Finger threw Matthew against a rock and advanced toward Mrs. Dean and Sally. The Shadows of Death billowed around them. Matthew slid his hand under the cuff of his trousers and unsheathed the knife. Jumping to his feet, he saw Mrs. Dean lean close to Sally and whisper in her ear. Matthew stared at the trembling lips.

I love you, Sally.

Her face calm and serene, Mrs. Dean kissed Sally on the forehead and pulled her backward. Wrapped tightly in each other's arms, their bodies dropped into the deafening roar of the Shadows of Death. A smile formed on Two-Finger's lips. As he turned, Matthew charged forward and thrust the knife into his throat.

Blood gushed in the air and splashed warm against Matthew's face. The force of the impact propelled both Matthew and Two-Finger over the edge of the cliff. Feeling cool mist strike his body, Matthew kicked free of the corpse. Holding onto the slack rope, he fell through the Shadows of Death.

Branches ripped across Matthew's arms and legs. The noose tightened, digging deeper into his neck. Matthew grabbed the rope with both hands just as his body jerked to a stop. Glancing up, he saw the rope had looped around a tree trunk jutting out of the cliff. On the other side, Two-Finger broke loose from the branches, and with feet dangling in the shadows, his body swung past Matthew in a wide arc. On its return swing, the lumpish corpse bumped against Matthew and stopped. The stitched fingers, blood dripping off the nails, pointed at Matthew's chest. Then the heavier body began to descend.

Reaching out, Matthew ripped the knife from Two-Finger's throat. As the Indian dropped lower, Matthew's body began to rise. His shoulders hit against the tree. Matthew pulled himself onto the trunk. Locking his feet together, he took a deep breath and cut the rope. Arms and legs swinging wildly, Two-Finger plummeted through the shadows and splashed silently into the rapids below. A frothing wave tossed the mangled body onto a wide, flat rock.

Dark shadowy forms swooped by Matthew. Two vultures spiraled downward, and wings flapping in the mist, they landed smoothly on the rock. Thrusting their beaks into Two-Finger's body, shaking their heads, they removed large wagging pieces of flesh.

Matthew replaced the knife in the sheath, loosened the rope from his neck, and slid down the trunk to a small cave. A thick cobweb, myriad insect bodies entwined on its surface, partially covered the entrance. Reaching out, Matthew brushed at the web. A black spider with beady red eyes ran across his hand and disappeared up the side of the cliff. There was a cool draft from the cave.

A wail sounded from above. The noise grew louder, and a frail body hit the branches of the tree and stuck there. Matthew saw his sister's face, disfigured and streaked with blood. Large imploring eyes stared at him. Then, hands tearing away branches, Beatrice plunged downward. A piece of white cloth remained. When a gust of wind blew from the rapids, the fabric made a flapping noise.

Violent tremors shook Matthew's body. A vulture flew out of a wide arc, and with yellow talons outstretched, it landed on the branch. Stretching its purplish head, the vulture began to shred the tattered cloth with its ivory beak. Then it pulled away and hissed loudly. The vulture defecated a great volume of feces and urine and angled its curved beak toward Matthew's face.

"No!" Matthew shouted, and swinging his fist, he struck the vulture in the neck. Flapping its wings, the vulture dropped into the shadows.

Matthew sat precariously at the base of the tree for a long period of time. Then he lowered his head and crawled inside the cave. In the gray light, he brushed his hand against the smooth surface of rock. Taking the knife from the sheath, tears welling in his eyes, he began to carve the letters. He moved the blade slowly, purposely, deeply. When he finished, Matthew fell back and looked at the outline of the cross and inscription below it.

+

Beatrice

Vapor collected on Matthew's body and saturated his ripped trousers. Huddled in a squatting position, he heard piercing screams from the summit. Wrapping his arms around his knees, he listened as the shrieks subsided and then turned deafening. An eerie silence followed.

Matthew released his grip on his knees, slid out on the ledge, and balanced himself on the tree. His chest pressed against the wet, slippery rock, Matthew inched his way up the side of the mountain. The ascent was delayed by a barrier of jutting rocks and thick brush. The thorns in the brush broke off and stuck in his hands and legs.

Soaked with perspiration, blood flowing from cuts and bruises, Matthew finally reached the summit. Slanting through the Shadows of Death, the rays of the setting sun cast a crimson glow that illuminated the sharp edge of the precipice. Matthew slid his hand over the top, and with a great effort, he pulled his body onto solid ground. His crushed lungs heaving, Matthew saw the pine tree and the two naked bodies attached to it.

Standing, his vision blurred, Matthew stumbled toward the tree. His arms twisted at grotesque angles, Will was bound to the trunk. An arrow stuck in Will's chest; a second arrow slanted out of his groin. Ants scurried over his body, forming black clusters on the pale skin. The darkest cluster of ants was on the forehead where the scalp had been torn away. Hanging above Will, Ben had a noose around his neck. Ben's feet lightly touched Will's shoulders. Trembling, Matthew undid the knot around Will's hands. The body dropped to a sitting position. Grasping Will around the shoulders, Matthew dragged the body a good distance from the ant mounds.

Matthew returned and climbed the tree. Brushing away ants that began to bite his hands, he cut the rope. Ben fell heavily to the earth. Matthew jumped down, and grabbing both wrists, he pulled the body across the ground, resting it next to Will's.

Matthew broke off a handful of leaves, and tears streaming down his face, he scraped the ants off the bodies. Some ants he killed when he squeezed the leaves together; others he crushed into the ground. Matthew broke the feathered ends of the arrows and pulled the shafts out of the bodies. He slid one arrow into his pocket. Glancing at the vultures that were circling closer, Matthew pulled the bodies deep into the woods and placed them under heavy brush. Then in the darkening light, he turned and began running down the mountain.

The moon was shining brightly when Matthew reached the deep pool at Twin River. On the opposite bluff at the school site, a fire cast a red glow over the bell tower. In the dim light, Matthew saw a canoe on the bank below the bluff.

Matthew waded into the river. Halfway across, water flowing against his chest, he submerged himself in the icy darkness. The cold pressure of the current numbed his body; a ringing noise filled his ears. His knees digging into the sandy bottom, Matthew held his breath for a long time. Then he stood and breathed deeply, warm air filling his lungs.

The fire on the bluff lifted sparks high in the air. Wading to the bank, Matthew saw the Indian asleep in the canoe, his head leaning lazily over the side. Matthew unsheathed his knife. He took long strides, his feet leaving deep prints in the sand. Reaching the canoe, he sank the knife powerfully into the Indian's chest. Wild-eyed, standing on wobbly legs, the Indian fell at Matthew's feet.

Matthew plunged the knife deeper and twisted the blade to the side, breaking a rib. When he removed the knife, a massive amount of blood gushed over the Indian's body. Matthew slid his hand in the gaping wound; blood flowed smoothly between his fingers. His heart pounding rapidly, he stood and smeared the warm liquid over his face and chest. Breathing evenly now, Matthew walked to the riverbank. Bright moonlight reflected off the still water. Looking at his image shimmering in the light, an image that stared at him with eyes burning red with hatred, Matthew saw the bloody specter of death.

"God's soldier," he whispered. Matthew replaced the knife in the sheath, walked across the sand, and began a slow crawl up the trail. When he reached the top of the bluff, he saw two Indians sleeping at the fire. A pale figure sat tied to the log support of the bell tower. Matthew looked closely, and through the flickering light, he saw Sarah.

Removing the broken arrow from his pocket, Matthew approached the fire. The rays of heat dried the blood on his body into a crust. Matthew kicked the Indian in the side; the Indian coughed and rolled over.

"I am God's soldier," Matthew whispered. The Indian grunted, and when his eyes opened, Matthew stuck the arrow into his throat. The Indian shrieked a piercing cry. Blood spewed from his mouth.

Awakened by the noise, the second Indian jumped to his feet and lunged at the thin boy. He missed awkwardly and fell into the fire pit. Matthew leapt onto his back, and clutching the Indian's neck, he forced his face into the burning coals. Flames flared over Matthew's hand. Pushing down savagely, he twisted the Indian's head back and forth. There was a popping sound. An ivory pupil burst from the Indian's eye socket and stuck in the red coals. With his nostrils and lips cauterized, the Indian twitched erratically and was still.

Matthew stood and backed away from the Indian's charred body. When he tried to raise his hand against the rising stench, a sharp pain shot the length of his arm. Glancing down, Matthew saw how the skin on his hand was blackened; wisps of smoke rose between his fingers.

"Matthew," a voice called from the bell tower. Sarah stood and motioned to him. "I don't believe it's you. I saw you fall over the cliff. How did you …"

"It wasn't my time to die," Matthew said in a whisper, walking toward her. After cutting the rope around her hands, he led her past the bodies at the fire.

"Good," she said. "It's good they're burnt, Matthew. You sent them to hell." Sarah followed him down the trail to the canoe. Noticing the blisters on his hand, she dragged the canoe to the water and got in. Matthew pushed off, slid in the back, and grabbed the paddle. When his charred fingers scraped against the wood, Matthew cried out, bright flashes clouding his vision. Matthew couldn't move. As the canoe approached the end of the deep pool, there was a loud roar. White water swirled around the canoe, splashing over the sides.

"We're going toward the rapids!" Sarah shouted.

Gritting his teeth, Matthew ripped the paddle through the water. A huge wave hit the canoe, turning them sideways. When the wave broke, the canoe descended sharply into a whirlpool. Matthew fell on his back. As the canoe descended, he saw the black cliffs and the dark shadows swirling overhead. Matthew dropped the paddle and cradled his injured hand against his stomach.

Water boiled around them. The canoe slowed, turned vertical, and stopped. There was a loud gurgling sound. With the sides vibrating, the canoe reversed direction, spun upward, and was propelled in the air. It splashed down in the wide channel and began to drift slowly downriver. Lying flat on the bottom of the canoe, Matthew saw the North Star and Big Dipper shining brightly in the night sky. Then Sarah's face appeared over him.

"Thank you, Matthew." Sarah kissed his forehead. "Thank you for saving me." The canoe rolled back and forth with the current. The roar of the rapids fell silent; the Shadows of Death dissipated. Sarah wiped at her eyes and leaned her head on the side of the canoe.

With his good hand, Matthew paddled the canoe on a meandering course. There was a slight breeze; the night echoed with owl and frog sounds. Then there was a crashing sound from the bank. Matthew watched a pack of wolves burst from the shadows and race down the stretch of sand.

There were louder thrashing noises, and Matthew watched two deer, one a fawn, break out of the heavy brush. The bigger deer splashed into the water and began swimming, but the fawn was slower. The lead wolf lunged and struck the fawn on the hind leg. The fawn fell sideways into the river, regained its balance, and began to swim. The wolf splashed toward it but stopped in the deeper water. The pack circling on the bank began a series of howls that echoed across the river.

The larger deer reached the far bank; the fawn was motionless in the current. As the canoe floated closer to the bobbing head, Matthew heard its rapid snorting. When the fawn slipped under the water, the sound abruptly stopped.

"Why, Captain?" Matthew whispered. "Why do bad things keep happenin'?"

The fawn's head surfaced, and a spray of mist gushed from its nostrils. The fawn moved inches forward and sank again. As the canoe drifted into the widening circle of bubbles, Matthew lowered his hand over the side. The cold water ripped into the burnt skin; Matthew clenched his lips. His fingers circling deeper in the river, he touched fur, slid his hand around the fawn's neck, and slowly began to lift the body upward. The fawn's head broke the surface of the river. When Matthew cradled the body against the side of the canoe, the fawn's eyes blinked open. Prancing along the bank, the lone deer followed the two shadows drifting in the water.

Minutes passed. Oval eyes glistening in the moonlight, the fawn snorted and straightened its head. Matthew released his grip and pushed the fawn toward the bank. It swam slowly with the current. When Matthew lifted his hand out of the water, he saw where large, opaque bubbles had formed on the skin.

Moments later there was loud splashing at the bank. Both deer pranced out of the river and disappeared in the tree line. There were flashes of light downriver; musket retorts sounded from Fort Standing Stone. The lanterns around the fort reflected a dim glow in the night sky. Wiping her hand across her eyes, Sarah sat up.

"Matthew," she said in a choked voice, "did you see the twins?"

"I took them down from the tree."

"There were white men with the Indians. They did terrible things, Matthew."

"I saw what they did. You don't have to talk about it."

"I must talk about it. Just to you, Matthew. You're the only one who will understand. The Indians and the white man did bad things. I saw Beatrice and Will run for the cliffs. But they were slow, Matthew. The white man stuck a knife in Will's leg. He fell, but he nudged Beatrice forward. She got away, Matthew. Your sister got away."

The canoe moved languidly in the current. Holding the paddle steady, Matthew lowered his head. The moon was high in the sky; another musket sounded from the fort.

"The Indians bound Will to the big tree. The Tory with the blond hair tied Ben's hands and put a noose around his neck. He gave the rope to the Indian. The Indian climbed the tree and pulled Ben up so his feet were resting on Will's shoulder. Then he tied the rope to the branch.

"The Indians shot arrows into Will. The Tory said Will couldn't hold Ben up but a few minutes. He said Will would collapse and hang his brother. But Will was standing strong. The Tory kicked open the big mounds and threw handfuls of ants on Will where the arrows were sticking. But Will still didn't move. Then the Tory grabbed a tomahawk and began to chop at Will's ankles. I closed my eyes at the screams."

Sarah began to sob; she buried her face in her hands. Matthew's heart beat rapidly. There was a light splash in the water, and the canoe turned sideways in the current. Watching the shoreline spin into view, Matthew had trouble breathing. Sarah spoke again; he could barely hear her words.

"When the screams lessened, I looked at the twins. Ben was crying. He said, 'It's not your fault, Will. I can do it. I can do it myself.' Ben jumped off Will's shoulders. But it didn't snap his neck. He swung back and forth kicking his legs. When the white man saw this, he grabbed his knife and began to scalp Will.

"Then everything went black. When I heard noises, I saw you at the fire. At first, I didn't recognize you." Waves lapped against the side of the canoe. Sarah pointed at the glow in the sky. Her voice was barely audible. "We'll be at the fort soon. We'll be safe."

We'll never be safe from the demons, Matthew thought. His hand was a knotted fist. He turned and noticed the paddle floating in the river.

It was midnight when the canoe slid alongside the wooden dock at Fort Standing Stone. A guard sounded the alarm, and armed Rangers ran down the steps. Captain Jack, white bandages covering the wounds on his face, lifted Sarah out of the canoe and carried her to the fort. Matthew was exhausted climbing the steps dug in the riverbank. When he reached the center courtyard, Rangers and a group of settlers, some holding small children, gathered in a circle and gawked at him. Pushing his way forward, Captain Jack looked at the gashes on the boy's face and the blisters that bubbled from the blackened hand.

Talking slowly, Matthew explained about the murders at the spring, the bodies falling into the Shadows of Death, and the massacre on the cliff. The Rangers listened intently; the settlers with children began moving away. As Matthew finished his story, a group of men mounted horses and galloped through the front gate. When the horses disappeared, Matthew turned to Captain Jack. Matthew's face was glistening with moisture; tears filled his eyes.

"I heard the bells ringing up and down the river," Matthew said, wiping at the tears. "No one came to help us."

"There was an attack in Woodcock Valley," Captain Jack began to explain. "It was a band of Seneca Indians, twenty or more. The militia went there before we heard about the smoke up your way. The militia just returned."

Matthew was silent. His jaws set tight, he glared at Captain Jack and the group of Rangers. The captain spoke softly.

"When the militia reached Woodcock Valley, the Indians were gone. Colonel Stephens found ten of Captain Phillips' Rangers tied to trees. The Rangers suffered greatly before they died. They all had family here, and …"

"You don't need to tell me about family," Matthew whispered, lowering his head.

"What did you say?"

Matthew didn't answer. The settlers began to move away; soon the courtyard was deserted. Matthew followed Captain Jack to a log building that had two rows of bunks inside. The captain led Matthew to the only unoccupied one. It had a heavy blanket, and the pillow at the end was crushed in the center. The white-and-blue Colonial flag was on the wall above the bed.

"Use my bunk tonight. The doctor will be here soon to treat your hand." Captain Jack turned and walked through the door. Some sitting on the bunks, some reclining, the Rangers watched the captain. Then their collective gaze settled on the thin boy struggling with his shoes. The young Ranger in the next bunk moved quickly, unlaced the shoes, and pulled them off. Grimacing when he saw the blackened hand up close, the Ranger nodded to the boy and returned to his bunk.

Late the next afternoon in a small cemetery outside of Hartslog, four wooden coffins were lowered into the ground. Captain Jack and a group of armed militia stood sentry around the burial plot. The sky was clear, and a light breeze carried the scent of lavender and mint from the nearby woods. Birds chirped; yellow butterflies fluttered around the grave site, some alighting on the moist mounds of earth.

Wearing a stiff brown shirt, Matthew stood next to his mother and uncle. Sarah Bebalt walked up to him. She wore a gray short gown with black lace embroidered on the sleeves and cuffs. Tears glistening on her face, she kissed Matthew on the cheek.

"You must take care of yourself. And if you need anything, anything at all, you must be sure to come to me first."

"I will," Matthew said. Holding onto her hand, he hesitated. "Sarah …"

"Yes, Matthew."

"I just remembered," Matthew said, his eyes focusing on the shovels jutting out of the mounds of dirt. "Dad was plannin' a great celebration for me. It's my birthday tomorrow."

The voices quieted around the graves. A minister stepped forward and read from the book of Matthew. Head bowed, he finished in a solemn voice: "Because strait is the gate, and narrow is the way, which leadeth unto life, and few there be that find it." Matthew listened attentively. Looking past the minister, he watched his mother drop a handful of dirt on the captain's coffin.

After the graves were filled, the large group of mourners moved slowly to the grove of trees where the horses and buckboards waited.

Matthew saw his horse tied to a tree grazing on patches of grass. Captain Jack approached him.

"We buried the savages where you killed them. I know the hatred you feel, Matthew. I lived with the Lenape Indians many years. Before I left, the chief told me there are two wolves in the heart of every person. The pale wolf is love. The dark wolf with burning red eyes is hate. They fight for control. I asked the chief which wolf wins." Captain Jack hesitated, his eyes searching Matthew's face.

"What did the chief tell you?" Matthew asked. "Which wolf wins?"

"The one you feed," Captain Jack answered in a sad voice. "I lived a wild, solitary life filled with hatred. I killed many Indians. I had the choice to stop, but I couldn't."

"I understand. Like you, my choice is to kill as many Indians as I can."

"You're just a boy."

"I'm God's soldier. I felt a great fear when I approached the Indians camped at the schoolhouse. But I felt greater joy when I killed them."

"It's wrong to feel joy from killing. Even when it is necessary to kill, you should never feel joy." Captain Jack lifted a rawhide cord from his neck. There was a smooth green arrowhead hanging from the cord. "The Lenape chief gave me this arrowhead. He said it would help me to survive in the wilderness."

"Did it help you?"

"My wife," Captain Jack muttered slowly, "and children are dead. Nothing can help me." He slid the rawhide around the boy's neck.

Matthew shook the captain's hand and walked to his horse in the grove of trees. It was a short ride to the schoolhouse. Four mounds of earth were next to the fire pit. Inside the pit, thin lines of smoke curled upward. Matthew tied the horse to the bell tower, walked to the edge of the bluff, and looked into the large pool formed by the two rivers. The water's surface reflected the Shadows of Death rising against the steep cliffs of Holy Pine Mountain. Dark-winged vultures circling the area were reflected in the fathomless depths of the pool.

The low howl of a wolf shattered the silence. Staring into the pool, Matthew watched the watery image of the wolf lope to the summit. The body was pitch-black, and when a breeze blew over the pool, the black hairs on the wolf's body trembled in a wavelike motion. Two blood-red eyes burned through the water's surface.

"Demon," Matthew whispered, his eyes tinted red in the fading light. Turning away, Matthew clutched the arrowhead in his fist. When he looked at the river again, the pool was dark and lifeless. Matthew walked back to the horse. Patting it gently on the neck, he climbed onto the saddle and rode out of the grove of trees into the dark night.

Chapter Two

DEATH VALLEY

1976

Shielding his eyes from the desert sun, the Reverend Towers watched the cloud of dust approach the house. The reverend's tailored white sport coat hung loosely on his tall, bony figure. Wrinkles crossed his face; his eyes were small and set deep in the forehead. When the mail van braked to a stop, the postman lowered the window and handed the Reverend Towers an envelope. After waiting for the van to leave, the reverend opened the envelope and pulled out the letter from Attorney Masters, of the Law Offices of Masters, Davis, and Archibald in Huntingdon, Pennsylvania.

After reading the letter, the Reverend Towers jumped the steps, slammed the door open, and burst into the kitchen. Startled, his wife, Irene, dropped the egg she was holding; it cracked white and yellow on the floor. His foot crushing the shell, the reverend grabbed Irene and hugged her. Then sitting next to her at the kitchen table, he explained that his older brother, Jonas, had passed away.

In his will, Jonas had left the reverend his mansion, a mountain, and two hundred acres of land along the Juniata River in Hartslog Valley, Pennsylvania. Irene was elated, and putting on her bonnet, she followed her husband down the porch steps. They got into the rusted church van, drove to the one-room diner, and ordered the day's special, which was rabbit, mashed potatoes, and a thick green cactus soup. The waitress brought two glasses of ice water and returned to the counter.

"You never talked about your brother," Irene said, taking a drink. "Why was that?"

"Jonas was a recluse. He didn't want anyone bothering him. Every year I would send him a simple birthday card. That was our only contact until today."

"But you knew he was wealthy?"

"Jonas was very wealthy. He lived on the top floor of the historic Water Street Inn before it was demolished. Then he built a stone mansion on the Juniata River. It's our home now. And the mountain we own is prime property. It's on the river directly across from Twin River High School."

"Prime property," Irene repeated, putting her hands together in silent prayer. Her head was bowed when the waitress brought the dishes of food and left the bill on the table.

Leaving the diner, the Reverend Towers and Irene went to the *Weekly Desert Post*. Bargaining with the editor, the reverend bought four inches of space on the back page. He filled the space with the announcement, "Holy Redemption Church Closed." Underneath he added, *"But God Is Still Open!"* The editor of the *Post* shrugged his shoulders and took the reverend's money. When they left the office, Irene went next door to the Dead Water Trading Post and bought a bottle of Desert Cabernet.

That evening Irene and the Reverend Jeremiah Towers sat on wicker chairs on the back porch of their single-story house. Flat desert sand, cacti, and clumps of chaparral stretched to the distant Funeral Mountain. Lightning flashed jagged lines of light through the darkening sky. A golden glow momentarily illuminated the solitary Joshua tree in the yard.

Although the reverend had a deep tan, Irene had a pale

complexion. Her frail body was buried deep in the soft cushions of the chair. When she spoke, her voice was high-pitched and cold. The round table in front of her had a cassette player, two glasses, and the bottle of Cabernet. Taking the bottle, the Reverend Towers filled the glasses. He smiled and gave his wife a glass; they clicked the glasses lightly.

"I can't wait to leave this place," Irene said, drinking the wine. Red drops appeared on her lips. "It was 118 degrees today. The sun here will burn your skin to the bone."

"But, Irene, we were called to do His work in the desert."

"In two years of doing His work, we buried three Christian Indians," she stated poignantly, placing the empty glass on the table. "And last Sunday, only seven people came to hear your service at Holy Redemption Church."

"But now we move on to greater glory in Hartslog Valley. We have a mountain to spread the gospel. We'll build the church there."

"What about Cain and Abel?" Irene asked. "They've been in the desert three days now. They disappear without a word."

"They always return."

"Why do they come back? When I order them to do something, even simple things, they walk away. They never listen. It's always in one ear and out the other."

"We made the decision to adopt them."

"*We?*" Irene said in a strident voice.

"*I* made the decision." The reverend filled his glass for the third time, took a long drink, and smiled condescendingly. "Cain and Abel are family now."

"That agency took our money, but they never explained why both their parents disappeared so suddenly. And your giving them biblical names only made it worse."

"They needed naming. They needed new and pure identities. We accepted them. And we can't abandon them now. They need proper schooling."

"You keep making excuses for them. They stole candles and paint from the trading post. They crippled the Shoshone boy, and no one knows what they did to Abbey Lee. And now she's gone missing. I'm scared of them." Irene's hand trembled slightly; she grabbed the bottle of Cabernet and refilled her glass.

On the horizon, flashes of lightning illuminated the grandiose peak of Funeral Mountain. A larger bolt suddenly materialized, sliced brilliantly downward, and struck the Joshua tree in the yard. As thunder rattled the house, there was an explosion of sparks, and the tree began to burn. The flames produced a cracking, melodic sound that filled the confines of the porch. Lowering his empty glass, the Reverend Towers stood in awe as the smoldering branches of the Joshua tree twisted into the shape of a cross. His eyes burning in the light, the Reverend Towers swayed back and forth.

"Lord, I understand," he muttered. "Flaming Cross will be the name of my new church in Hartslog Valley."

The fire flared suddenly, the flames generating a red-and-white halo that glowed in the night sky. Bubbling down the blackened bark, lines of sap created a pleasant aroma. Breathing deeply, sipping the wine, Irene hit the play button on the cassette recorder and leaned back in the chair. Gospel music drifted across the yard.

> Sowing in the morning, sowing seeds of kindness,
> Sowing in the noontide, and the dewy eve;
> Waiting for the harvest, and the time of reaping,
> We shall come rejoicing, bringing in the sheaves.

"My favorite hymn," Irene commented, humming the refrain with sincere enthusiasm.

At the base of Funeral Mountain, there was a dark opening in the maze of cracks formed by the rock slide. Cain and Abel stooped low and entered a narrow passageway. The twins had dark tans and muscular six-foot-four-inch, two-hundred-pound bodies. They both had black hair, narrow green eyes, and scowling mouths. Abel coughed loudly and covered his mouth.

The stench of decay permeated the air. Dried, colorless stems of desert flowers littered the floor. As they walked, Abel lit candles set in the stone walls. The candles cast a pallid, flickering glow. Reaching the end of the passageway, the twins entered a circular cavern. A full-sized image of a human body was cut in the stone wall.

The head indentation was dark and empty, but the center piece below was filled with a girl's body. The heart had been ripped out of Abbey Lee; flies buzzed in and out of the mutilated rib cavity. Rounded from a late pregnancy, the girl's stomach protruded grotesquely. Abbey Lee's hands faced upward. Thin, pasty fingers reached toward the ceiling. The words "Temple of Shinar" were painted in bright red on the wall.

There was a wooden cage directly under the Temple of Shinar. The coyote inside snarled and bit into the wood. As Cain and Abel approached, the coyote bared its teeth, dark hair rising along its back. Hovering over the cage, each twin grasped a razor-edged Sharpfinger skinning knife.

"We needed a wolf, but there's no such beast in these parts," Abel said. He stuck the Sharpfinger deep into the coyote's back, paralyzing it. Abel unlatched the door, pulled out the coyote, and held it by its front paws. Thrusting the knife through the coyote's neck, Cain quickly cut off the head and stuffed it into the black hole above the girl's body. It lodged there, jaws protruding outward, the dark skin draping over the girl's shoulders.

"Perfect!" Cain exclaimed. He guided his hand deep down the coyote's neck and extracted the beating heart. Caressing the spongy organ, he delicately positioned the heart in the girl's breast cavity. Blood spurted intermittently from the ripped valve and flowed in thin lines over the pale skin of the girl's bloated stomach. Abel watched with admiration.

"Cain, how do you know to do the sacrifice this way? The Reverend Jeremiah Towers reads his King James Bible. What book do you read?"

"There's no book, Twin Brother. I hear voices. The voices tell me what to do."

"I'm with you all the time. I never hear voices."

"But you do hear voices," Cain said and smiled. "You hear my voice."

Thunder roared over Funeral Mountain, the noise echoing through the cave. The coyote's eyes glared red; blood trickled from its heart. Savoring every detail of their offering, Cain and Abel stood quietly for a few moments. Then they pinched the candlewicks and went outside. There was the dim glow of a cross in the distance. The refrain, *We shall come rejoicing, bringing in the sheaves,* was a soft echo over the desert sand.

Chapter Three

Shadows of Death

1980

A heavy mist lifted over the Juniata River. It rose in thick layers before dissipating on the sheer cliffs of Blood Mountain. Their wings casting dark shadows, vultures soared in and out of the mist. The trail on the side of the mountain was steep and bathed in bright sunshine. Advancing laboriously up the trail, two Twin River High School sophomores dropped their bicycles loaded with camping gear against a boulder.

"Jeez, it's hot," Conner Brooks said, removing his long-sleeved shirt. He had thick black hair that drooped low over his ears. At an even six foot, Conner was the taller of the two boys. He also was stronger, his chest and biceps showing smooth definition as he twisted the moisture from the shirt.

"It's too damn hot," Matt grumbled. Matthew Henry was five-feet-eight inches, and he was thin. He had a soft, clear child's face and large brown hypnotic eyes. Streaked with perspiration, his brown hair lay flat over his forehead.

"My dad says this is the hottest Indian summer he's ever seen," Conner commented.

"Your dad knows what he's talking about," Matt said. "He's pretty smart for a janitor." Matt's white T-shirt was plastered to his skin.

When Matt stepped in front of him, Conner saw wide, dark lines through the cloth.

"Don't move, Matt," Conner instructed, and he lifted the T-shirt. Black-and-blue welts crisscrossed Matt's back. "Jeez, Matt! Your skin's all tore up!"

"It's nothing," Matt said, pulling the shirt down.

"I've heard talk about your dad being mean. He did it to you, didn't he?" Conner didn't wait for an answer. "I never liked that man. It's real scary when he looks at you, because his right eye is all dark and it never moves."

"That's because it's a glass eye, Conner. Sometimes he takes it out and shoves it in my face to frighten me."

"That's crazy. You need to tell the sheriff."

"Sheriff Parks don't care. He plays cards with Mr. Henry every weekend. The only reason I'm here now is because they went to play poker in Atlantic City."

"You worship at Redemption Mountain. Talk with the Reverend Towers."

"Jeremiah Towers won't do anything either. Mr. Henry gave him the cheap loans to build his church up there on the mountain." Matt grabbed the handlebars and began pushing the bicycle up the trail. Conner caught up to him. After a short distance, Matt stopped at a large boulder on the edge of the trail.

"Conner," Matt said, getting behind the boulder, "let's roll it down the mountain." Conner nodded and stepped next to Matt. Groaning, Matt pushed on the boulder; Conner threw his shoulder into the rock surface. The boulder moved slightly and settled back.

"Jeez, it's too heavy."

"Wait," Matt said. He picked up a branch and jammed the edge under the boulder.

"You're smarter than you look." Conner got behind the boulder and pushed. Matt slid his shoulder under the branch and heaved upward. The boulder swayed, tipped forward, and went over the edge. There was a loud rumbling sound. The boulder hit the trail below and flattened a tree. A flock of birds scattered high in the air. Matt began laughing and clapping his hands.

"That was awesome!" Matt shouted joyfully. Conner noticed a coiled shape at Matt's feet and grabbed him by the shoulder.

"Matt, stop jumping around," Conner whispered. When Matt glanced down, his body tensed; his face turned ashen. Conner took the branch from Matt's hand. "Just stay still, Matt. Dad says snakes have bad vision and only strike out when something moves."

"I ain't moving!"

"Not even an inch," Conner cautioned. A strong wind blew over the mountain. Moving quickly, Conner slid the branch under the snake and tossed it in the air. Suddenly, the rising wind caught the twisting body and flung it back toward Matt.

"Son of a b—" Matt screamed. The snake hit him on the chest, the flaky skin scraping against his shoulder, the hollow tail rattling in the wind. Conner flicked the snake off Matt's chest and laughed.

"You should see your face!"

"Nothing but an old dry skin," Matt said, and he crushed it under his sneaker. He had a relieved expression on his face. "How much farther to the top?"

"Not too far," Conner said. He and Matt began moving up the trail. "I have a question, Matt. How come you never finish what you're saying? You get all excited and shout, '*Son of a b*—,' and then you just shut up. I'm waiting and waiting, but you never say the *bitch* word."

"I'm not allowed to say it."

"What do you mean, you're not allowed?"

Matt didn't answer. They pushed their bicycles into a shaded area. Dark clouds drifted over the mountain; the wind made a roaring noise through the branches. Barely audible above the noise, Matt spoke in a soft voice.

"I called Mr. Henry that name the first time he hit me. He wouldn't stop until I promised never to call him that again." The wind subsided, leaving an awkward silence. Matt lowered his head.

"Mr. Henry swore it was necessary to punish me. He hurts me in different ways. I hate him."

"I'm sorry, Matt. I didn't know." Conner pushed the bicycle up the trail. The sun was setting when he and Matt reached the summit, a football-sized clearing cluttered with boulders, patches of brush, and trees. Pinecones lay on the ground. Long brown needles crunched under the wheels of the bicycle.

"Over there," Matt said, pointing to the largest tree in the clearing. He pushed his bike past two mounds of dirt. "Watch out for these ants." Matt reached the pine tree and dropped the bicycle against the gnarled roots. "It's a white pine. I've never seen one this big." Matt looked up and pointed. "Conner, someone tied a rope on that bottom branch."

"You need glasses," Conner said, laughing. "It's only a vine." Hanging from the branch, the end of the vine curled in the form of a circle. Thunder sounded in the darkening sky, and a gust of wind dropped pine needles from the tree. The vine began to swing back and forth.

"We'd better hurry," Conner suggested. He took the tent from the bicycle, and he and Matt stretched it flat on the ground. Grabbing a pile of pegs, Matt began to work on his side of the tent. After a few minutes, Conner still had pegs in his hand when Matt hammered his last one into the ground.

"I'll help you," Matt said, walking over and taking a peg from Conner.

"You're good at this."

"I like putting things together. Nothing interests me at school, except maybe wood shop when I'm building something. School's pretty boring."

"I tell my dad that all the time."

"What do you tell your mom?"

"Nothing," Conner said. "She left us."

"Why'd she leave?"

"I don't know. Dad took two of his best friends hunting in Polecat Hollow. Something real bad happened there. They were murdered."

"How do you know that?"

"I don't for sure. I just suspect they were murdered. The day it happened Dad came home all angry and crazy. He shouted at me, and he was even shouting at Mom. He went into the woods and stayed there a long time. He came back all bloody. That's why Lucy … that's my mom's name … I think that's why she left. Now Dad sits on the porch and plays this *Lucille* song all the time." Swinging the hammer, Conner hit the final metal peg into place. He nudged Matt in the shoulder. "What about your mom? Why doesn't she help when Mr. Henry hits you?"

"She can't help me." Matt hesitated, lowering his head, shuffling his shoes. "My mom died in childbirth."

The sun set with a hazy glow. Thunder cracked in the distance. Conner went to the bicycles and returned with the sleeping bags, a backpack, and a blue-and-white cooler. After he dropped everything in the tent and zipped the opening shut, Conner motioned to the cliff and the dark cloud of mist rising in the air.

"Let's check out the Shadows of Death." Conner started walking, and Matt followed a few steps behind. They maneuvered around patches of brush and huge, waist-high boulders. The ground became moist and slippery.

"This is close enough," Conner said, stopping a few yards from the cliff. Matt stepped past him and went to the edge. He stood there motionless as vapor from the Shadows of Death settled over his body.

"Wow," Matt said.

"Wow what?" Conner asked, and he slid his feet forward. Through the mist, he saw the wide, circular pool at the confluence of the Little Juniata and Juniata Rivers. On the bluff overlooking the pool, yellow security lights lit up the corners of the school.

"Twin River," Matt said. "And there's Redemption Mountain across the river."

The mountain and the gigantic cross at the summit were dark shadows. Suddenly, four rows of lights blinked on, and ascending rapidly up the sides of the cross, the lights merged at the top in a brilliant display.

"The Flaming Cross," Conner said. "It's beautiful."

"Reverend Tower's church," Matt said. "It's more like a cathedral. I watched the trucks come in and unload blocks of marble from Italy. The reverend carved out a burial grotto next to the cathedral. He modeled it like the Roman catacombs. His wife was the first one buried there. Mrs. Towers fell off the mountain. The fire police and volunteers searched for a long time, but it was Cain who found her body. He knew right where to look."

"Cain and his brother, Abel, are weird. And dangerous. They're always picking on someone. I can't figure them being sons of a minister."

"They're not his sons, Conner. Reverend Towers adopted the twins. They were in some kind of reformatory because they killed and sacrificed animals. The reverend told Mr. Henry that was all in the past. Living at Flaming Cross would make them good Christians. He changed their names to Cain and Abel. But those are terrible names. Cain bashed his brother's head in. It was the first murder in the biblical history of the world."

"How do you know so much about the Bible?"

"When Mr. Henry gets drunk, he makes me read scripture to him. Mostly he wants me to read from the book of Revelation. He likes listening to Revelation because it relaxes him and puts him to sleep."

Lightning flashed over the mountain. For a brief second the river below was a line of molten silver. Then the brightness was gone; the river turned black, and thunder echoed down the valley. A dark shadow and then another larger shadow swooped down from the sky. When the birds glided toward Conner, beady eyes focusing on his face, Conner flung his hands in the air and stepped back, pulling Matt with him.

"Don't worry, Conner. They're turkey vultures. They only eat dead things."

"Why are they coming toward me? I'm not dead. Let's get out

of here!" As he and Matt turned, they walked into a swarm of mosquitoes and began running toward the tent. After Matt jumped in, Conner zipped the flap shut. In the darkness, he opened the cooler and took out a heavy-duty flashlight. Conner clicked it on and beamed the light around the tent before placing it on the ground.

Three miles upriver, Gene Brooks entered his two-story, wooden-framed house. Gene was six-feet-two inches tall, and he had an agile, muscular frame. His face was clear, the skin smooth and tight. Loud thunder cracked outside, and drops of rain began to spatter against the roof.

Walking to the fireplace, Gene looked at the row of pictures on the shelf. The first picture was of Lucy and Gene. Inches shorter than Gene, Lucy wore a yellow blouse open at the bottom. She had a graceful, angular body. Lucy was holding baby Conner in her arms. Gene had an arm wrapped around Lucy; they both were smiling. Lucy's smile was exuberant; her eyes gleamed in the light.

"You're beautiful," Gene whispered.

The second picture was taken when Gene was on leave from Vietnam. Gene and Lucy stood holding hands on the steps of Holy Waters Church in Barree. Lucy was dressed in a white gown; Gene wore a military uniform. Gene's older brother, Pastor Andrew Brooks, who had conducted the marriage ceremony, and his wife, Joyce, stood next to Conner. Conner, who was now four years old, had his head lowered, looking at the ground.

There was a group wedding picture on the wall. Conner was not in the picture. Gene's best man, Pete Rogers, stood next to him. Lucy and her family from Water Street filled the first two rows. Standing at the end of the row, Lucy's younger brother, Wally, had a cropped haircut. He was eighteen years old and a star on the Twin River football team.

Wally had a glazed look on his face. At the reception, Gene had given him drink after drink of Jack Daniels, and Wally had thrown up all over the porch. Wally thanked Uncle Gene and told him he had the best time ever. Gene told Wally that he was a brother-in-law and not an uncle. Wally laughed and said they were all family together.

Three days after the wedding, Gene was dressed in a military uniform again. Waiting at the Huntingdon Train Station, he stood with Lucy and Conner, Andrew and Joyce, and a sober Wally. Gene shook Andrew's and Wally's hand. When the train came to a screeching stop, Conner began to cry.

"Be still, soldier," Gene ordered. Conner wiped at the tears on his face.

Gene held Lucy's hand until the conductor called to him. Kissing Lucy quickly, Gene jumped up the steps and disappeared inside the coach. Lucy and Conner waved at the train as it moved down the tracks. Bright sunlight filtering through the glass, Gene sat at the window. His eyes were tightly closed against the light.

Wind howled, and rain blew in through the open window. Gene pulled the window shut, went to the kitchen, and took an Iron City beer out of the refrigerator. Walking back to the living room, he switched on the TV and VCR. The show was a rerun of the first episode of *The Dukes of Hazzard*. With cars racing down the road, the credits flashed on the screen, and the theme song filled the room:

> Just the good ole boys,
> Never meanin' no harm.
> Beats all you ever saw,
> Been in trouble with the law
> Since the day they was born.

Gene took a drink of Iron City and laughed. The orange 1969 Dodge Charger, big "01" stenciled on the side door, Confederate flag on the roof, was racing away from the sheriff's car. It was a wild chase that ended with the sheriff's car crashing through a construction site, flipping in the air, and landing on its side.

"You are so damn dumb," Gene said when Sheriff Rosco appeared on the screen. The sheriff entered the Boars Nest, where Jefferson Davis Hogg was sitting at a table. The plate in front of him had three slices of liver floating in a pool of blood. Boss Hogg smiled and forked a piece of liver; Sheriff Rosco had a horrified look on his face. A flash of lightning blazed through the window. In the roar of thunder, the television went dark.

"Damn it," Gene said. He took his shotgun off the rack, shoved the cassette player under his arm, and went to the porch. A tightly woven brown hammock stretched from the wall to the railing. Taking a drink of Iron City, Gene sat comfortably on the hammock and clicked on the cassette player. The lyrics began slowly: *You picked a fine time to leave me, Lu-cille.* Lightning crisscrossed the night sky. Across the road, the Little Juniata River cracked silver waves the length of the grassy bank.

Thunder boomed over Blood Mountain; dark shadows fell from the tree. The steady beam from the flashlight filled the tent with a bright glow. Conner pulled out a hoagie and a can of Mountain Dew from the cooler. He took a bite of hoagie and looked at Matt.

"What's that you're eating?"

"Soy burger," Matt answered. He lifted the top of the sandwich and showed Conner some flattened lettuce and a thin, square patty.

Shaking his head, Conner bit into his hoagie stuffed with ham, cheese, a double-thick layer of mayonnaise, jalapeño peppers, black olives, lettuce, and tomatoes. He watched Matt put the last piece of soy burger into his mouth.

"That wasn't much of a meal, Matt. I didn't see any meat in there."

"I don't eat meat."

"That's crazy, not eating meat," Conner said, taking a big bite, mayonnaise sticking to his lower lip. "Now I know why you're so thin."

"Who do you think were the greatest fighters ever?" Matt asked.

"I don't know. Maybe André the Giant or Hulk Hogan."

"No." Matt laughed. "Not the fake TV fighting. I'm talking about the Roman gladiators. Archeologists found a gladiator cemetery in Turkey. When the scientists analyzed the bones, they discovered the gladiators ate mostly barley, beans, and fruit. They were vegetarians."

"Is that why you don't eat meat? You're practicing to be a gladiator?" Conner finished his hoagie and drank some Mountain Dew, placing the can on the ground.

"I'm already a gladiator," Matt said. He opened his backpack and pulled out a black double-headed hammer; the short wooden handle fit comfortably in his grip. One side of the hammer had a sharpened point; the other side was smooth. "This is Dis Pater. I made it myself." Matt lifted the hammer in the air and swung it into the Mountain Dew can. The can flattened, the impact burying it deep in the ground.

"Dis Pater? What's Dis Pater?"

"He was the Roman god of death. If a gladiator had fatal wounds, Dis Pater, who was an attendee, dispatched him with one blow from the death hammer."

"Why did you make a death hammer, Matt? Are you planning to dispatch someone?" Conner asked, a look of amusement on his face.

"Maybe I am," Matt said, sliding the hammer under his belt. "When it's time, when I have the skill, I will be Dis Pater. I will dispatch someone."

There was a flash of lightning followed by a rolling crack of thunder. A strong gust of wind roared through the pine tree. A branch and some twigs hit the top of the tent. Turning his head, a pained expression on his face, Matt followed the scraping sound.

"Have you ever camped here before?"

"Two times," Conner answered. "The first time was with Dad. He made me go to the edge of the cliff. The shadows from the rapids smothered me. I was afraid and tried to leave, but Dad held me there. He said a real soldier controls his fear. The second time I camped here was after Mom left. I was by myself."

"I could never stay here alone." Matt unrolled his sleeping bag and got inside. A strong gust of wind partially lifted the tent off the ground; a larger branch hit the tent, scratching a hole in the canvas. "I don't like this, Conner. The way the wind's blowing, it could pick up this tent and drop us right in the Shadows. I'm thinking we should get some rope and tie the tent to the pine tree."

"No way." Conner slid into his sleeping bag. "I'm not going near that tree. The Dean massacre happened there. Dad told me the whole story. After listening to the way he told it in the dark, I swore never to go camping with him again."

"Was it that bad?"

"It was worse than bad. The Indians and white Tory renegades chased the Dean family right to this spot. Back then it was called Holy Pine Mountain. After the massacre, the settlers changed the name to Blood Mountain. And for good reason, my dad said."

"I heard thirty settlers were massacred here."

"Not thirty, Matt. Quit your exaggerating. There were only twenty. And the women and children weren't massacred. They jumped to their death. But the Dean twins never jumped. They fought until they ran out of ammunition. The Indians and Tories captured them and tied them to the pine tree. The white Tory cut the twins bad and then threw piles of those damn ants on the bodies. Then he scalped them. The twins suffered. They bled to death."

"That's a terrible story. Why do men act that way?"

"Dad says he's seen it over and over. It's man's nature. Dad says certain people don't deserve to live."

"I agree with your dad. It says so in the Bible."

Lightning cracked over the tent. Thunder boomed immediately; a horrific wind rolled across the clearing. Two of the metal pegs tore out of the ground; the front fabric of the tent ripped open. Conner felt a layer of air flow under his body. The flashlight rolled against his sleeping bag; Conner picked it up.

A heavy branch at the top of the tree broke loose and ricocheted downward. It pierced through the tent and stuck solidly in the ground between the two sleeping bags. When lightning flashed again, Conner saw a thin, angular shape clinging to the branch. Wind whirled through the slit in the tent, tilting the branch toward Matt.

Conner focused the flashlight on the branch. In the wavering light, he saw the angular shape was a skeleton. Silver coils of wire held the bones against the bark. Both legs were missing. The white skull, jaws clattering open, stopped even with Matt's face.

"Son of a bitch," Matt gasped. He grabbed the death hammer and smashed it repeatedly into the skeleton. Fragments of skull and rib bone bounced off the side of the tent. Conner's hand began to shake; the flashlight swung erratically.

Through the flickering light, Conner saw the bony remains of a second skeleton embracing the branch. It was headless. Another peg broke loose, and the tent lifted off the ground. Shoving the flashlight under his belt, Conner grabbed Matt and pulled him outside. Tearing through the branch, the tent flapped noisily and disappeared into the abyss.

The gale-force wind knocked Conner and Matt on the ground, rolled them a short distance, and slammed them hard against a mammoth boulder. His back flat against the rock, Conner watched as dark particles flew at them. When there was a flash of lightning, he saw ant bodies stuck to Matt's shirt. Then a loud wailing noise moved over the mountain. The wind sucked the branch off the ground. Lashed to the wood, the headless skeleton danced vertically across the clearing and pirouetted into the Shadows of Death.

As suddenly as it had begun, the wind slackened. There was a dim glow of light in the sky, and thunder sounded in the distance. Conner stood and pulled Matt to his feet. Matt's eyes were open wide; both hands clutched the death hammer.

Conner took the flashlight from his belt and pointed it toward the tree. The two bicycles were twisted under the roots. He and Matt walked across the clearing, and jerking on the handlebars, they pulled the bicycles free. When Conner saw black-and-red ants crawling on the frame, he flashed the light on the broken sections of the mound. Laboring in long lines, ants carried particles of debris up and down the side of the mound.

"Let's get the hell out of here," Conner said. He pushed the bicycle toward the trail. Matt followed him. There was a light drizzle, and heavy drops of rain fell from the trees. Trying to hold the flashlight steady, Conner walked slowly, the light throwing a faint glow on the trail. Matt pushed up next to him and grabbed the handlebar.

"Conner."

"Yeah." He swung the light around, shining it in Matt's face.

"There were two skeletons in the tree. One skeleton didn't have any legs. And one didn't have a head! The vultures did it, Conner. The vultures ate the flesh off the bodies." Matt's hair was plastered flat by the rain; his face glimmered in the light; and his eyes darted right and left. "If the storm had killed us, vultures would have eaten our flesh, too."

"Jeez, Matt ..." Conner shook his head and pushed the bicycle down the mountain. Matt was close behind him. Reaching the base of Blood Mountain, they climbed onto their bicycles and pedaled rapidly. There were a few barn lights, but mostly they went through dark woods. The rain was steady, and there was the occasional flash of lightning. As they approached the intersection at Petersburg, music echoed in the darkness. Headlights glowed brighter on the winding road, and the music became loud and distinct.

> We don't need no education;
> We don't need no thought control.
> Teacher, leave those kids alone.

Splashing water high in the air, a red pickup truck came into view. Above the roar of the engine, Pink Floyd shouted through the open window: *Hey, Teacher, leave those kids alone!* When the truck careened through the intersection, a black garbage bag flew out of the back. It hit the road and split open. Conner watched a pale object spin free of the plastic. The bright headlights raced away; Pink Floyd's voice became weaker: *All in all you're just another brick in the wall.* The music disappeared in the falling rain. When Conner pushed his bicycle to the ripped garbage bag, he saw a hand resting on the wet asphalt.

"What the hell!" he exclaimed. Conner knelt down, grabbed the hand, and slid it inside the bag. Matt watched the fingers disappear and shouted, "Conner, are you crazy?"

"Jeez, Matt, we can't just leave it here," Conner said, tying the bag to his carrier. "It ain't roadkill." He jumped onto the bicycle and began pedaling furiously. The road followed the Little Juniata River, and when lightning flashed, a bright glow reflected off the water.

Breathing heavily, glancing at the shiny surface of the garbage bag, Matt saw the flaps flare open. Lightning blazed across the road, and the hand waved wet fingers at him. Matt made a wheezing noise and pedaled harder.

The red pickup truck slowed at the twenty-acre parking lot at the base of Redemption Mountain. Off to the side, the Reverend Tower's residence, a sprawling three-story, stone house with seventeen rooms, was flooded with security lights. Leaning forward, Cain turned the wheel sharply, and the truck sped up Commandment Road.

"You lost a bag at the intersection," Abel said. "I recognized the boy on the bicycle. It was that creep son of the janitor. The bag fell at his feet."

"He's a wimp. We'll talk to him tomorrow." Cain slammed down on the gas, racing the truck up the wide circular road.

There were large stone tablets spaced the length of the road. Each tablet displayed one of the Commandments. Sliding onto the berm, the truck scraped the first tablet: "I am the Lord thy God." Sparks and particles of sand flew in the air. Abel grabbed the dash with both hands. Cain laughed and accelerated. Reaching the summit in record time, he braked in front of the security gate. The Flaming Cross filled the area with light. Glittering off the puddles, the magnified cross glowed the length of the courtyard. Cain grabbed the remote off the dash.

"Open, sez-me." Cain pressed the remote; the wheels on the gate began to move. Before the gate was half-open, Cain gunned the engine. The truck lurched high over the speed bump, scraped the gate, and splashed through the puddles, shattering the Flaming Cross into shards of light. Still laughing, Cain slid the truck to a stop in front of a large portal. There was a golden sign with black lettering, "Catacombs of Rapture," above the portal. Cain pressed another button on the remote, and the two doors of the portal swung open. Cold air seeped out, clouding the security lights in mist.

"Grab the bag!" Cain ordered, getting out of the truck. Entering the cavernous room, Cain pushed the switch on the wall, and the fluorescent lights on the ceiling flickered into brightness. The walls on each section of the catacombs had ivory crosses and the large Roman letters *A, B, C, D* inlaid in the stone. Each burial chamber had a thick glass door. As Cain and Abel walked down the passageway, they approached a chamber with a gold cross above it. The inscription on the door was written in bold letters:

Irene Towers
Beloved Wife of Jeremiah Towers
Beloved Mother of Cain and Abel Towers

When Cain and Abel were directly in front of the door, there was a clicking noise, and *Bringing in the Sheaves* sounded softly from two recessed speakers.

"Damn it, Abel. Why did you put in that damn sensor?"

"The reverend likes to listen to Mom's gospel music." Abel hesitated before he spoke. "That day on the mountain, Cain, why'd you do it? Why'd you push Mom?"

"The opportunity presented itself."

"But why? She was loving it here."

"She was always ordering me to do things. When she squeaked, 'In one ear and out the other' for the hundredth time, I nudged her just a little." Cain laughed and shoved Abel down the passageway. The gospel music stopped; the cross dimmed behind them.

Cain and Abel walked to the Children of God section at the end of Catacomb B. They stopped in front of a burial chamber that had a picture of a young girl on the glass door. She had a bright smile on her face. The inscription under the picture read,

Our Beloved Daughter
Emily Johnson
1973–1980
At Peace in the Hands of the Lord

Cain pressed the code numbers, slid the glass door to the side, and opened the casket. Abel tossed the garbage bag onto a white, lacy dress. The stench of formaldehyde drifted into the passageway. Cain closed the coffin and locked the glass doors.

"It wasn't done right," Able commented as he and Cain walked away. "Emily's hands were too short. They didn't fit. We couldn't do the ceremony like we should."

"I know that, Abel. But we got the legs in place, didn't we? Just to be sure, I measured the body cavity. Becky will fit perfectly."

"I like her," Abel commented. "She's way prettier than Abbey Lee ever was. And I like how we set those traps for the wolf. We should get some rabbits to feed it."

"That'll be your job," Cain said. They hurried past Irene's burial chamber. Cain was quiet when *Bringing in the Sheaves* sounded from the speakers. At the portal, Cain pushed the red button, switching off the lights. After closing the portal, he and Abel got into the truck and began the drive down Commandment Road. On their wild descent, Abel cautioned his brother when the dark shape of a deer appeared on the road. Cain shouted, accelerated, and smashed the fender into its hind leg. Drumming his hands on the steering wheel, he raced the truck past the looming stone tablets.

Conner heard heavy breathing behind him as Matt pedaled to keep up. Both boys were soaked when they turned on River Road. The cement gave way to cracked sections of asphalt that had huge potholes overflowing with water. Conner slowed when he saw the dim porch light in the distance. The familiar lyrics of Kenny Rogers's *Lucille* drifted through the night shadows.

> You picked a fine time to leave me, Lu-cille.
> Four hungry children and a crop in the field.
> I've had some bad times, lived thru some sad times,
> But this time your hurtin' won't heal.

Conner turned into the lane. Through the mist, he saw the house and the decrepit garage that slanted to the right. There was no door on the garage; the orange-styled *Dukes of Hazzard* jeep, "01" spray-painted on the side, a white "National Rifle Association of America MEMBER" logo on the window, glistened in the rain. A rusty basketball hoop hung under the rainspout, and a red wagon was nailed to the roof. Black turtle shells covered the side of the garage.

There was a clicking sound; the whining notes of *Lucille* stopped suddenly. Rain streaming down his face, Conner dropped the bicycle in the wet grass, grabbed the black garbage bag, and ran up the porch steps. His dad sat on the hammock, a shotgun balanced across his lap, the barrel pointed to the road, empty bottles of Iron City on the floor. Matt ran up the steps. His eyes on both of them, Gene Brooks pushed the rewind button on the cassette player.

"You're back kind of early, aren't you, soldier?"

"Yeah, we're back early," Conner said. With a quick motion, he pointed to Matt. "This is my friend Matthew, the banker's son. It's too late for him to go home, so he's sleeping here. Good night, Dad." Pulling open the screen door, Conner pushed Matt inside.

"Your girlfriend Cindy was here looking for you," his dad called after him. "Why don't you tell people—" The screen door slammed shut before he could finish. Dripping water on the floor, Conner removed his shoes and wet socks. Matt did the same.

"Wait here," Conner said. Holding the garbage bag tightly in his hand, he ran down the steps to the basement.

Chilled and dripping wet, Matt stood in the living room. There was a brown sofa, a La-Z-Boy with faded cushions, a corner table with a lamp, a VCR, and a small television with rabbit ears. Looking at the pictures on the shelf above the fireplace, Matt recognized Mr. Brooks in his army uniform and the diminutive Conner. Three rows of deer trophies, their antlers reaching far into the room, were mounted on the wall.

A glass display case was set in the middle row of antlers. Stepping closer, Matt looked inside the case and saw two large knives with gleaming silver blades and ivory handles. The metal inscription on the case read, "Arkansas Toothpick—1830." Matt turned when Conner pushed open the basement door.

"Where's the hand?"

"I put it in the freezer under a pile of deer steaks."

"What!"

"It'll be frozen soon and won't smell so bad," Conner explained. He walked up the staircase to the bedroom. His bed was next to a window overlooking the road and the Little Juniata River. There was a cot on the other side of the room. A wooden dresser was pushed against the back wall. Conner pulled shorts and T-shirts out of the dresser and gave one pair to Matt. They threw their wet jeans and shirts in the corner and put on the dry clothes.

"You have the cot. The mattress is real solid."

"Great." Matt got on the cot and slid under the sheet. "What a crazy camping trip! I'm still shaking. What the hell happened?"

"Are you asking about the hand on the road or the skeletons on Blood Mountain?"

"Mostly the skeletons."

"It was no big deal, Matt. The skeletons dropped out of the sky and nearly crushed us to death, that's all."

"Shouldn't you tell your dad?"

"We don't talk much. When he first came back from Vietnam, I tried talking with him. Mom tried, too. But he ignored us. Most nights he's on the porch with the gun. He drinks and talks to himself. He's always ranting about this guy called Harry."

"Who's Harry?"

"I don't know, but Dad's crazy when he gets to Harry. He takes off for the mountain. Sometimes he's gone for days. I don't know what he does up there."

"You should find out."

"I told you he won't talk about it. Once he said he was on the porch to protect Mom and me because it was dangerous here like in Vietnam. When I asked him what happened in Vietnam to make things so dangerous here in Hartslog Valley, he just shut up."

"Conner," Matt said, leaning forward, "I know why he won't talk about Vietnam."

"You never met my dad until tonight. How can you know anything?"

"Because I know!" Matt exclaimed in a voice that was too loud. He was quiet for a moment, caught his breath, and looked across the room. The sound of *Lucille* drifted softly though the night air. "When bad things happen, sometimes it's hard to talk about them."

"Dad did say there were bad things." Sitting up, Conner stared at Matt, who now lay rigidly on the cot. "He said when bad things happened, they happened fast. When you talk about them later, you have to find the words. And not just any words. He said finding the right words is slow and painful. How did you know about that, Matt?"

"What I told you on the mountain, I never told anyone. I was being careful, real careful, but it was difficult. The words hurt me a lot when I said them for the first time." His eyes open wide, Matt turned onto his side, cushioning his head under his forearm. Conner sat up straight and stared across the room.

"I'm sorry, Matt. I didn't know. We've got to get you out of that house."

"I'll never get away. Mr. Henry's too rich and powerful. He owns this town."

"He doesn't own us. We'll fight him together. We'll be like Batman and Robin. They're my favorites. They always win. And Cindy was here tonight. She'll help us."

"She can be Catwoman."

"No, she's allergic to cats. She'll just be herself." Conner yawned. "We should get some sleep. Good night, Matt."

"Good night, Conner." Matt laughed and clapped his hands. "Wow, that's the first time I've said those words in years."

"What words?"

"Good night."

"We've got to get you out of that house," Conner repeated, and he looked out the window. The frogs chirped along the banks of the Little Juniata. *Lucille* clicked off. Conner heard footsteps on the porch and watched his dad, binoculars around his neck and shotgun in his hand, splash across the yard. Conner yawned and closed his eyes. He slept fitfully. Hours later, he sat up rigid as the sharp echo of a gun blasted into the room.

Carrying a rifle, the man brushed stealthily through the stalks of corn. He had a mustache, plump red lips, and a bushy beard. His gray hair was thick and unruly. At the edge of the cornfield, the man dropped to one knee and swung his rifle across the front of Twin River High School. A night light was on in Mrs. Walters's room. Her desk and black leather swivel chair were in shadow. A plaster bust of Shakespeare sat on the desk. The man fired. The bullet went through the window, shattered the bust, and embedded itself in the swivel chair, which spun around rapidly. The man shouldered the rifle and hurried through the cornfield, his boots leaving deep prints in the mud.

Stopping on a narrow trail on the mountainside, Gene Brooks lifted his binoculars when he heard the gunshot. Gene focused on the figure approaching the truck at the edge of the cornfield. A large oval red-and-silver "NRA Bull's-Eye Marksman" logo was on the back window. Swinging the door open, the man got into the truck and drove away.

Charlie Hesston, what the hell are you up to? Lowering the binoculars, Gene sat down, his back resting against a tree. A flash of lightning momentarily lit up the sky, and then the mountain was in total darkness. Rain dripped steadily through the leaves. Gene closed his eyes, and within minutes, he drifted back to the war and the Ho Chi Minh Trail.

Chapter Four

Ho Chi Minh Trail, Laos

1971

Towering trees rose from the jungle floor. Their branches formed a green, interlocking canopy that shut out the sun and dropped dark shadows across the lush mat of ferns and moss. Vines and creepers and an occasional orchid clung to the trees. When wind or lightning toppled a tree, thick patches of bamboo formed in the empty space. Narrow animal trails skirted the impenetrable bamboo.

Camouflaged as a leaf fragment high in the bamboo, a jumping spider, *Portia fimbriata*, perched motionless over a gigantic web. When a fly hit the web, its wings vibrating the sticky silk thread, a large funnel web spider moved cautiously from its refuge. As it approached the fly, *Portia fimbriata* jumped on the back of the funnel web spider and buried fangs in its neck. After *Portia* devoured the head and body delicacies of the funnel spider, it crept toward the fly, which emitted an erratic buzzing noise.

Gene and JJ Jackson stepped into a clearing that was choked by jungle and low-hanging branches. JJ, a trim twenty-four-year-old Negro, was breathing evenly after two hours of mountain trekking. He had a serious face and narrow clear eyes that darted left and right across the clearing. JJ wore a green Viet Cong bush hat, a brown shirt and fatigues, and a pair of black Converse tennis shoes. Except for the Converse tag, there were no labels on his clothing. He had a Colt M1911 on his belt. JJ nudged Gene in the shoulder.

"Why are we stopping?" he whispered.

"Stay here and don't move. Whatever happens, don't move an inch."

"Why can't I move?"

"Because one, maybe two VC are watching us."

Gene slid into the jungle. There was a slight brushing sound, and JJ looked at the line of trees across the clearing. The branches parted; a Viet Cong soldier stepped forward. The oversized green uniform draped loosely over his body, the AK-47 strapped on his shoulder, the soldier stood there quietly. He was staring directly at JJ. JJ didn't breathe.

When another VC soldier stepped next to the first, JJ felt his lungs collapse. He remained perfectly still. The second VC slid the AK-47 off his shoulder, smiled, and aimed it casually at JJ. JJ remained frozen in place.

Out in the open. An easy target. And I'm ordered not to move an inch, JJ thought. The images of his wife and two sons flashed in front of him. *I'm sorry. I'm so sorry.*

Then JJ heard a light whishing sound and saw a glint of silver fly across the clearing. The knife sliced deep into the chest of the VC, lifting him off the ground. Mouth dropping open, the second VC began moving his AK-47 into position when another knife shot in a straight line the length of the clearing. It struck the VC in the throat. Blood gushed in the air. Still clutching the AK-47, the soldier was spun sideways before his body hit the ground.

Gene materialized from the shadows and nodded to JJ, who wobbled slightly before following him across the clearing. Removing the knives, Gene cut the straps of the bulky VC backpacks. Then he placed a heavy plastic bag next to the first VC. He gave an identical plastic bag to JJ.

"Body bags," Gene said. "Just do as I do, and we can clean up this mess." Gene stripped away the VC uniform, slid the body into the plastic bag, and zipped the bag shut. Watching everything closely, JJ did the same. Gene pulled a smaller bag from his pocket, collected the bloodied uniforms, and threw them inside.

"Let's go," Gene said. Picking up the VC backpacks, he gave one to JJ. Gene slid the backpack into place, draped the body bag over his shoulder, and began walking at a fast pace.

"Slow down," JJ said. Body bag bouncing off his chest, he hurried to catch up.

Gene led JJ through a hilly terrain of hanging vines and towering trees. Mumbling to himself, JJ wiped the sweat from his eyes. Hours later, Gene dropped the body bag at the base of a massive tree. There were no low branches; the trunk angled straight in the air, disappearing in the canopy of leaves. Unzipping the bags, Gene pulled out the bodies and leaned them against the tree. Straightening, he lowered his backpack to the ground.

"Wait here." Gene walked to the neighboring tree and pulled himself onto a branch. JJ listened as the branches shook under Gene's weight. Immense black flies buzzed out of the jungle and swarmed over the bloody bodies.

"Catch," Gene shouted from above. A rope twisted in the shape of a harness dropped down from the shadows.

"Got it," JJ said, grabbing the rope. "Now what?"

"Tie the harness around the VC's shoulders."

"Say what!" JJ exclaimed.

"Just make sure the harness is tight. I don't want one of these bodies falling on you."

"Damn," JJ said. Swatting at the flies, he maneuvered the rope over the shoulders of the first VC and tied the ends together. "Done," he said.

Releasing the harness, JJ stepped back and watched the naked VC body disappear in the tree. Ten minutes later the empty harness dropped to the ground. JJ hooked up the second VC and gave the rope a sharp tug. The body, legs spinning in circles, swung upward through the branches.

JJ walked to a shady area and sat down. After twenty minutes, a redbreasted parakeet screeched and flew out of the tree. Gene jumped to the ground, rolled up the body bags, and joined JJ. JJ shook his head.

"Why do you go up one tree and come down the other?"

"I made it impossible for anyone to climb the VC tree house. I use the smaller tree. There's a solid crossover branch halfway up. It's easy to hoist the bodies from there."

"In civilized countries, we bury the dead, even those of our enemies."

"Forget civilization. This is the jungle. Animals would dig up the bodies. VC trackers would find them."

"So you dispose of them in the tree?"

"I wire the bodies to the top branches. The birds and big cats eat them. It's sanitary. The bodies just disappear. I take the uniforms back to base camp and burn them."

"A clinical operation. How many you got wired up there?"

"A bunch."

"You make them sound like bananas," JJ said, a smile on his face. "The Viet Cong have a name for you. We interrogated a prisoner, and he explained this fear of the Jungle Ghost." JJ studied the towering tree. "Would you have put me up there?"

"You weren't in any real danger, JJ. You followed directions. You didn't move an inch. Alpha trained you well."

"Who trained *you*? You know more about the Trail than anyone at Alpha."

"I watched the VC. I studied everything they did. They trained me."

"Then you're as ruthless as your enemy. Except for that battle on Hill 101, you've always come out a winner."

"How do you know about Hill 101?"

"I read the classified government document not once, but twice. There were only two survivors on Hill 101—you and Lieutenant Chase Butler. It must have been one hellish fight. A news reporter took a picture of two Vietnamese heads spiked in the ground. What do you know about that?"

"I put the heads on the spikes."

"Say what! I'm missing something here, Gene. Those two heads were South Vietnamese. They were our allies."

"They weren't our allies when I killed them."

"Do you care to explain that?"

"No," Gene said. "We should get back." He stood, positioned the backpack, and motioned to the jungle.

———

Hours later, the setting sun cast a red glow over the mountains. Gene approached a dense thicket of bamboo. At the higher levels, the bamboo was covered with spiderwebs dotted with gray mounds of tightly wrapped insects. A black mouse tail protruded from one of the mounds. Gene dropped to the ground, lifted a section of bamboo, and crawled under it. JJ followed, lowering the bamboo behind him. The trail was narrow, the bamboo stems scraping against their bodies. Gene walked a short distance and stopped in front of a thin wire. He disarmed the claymore, navigated a series of turns, and stepped into a cleared area. Green knotted poles of bamboo formed a solid wall. An intricate maze of spiderwebs was woven in the bamboo. Overhead, the branches bent outward, leaving a panoramic view of the sky. Gene slid off the backpack and sat down. His eyes focusing on the bamboo, JJ dropped next to him.

"I never saw so many webs. I hate spiders. Don't they bother you?"

"Spiders are only dangerous when they're stalking prey. You and I don't qualify as food. I've been studying these spiders for over a year now. Some of them are doing strange things, really strange things." Gene pointed to a large funnel-shaped web high in the bamboo. "A fist-sized, black-and-white-banded spider lives in that funnel. Keep your eyes open. Let me know if his web starts to vibrate."

"I'll keep my eyes open," JJ promised, rubbing his hands nervously.

"What's worrying you? I told you the spiders were no threat."

"It's not the spiders so much, Gene. It's you. You worry me. At Alpha Base in Thailand, I read that you never carry a gun. Why is that, Gene? I sure would have felt better if you'd had a gun back there. Why don't you carry a gun like the rest of us normal soldiers?"

"I don't like all that noise. The Colt you have is fine, but after one shot, the VC would know your exact location. They would track you down and kill you." Gene reached back and pulled one of the knives from the double holster strapped to his back. The polished silver blade was twenty inches long and razor sharp on both sides. In a quick motion, Gene sliced through a trunk of bamboo.

"Say what!" JJ exclaimed, watching the bamboo fall to the ground.

"It's an Arkansas Toothpick," Gene said. "It's great for cutting and slashing and perfectly balanced for throwing. When a VC gets within range, say thirty feet, I can slide the knife out and throw it in one motion. The VC soldier is dead before he can lift his AK-47."

"Okay, I saw the Toothpick in action," JJ said, staring at Gene. "I would like to learn more about our last topic, Hill 101. I know that Captain Din was in command. He was murdered with a knife. The report said the wound was in his back."

"I can clarify that, JJ. The entry wound was in Din's chest. The tip of the blade pierced through his back. I shoved the Toothpick in with a lot of force."

"Then you killed him?"

"Yes, he was a traitor. There were others. It was a rough day. I nearly killed the photographer, the one who took the picture of the spiked heads."

"It's fortunate you didn't kill him. The picture he took was mesmerizing. It was in all the newspapers. He won a prestigious award."

"Good for him," Gene said in a derisive tone.

"With all your activity on Hill 101, you were barely mentioned in the final report. Lieutenant Butler got all the attention. The army investigators concluded that Butler was too young and inexperienced to be in command. He wasn't prepared for the attack."

"The military is always looking for scapegoats." Gene spoke in an even, precise voice. "You don't measure an officer's competency by his age. No one would have been prepared for what happened that night. Any more questions?" Gene glared at JJ.

"No." JJ leaned against the VC backpack. Gazing across the clearing, he detected motion at the large funnel web.

A small, dark object fell from a leaf, stuck on the edge of the silky threads, and began to move erratically. Vibrations moved up and down the web. A black shape appeared at the mouth of the funnel. Two long woolly feet stretched out of the opening; black fangs, small beady eyes, and a tennis-ball-sized head followed.

"Gene," JJ whispered. "The web—it's moving." JJ watched the gigantic spider crawl slowly across the web. "Gene, it's way bigger than I thought."

His eyes open wide in anticipation, Gene didn't say anything. The spider stopped, clicked its fangs open and shut, and then moved forward cautiously. The black object at the edge of the web jerked violently and was motionless. JJ sat up, his back rigid.

"Something bad is going to happen," he said.

When the black-and-white-banded spider was within a few feet of the edge of the web, the small object elevated and then, incredibly, leaped in the air. It landed on the back of the banded spider and buried its fangs in the neck. The large spider fell flat against the silky threads. Voracious fangs began to eat into its neck and head. JJ's mouth dropped open.

"I call it the jumping spider," Gene commented.

"I don't believe this. That jumper, whatever you call it, is twenty times smaller."

"But twenty times smarter. It lured the banded spider out of the funnel and killed it."

"You're telling me that spider can think?"

"Maybe it just does things better. The big spider spins a nice web, but I think it's dumb. It doesn't sense danger. Dumb can get you killed in the jungle."

"I agree." JJ watched as the head of the banded spider slowly disappeared, leaving two black eyes perched on the front of the empty skull. Fangs opened over one eye and sliced it in half. JJ shuddered and leaned on the backpack. "I was scheduled to be here two weeks ago. But you had left the Trail."

"I went on R & R in Saigon. I spent most of the week at a Chinese restaurant, the Green Dragon. It had great food downstairs and a whorehouse upstairs."

"Then you had a good time?"

"I had a miserable time, JJ. I couldn't reach my wife or my son, Conner. But I reached my sister-in-law. She informed me Lucy was dating the local sheriff, whom I despise. I immediately took the cheapest whore to the cheapest room in the Green Dragon."

"You were that pissed?"

"I was scared, JJ. I was scared to death I had lost her and my son."

"Let's stay away from that subject, too. What about this one? Your report on the pipeline got everyone's attention. We all went to the bar, drank ourselves drunk, and laughed for hours. No one at Alpha thought it was possible to build a pipeline in this kind of terrain. How did you find it?"

"At first I was curious why the gas trucks had disappeared. I couldn't figure it. The war was escalating, and I expected more traffic. Then I had some luck. I was wading across one of those submerged bridges. A US helicopter came by, and the door gunner began blasting away at me. I jumped into the river and hid under the bridge. When I tried to surface, my head bumped into a piece of plastic pipe. At first I thought it was just a bridge support, but when I cut a hole in the plastic, gasoline poured out. So I wrote the colonel a full report. I was always suspicious of Alpha, but when I got his response … that's when I knew for sure."

"Knew what?"

"You people at Task Force Alpha are a bunch of dumb-fucks."

"Say what!" JJ exclaimed. "That can't be true. Task Force Alpha doesn't even exist." JJ thought for a moment and looked at Gene. "But if it did happen to exist, I'd have to agree with you. No one at Alpha gave your plastic-pipe report any credence, but we went along. You sent us the coordinates, and we passed them to the Laos air force. When the B-28s showed up, the pilots saw a cloud of smoke right where you said it would be."

"I sliced through a section of pipe, threw a match on the gushing petroleum, and got the hell out of there."

"The pilots were astounded. They dropped the first bombs and reported smoke and fire everywhere. We called in the B-52 bombers to finish the job."

"It'll never be finished, JJ. The PAVN have cutoff values and alternate routes all along the Trail. They adjusted the flow of petroleum after the bombing."

"But it still was an eye-opener." JJ stretched and patted his stomach. "It's been a rough day. But I'll admit one thing. I really have an appetite now."

"I have the perfect remedy for hunger." Gene reached into his jacket and took out two silver packets. Unzipping the packets, he poured in some water, closed them, shook the contents, and handed one packet to JJ.

"Thanks," JJ said. He tasted the mixture, and a big smile formed on his face. He ate another spoonful. "I don't believe this. It's sweet-and-sour pork." JJ chewed slowly. "This was meant for NVA officers. When did you get their rations?"

"Right after I killed them," Gene said matter-of-factly. He finished eating, took the empty packets, and stashed them in his pack. "JJ, I'm amazed at how many planes fly over the Trail. The bombing is nonstop."

"It is nonstop. Air Force Chief of Staff Curtis LeMay, in his own words, hopes to bomb the Vietnamese back into the Stone Age. By some estimates, we've hit those people with over six million tons of explosives. That's more than all of World War II."

"Our munitions factories must be loving it."

"Of course they are, Gene. The managers, mostly retired military officers, have become instant millionaires."

"When I see all the traffic moving down the Trail, I don't think six million tons has had much effect, JJ. What do you think?"

"I think you're right. At the beginning of the war, the Trail was called Blood Road. It took months for a soldier to get south. Now he's outside Saigon in a few weeks." JJ glanced at the funnel web. The dark spider was motionless; two shiny oval eyes stared from the web. JJ shuddered again and looked away. "How long have you been out here?"

"Too long."

"Maybe it's time to leave."

"I can't leave yet. I'm tracking a traitor named Harry. He was responsible for the butchery on Hill 101."

"Colonel Haskins contends the white VC, whom both you and Lieutenant Butler cited in the debriefing, doesn't exist. But I did read one report about a soldier, Harry Wintergreen, who's AWOL. Harry was born in the Finger Lakes region of New York. He's part Seneca."

"That's the Indian I'm going to kill," Gene said. He was quiet for a moment. "JJ, there's something else I wanted to report before you left. Last week, I heard this noise. I put my ear flat on the ground and heard this very distinct noise. That was the first time ..." Gene hesitated, biting his lip.

"First time, what?"

"The first time I felt we would lose."

"What was it you heard?"

"The sound of a tank," Gene answered. JJ looked at him momentarily. Then a huge smile appeared on his face, and JJ laughed.

"Of course, you're joking. The VC have trouble getting their Czech-made bicycles down the Trail. No way can a tank get through."

"I heard a tank, JJ." There was a rustling sound in the bamboo, followed by a low growling noise.

"What that hell is that?" JJ asked, reaching for his gun.

"Don't worry. Just be still."

"First, it was 'don't move an inch'; now it's 'just be still.' Is remaining stationary your secret for jungle survival?"

"One of them," Gene said. He patted the ground with his hand and whispered, "Hondo. Hondo." The bamboo leaves parted, and a dog's head appeared. The black German shepherd crawled forward and stopped, its body tensing, its jaws snarling.

"Quiet," Gene said, petting the dog's head. Hondo's tail moved back and forth.

"That's a mean-looking dog. I'll bet you got his name from the John Wayne western."

"I did. The Duke is one of my favorite people."

"You got it all wrong, Gene. John Wayne was Hondo. The dog's name was Sam. But anyway, how did you find Hondo in this jungle?"

"The Special Forces had a supply base a few mountains away. There were six German shepherds guarding the perimeter. After the VC overran the base, they tethered the dogs and carried them out. It took me a while to find the camp. There were three VC around a fire. Hondo was on the ground, legs bound together. One of the VC grabbed a machete and started toward Hondo. I killed him first. Then I killed the other two.

"Hondo was starving. Since the fire was ready, I hacked off a section of VC and fed Hondo blackened calf muscle. He wolfed it down and wagged his tail for more. So I fed him blackened shoulder muscle. He loved it. I think that's when we bonded." Gene whispered in Hondo's ear. His eyes on JJ, Hondo growled and backed out of the bamboo. JJ sat motionless until the dog was out of sight.

"You say you're a fan of the Duke. What about his latest film, *The Green Berets*? It's been playing at the base all month. I just finished watching it for the third time."

"I saw it at Da Nang," Gene said. "I laughed when I saw the jungle. The movie was filmed in Georgia. I stuck it out until the Green Beret put the orphan on the helicopter and told the pilot to 'take care of the kid. No matter what happens, take care of the kid.' When I heard those words, I stumbled out of the theater." Gene's tone turned bitter. "I don't plan on watching the movie again."

"In a way, the battle scenes could have been scripted from your report on Hill 101. Both were defended by the same mixture of Vietnamese, Americans, and hill people. Both were overrun and then destroyed by American bombs. But there was a difference. You didn't have any kids to take care of."

"We had kids there," Gene spoke softly. He grabbed the VC backpack and pulled out a brown hammock with heavy cords at each end. Tying the cords to the bamboo, he flattened the hammock with his hand. "VC beds," he said.

"It looks solid." JJ unrolled his hammock and tied the cords to the bamboo.

"They're made in China. They're indestructible." Gene pulled the mosquito netting over the top and stretched out on the hammock.

"Well, here goes," JJ said with some anxiety, and he sat on the hammock. The cords tightened; the bamboo bent. Taking a deep breath, he settled his body in the folds. "This is really neat." Flat on his back, JJ stared at the night sky ablaze with light. "What a show! The stars are brilliant."

"It's like this every night during the cold season. Directly overhead, the brightest constellation is Orion, The Hunter. The line of three stars around Orion's waist make up his belt. You can see the sword. Orion was an expert hunter."

"So are you, Gene. And you both favor the same weapon." JJ turned on his side; the hammock flipped over and dropped him on the ground. Grabbing the hammock securely, he slid back on. "Do you want to know what I think? Between you, me, Orion, and Hondo, I think you've been out here too long."

"I'll be done soon," Gene said dryly. "Before you doze off, can you tell me something? Do you snore at all?"

"Hell, no," JJ answered with confidence. "I'm dead quiet when I sleep."

"Good. I feel better knowing you won't attract a big cat or a VC tracker."

It was warm inside the netting. Gene recognized the familiar animal stalking sounds and the occasional squeal of a kill. After a few minutes, JJ hiccuped once, twice, and began to snore. Hondo made a low growling noise and was quiet. Gene closed his eyes. Overhead, Orion was a flickering beacon in the night sky.

———————

There was a loud crashing noise in the brush. Immediately awake, staring into the shadows, Gene saw a large buck and three does pass in front of him. Far below, the lights around Twin River High School glowed in the darkness. Gene got up, stretched, and began the trek back to the house.

Chapter Five

On Sunday, Conner and Matt woke up late. The sun was shining, and the air was clear and fresh after the night's rain. Mr. Brooks made them an egg-and-bacon breakfast. Conner and Matt finished eating and were cleaning the table when they heard voices in the yard. Going to the porch, they saw Cindy Hoover and Alice Byrd pushing their bicycles down the walk.

Alice was dressed in blue shorts. The top buttons of her pinkish blouse swung loose, revealing a low neckline and the outline of healthy breasts. Her face was lively, her smile natural. Cindy wore tight yellow shorts and a white blouse. Sleek and mature for her age, she reached the top step and kissed Conner on the cheek.

"Good morning," she said. "Good morning, Matt. Do you know Alice?"

"Yes," Matt said, nodding to Alice. "I'm in your English class. Yesterday I heard what you said to Abel Towers."

"What'd you hear?"

"You sounded angry. You told Abel he'd have to buy a ticket if he kept looking at your breasts."

"Matt …" Conner admonished.

"No, he's right. I did say that. Abel's so horny."

"When Cain and Abel first moved here, they could date any of the girls," Cindy said. She looked at Conner. "Except for me and

Alice, of course. They're both handsome and well-built. But Cain's arrogant, and Abel's obnoxious. Abel calls himself the SF Man."

"What's *SF* mean?" Matt asked. "Satan's freak?"

"No."

"I know what *SF* means," Conner said.

"What?"

"Stupid fucker."

"Wow, Conner," Cindy observed. "I didn't know you had a problem with Abel."

"Maybe I do."

"Everyone has a problem with Abel," Alice said. "So what's *SF* really mean?"

"Shock force," Cindy said. "Abel tells people he likes to create shock. He runs the special effects at his dad's church on Redemption Mountain. It's loud and terrifying. Cain's like the director of the show."

"They're both creepy," Matt said in a low whisper.

"They sure are," Alice agreed quickly, turning a pleasant smile toward Matt. "We're going swimming after church. Do you want to join us?"

"If Mr. Henry gives me permission."

"I hope you can go," Alice said. "I see you at lunch, Matt, but you seldom look up. You never talk to anyone. Why are you so quiet?"

Matt didn't answer. Sunlight flooded the porch. Frogs splashed in the puddles in the yard. Chattering loudly, a bluebird flew from the tree. Beads of perspiration formed on Matt's face, and he lowered his head.

"Sometimes it's just that I don't know what to say."

"Everyone has something to say. You just need to practice. Maybe I can help you."

"Maybe," Matt said, looking at his watch. "But I can't start now. I left the house without permission. I have to get back before Mr. Henry finds out."

"I'm leaving, too. Can I ride with you to Barree?"

"Sure," Matt said. Waving to Conner and Cindy, Matt and Alice got on their bicycles. Conner watched the bicycles disappear down the road, and then he turned to Cindy.

"Matt finally talked to a girl. Do you think Alice will like him?"

"You can't help but like Matt. He has those big, soft eyes and such a cute face. But he always looks so unhappy. The corners of his mouth droop down, and he has this sad frown on his face."

"I know why he's sad," Conner said. Gene Brooks pushed open the screen door and walked onto the porch. "Dad, we were just talking about Matt. He's got a problem at home."

"What problem?"

"When we were camping on the mountain yesterday, I saw these bruises on Matt's back. Mr. Henry beats him. What can we do, Dad?"

"Until abuse is reported to the police, there's not much you can do."

"Matt won't report anything to Sheriff Parks. He doesn't trust him."

"I wouldn't trust Parks, either," Gene said. "I don't know who you can trust around here." Gene walked down the steps and across the yard to the garage. He backed the jeep out and drove down River Road.

Pedaling in silence, Matt and Alice reached the one-lane bridge over the Little Juniata River. They bumped their bicycles over the wooden planks and entered Barree. Main Street consisted of Holy Waters Church and a dozen houses. There was one truck in the church parking lot. A few of the houses had doors and windows boarded shut. Opposite the houses, shrubs and trees grew wild on the banks of the river. A dented Pontiac with a blue-and-white Penn State parking sticker on the windshield was abandoned there. All four tires and the doors were missing. When Alice stopped at the Pontiac, Matt pulled in beside her.

"Why isn't there anyone at the church?" he asked.

"It's been closed a few months now. Andrew Brooks, the pastor, is Conner's uncle. I don't know what he plans to do."

Loud barking sounded from one of the houses down the road. The door banged open, and Dan Boonie ran down the steps. Dan was tall; had a muscular, athletic body; and had his blond hair cut short. A huge dog with a shaggy white coat chased him. The dog jumped, placing soft paws on Dan's shoulders, and proceeded to lick his face.

"That dog is massive," Matt said.

"It's an Irish wolfhound named Ruggs. Dan's had him for years."

"I remember Dan. He graduated a few years ago. He was easy-going. He got along with everyone, even the teachers. What's he doing now?"

"I don't know," Alice answered. "Dan!" she called. "Did you get a job yet?"

"I just got hired at the Green Hollow Correctional Camp."

"That's a place for delinquents."

"I know," Dan responded, laughing. "I'll be right at home." Dan pushed Ruggs, ran down the bank, and dove into the river. Barking playfully, Ruggs leaped powerfully and hit the water as Dan surfaced. Dan let out a substantial yelp that echoed down the river.

"It's got to be cold." Alice took her gaze off the river and looked at Matt, a smile on her face. "Can we see each other again?'

"Sure. It's just that I don't get out very often."

"We'll find the time." Alice smiled, leaned closer, and kissed him on the cheek. His eyes opening wide, Matt blushed. He watched her cross the road to her house. When she reached the door, she turned and waved at him.

Matt waved back and pedaled slowly down Main Street. He jumped the railroad tracks and turned onto a gravel road. The road went through a large pasture and angled up a steep hill with dense woods on both sides. Matt was out of breath when he reached the top of the hill. Approaching the ten-foot brick wall that encircled the house, he heard barking.

"Damn it," he said, and his heart began beating faster. Matt stopped at the entrance and hit a series of numbers on the control box. When the massive iron gate scraped open, he pushed the bicycle inside. Before the gate closed completely, he heard a bark and saw the collie racing toward him. The dog lunged high; Matt caught it in midair.

"Quiet," he whispered. "SenSay, you have to be quiet."

Getting on the bicycle, SenSay running beside him, Matt pedaled up the tree-shaded lane. Breathing heavily when he reached the four-story mansion, Matt saw the white Cadillac convertible parked under the portico. Pushing the bicycle to the servants' entrance in the back, Matt was at the steps when the door opened. Unshaven and red-faced, Mr. Henry stomped onto the porch. He was shirtless, the white folds of his belly sliding over his trousers. His right eye was misshapen, the black pupil stretching the socket.

"What do you mean, staying out all night!" he shouted, sliding his belt loose. SenSay barked loudly.

Lowering his head, Matt heard a loud whirring sound, and the belt buckle whipped across his shoulder. Matt staggered backward. SenSay began snarling and circling the steps. Mr. Henry swung the belt again, hitting SenSay across the back, sending the dog howling across the grass.

"You son of a bitch!" Matt shouted.

His face turning a bright crimson, Mr. Henry wrapped the belt around his fist. Moving closer, making grunting sounds, he steadied his feet and lashed out. The belt made contact below Matt's eye and knocked him down the steps. Blood spattered in the air. Rough hands pulled Matt up the steps into the house; the door slammed shut. Tail scraping the ground, SenSay moved slowly to the porch, crouched low, and stared at the door.

Waves of cool air flowed through the open windows of the jeep. Gene crested the hill on Route 305 and turned into the Twin River High School parking lot. Puddles from last night's rain glistened in the morning light. Gene stopped at the main entrance and looked at the cracked glass in Mrs. Walters's window.

"Charlie Hesston," Gene said, shaking his head, "you did hit something last night." Gene entered the building, walked down the hall, and unlocked the door to Mrs. Walters's room. Sunlight flashed over the rip in the cushioned chair and the plaster fragments of William Shakespeare.

Taking the wall phone off the hook, Gene called Arthur Port. After he told the principal about Shakespeare and the cracked window, he walked across Route 305 to the cornfield. Brushing some stalks aside, he saw the line of footprints in the mud.

Conner and Cindy talked on the porch for a few minutes. Then they went to the kitchen and began washing dishes. Sunlight streamed through the window, warming the room. Conner turned the faucet to high, and the burst of water sprayed wet patterns on Cindy's blouse. She laughed and splashed water on his face.

"Let's go in the living room." Cindy grabbed a towel and wiped the water off Conner's face. Dropping the towel on the table and taking his hand, she led Conner to the sofa. After pushing him onto the cushions, she brushed her body against his. Conner put his arm around her. Kissing, nibbling his ear, Cindy lowered her hand to his jeans.

"Cindy ..." Conner whispered.

"What?" Cindy asked, her fingers sliding deeper into the fabric of his jeans.

"Cindy," he said in a louder tone, lifting her hand, "I don't think ..."

"What don't you think, Conner?"

"I don't think it's time."

"Why do you think so much about time?" she complained, removing her hand. "You never think about me. You never want to do anything. Maybe you don't love me as much as I love you. Maybe you've never loved me."

"That's not true," Conner said, taking a deep breath. "I've loved you for years."

"You always talk about love, but it doesn't mean anything. I don't know what's wrong with you."

"Jeez, Cindy, there's nothing wrong."

"There is something wrong, Conner. Why is it you never consider my feelings? I don't know why I even come here. You don't enjoy being alone with me." Cindy got up, hurried to the door, and turned. "Just don't forget we're going swimming this afternoon!" Slamming the door, she ran across the yard to her bicycle. Conner collapsed on the sofa. The bicycle chain made a harsh clicking noise as Cindy crossed the yard. Wiping the perspiration from his face, Conner jumped up and rushed to the porch.

"Cindy," he called. When he called her name the second time, the bicycle turned the bend on River Road and disappeared. Conner went upstairs to the bedroom and rummaged through the drawer until he found his swimming trunks.

Chapter Six

That same Sunday morning, Jeffery Turner, a twenty-year-old sophomore at Penn State University, parked an orange-and-black FritoLay van in the back of the QuikStop on Route 22. Going inside, he bought the Sunday *Altoona Mirror*. When he returned to the van, the two puppies in the back wagged their tails and barked loudly.

Starting the engine, Jeffery drove into Alexandria, stopped at the intersection, and watched the parishioners enter Christ Reformed Church. Bells echoed down Main Street; the parking lot was full. When Jeffery saw the last group of girls climb the church steps, he pulled the van to the curb.

Right on schedule, he thought. Jeffery wore a blue Penn State sweatshirt and sported a pair of dark sunglasses. The hood of the sweatshirt completely covered his head and cast shadows over his face. A member of the swimming team, Jeffery had a trim physique, sculptured chest, and broad shoulders. Looking at his reflection in the rearview mirror, Jeffery thought back to the party and shook his head. "You are so damn dumb," he muttered.

The hot tub party for scholarship candidates started at seven. By midnight the kegs were empty, and everyone was drinking straight vodka. In the morning, Jeffery woke up next to April, a firm-breasted, seventeen-year-old one-hundred-meter state champion from Mt. Lebanon High School. April was crying when she called her parents. Her parents called the police and the coach. Late that afternoon, Coach Abraham informed Jeffery he had lost his scholarship and was facing criminal charges.

In the evening at the Pump House, Jeffery was alone at the bar when a stranger sat down, introduced himself as Nathaniel, and started buying rum and Cokes. As they drank, Nathaniel offered Jeffery a job as driver/actor for Xanadu Video Productions. Nathaniel explained that Xanadu had a wealthy clientele who paid a monthly fee to view sophisticated seduction videos. Jeffery would not only procure young actresses, he would also be their sex partner in the videos.

"It sounds like porn. I don't do that."

"It's not porn, Jeffery. It's nothing more than what you did at the party. You'll become rich. And don't worry about your legal problems. We'll take care of this lawsuit. It's a simple matter of getting money to the right people."

"I don't want a criminal record," Jeffery said, deep in thought. "More than anything, I don't want a criminal record," he repeated in a whisper. After draining his rum and Coke, he turned to Nathaniel. "If you get the charges dropped, I'll work for Xanadu."

"That's great. You won't regret this decision." Nathaniel shook Jeffery's hand, dropped a hundred-dollar bill on the counter, and asked for the change in Pump House tokens. When the bartender returned with the tokens, Nathaniel gave them to Jeffery.

"This month the drinks are on Xanadu Video Productions."

"Thanks," Jeffery said, pocketing the tokens.

"Come outside. I want to show you another Xanadu benefit."

Jeffery slid off the stool and followed Nathaniel to the exit. Pushing the door open, Nathaniel pointed to a silver Porsche. "I own a profitable car dealership in State College, Jeffery. When you're working, you'll be driving a secondhand FritoLay van. But that Porsche is yours for recreational use as long as you're employed by Xanadu."

"Fantastic!" Jeffery exclaimed. "This is fantastic!"

Two men with contrasting physiques were standing next to the 1980 silver Porsche. Nathaniel introduced Max Wright, a thin man with shifty eyes, and Luther Cicconi, a muscular man with a dark mustache. Luther was smoking a Marlboro. Both men took turns crushing Jeffery's hand. Nathaniel opened the door and gave Jeffery the keys. Jeffery slid in the front seat and started the engine. The Porsche made a soft humming sound; Jeffery smiled and drove off in the evening light.

"You are so damn dumb," Jeffery repeated loudly. Hearing his voice, the puppies began barking and jumped on the armrest trying to lick Jeffery's face. "Skippy and Tippy, you're the only friends I have."

Jeffery pulled away from the curb, drove through the intersection, and turned down Canal Street. Empty and quiet, the street was lined with wooden garages and grassy lawns. Some of the yards had small gardens with wire fences around them. Parking the van under a tree, Jeffery opened the back door, grabbed the leashes, and led the puppies outside. Tippy and Skippy were golden retrievers. They were covered in soft white fur and had long floppy ears. When they chased each other, making only light whimpering noises, their tongues appeared wet and pink.

Jeffery surveyed the yard. There was a brick sidewalk that disappeared in a grove of apple trees. The thick foliage turning bright autumn colors made it difficult to see the house. Jeffery walked a short distance in the yard and tied the puppies to a sapling at the edge of the grove. Talking in a soothing voice, he pushed Tippy flat on the grass. The puppy lowered its head between its front paws. Skippy circled around and sat next to Tippy.

"You two are priceless," Jeffery said. He walked back to the van, sat in the driver's seat, and began reading the *Altoona Mirror* headline, "Sanctions Ineffective Against Iran":

Captured when three hundred armed students stormed the embassy in November, fifty-one Americans have been held hostage in Tehran for over five months. During this time, President Jimmy Carter canceled all oil imports, expelled Iranians from the country, and froze $8 billion of Iranian assets. In response, Ayatollah Khomeini branded America the Great Satan and refused to negotiate the release of the hostages. Instead, the ayatollah has demanded an apology.

Bells pealed; people began to exit the church. Dropping the newspaper, Jeffery watched the group of girls approaching the intersection. Three of them waved their hands and continued walking. The last girl waved back and approached the van.

Jeffery knew her name was Sally, and he also knew that she was thirteen years old. She was slight of build, had curly brown hair and brown eyes, and today she wore a pink dress. Nearing the sidewalk, she saw the puppies, laughed, and ran to them. Skippy jumped up and yelped, but Tippy remained motionless, his head buried between his paws.

"Skippy and Tippy," Jeffery called to the girl. "That's their names." Tippy lifted his head and barked. The puppies danced around the girl. "They like you," Jeffery said, glancing up and down the empty road. "Can you bring them to the van?"

"Skippy and Tippy," she ordered playfully, "come with me." Sally untied the leashes from the sapling. Tippy began licking her face; Sally was laughing. Jeffery stepped out of the van, walked to the back, and opened the door. Sally approached, and when she handed him the leashes, he grabbed her and threw her into the van. Sally began to kick wildly.

"Be still," Jeffery commanded, wrapping tape around her mouth. After he bound her hands and feet and dropped the puppies next to her, Jeffery slammed the doors, got in the driver's seat, and drove slowly down Canal Street. Sally made muffled sounds; the puppies barked and licked the tape around her mouth.

At the end of the street, Jeffery turned onto Route 305. He had gone only a short distance when he heard the loud siren. Looking through the side mirror, he saw the flashing lights of the police car behind him. Skippy and Tippy began to bark. Sally kicked her feet against the empty boxes. His heart beating rapidly, Jeffery edged the FritoLay van to the side of the road. The shrill noise of the siren filled the van; the police car raced by.

Perspiration streaming down his face, Jeffery waited a few minutes and pulled back onto the road. Driving past Twin River High School, he saw the police car, an orange jeep, and two other vehicles parked in front of the building. The stalks of corn parted at the side of the road, and a man emerged from the field. Skippy barked again, and the man locked his eyes onto the van. Covering his face, pushing down on the gas, Jeffery accelerated the FritoLay van past the school.

Gene reached the road at the same time as the FritoLay van. He saw the hooded driver and the dark glasses, and he heard a dog barking. The van went by quickly. The last thing Gene saw was a Penn State Nittany Lions football sticker on the back door.

1969

UNDEFEATED

11–0

Gene walked across Route 305 to the parking lot. A group of people stood at the school entrance, and behind them wide bands of yellow police tape stretched across the lawn in front of the cracked window. As he approached the group, Sheriff Parks stepped forward and shouted his name, followed by an expletive.

Jeffery exited the village of Petersburg. He raced by farms, pasturelands, and numerous hunting cabins. As he neared the state game lands at Hare Valley, he stopped the van in front of a heavy pole barrier across a gutted dirt road. Jeffery unlocked the chain and swung the pole to the side. Driving through dense woods for another ten minutes, he approached a chain fence with strands of barbed wire looped over the top.

After opening the gate with a remote, Jeffery drove up the lane to a one-story cabin. The cabin had a wide wraparound porch. The windows had thick security glass; the metal bars that covered each window were inset deep into the wall. Jeffery steered the FritoLay van around the cabin and turned down a steep grade into the basement garage. The motion sensors clicked on the lights and a video camera.

Two rooms were in the back of the garage. "Shangri-la" was painted in bold letters on the red door. The yellow door was labeled "Nymph." Opposite the two rooms, a stairway led upstairs to the living room. There was a worktable cluttered with video equipment against the wall. A dog cage was in the corner of the basement; Tippy and Skippy began barking loudly.

"You both did good today," Jeffery said. Taking snacks from his pocket, he broke them into pieces and dropped them on the floor. As the two pups scrambled out of the van, Jeffery went to the wall phone and dialed a number. Hearing Nathaniel's gruff voice at the other end, he spoke quietly.

"The package is in the garage," Jeffery said, and he replaced the phone. There was movement and noise from the back of the van. Boxes were kicked around; one flew out of the open door.

"Sally, Sally, Sally," Jeffery said, shaking his head. "Don't waste so much energy. No one can hear you down here."

Mounted on the walls of the Shangri-la Room, two video cameras focused on the nude girl in the bed. Seeing the dim light from the garage, Brenda Larson sat up and wiped at her eyes. She had an electronic collar around her neck. The cameras followed her when she stood on the bed and looked out the gray-tinted window.

Balancing on her toes, Brenda saw the FritoLay van and Tippy and Skippy chasing each other. Jeffery walked into view and picked up the puppies. He hugged them and talked to them before placing them in the cage. Jumping on the bed, Brenda shouted and pounded on the window with her fists. Her screams echoed off the thick glass.

Jeffery opened the door to the Nymph Room and carried Sally inside. A full-length wall mirror magnified Jeffery's image. A plush white carpet covered the floor. There was a toilet, shower, and marble sink. The refrigerator was stocked with milk, soda, fresh apples, lunch meat, and bread. The temperature in the Nymph Room was a constant seventy-five.

The fifty-two-inch TV mounted on the wall showed couples performing sexual acts. A pleasant female voice explained the pleasures of the various sexual positions. Jeffery carried Sally to the king-sized bed in the middle of the room. When he took the sensor from the pillow and fastened it around her neck, the video camera clicked into motion. Jeffery teasingly loosened the buttons on Sally's blouse. The actress on the TV screen gasped with anticipation. Jeffery felt his growing arousal and removed his sunglasses. Staring at his reflection in the mirror, Jeffery heard Nathaniel's directives:

Under no circumstances must the girls be injured or rushed into performing. You will wait until they accept you. Our clientele want to see innocence and the slow process of seduction. You're the right actor for this part, Jeffery. Your face has these boy features, and you have a smooth swimmer's body. It's a perfect mix: the handsome prince wins over the young princess. These videos bring in a lot of money. You'll be rich, Jeffery.

The music was soft and enticing. Jeffery removed his sweatshirt. A moist sheen formed on his chest and ribbed abdominal muscles. Sliding his hand the length of his body, he listened to the music and the girl's erratic breathing. Jeffrey unbuttoned his jeans and was pulling down the zipper when the girl opened her eyes. She stared at his naked torso and screamed, tears filling her eyes.

"Damn it!" Jeffery exclaimed. "She's scared to death!"

Grabbing his sweatshirt, listening to the sobbing voice, Jeffery left the Nymph Room, slammed the door shut, climbed the steps, and walked in a worried, uneasy manner to the bathroom. Tossing his clothes on the floor, Jeffery stepped in the shower, turned the faucet, and stood under the cold spray for a long time.

"You dumb son of a bitch!" Sheriff Roger Parks shouted at Gene. "This is my crime scene. You can't be walking around trashing the evidence."

Towering over everyone, the sheriff was a broad-shouldered, dominating presence. He wore a white Stetson cavalry felt cowboy hat, a blue shirt with a polished silver badge, a belt with a revolver, and designer jeans. His $800 bone-white alligator boots were spotless.

"It wasn't a crime scene until you got here, Rosco."

"Quit calling me Rosco. You have no respect for anyone. You've always been a wise-ass." Sheriff Parks turned to the principal. "You have a big problem with this shooting, Mr. Port. I need time to investigate. I think you should close the school."

"Because of a cracked window?" Mr. Port asked. He wore a blue-

and-white Penn State polo shirt; his Converse tennis shoes were spattered with mud.

"It's more than a cracked window. We have a wacko loose in the community. He can strike again at any time."

"The sheriff's right," Joe Stedman said. The assistant principal was a short, stocky man with narrow eyes, thin lips, and a sunken chin. "This could have been a massacre."

"The shooter knew what he was doing, Mr. Stedman," Gene responded quickly. "He shot out a window and blew away Shakespeare. I don't see any massacre."

"You're just a janitor," Steadman ridiculed. "You wouldn't know danger if it looked you in the face."

"Enough arguing," the principal said. "If I close school because of some broken glass, we'll never reopen. The kids would take turns shooting out windows. We'll have school tomorrow as usual."

"You'll regret this," Sheriff Parks warned.

"I agree with the sheriff," Joe Stedman said in a firm voice. "It's not safe yet."

"Joe, take a sick day tomorrow if you're afraid," the principal advised.

"But I only meant—" Mr. Stedman's words were interrupted by loud static from the police radio. Then the deputy's voice cracked shrilly in the morning air.

"Sheriff, you'd better get down here fast. Mrs. Henderson said her daughter, Sally, left church and no one's seen her since. She's missing like Brenda Larson."

Moving quickly, Sheriff Parks jumped into the car and pulled the door shut. He turned on the spinning lights and siren and slammed the gas pedal to the floor. The tires tossed stone and gravel in the air.

"Good luck, Sheriff Rosco," Gene muttered. Across the river, church bells sounded from Redemption Mountain; the melodious ringing grew louder and echoed the length of Hartslog Valley.

Chapter Seven

Conner was sitting on the hammock when he heard the church bells. Standing, he looked downriver where the cross on Redemption Mountain gleamed silver in the blue sky. The church bells stopped. Conner went down the steps and got on his bicycle. Skirting the rain-filled potholes, he pedaled to Barree, stopped at Holy Waters Church, and dropped the bicycle next to a wooden sign that had "Pastor Andrew Brooks" written in bold letters at the top. The hours of worship under the pastor's name had been scratched out.

Holy Waters was a narrow wooden structure with large windows. Pushing through the unlocked doors, Conner looked at the empty pews. Bibles lay at odd angles on the benches. A stained-glass window of Jesus with arms outstretched to a group of children was behind the podium. Streaming through the glass, rays of sunlight brightened the expressions of joy on the young faces. The inscription on the plaque was in gold letters:

Suffer the little children to come unto me.
For such is the kingdom of heaven.
—Mark 10:14

Conner walked down the center aisle; thin swirls of dust spiraled in the air. Opening the back door, Conner descended the steps to the basement, which consisted of an open living room and kitchen, a corner bathroom, and large bedroom. Uncle Andrew and Aunt Joyce were sitting at the kitchen table drinking coffee. Uncle Andrew was two years older than his brother. He had gray eyes, and his dark hair was trimmed neatly above the ears. Not as athletic as Gene, Andrew carried more weight, his waist rounded and pushing against the belt. Aunt Joyce was the same age as her husband. Her face was sunburned; furrows cut deep across her forehead. She filled a glass with orange juice and gave it to Conner.

"You look worried this morning," she said.

"It's nothing," Conner said. They sat there waiting for him to continue. "Cindy and I had an argument."

"Again?" she asked.

"Same old stuff." Conner drank some juice. "I can't seem to please her."

"Cindy's a nice girl, and she comes from a good family," Uncle Andrew said. "So it must be your fault."

"It's always the man's fault," Joyce said. She smiled, and the hard lines disappeared. Then her jaw set, and the lines closed back in place. "You two have been together since childhood. She'll get over it."

"I'm not used to her moods," Conner said. He looked across the table. "It's so quiet here now. There should be organ music. The church should be full."

"The congregation goes to Redemption Mountain now. I hear they worship on a grander scale up there," his uncle said. "When they officially closed Holy Waters Church, I wasn't sure what to do, where to go."

"So we decided to stay put," Joyce said. "I got hired at Twin River High School as a nurse. We took our life's savings and placed a down payment on the building. We plan to grow old here and be buried here. There's only one problem. We're three months delinquent on the mortgage. Mr. Henry warned us yesterday the bank would foreclose if we don't come up with the money."

"I don't like that man, Mr. Henry," Conner said. "Did you ask Dad to help?"

"My brother is good at what he does. But a school custodian doesn't earn much."

"You should ask him anyway. If you don't, I will."

"Is he still disappearing at night?"

"Yes. I think that's what drove Mom off. I'll probably be the next to go. Dad don't care. He's selfish and mean and don't care about anyone but himself."

"You're too hard on him."

"You're family, Uncle Andrew. You have to stick up for him."

"What about you, Conner? You're his son. Who's closer family, you or me?"

"I don't know. I guess I am," Conner said softly. Aunt Joyce was quiet for a moment. She glanced at Conner.

"Your dad's not a mean person. He has his reasons."

"Joyce, it's not our place to talk about others."

"That's true, but, Conner, you should know what's really troubling your dad. Sure, you have an empty house now, but it's not all his fault."

"What do you mean?"

"Lucy was seen with Sheriff Parks. Your dad heard about it. Actually, I told him. I think that's what started the fighting and arguing."

"Is it true?" Conner asked, looking at his uncle.

"Lucy was lonely, Conner. She needed someone to talk to. That's all it was." Andrew put his cup on the table and stood. "I'm driving to Redemption Mountain to see what the big deal is. Cindy and her parents went earlier. Want to come along?"

"Sure," Conner said. He kissed his aunt on the cheek, and he and Uncle Andrew walked outside to the truck.

The parking lot at the base of Redemption Mountain was filled. Andrew turned the vehicle onto Commandment Road. Staring through the window, Conner saw the stone tablet come into view.

"Look at it closely," Andrew said.

"What?" Conner asked. Then the tablet "Honor thy Father and Mother" loomed in front of him. *I wish I could*, Conner thought. After a few minutes on the winding road, Andrew drove past the last commandment. When they reached the gate at the top, he bounced over the speed bump and parked the truck next to a line of shuttle buses.

Getting out of the truck, Conner looked at the large central plaza, the domed church, and the curved portal to the Catacombs of Rapture. There was a narrow gravel path behind the parking area. It led to the summit, where thick steel girders supported the monumental cross. When Conner and his uncle climbed the steep row of steps to the church, an usher in a black suit watched them closely.

"Hurry up!" he ordered, opening the door. "We don't let anyone in once the Reverend Towers begins his sermon." Conner and his uncle stepped inside, and the door closed quietly behind them.

A black marble altar was prominent in the front of the church. Behind it, a staircase with illuminated rectangular steps led to a balcony. Dressed in a dark blue suit, red shirt, and blue tie, the Reverend Jeremiah Towers began a slow walk upward. With each step, the light on the staircase dimmed. When he reached the balcony, the church, except for the halo that covered the Reverend Towers, was in darkness. Caressing the microphone, the reverend spoke in a solemn tone. His words, amplified by large speakers, descended powerfully over the crowded pews.

"Welcome, my friends, welcome to the Church of the Flaming Cross. My story is one of humility and faith in the Lord. Years ago, I undertook a pilgrimage in the great wasteland of Death Valley. On the fourth day of my wandering, there was a sudden, inexplicable fire. I was blinded and very fearful. But then God's voice thundered from the heavens. He directed me to construct a church on Redemption Mountain. God also directed me to place a cross next to the church. Not just any cross. It had to be a magnificent flaming cross. Your donations today will make the light shine more brightly."

Glaring from his perch, the Reverend Towers monitored the ushers, who brandished long-handled baskets. A dim ring of light circled the top of the baskets. In the darkness, the lights paused and shook in front of parishioners. When money was dropped, the lights brightened; faces glowed in the shadows. The reverend noticed the owner of the Petersburg Deli standing motionless in front of the ring of light.

"Mr. Stout, God sees everything. Your light wavers dim in His church."

Admonished, his hands moving quickly, the grocer dropped a handful of coins and bills. The basket glowed brightly. The reverend smiled as more baskets reached full intensity. Leaning forward, he spoke in a stern voice.

"In Genesis, because of the transgressions of Adam and Eve, God placed cherubim and a flaming sword at the gate to the Garden of Eden. No man could enter and gain knowledge from the Tree of Life. But Jesus showed us another way to salvation. His Flaming Cross on Redemption Mountain is a beacon of light that guides all believers."

The dome projected a night sky of stars and constellations. The North Star and Big Dipper glittered prominently. Trumpets sounded, and the towering cross on Redemption Mountain burst the length of the dome. The light covering the congregation in a warm glow, the Reverend Jeremiah Towers spoke passionately about his work as God's missionary in Hartslog Valley.

The reverend praised the settlers for bringing God's word to the Valley. He deplored that the savages rejected Christianity. The lights dimmed, and the reverend began a diatribe against the Indians. Citing historical journals, he recounted the story of the Dean massacre. When he finished the bloody account, the church was in total silence. Then, his voice assailing the silence, he told the story of the boy Matthew Simonton.

"Young Matthew"—the Reverend Towers annunciated the name slowly—"was a true soldier of God. Matthew suffered greatly. Indians murdered his father and his beloved sister Beatrice on Blood

Mountain. The first Christian settlers called it Holy Pine Mountain because the tree at the summit was magnificent and its branches reached to the heavens. But after the massacre of the settlers, the name was changed to Blood Mountain.

"The heinous massacre of the early settlers was the work of devils. And today, against all Christian understanding, Twin River High School honors these savages. The school's mascot is a devilish one-eyed Indian, and the Indians who murdered the Dean family are buried in the exact spot where Matthew slew them. As stated in the book of Revelation, God demands retribution for any grave injustice.

Misshaped devils and packs of ravenous wolves appeared from the shadows and began to stalk the dark confines of the church. The demons and beasts grew larger and hovered over the parishioners. Their eyes blazed red, and their gaping mouths sprayed a warm, foul-smelling vapor. Children began to wail; the adults swayed in awe.

Packed with sensitive equipment, the special effects Room of the Holy Prophets was hidden behind the pulpit. Comfortable in cushioned swivel chairs, Cain and Abel Towers watched the mayhem. His fingers moving with deft precision, orchestrating every image and note, Abel smoked a joint.

"Shock force," Abel said, pointing to the hysteria below. "Look at them. They are afraid. They don't know where to hide."

"There's no place to hide," Cain commented. "The reverend has buried the demons deep in their souls. And there they fester and grow strong."

Standing tall, the Reverend Towers lifted his hands, and four giant horses appeared on the dome's surface. Hooves rearing high, nostrils blazing fire, the horses were white, red, and black, and the last one was a sickly pale color. The rider on the red horse brandished a gigantic silver sword, and swinging it in a frenzied manner, he slayed the people attempting to flee God's wrath. Wild animals and vultures scoured the chaos and devoured the bodies. The sound deadening his ears, Conner stood motionless.

"Conner!" his uncle shouted. He shouted a second time. When

Conner didn't respond, his uncle grabbed him by the arm and pulled him through the crowd. Shoving past the usher, his uncle pushed on the door forcibly, and it banged open. Bright light streamed into the church. Shielding his eyes from the sun, Conner followed his uncle across the courtyard and up the path to the summit. When they reached the Flaming Cross, they sat on one of the wooden benches. Across the river, clouds of mist rolled up the side of Blood Mountain; dark shadows of vultures circled the treetops. Andrew spoke in a subdued voice.

"Do you know what the main cause of mental illness in America is?"

"No," Conner answered, shaking his head.

"Fear."

"Like what happened in the church?"

"Yes."

"Why does the Reverend Towers minister that way?"

"Because fear is effective, Conner. The church is packed. Money is dropped in the collection basket. But I believe it's wrong. People, especially children, should never associate fear with the church. Instead, they should learn about Jesus and embrace His message of love and kindness and forgiveness."

"Holy Waters Church was like that. But now it's empty."

"No, it's not empty. Jesus will always be there."

"Is Jesus here, too?" Conner asked. "I mean, both you and the Reverend Towers teach the Bible."

"The Reverend Towers preaches the book of Revelation. I don't teach Revelation. John was a good man, but I never believed that terror and fear were necessary to love God. Even the early church leaders did not readily accept Revelation."

"Inside the church, I couldn't stop from watching. It was like some beast would strike me dead. What happened to John that he saw such terrible things?"

"His was a tormented vision that came from spending days and nights in the desert, some say in a prison cave. In his hallucinations, he saw the beast with seven heads and ten horns. He saw the Horsemen of the Apocalypse bringing war and famine. These visions came from darkness. I prefer to teach from light, the true light of Jesus. Instead of pain and hellfire, Jesus talks of love and forgiveness. That is the message everyone should hear."

"But both messages come from the Bible. What should I believe?"

"It's the choice everyone must make. Listen to both messages, but follow the one closer to your heart."

"Then I will follow Jesus."

"You have made a good choice, Conner. The book of Revelation contradicts everything Jesus taught. I think it belongs on the shelf. With its emphasis on terror and fear, it should only be taken down for Halloween."

"Uncle Andrew?" Conner stuttered. "How can you say that about the Bible?"

"Don't worry, Conner. I don't think God will damn me because I love his Son. It was Jesus who died on the cross for us. Even after His great suffering, Jesus didn't rant or condemn or try to frighten anyone. Instead, Jesus said, 'I am the way.' Remember those words above all the words in the Bible. Do you understand?"

"Yes, I do," Conner answered emphatically. It was blissfully quiet on Redemption Mountain. Conner marveled at the radiant splendor of the cross.

Inside the Room of the Holy Prophets, Abel pressed a button, and the shrill sound of bells shattered the morning calm. The main door and side exits swinging open, the parishioners rushed out of the darkness into the light. Their faces streaked with moisture, they began the journey down Commandment Road.

"Why are they walking?" Conner asked. "Why don't they take the shuttle?"

"The shuttle doors are locked. The Reverend Towers wants the people to walk and take note of the Commandments." Andrew watched the rush of people on the road. As the crowd approached the first stone tablet, there was a herald of trumpets and a booming voice sounded from a hidden speaker.

"I am the Lord thy God. Thou shalt not have any other gods besides me."

"That's loud," Conner said. "Are there motion sensors on the road?"

"There must be," Andrew answered. "As you witnessed in his church, the reverend is very fond of technology." Andrew got up from the bench, and he and Conner walked down the path to the courtyard. Cindy and Alice saw them and broke away from the crowd. Cindy took Conner's hand.

"It's time to go swimming," she said. "I have to wash off that awful spray."

"Can we invite Matt?" Alice asked.

"We sure can," Conner said. "Let's ride up to his mansion."

It was noon when Uncle Andrew parked his truck at Holy Waters Church. Conner and the girls got on their bicycles, bumped across the railroad tracks, and pedaled up the steep grade of the hill. Pine trees cast dark shadows on the road.

"This is hard work," Cindy said. "Have you ever been to Matt's house?"

"No," Conner answered. "Matt said Mr. Henry doesn't want any visitors."

When they reached the top of the hill, Conner and the girls leaned their bicycles against the brick wall. Conner noticed a crack in the security gate and walked toward it. Ignoring the black box and keypad, he turned sideways and slid through the opening to the road. Cindy and Alice followed. Patches of light beamed through the thick cover of trees. They were a short distance down the road when Conner heard a gunshot.

"Jeez!" he shouted, pushing the girls behind a pine tree. A second shot, louder than the first, hit the pine tree; a splinter of wood pierced Conner's neck.

"Run!" Conner grabbed Cindy's hand, and they scrambled back to the gate. As they were sliding through the narrow opening, another shot ricocheted off the metal links. The gate began to close with a grating noise. Conner and the girls jumped on their bicycles and raced down the hill. When they reached the pasture at the bottom, Conner braked. Red-faced and breathing heavily, Cindy and Alice stopped next to him.

"You're bleeding!" Cindy exclaimed, seeing the spot of blood on Conner's neck.

"Jeez, it's only a scratch," Conner said, pulling out a sliver of wood. "I'll bet it was Mr. Henry trying to scare us. Now I know what Matt's going through." Conner looked up the hill and the dense grove of trees concealing the mansion. Massaging his neck, he turned back to the girls. "Do you still want to go swimming?"

"We should go," Cindy said. "We need to relax in the river."

Pushing off, they pedaled through Barree and followed the River Road to Twin River High School. Reaching the baseball field, they dropped their bicycles at the dugout and walked down a narrow, sloping path to a clearing. Conner pointed to a gray stone enclosed by a wooden fence. Two crossed tomahawks and the year 1778 were carved into the face of the stone.

"The Reverend Towers spoke about the Indian Memorial this morning. He was real angry about it."

There were voices on the trail, and Wayne Wilson and his sister, Becky, walked into the clearing. Wayne was six feet tall and had a bony frame. His face and arms were deeply tanned. Becky was shorter than her brother. She had clear skin, bright blue eyes, and an engaging smile. She wore shorts and a loose-fitting blouse that stretched with the motion of her breasts. Wayne waved his hand.

"There's open gym Monday, Conner. Are you going?"

"Sure am," Conner said. "Basketball's the only sport I know anything about. I can't see how you play three sports."

"My backward brother is up at five every morning," Becky said in a complaining tone. "And he's noisy getting his bicycle. Sometimes he wakes me up."

"Dad's too busy working to pick me up after practice. So I have to take the bicycle. It's not that bad."

"Maybe not now, but riding that road during a blizzard is worse than bad." Becky shrugged. "That's enough talking about Wayne's problems. Let's go swimming."

They walked down the path. When they reached the sandy bank, Becky tossed off her shoes, Wayne stripped down to his shorts, and they waded into the water. Conner and the other two girls undressed to their swimming suits and joined them.

"It feels great," Alice said. "I wish Matt was here."

"Watch this!" Wayne shouted. He swam under Becky and lifted her out of the water.

Perched on his shoulders and laughing, her blouse wet and dripping water, Becky grabbed Wayne's hands and slowly pulled herself to a standing position.

"That way," Becky said, pointing to the middle of the pool. After Wayne pivoted, Becky bent low and sprang high in the air. She did a perfect dive, her body splashing smoothly in the water. They all clapped.

Cain turned into Twin River High School and roared the truck across the empty parking lot to the baseball field. He shut off the ignition, and slamming doors, he and Abel walked past the dugout and down the path to the clearing.

"There it is," Cain said, pointing to the burial plot. They rushed over; Abel kicked at the stone marker. It loosened, and Cain lifted it to his shoulder. Hearing noise from the river, they walked to the edge of the bluff. Cain laughed when he saw the girls.

"Our bitches are here," he said, and they sauntered down the path. Reaching the riverbank, Cain hoisted the Indian marker over his head and shattered it against the rocks. Then he and Abel picked up some of the flatter stones and began skimming them across the water. One of them splashed close to Wayne.

"Hey! Watch what you're doing!" Wayne shouted.

"You watch this!" Cain shouted back. He picked up a bigger rock and threw it at Wayne. Wayne ducked, and the rock sailed inches over his head.

"What's wrong with you two?" Alice shouted.

"We're just having some fun." Abel laughed. "You want to go to Raystown with us, Alice? We're diving off the cliffs. The lake's way better than this muddy shit hole."

"No, thanks."

"How about you, Becky?" Cain asked. "I guarantee you a good time."

"Well, maybe," Becky said, and she started toward the bank.

"Don't go with him, Becky." Wayne grabbed her hand. "He's a jerk."

"Leave her alone, farm-boy," Cain ordered.

Becky pulled free from Wayne and reached the bank. Cain took her hand, and they walked up the bluff. When they were out of sight, Abel charged into the water at Wayne.

"Don't you ever sass me, you farm-fuck!" Abel bellowed. Wayne's hands were at his side when Abel swung and cracked him in the mouth. Then Abel grabbed Wayne by the shoulders and shoved him underwater.

"How do you like that, farm-boy?" Abel asked. He put his foot in Wayne's back and crushed his body into the sandy bottom. Bubbles exploded to the surface.

"Let him up!" Conner shouted, splashing through the water. A loud blast from the truck horn sounded from the baseball field.

"Sure, I'll let him up," Abel said. He grabbed Wayne by the neck and pulled him, coughing, to his feet. "Nothing to be concerned about. Just having a good time, that's all." Abel gave them the finger, laughed, and walked toward the bluff. Conner and the girls hurried to Wayne; blood covered his bottom lip.

"Are you okay?"

"I'm fine," Wayne murmured. Getting to his feet, he splashed water on his face. "I ought to be going home."

Conner and the girls followed him to the riverbank. After Wayne dressed, drops of blood forming circles on his T-shirt, he lowered his head and walked up the path. Buttoning her blouse, Cindy looked at Conner.

"What were you going to do, Conner? Abel would have killed you."

"He's not so tough."

"He's a bully," Cindy said. "I can't believe Becky went with him."

They finished dressing, climbed the hill, and walked past the broken fence at the Indian mound. When they reached the baseball field, Conner saw his bicycle on the roof of the dugout. He pulled it down and straightened the handlebars, and he and the girls pedaled across the parking lot.

Chapter Eight

On Monday morning Gene drove around the crowded pump stations at the Route 22 QuikStop and parked the jeep next to an orange-and-black FritoLay van. He entered the QuikStop, filled a large cup with coffee, and got in line. While he waited, he watched Pete Rogers stocking the shelves with chips and pretzels. Pete had a medium build and a muscular body. His animated blue eyes and neatly trimmed mustache contrasted with the rugged lines on his face. He wore a Boston Red Sox baseball cap.

"Big crowd today," Gene said, handing the cashier two bills.

"I don't know where they're coming from, Mr. Brooks." She smiled and gave him his change. "It's worse than fair week. Have a good day at Twin River."

"Thanks," Gene said, and he went outside. Minutes later, Pete returned to the FritoLay van and began to stack boxes on the empty cart. Gene walked over and shook his hand. "Is there another FritoLay van working this area?"

"No, why do you ask?"

"One went by the school yesterday. What kind of delivery schedule are you on, Pete? I've never seen you this late."

"Sarah's sick. I had to get the kids ready for school."

"I do that all the time."

"You only have Conner to worry about." Pete hesitated. "Any word from Lucy?"

"Why bring my wife into the conversation?"

"Because I was best man at your wedding, and I like her."

"Then tell me why she's not answering the phone. It's killing Conner, and my life couldn't be more miserable. I'm driving to Lancaster after school. I need to convince her to come home."

"Good luck, Gene. I hope she does come back." Pete reached in a box and gave Gene a bag of chips. "I don't have any M&M's. Try these on the drive. They'll keep you awake. They're jalapeño parmesan pizza."

"Thanks." As Gene walked to his jeep, a state police cruiser pulled next him, and Sergeant Vincent Delaware Smith, the only Negro officer in the Huntingdon barracks, got out. Sergeant Smith was six feet four inches tall, had a thick neck, and weighed two hundred and forty pounds. The sergeant wore sunglasses with thick metal frames. He put his hand on the door and stared through the open window.

"What's happening out at Twin River High School, Gene? You've got girls being kidnapped. You've got a sniper shooting out windows."

"I don't know anything about the girls. But the sniper's the history teacher, Charlie Hesston. He took a shot at the window Saturday night."

"Why would he do a crazy thing like that?"

"I don't know."

"If you find out why, will you give me a call?"

"Sure."

"I haven't seen you since the accident, Gene. I'm real sorry about those two friends of yours. I didn't believe what the hogs did to their bodies. No one should die that way. You knew them pretty well, didn't you?"

"I grew up with Sam and Robert. They moved away after graduation but always came back for buck season. I got permission from Mr. Wilson for them to hunt at Polecat Hollow." Gene shook his head. "Thanks for not giving the story to the newspapers."

"The public didn't need to know the gory details." Del reached up and adjusted his glasses. "Your Lucy left town about that time, didn't she?"

"She left that night."

"Why was that?"

"It was hard on Lucy. She grew up with Sam's wife." Gene looked at the sergeant. "What about the killers?"

"It had to be the two Calvin boys. Sam and Robert's body parts were found in their pen. But you know what is really strange, Gene? The Calvins' four prize hogs are missing. What do you think about that?"

"No idea."

"My idea is that a third person was there. He opened the gate. We found broken teeth and all kinds of prints. The Calvins were barefooted. But we've got some good boot casts from the mud." Del hesitated, glancing at Gene's military boots. "As for the Calvin boys themselves, I think they're dead."

"Why do you think that?"

"Their truck is parked at the house, and their two Harleys are inside the garage. They never left Polecat Hollow. There's no sign of them. Aboveground, that is."

"My guess is that they're way aboveground," Gene commented. Del searched Gene's face for an explanation. A horn sounded, and the FritoLay van drove past them. Gene waved; Del straightened his sunglasses.

"I'm ready for a break from this case, Gene. Can I make plans to do some serious hunting in your mountains?"

"Anytime. Just let me know when."

"I will. You still use that big knife, or Toothpick, as you call it?"

"Yes."

"I didn't believe that morning when we were on the mountain and this huge buck approached. I stepped on a stick, and just as the buck turned, the Toothpick was sticking in its throat. All in a matter of seconds."

"I've had a lot of practice," Gene said.

"I'll bet you have," Del said, and he walked to his car.

At eight o'clock that morning, Conner chained and locked his bicycle to the iron rack in front of the school. A few minutes later, Wayne pedaled up to the bike rack. Even though the weather was cool, Wayne's blue shirt was wet with perspiration. There was a gash on his lip. When Wayne locked the bicycle, the pedals spun around, and Conner saw dried chunks of cow manure fall to the sidewalk.

"Hey, Wayne. How's your lip?"

"It's fine."

"How's Becky?"

"She snuck in after dark. Cain and Abel had better stay away from her," Wayne said angrily. "I'll see you after school in the gym." He nodded his head and walked in the building. Conner waited at the entrance. The last bus parked at the curb, and Cindy and Alice came down the steps. Alice had a worried look on her face.

"Matt wasn't at the bus stop. Did Mr. Henry bring him to school?"

"I haven't seen Matt," Conner said. The bell rang, and they hurried inside. Conner got to homeroom and took his seat just as the teacher began taking attendance. Hearing a horn, he looked out the window and saw a red truck careen around the turn and head for the student parking lot. Abel Towers was hanging out the window giving the finger to Twin River High School.

At lunch, Conner was sitting with Cindy, Alice, and Wayne. Scattering the students at the door, Cain and Abel came into the cafeteria and headed toward them. When they reached the table, Abel stopped in front of Alice.

"Hi, honey. Missed you yesterday, but we had a good time anyway."

Alice didn't look up. She reached into her lunch bag and pulled out a bag of chips. Wayne stopped eating his sandwich and stared belligerently at the twins.

"You got something to say?" Cain walked over and bumped roughly against Wayne's shoulder; Wayne lowered his head.

"I didn't think so." Cain turned and pointed at Conner. "I want to talk to you."

"Go ahead and talk."

"I mean in private," Cain said. He nodded to Abel, who grabbed Conner by the shoulders and lifted him out of the seat. Pushing at times, they ushered him to the hall. Abel backed Conner against the wall and got in his face.

"Were you at the Petersburg intersection Saturday night?"

"Maybe I was."

"We lost something from our truck. Did you see a black garbage bag on the road?" Abel nudged Conner in the chest. Conner remained quiet, staring at the twins.

"You don't hear very well, do you?" Cain muttered through tightly closed lips. "Why is it Abel's words go in one ear and out the other? This is your last chance to answer. What were you doing at the intersection?" Conner shrugged his shoulders and lowered his head. Cain grabbed him by the neck. "Let's take Conner outside and punch him around."

"That's a good idea." Just as Abel gripped Conner's arm, the exit door swung open, and Mr. Brooks walked toward them. Exchanging glances, Cain and Abel released Conner. Mr. Brooks stopped in front of the twins.

"Shouldn't you boys be eating lunch?"

"Yes," Abel said meekly. "We were just talking with Conner here. We can finish our conversation later." Watching Mr. Brooks closely, Cain and Abel walked away. Advancing a short distance, Abel punched a locker, the noise echoing the length of the hall. Gene didn't turn around.

"You all right, soldier?" he asked, looking at the red coloration on Conner's neck.

"I'm hungry."

"Stay away from those two. They're nothing but trouble. Yesterday, I saw a Sharpfinger in their truck."

"What's a Sharpfinger?"

"It's a knife. It's popular with Hell's Angels."

"Oh," Conner said. "Why doesn't it surprise me that you would recognize a Sharpfinger?" He looked at his dad. "I meant to tell you. I was with Uncle Andrew yesterday. He was really worried."

"About what?"

"He's behind in the mortgage payments. The bank might take Holy Waters Church from him. He needs help. You should go visit him."

"And you should go eat your lunch," Gene said, and he walked away.

Junior high preseason basketball practice was in the small gym at the elementary school. It was hot, and the side doors were swung open. After twenty minutes of drills, Coach Eckin blew his whistle and divided the teams into shirts and skins.

"Ten baskets!" he shouted. "Losing team has twenty suicides. And if any player commits a stupid foul, his team has ten push-ups." As Coach Eckin walked to the jump-ball circle, Principal Port appeared at the door.

Conner and Wayne were on the skin team. Billy, Clyde, and heavyweight George were the other skins. After ten minutes, Wayne made a layup and tied the game at 9–9. On the inbounds pass, Conner crowded Randy Parks, the sheriff's son. Randy shouted and made a face; Coach Eckin called a foul on Conner.

It was Conner's fourth foul; the players moaned and did push-ups. Coach Eckin grabbed a towel and wiped the pools of sweat off the floor. Billy, a tall player with crooked teeth, walked up to Conner.

His friend George, who was four inches shorter and thirty pounds heavier, followed him.

"Quit your stupid fouls," Billy demanded loudly. He swung his hand and flicked sweat in Conner's face. "You cost us forty push-ups, you asshole!"

"And you ain't even scored one basket," George added. He was sweating profusely, water pouring over his pink, rounded belly. "I hate these damn push-ups."

Coach Eckin blew the whistle, and the shirts inbounded the ball to Randy, who dribbled wildly the length of the court. Lowering his head, he ran over Conner at the foul line and scored the winning basket. Blowing the whistle for a long second, Coach Eckin stared at Conner sprawled on the floor.

"Foul on the defense!" he shouted. The shirts laughed, high-fived at midcourt, and went to the locker room. The skins began their suicides. When they finished, Principal Port walked up to Conner.

"You play some tough basketball."

"But, Jeez, we lost."

"When you play hard defense like that, you're a winner no matter what the score. I coached your dad. I always put him on the other team's best scorer."

"I heard Dad fouled out 'most every game."

"That's true, but his man didn't score. That's why we won a lot of games."

"Not the section championship."

"No, we didn't win the big one," Principal Port admitted. "But that wasn't your dad's fault. He did all he could. You remind me of him. Keep up the good work."

"Thanks," Conner said.

Gene exited the Pennsylvania Turnpike at the Reading interchange. After twenty minutes on Route 23, he turned into the Shady Maple

Smorgasbord. Going inside, Gene paid for his dinner at the counter, and a hostess showed him to an empty booth.

Removing his jacket, Gene entered the expansive buffet area, where he put sweet potatoes, turkey and stuffing, and a helping of barbecued chicken on his plate. Filling a cup with black coffee, he returned to his booth. Gene finished his dinner, had a slice of shoofly pie, and was on his second cup of coffee when Lucy walked down the aisle and sat opposite him. She wore a green dress with a white collar. Her complexion was clear and fresh. There was a rose fragrance in the air.

"I have to close the gift shop in ten minutes," Lucy said. "What are you doing here?"

"I had to see you. Things haven't been going so well since you left. When are you coming home?"

"When are you going to act like a husband again?"

"I don't understand."

"Then keep a journal. Write down how many hours you're roaming the woods. Write down how many hours you spend drinking on the porch and guarding the house."

"There are things I have to do."

"You told me you have to protect your family."

"Family's the most important thing to me. I've already lost one family member—"

"What do you mean?" Lucy interrupted, alarm in her voice.

"Nothing," Gene said softly but firmly. "I need to keep you and Conner safe."

"We are safe, Gene. I mean, we were safe until you came home from Vietnam. Then you took out your guns and knives and scared everyone away. You even scared me."

"I admit we had some problems. But I didn't cause all of them. When were you going to tell me about Sheriff Parks?"

"Jeez, he took me to dinner once. How's that a problem?"

"Parks looking at you is a problem." Gene's face hardened; he stared across the table at Lucy. "I swear if he ever touches you, I'll kill him."

"That's where your problem is, Gene. You overreact. People get uncomfortable around you. Conner doesn't understand you at all."

"He really misses you." Gene took a drink of coffee. "Please come home, Lucy. I'll try harder. I'll keep that journal. I'll write down everything like you said. We can be a family again."

"I loved you once, but now I don't know who you are."

"I'm the same person."

"No, you're not."

"I can be that person again," Gene said. He reached across the table and took her hand. "I just have to work out some things. Please, say you'll come home."

"My break's over," Lucy said, pulling her hand free. She stood, kissed him on the forehead, and walked away. Staring at the empty seat, Gene didn't move. Minutes passed. Then he finished his coffee, thanked the hostess at the door, and walked to the jeep.

There was little traffic on the turnpike. A fast-moving storm hit the area; large drops of rain spattered on the windshield. After an hour of staring at the wet glare on the highway, Gene had trouble keeping his eyes open. He opened the bag of jalapeño parmesan pizza chips and ate a handful. Gene coughed loudly. Approaching Harrisburg, he pulled into a rest area, parked the jeep next to a picnic table, and fell asleep.

Chapter Nine

It was three in the morning when Gene turned the jeep onto River Road. The air was chilly, and a light mist drifted over the river. When he neared the house, he saw a gray government car parked in the driveway. He pulled the jeep onto the grass and walked to the porch. The light cast a sharp glow over the man standing at the top of the steps.

"JJ Jackson," Gene said, and he grabbed the extended hand.

"I see you're still a night person," JJ said.

"I can't shake the old habits. Sit down on the hammock and get comfortable. I'll be right back." Gene went inside and shouted Conner's name. After he shouted again, the door opened. Wiping his eyes, Conner came down the steps in shorts and a T-shirt. Gene went to the refrigerator and pulled out two Iron City bottles.

"Jeez," Conner mumbled. "Do you know what time it is?"

"Quit complaining, soldier," Gene ordered, nudging him through the screen door. "Conner, I want you to meet a buddy from Vietnam, Mr. JJ Jackson."

"Glad to know you, Mr. JJ," Conner said, shaking hands. "I hope you two have a good reunion. I'm going back to bed." When Conner turned, Gene saw the bruise.

"What happened, Conner? What happened to your neck?"

"It's nothing."

"What do you mean, nothing?"

"It happened yesterday, Dad. We went up to Matt's house. The gate was open, and we went inside. I don't know. Maybe we were trespassing." Conner was silent for a moment. He glanced at JJ and then at his father. "Someone fired a shot at us. The bullet hit a tree real close. A splinter stuck in my neck. I guess Mr. Henry doesn't want visitors."

"That bastard," Gene said, anger rising in his voice.

"We never did see Matt. He wasn't in school today. I'm worried about him."

"I'll check about his absence in the office."

"Thanks, Dad. Good night, Mr. JJ," Conner said, and he went inside the house. Gene sat down in the chair opposite the hammock.

"Having some problems with the neighbors?"

"Nothing I can't handle."

"Sounds familiar. You don't have any big trees around here, do you?" JJ laughed. Seeing the scowl on Gene's face, he took a long drink of Iron City. "Your son got shot at. It didn't seem to bother him."

"Conner's okay, but he's a little confused now."

"Why's that?"

"He's got his mom's softness and some of my toughness. In time, one or the other will shape his life." Gene took a drink of Iron City. "How long have you been here?"

"A few hours," JJ said, leaning back on the hammock, slapping the fabric with his hand. "Made in China. Strong as ever. This brings back nasty memories of the Trail. You don't sleep out here, do you?"

"Sometimes."

"I couldn't do it."

"I have the same memories inside the house."

"Yeah, I guess you would. It doesn't matter if you're on a hammock or on a mattress. The past has a way of sticking to a person." JJ looked into the yard; dark shadows fell from the trees. "I came to warn you about a problem from your past. Leroy escaped. We think he's looking for you. Wasn't it your testimony that sent him to prison?"

"Yes, it was my testimony. Our outfit was making a sweep through this village in Tay Ninh Province. I heard shots, ran around this hut, and saw Leroy standing over two bodies. They were unarmed boys. I was carrying a gun then. When I saw what he had done, I aimed at Leroy. He smiled and raised his hands. I wanted to, but I couldn't shoot him."

"At the trial, Leroy swore he killed the boys in self-defense."

"Their hands were tied. Both were shot in the back of the head. When the court found him guilty, Leroy went psycho. He jumped up and swore he was going to kill me. I thought they put him away. And now he's out?"

"He escaped six days ago. The bastard jumped a train, got off in Huntingdon, and stole a truck right there at the station." JJ took a drink of Iron City and put the empty bottle on the floor. "We're alerting the police and all the area schools. Plus, we have two government cars patrolling the area."

"It won't be easy finding Leroy. In a way these mountains are like Nam. You can disappear here."

"That's what you did," JJ said. He scraped his shoes on the floor, stopped the sway of the hammock, and stared at Gene. "When Saigon fell, I saw the breaking news on our big-screen TV. I saw a Russian T-55 tank crash through the gate of the presidential palace."

"I told you about that rumbling noise. After you returned to Alpha, I watched a tank cross a river. It was completely submerged except for the turret. The Russian engineers made the T-55 waterproof and equipped it with a snorkel. I tried to tell you."

"Dumb-fucks," JJ said. He leaned back on the hammock and yawned. "It's too late to go back to the motel. Can I use the sofa tonight?"

"Sure."

"Thanks," JJ said. "When I pulled in, I thought I'd see Hondo on the porch. What happened to your friend? Couldn't you bring him over?"

"I wanted to," Gene said. "But the VC killed Hondo in 1972. Exactly eight years ago. It was a simple animal snare. I followed the trail all day, but I couldn't find anything. I was listening for any sound, but Hondo never barked. He would have loved these woods."

"You never got another dog?"

"No," Gene said. He and JJ went inside the house. JJ yawned and stretched out on the sofa. Gene threw him a blanket. As JJ tucked it under his chin, he had a puzzled expression.

"Gene, I was curious. Did you ever find Harry Wintergreen, that Indian you were looking for?"

"I wouldn't be here if I hadn't found him," Gene answered laconically. JJ nodded his head and pulled the blanket higher, exposing his feet. Within minutes he began to snore. Shaking his head at the noise, Gene grabbed his shotgun, returned to the porch, and switched off the light. Sitting on the hammock, he stared into the darkness.

The morning sky was gray when Gene heard the beeper. Going inside the house, he saw JJ with the telephone. JJ listened intently and slammed the phone down.

"Let's go. Captain Walters found the stolen truck at a school in Belleville."

"It's a Mennonite school, JJ. I know where it is. I'll get you there in no time."

Gene took one of the Arkansas Toothpicks out of the cabinet and slipped the harness over his shoulder. After grabbing his binoculars, he followed JJ to the car. JJ started the engine and raced the car down River Road. Gene directed him to an old logging road across Captain Jack Mountain. It was seven fifteen when the car stopped on the hill overlooking the school. The clouds opened, and bright sunlight flooded the school yard.

Getting out of the car, Gene focused the binoculars. He saw the government car at the entrance. He saw the log fence and the truck parked next to it. The school ground was wet from the rain; a large glistening puddle lay at the bottom of the sliding board. Gene zoomed in on the side of the building. A pale face, eyes blindfolded, cheek smeared with tears, was behind the first window. Looking at the next window, Gene saw the second boy. He swore, jumped into the car, and shouted at JJ.

"He's got the students tied up execution style."

"I'll drop you at the back exit. Then I'll go around front and alert Walters." JJ raced down the hill and stopped the car behind the school. Adjusting the knife harness, Gene got out. There was the dull sound of a siren in the distance. JJ drove off.

Gene jumped a ditch and was climbing over the log fence when he heard a gunshot. He pulled out the Arkansas Toothpick and took off running. At full stride, he kicked the door open and burst into the classroom. Gene immediately saw the twisted expression on Leroy's face. The man leveled his weapon in a smooth, quick motion.

"You bastard!" Gene shouted. As he hurled the knife, he heard the crack of gunfire. Gene felt pressure rip into his shoulder, and he fell backward. His head hit the wall; there was total darkness.

When Gene regained consciousness, he was in the backseat of the government car. His shirt was off; the knife harness was rolled up on the floor. There was a thick bandage on his head and another one around his shoulder. Gene looked out the tinted window and saw the flashing lights from the ambulances and police cars. Medics and state troopers hurried past the car. Holding cameras, reporters hovered around the area.

There was movement at the front entrance of the school, and Sergeant Delaware Smith walked through the door and stood on the steps. Right behind him, medics carried a stretcher and maneuvered it down the steps.

Two figures, one in a police uniform, stopped at the government car. Sheriff Parks stared at the window. Charlie Hesston stood next to him. The sheriff stepped closer to the car and wiped his finger over a dark spot on the glass.

"Damn Rosco," Gene said, noticing the blood smear on the inside of the window.

Leaning closer, Sheriff Parks cupped his hand and peered through the glass. His nose was pressed flat on the window. There was a loud commotion at the school. Straightening quickly, the sheriff grabbed Charlie, and they rushed to join the reporters.

A group of Mennonite men in suspenders and black trousers and women wearing bonnets and long blue dresses stood in the playground next to the sliding board. There was a row of horses and buggies behind them. Heads bent low to the ground, the horses were grazing. The front door of the car swung open. JJ got in and slammed the door.

"You okay, Gene?"

"I have a hell of a headache."

"I'll bet you do. What happened in there?"

"I heard the shot and crashed through the door. I threw the knife a split second before the gun went off. The bastard shot me."

"You had some force behind the throw," JJ said. He lifted his finger and stuck it against his throat. "The blade went right through here and severed the spinal cord. Leroy was dead before he hit the floor."

"What about the kids?"

"He killed one boy—shot him in the back of the head. It was an ugly scene. The floor was covered with blood and sections of scalp. We untied the kids and walked them through the door. We didn't remove their blindfolds until we got outside. Also, there was a teacher in the back of the room. She saw everything. She's the only one who knows what you did. I looked for her, but she was gone."

"This never should have happened," Gene said. "I'm responsible. If I had killed Leroy in Nam when I had the chance, the boy would still be alive."

"No way is the boy's death your fault. You can't think like that."

"But I do think like that. I won't make that mistake again."

"Fine, don't make that mistake again," JJ said. "The medic cleaned you up pretty good … said the bullet went right through the shoulder. The gash on your head took some sutures. But he didn't scrape off too much hair, so they're hard to see. How do you feel now? Are you ready to go home?"

"I'm ready," Gene said. "What about Leroy and the hole in his throat?"

"The local police get Leroy's body for twenty-four hours. Before they secured the scene, I fired two rounds in Leroy's throat. I didn't want to involve you, so I told this big sergeant that I shot and killed Leroy." JJ smiled. "I could get a pay raise."

"I hope you do," Gene said. "I'm glad you got me out of there. The sergeant knows I'm proficient with a knife. He would never confuse a knife wound with a gunshot wound."

"He can investigate the wound all he wants. I'm not changing my statement." JJ started the car. "I'm taking Leroy's body to Philadelphia on Wednesday. The train leaves at ten thirty. I'd like to buy you breakfast before I go."

"Sure," Gene said. He looked out the window at the blur of fence posts and farmhouses. JJ drove around a horse and buggy. Gene had trouble making out the driver's face. "I'm getting dizzy."

"I ordered the medic to give you a double dose of painkiller."

"Great," Gene said. He leaned back and closed his eyes.

Chapter Ten

Ho Chi Minh Trail, Hill 101

1970

Defended by a complex network of barbed wire and claymore mines, the camp on Hill 101 was on a plateau surrounded by jungle. A mile to the east, the guns of Firebase Hazzard covered its perimeter. The eleven South Vietnamese, seven tribesmen, and five American soldiers stationed on Hill 101 were under the command of Captain Din. The captain addressed the Americans in English and sometimes French, but he spoke only Vietnamese to his subordinates and the tribesmen. Lieutenant Chase Butler nudged Gene.

"You understand their language, Gene. Why don't you use it with the captain?" Born in a beach house in Wildwood, New Jersey, and married with two children, Chase Butler had a youthful appearance. He was tall, over six feet, slender, and had broad shoulders. Rain pelted him in the face. The lieutenant repeated the question.

"Why don't you use their language?"

"I want them to think I'm ignorant like the rest of you *farangs*. When they talk and scheme in front of me, I learn fast who I can trust."

"Who do you trust?"

"None of them."

"Not even Captain Din?"

"Especially him. He hasn't been on patrol once. And there's something else about our leader. He had an escape tunnel built under his cot. It comes out on the South Trail."

"That wily, sneaky bastard. When were you going to tell me?"

"I was hoping I never had to."

"Right." Chase smiled. The rain was a steady downpour; a thick cloud of mist rose from the jungle. There were voices in the bunker below them.

"What about the tribesmen, the Montagnards?"

"Don't call them Montagnards, Lieutenant. That's the term the French forced on them. It's insulting. They're H'mong."

"Can we trust them?"

"Yes, we can trust them. They have historical reasons to hate the Vietnamese."

"On Hill 101, we have the H'mong, the Vietnamese, and the Americans—each working on a different agenda."

"And you're the lucky West Point graduate who shares responsibility with Captain Din for our safety. Did you build your escape tunnel yet?"

"No, not yet." Chase laughed. "Are you going on patrol when Frank gets back?"

"No, not tonight."

"Frank thinks you're way over the edge. You go out on patrol alone, and you only carry those knives."

"The Arkansas Toothpick," Gene said, removing one knife from the sheath. "It's a great killing tool. The state of Arkansas figured that out years ago. To ensure the safety of its peaceful residents, Arkansas prohibited its manufacture in 1830. Of course, that only made it more popular." Gene offered the knife to Chase. The lieutenant swung it through the air.

"It feels natural, like an extension of the arm. Where did you get it?"

"From a metalworker in Hue. The guy was a genius. He gave it perfect balance. The blade's sharp as a razor, and the handle's a thing of beauty. I think it's 100 percent ivory."

"You should take me on your next patrol." Chase gave the Toothpick to Gene. "I'd love to see how you operate out there."

"There's not much to see. One second the Cong soldier is standing there thinking all *farangs* are clumsy, noisy bastards. The next second he's dead."

"That's it—no sound at all?"

"There's the sound of the body hitting the ground," Gene said matter-of-factly. Black clouds moved over the jungle. Thin lines of lightning flashed into the dark canopy of trees, and the roll of thunder cracked closer to Hill 101.

"The storm's getting worse," Chase said. "We should check the perimeter." He and Gene sloshed through the trench. When they reached the South Trail, Chase stopped and studied the rows of barbed wire.

"What are you looking for?" Gene asked.

"Captain Din's tunnel."

"You can't see it from here. The entrance slopes with the hill and is covered with bamboo. But to give you an idea, the door's halfway down the hill where the coils of barbed wire are doubled."

"That wily, sneaky bastard," Lieutenant Butler reiterated. He and Gene continued the inspection. Thunder cracked overhead, and the rain intensified. Clumps of mud washed into the trench. The lieutenant stopped at a sandbagged tower where one of the Vietnamese soldiers was snoring. Chase swore and rudely shook him awake.

Leaving the tower, the lieutenant and Gene pushed through a sturdy wooden door into a large bunker that had two cots and a desk cluttered with radio equipment. Sitting at the desk, Junior Johnston, a nineteen-year-old Negro, was cheerful and quick-witted. He was drafted five months ago in Detroit. Chase nodded to Junior and turned to Gene.

"I had to knock that soldier pretty hard. He looked angry and whispered something to his friend. Did you hear what he said, Gene?"

"Yes, I heard every word. He gave you a compliment."

"He did? That's my first one. What was it?"

"It was good. He called you an ugly, white-faced *farang* fucker of water buffalo."

"That has a nice ring to it," Chase admitted. They laughed. The noise woke Oscar Jordan, a former resident of San Diego, who was stretched out on one of the cots. His face was tan and clear, his green eyes wide and alert. He wore a dark "Mad About Pandas" T-shirt. Just a few months ago he had been partying on the beach at Fletcher Cove.

"Can you keep the noise down?" Oscar requested.

"Relax, surfer boy," Junior said. "Look at you sleeping. What I don't understand is why you're not on patrol with Frank and the hill people."

"There's no sunshine today. My recruiting officer guaranteed me that I would only have to work in blue sky and sunshine."

"Did he recruit you on the beach?" Junior asked.

"His office was a block away. He gave me a big signing bonus."

"What good's a bonus on this hill?"

"I don't know, Junior. But the bonus is gone anyway. I used it in Hawaii. I danced with a native girl for hours, and she gave me a lei."

"In Detroit the native girls give out more than one lei," Junior bragged. They laughed; Oscar pointed to the image of the over-sized docile panda on his T-shirt.

"Eat my panda."

"Your mom ..." Junior began but was interrupted by a blare of static from the radio. He quickly turned the dials. The static became louder. Switching off the radio, Junior looked up. "Hazzard's been silent for six hours. What's that mean, Lieutenant?"

"It's overrun," Chase answered quietly. "Frank's patrol went to check for survivors."

"Now that we lost our artillery, how long before the VC launch an attack?" Junior looked at Lieutenant Butler, who was silent. Then he looked at Gene.

"Tonight," Gene said. "Tomorrow at the latest."

The door from the adjoining room opened. Dressed in a neatly tailored uniform, Captain Din entered the room. The captain had a pudgy face. He had recently shaved; the fragrance of French cologne filled the room.

"*Mon ami, excusez-moi,*" Captain Din began. Then he spoke English in a slow, precise manner. "Sergeant Whon just informed me that the patrol is back from Hazzard. They found one survivor, a *farang*," the captain explained, a hint of contempt in his voice.

Gene grabbed his binoculars, and he and the lieutenant went outside. The rain was steady. They splashed through water that was now a foot deep. Gene looked down at the rolls of barbed wire and the line of green Claymores, FRONT TOWARD ENEMY, that angled at the jungle. Focusing his binoculars, he watched a line of soldiers move up the hill.

Gene recognized Frank Williams. The helmets of two H'mong soldiers bobbed in and out of sight, and then Gene saw a tall figure. The man's hair was wet and dripping water. When rain washed away the dark streaks of mud, Gene saw the face clearly.

"Fuck!" he shouted. Gene slid down against the wall of the trench. Muddy water splashed over his fatigues.

"What's wrong?" Chase asked, sitting next to him.

"The survivor from Hazzard … I know him."

"What do you mean, you know him?"

"I married his sister, Lucy. I gave Wally his first taste of whiskey at the wedding. He got drunk and threw up all over the place. That made us family. He calls me uncle now."

Dripping water and mud, Gene stood up. He peered over the top of the sandbag and watched Frank's patrol make its way up the trail. The last member, a H'mong nicknamed Cochise, angled the claymores back in position. After a few minutes, Frank appeared and slid into the trench. The patrol followed behind him. Moving clumsily, Wally lowered his head and fell against a sandbag.

"Wally," Gene called, splashing through the water. Wally looked up.

"Uncle Gene!"

"Let's get you out of the rain." Gene grabbed Wally around the shoulders and led him to the guard tower. After words with the two Vietnamese soldiers, who left quickly, he pushed Wally inside. Gene moved the cots closer and sat opposite Wally. There was an awkward moment of silence; then Wally couldn't stop talking. He talked about home, about his graduation at Twin River High School, about losing his football scholarship to Penn State, and he talked about Lucy and Conner. Pausing a moment, Wally reached into his pocket and gave Gene a golden chain and blue medallion.

"Conner asked me to find you and give you his Batman medallion. He said it was his most-prized possession. He said he missed you. He wants you to come home."

The wind lashed out; rain spattered through the crack in the door. Gene lifted the medallion, a black bat with large expanding wings emblazoned on the front. Hand trembling, Gene placed the gold chain around his neck. After wiping the blue medallion, he slid it under his shirt. Then he lowered his head in his hands; Wally remained silent.

The sky was turning dark. Moving quietly in the shadows, Viet Cong soldiers crawled to the base of the hill and dug trenches in the mud. A tall, white *farang* with blond hair joined an officer in a makeshift shelter. Studying a detailed map, they traced the South Trail, which curved to the summit of Hill 101. Straightening, the VC officer told a crude joke about American fighting spirit and laughed. Showing respect, the *farang* laughed ardently, his blue eyes glistening in the light from the oil lamp.

It was midnight when Gene and Wally finished eating the packaged meal of ham and potatoes. They left the radio room, splashed through the trench, and stared at the black patch of jungle at the base of the hill. The rain was a steady deluge. Wally wiped his face.

"It was dark like this at Hazzard. The VC shelled us for hours, and then someone blew a bugle and hundreds of them charged. When I was out of ammunition, I crawled away, played dead, and crawled some more." Wally spoke in a whisper. "It took me a long time to reach the jungle. Then I ran like hell."

"You did good, Wally. I'm proud of you. I wish we had time to celebrate … maybe have a few drinks."

"That would be great. I don't get drunk as easy as before." Wally smiled nervously.

"You're safe here, Wally. When the weather clears tomorrow, the planes will napalm the hell out of this jungle. We'll smell freshly cooked Viet Cong when we eat breakfast."

"I'll drink to that."

"When this is over, we'll get drunk together," Gene promised. Suddenly, there was a cracking, static noise, and a microphone clicked on. Through the pitter-patter of the rain and a booming thunderclap in the distance, the Vietnamese officer issued directives in a shrill voice. Lieutenant Chase rushed out of the bunker.

"What's he shouting about?" Chase asked. His lips tight, his face turning hard, Gene raised his hand, listening. The rain intensified. When the microphone clicked off, Gene turned to the lieutenant.

"He mostly addressed the South Vietnamese soldiers. He wants them to throw away their USA uniforms and join the Viet Cong. There was more, but I didn't get it. You can ask Captain Din for his translation."

"I'll ask him right now," Chase said, retreating inside the bunker. Staring into the darkness, Wally spoke in a hesitant voice.

"Will the soldiers join the VC?"

"Probably," Gene answered. The microphone clicked on again, and a clear voice boomed up the hillside.

"My friends."

"What the hell!" Wally blurted. "He's speaking English!" Lightning cracked bright lines over Hill 101; the voice sliced through the rumble of thunder.

"You are fighting a war you cannot win. All Vietnamese and all people in the USA want the war to end. Our leader, Colonel Minh, guarantees that if you surrender now, you will not be harmed. You will have safe escort to your lines."

"Who is it, Uncle Gene?"

"A deserter," Gene answered. "A damn traitor." The door splashed open, and Lieutenant Chase came out. He lifted a megaphone; rain rapped off the yellow surface.

"You told us the colonel's name. What's your name?"

"Harry," the voice answered. "My name's Harry. I have been cooperating with the North Vietnamese. They are like family. You can trust them."

"Go fuck yourself, Harry!" Lieutenant Chase shouted. Rain spattered off the smooth surface of the megaphone.

"That's not a good answer," Harry admonished. "Don't be foolish. There is no way you can win. We have three hundred soldiers. You have twenty-three. Colonel Minh says you should have time to consider his offer. While you think it over, I'll play music for you. The song *I'll Be There* is number one in America now." There was a clicking noise, and a smooth, melodious voice sounded through the falling rain and distant thunder.

> You and I must make a pact;
> We must bring salvation back.
> Just call my name, and I'll be there.

"The Jackson Five," Lieutenant Chase said, drops of rain spraying off his face. "This isn't happening!" The music grew louder. A security light flashed at the bottom of the hill. Three black-pajama-clad soldiers were caught in the glow. Cochise opened fire, and the VC were knocked into the barbed wire. Gene pulled Lieutenant Chase to the side.

"I need to check the South Trail. If the VC make it to the bunker, you should get the men and escape through Captain Din's tunnel."

"I will. And, Gene, I left a standing order with Colonel Potter. If we ever lost radio contact, the B-52s were to level this hill."

"When were you going to tell the rest of us?"

"I was hoping I never had to." Chase nodded his head and smiled.

"Right," Gene said, focusing his eyes on the lieutenant. "There's one more thing. Wally's just a boy. He's been through a lot. Can you look after him?"

"Sure, I'll keep him right next to me. He'll be safe."

"Thanks," Gene said, and he splashed his way down the trench. Wally saw him coming and stepped in front of him.

"Where are you going, Uncle Gene?"

"The South Trail."

"Take me with you. We should stay together." Wally lowered his head. "I don't want to be alone again."

"Don't worry. I'll be back for you." Gene grabbed Wally and hugged him. The rain drenched them; water streamed down Gene's face. "Be brave, soldier," he said softly.

The Jackson Five sang with clarity, *Whenever you need me, I'll be there.* Gene released Wally and walked down the trench, his boots splashing waves against the mud walls. The South Trail was barely visible in the black drenching rain. Gene slid onto the trail, and descending a few yards, he saw the gap in the barbed wire and the disarmed claymores. Cracked pieces of glass from the security lights lay in the mud. When he heard voices, Gene gripped the Arkansas Toothpick and crept forward. The music cranked louder; Jackson's shrill voice echoed through the darkness, *Just call my name, and I'll be there.*

"I hate this fucking song," Gene whispered silently.

Two South Vietnamese soldiers were huddled together. One had a cigarette sheltered in his cupped hands. Gene stood, and with a smooth, powerful motion, he sliced through his neck. The cigarette bounced off the soldier's fatigues; the head splashed in the mud. Continuing in the same fluid motion, Gene ripped the Toothpick across the throat of the second soldier. Blood spurted in the air; the soldier's head rolled next to the first.

The rain turned to a misty drizzle. With a screeching last note, *Where there is love, I'll be there*, the song suddenly ended. It was replaced by the piercing sound of a bugle. Gunfire erupted; mortars exploded in staccato bursts on the north side of Hill 101.

Gene put the Toothpick in the sheath. Metal spikes buried deep in the ground held the barbed wire in place. Picking up the two heads, Gene rammed the smoker's head on the closest spike and the second head on the spike directly opposite it. Tongues dangled loosely and dripped blood on the trail. A thin line of smoke emanated from one mouth.

Two sentries from hell, Gene thought. Listening to the battle noise, he reset the nearest security light, retrieved the M16 of the dead Vietnamese soldier, and crouched behind the headless bodies. Within minutes, the group of deserters rushed wildly down the trail. The lead soldier tripped the security light; two impaled heads glared at him. Screaming, he charged past them. Gene shot him in the chest; the soldier's body fell over the security light. In the sudden darkness, the line of deserters scrambled back up the hill.

The claymores on the north side detonated near the summit. Loud yells echoed through the night; a blistering exchange of gunfire resonated from the top bunker.

They've breached the perimeter, Gene thought. He saw a glow at the escape tunnel. Dark shapes disappeared inside the bamboo door. Running toward the tunnel, Gene lost his balance and slid awkwardly into coils of barbed wire. The M16 flew out of his hands.

A bugle sounded; VC raced up the South Trail and were met by withering fire. Gene extracted himself from the barbed wire. Holding the Arkansas Toothpick, he walked to the tunnel and kicked through the bamboo door. Captain Din sat on an oil drum meticulously turning and lighting a French cigar. Looking up, he reached for his revolver. Gene thrust the Toothpick into Din's chest. Din bit down, his teeth mashing the cigar into pulp.

"*Farang imperialiste*," Din wheezed with contempt.

"You traitor," Gene hissed. He gave the Toothpick an extra hard push; the blade tip protruded through Din's back. It was momentarily quiet, and then piercing screams echoed the length of the tunnel.

Sheathing the Toothpick, Gene grabbed the captain's .45 Browning and ran. Sweat dropped from his forehead and burned his eyes.

When Gene approached the end of the tunnel, he saw a VC soldier sitting at the base of a wooden ladder. Listening to the screams, the soldier smirked knowingly and laughed. Gene shot him with the Browning. Stepping over the body, he climbed the ladder and looked into Captain Din's quarters. A lantern cast shadows across the room. Bound by a single coil of barbed wire, the American soldiers were propped on the captain's cot. Their scalps had been ripped away. Wally's body leaned grotesquely against the dirt wall. Next to him, Lieutenant Chase sat quietly. Advancing slowly, wielding a knife, the blond-haired American had a crazed smile on his face.

"Hold him!" he ordered. A VC soldier grabbed Lieutenant Chase. The American, three scalps tucked under his hemp belt, positioned his knife against the lieutenant's forehead. "You tell me to go fuck myself" Harry squealed, and he lowered the knife.

Gene stepped to the top rung of the ladder and fired twice. The VC soldier holding the lieutenant was hit in the forehead and left eye. Harry turned quickly, and Gene fired again. The blade of the knife deflecting the bullet, Harry dropped to the ground. The door burst open, and Cochise backed inside. A grenade flashed brightly, and Cochise's body was propelled through the air. Smoke filled the room; Harry crawled away.

Gene rushed to the prisoners and uncoiled the wire. Pieces of flesh stuck to the barbs. Gene ripped the last barb out of the lieutenant's chest, and Chase struggled to his feet. Wally's head dipped slightly. Small bubbles appeared on his lips, expanded, and popped. Tears clouding his vision, Gene slid next to him. He cradled the bloodied head against his chest and rocked back and forth. There was a slight gasping sound, and Wally stopped breathing. Hazy lines of smoke drifted over the cot; an eerie calm filled the room. Time passed slowly. Blood covered Gene's shirt; it dripped from the tips of his fingers.

Gene stood, rummaged through the wreckage of the room, and found the first-aid kit. Taking a stretch bandage, he wrapped it around the lieutenant's forehead. A series of explosions shook Captain Din's sleeping quarters.

"Your B-52s," Gene said. Lieutenant Chase didn't respond. A thin line of blood seeped through the bandage, moved in a jagged line down his forehead, and flowed into the corner of his eye. Chase spoke quietly, his lips barely moving.

"I'm sorry about Wally."

"Let's not talk about Wally. Not now. Not ever."

Bombs blasted the hillside; the lantern shook, and dirt dropped from the ceiling. Gene spotted Harry's scalping knife on the ground. He picked it up and slid it under his belt. When the bombing stopped, Gene and Lieutenant Chase went to the radio room. The door and sections of wall were blown away; rays of sunshine pierced through the darkness.

Covering his eyes, Gene walked outside. The air was moist and putrid; craters dotted the hillside. Sunlight reflected off the barbed wire. Blood-covered torsos stuck in the silver coils. A torn section of a T-shirt, a black hole disfiguring the panda's head, hung dry and straight in the light. Lieutenant Chase exited the radio room, and he and Gene walked to the South Trail. Lieutenant Chase pointed to the two heads on the spikes. The bombing had loosened the dirt. The spikes slanted across each other, forming a bizarre *X* that swarmed with flies. Purple tongues protruded from the gaping months; the bulging eyes were pearly white in the sunlight. The buzzing noise of the flies alternated from shrill to dull.

"You did that?"

"Yeah," Gene said. "They were on their way to join the VC. They were traitors."

"Most of them came back. They fought well."

There was a distant hum, and a line of helicopters appeared in the blue sky. The choppers circled the hill before landing in the bombed-out craters. Soldiers and medics poured out of the doors and began sorting through the dead. Shouting when they saw the first American, they slid Oscar Jordan into a body bag.

His camera clicking rapidly, a photographer walked into view.

He stopped abruptly at the slanted heads on the *X*-shaped spikes and composed a series of pictures. Followed by his aide, Colonel Potter strutted toward him. Leaning awkwardly, the photographer focused the camera on the colonel, who posed proudly behind the mutilated heads.

"Take good pictures," Colonel Potter advised. "These poor bastards, even though their body parts are scattered all over this hillside, are heroes. They represent everything we're trying to accomplish in this godforsaken country." The colonel paused; the aide had a puzzled expression on his face. Flies buzzed around the colonel, and showing considerable agitation, he swiped at them with his hand. The aide stepped forward with a can of Repel Sportsman Max and sprayed the area. The colonel coughed.

"We'll distribute their pictures to every major newspaper. It'll show the world how brave the South Vietnamese are. I'll need their names. I want full benefits to go to their families. What's the bonus we're paying for heroes now?"

"It's a lot of money. I think it's up to two hundred dollars."

"Well, they earned it. Don't give the money to the officers. It'll disappear. Give it directly to the families."

Dressed in black garments, their silver necklaces and bracelets reflecting sunlight, a group of H'mong women appeared at the edge of the jungle. Faces dark and stoic, they stood patiently and waited. A fog hung over the jungle; bird sounds emanated from the mist.

Gene and Lieutenant Chase walked down the trench, their boots sinking in the mud. When he rounded the corner, Gene saw the photographer and a group of soldiers enter the radio room; Gene ran quickly. Just as he entered the bunker, a brilliant flash lit up the darkness. Gene charged into the photographer and knocked him to the ground.

"No pictures in here!" Gene shouted. Lieutenant Chase hurried through the door, helped the photographer to his feet, and ushered him outside. Working quickly, the medics closed Frank and Junior in black body bags. A pale-faced soldier gripped Wally by the shoulders.

Spasms shaking his body, the soldier dropped Wally and fell to his knees.

"I'll do that," Gene said in a barely audible whisper. Pushing the soldier aside, Gene slid Wally inside the body bag. The zipper made a smooth gliding noise. When Gene bent lower, the Batman medallion swung free and plopped in a bloody pool on the exposed section of Wally's brain. Gene grabbed the medallion and stuffed it under his shirt.

No one will ever see you like this, he promised, and he closed the bag. The medics lifted the bag at the corners and rushed outside. Gene walked to the cot and sat down. A warm stench rose from the mattress; moisture covered Gene's face.

"Are you ready, Gene?" Lieutenant Chase asked, standing at the door. The whirring hum of helicopter blades filled the bunker. "The colonel ordered everyone to the choppers."

"I'm staying here."

"Gene, your tour's up. It's time to go home."

"I'll go home when Harry's dead."

The first helicopter lifted off Hill 101. There was a roar of noise, and the second and third helicopters followed. Moments passed; a burst of gunfire sounded from the last helicopter. Hesitating at the door, the lieutenant stared at Gene, who sat motionless.

"I told you I'm staying."

Looking at Gene's sullen expression, Lieutenant Chase nodded and walked away. Minutes later, with a loud roar from the whirling blades, the helicopter lifted and swung toward the jungle. The roaring diminished to a soft echo and ceased completely.

In the absolute quiet of Hill 101, Gene grabbed the medallion. Carrying their dead, the H'mong women shuffled silently by the door. Waves of tropical heat flooded the bunker. Rubbing his fingers in a circular motion, Gene scraped the blood from the medallion. When he clearly saw the Batman image, he slid the medallion under his shirt and stared at the shadows that swirled in the recesses of the collapsed bunker.

Chapter Eleven

"All faculty and students are to report to the auditorium immediately!" Principal Port announced through the intercom at eleven o'clock on Tuesday morning. The homeroom teachers dismissed the junior high students first. When they were seated in the side rows of the auditorium, the sophomores and juniors were dismissed. The last group of students, the seniors, sat in the reserved front six rows. On the stage, the head of the Indian chief mascot was embroidered on the closed curtain. Cindy looked at the chief's mutilated eye socket and turned to Conner.

"I hate that Indian. How did he ever become our mascot?"

"The chief's a legend. He lost his eye preventing a massacre at Fort Standing Stone."

"I don't care if he's a hero. That black hole is grotesque."

"In the colonial days," Conner explained, "the Indians and settlers fought over Hartslog Valley. They did really gross things to each other."

"Nothing's changed," Cindy commented. "Gross things are still happening here. The TV news said something about a murder at the Mennonite school. And Sally was abducted on Sunday. She's missing two days now."

"Brenda's been missing a week," Conner added. "There's never been a kidnapping at Twin River, and now we have two."

There was a scraping noise on the stage, and the curtain opened, splitting the chief's head down the middle. The principal, Mr. Port; the assistant principal, Mr. Stedman; and Sheriff Parks walked through the opening. The principal advanced to the podium while the others sat in folding chairs. There was some whispering as the curtain closed behind them. The deeply grained face and blackened eye of the Indian chief folded neatly in place. Principal Port turned on the microphone; the students quieted.

"I called this assembly to make you aware of what happened this morning at Belleville. There was a tragedy at the Mennonite school."

As Principal Port explained about the death of the student, the auditorium hushed to a deep silence. A girl in the back of the auditorium began sobbing. When the principal finished, Mr. Stedman marched to the podium. He informed the students that Mr. Henry, the bank manager, had offered five thousand dollars reward money for anyone with relevant information on the kidnappers. Then he stated that certain measures would be taken to ensure the safety of the students at Twin River.

"All side exits are now chained and locked," Stedman explained. "Only the front and back exits can be used during the day."

"Oh, that's great!" a student behind Conner remarked. "I feel safe now."

The boy next to him gave a muffled laugh. His straggly gray beard masking his face, Mr. Hesston appeared out of nowhere and pointed to the offenders. After giving them the "out" signal, he ushered both boys to the office. With a smirk on his face, Mr. Stedman left the podium. Principal Port nodded to Sheriff Parks, who got up brusquely from his chair. His Stetson cavalry cowboy hat balanced perfectly, the sheriff reached the podium and grabbed the microphone, which emitted a shrill piercing noise.

"Ouch!" Conner said, grabbing his forehead. "That hurt."

The students around him laughed. Beard swinging wildly, red lips closed tightly, Charlie Hesston stomped down the aisle and searched the row of frozen faces. After hovering there for a few minutes, he returned to the wall. Cain Towers nudged his brother.

"Just another prick in the wall," Cain whispered, and Abel laughed.

Sheriff Parks stretched the microphone higher. Ignoring the loud screech, he repeated Principal Port's rendition of the tragedy at the Mennonite school. Sheriff Parks often used the word *massacre*. When he finished and asked if there were any questions, a flurry of hands began waving in the air.

"How many students were killed?"

"One."

"But you called it a massacre."

"He was massacred."

"How many killers were there?"

"One," the sheriff said. "He was a veteran. He learned how to kill in Vietnam."

"Sheriff Parks," Conner muttered under his breath. "You rotten bastard."

"Are we in any danger here?" a student asked.

"I want to assure you that you have nothing to fear at Twin River."

"What about Brenda and Sally?"

"We're working on that case. We just got an important tip this morning."

"What was it?"

"We can't talk about an ongoing investigation," Sheriff Parks answered in a stern voice. "But we'll make an arrest soon."

"What's to stop the kidnapper from taking another girl?"

"For your safety, we'll have an unmarked patrol car in the area at all times." The auditorium turned quiet. Sensing a mistake had been made, the sheriff looked over the rows of students. Getting up quickly, Principal Port walked to the podium and thanked Sheriff Parks. Charlie Hesston clapped his hands, and that led to a brief ovation. After the ovation, the teachers walked to their rows and began escorting the students back to the classrooms.

The white Cadillac stopped at the side entrance to the school. Wearing an oversized sweatshirt, Matt stepped out, his tennis shoes clumsily scraping against the cement. When the Cadillac pulled away, Matt walked to the door and pulled the handle. The door opened a crack and stuck. Looking through the glass, he saw the heavy chains on the push bars.

Matt walked to the front entrance, opened the door, and went inside. Stopping in the main office, he handed his excuse to the secretary. While she wrote an admission form, she glanced at the cut lip and the bandage on his forehead. She asked him about the injuries, but shrugging his shoulders and slipping the paper into his pocket, Matt left the office.

Gene felt drowsy when he awoke at noon. Examining the bandage around his shoulder, he saw where blood had formed a wet smear on the white cloth. Gene went to the kitchen, filled his cup with coffee, and walked to the porch. With a sigh, he settled in the hammock. Hearing laughter from the river, Gene looked up. A green canoe floated high in the sparkling water. A young couple was rowing, and sitting between them, a small boy splashed his hands in the current and laughed. Gene sipped the coffee, steam rising from the cup. Rays of sunlight slanted through the trees and dried the blood on the bandage.

After finishing the coffee, Gene dressed, got into the jeep, and drove the short distance to Twin River High School. Entering the building, he went to the maintenance room, pulled open the desk drawer, and took out a bag of M&M's. The bells rang, and the hall filled with students. When the late bell sounded, Gene left the room and climbed the steps to the second floor. As he neared a lighted display case, he saw Matthew sitting there, his back against the wall. Gene frowned when he noticed the cut lip and the bandage over Matt's eye.

"You don't look so good, Matthew."

"You don't look so good yourself. You look like you've been hit by a tractor."

"Maybe I was hit by something big. What about you? Why don't we talk about what happened to your forehead?"

"You won't take me to the office?"

"No, I won't take you to the office. Let's go outside where it's quiet."

"Okay." Brushing off his jeans, Matt got up from the floor. In the light from the display case, the cut on his lip was a deep purple. As they walked down the hall, Gene took the bag from his pocket and handed it to Matt.

"Here, Matthew, have some M&M's."

"Thanks. You can call me Matt."

Gene took Matt to the back exit, and they walked to the riverbank. A row of wooden steps led down the sloping grass terrace to the water's edge. They sat on the top step. Across the river, the Flaming Cross at the summit of Redemption Mountain reflected a brilliant light in the blue sky. Below them, the Juniata River flowed slowly, forming the big pool where it joined the Little Juniata. Beyond the pool, rapids crashed against the rocks, creating clouds of mist. The mist blanketed the island and lifted dark, amorphous shadows against the stone face of Blood Mountain. Vultures glided in and out of the shadows.

"Why are there so many vultures?" Matt asked. He tore the top off the bag, picked out three red M&M's, and put them into his mouth.

"There's an abundant supply of food. You and Conner were on the mountain Saturday night. Did the vultures frighten you?"

"No," Matt answered. "I wasn't scared." He chewed the chocolate slowly. There was an open space at the bottom of the bandage; Gene saw the deep gash on his forehead.

"Who hit you, Matt?"

"Mr. Henry told the nurse in the emergency room that I fell down the steps."

"He lied to her. Your dad hit you, didn't he?" When Matt didn't answer, Gene continued. "There's only one way to stop him from hitting you again. You have to report what happened."

"I can't do that."

"Are you afraid?"

"No." Matt reached into the bag and picked out three green M&M's. "Maybe I was afraid of him before, but I'm not anymore."

"Good. The school nurse is married to my brother, Andrew. She's a very nice lady. She won't ask any questions about Mr. Henry. Will you let her look at the bandage?"

"Do you have any more M&M's?"

"A whole drawerful. I'll give you another bag."

"Great. They all taste the same, but I like some colors better."

After they entered the building, Gene went to the maintenance room, grabbed another bag of M&M's, and gave it to Matt. Then he and Matt walked down the hall and entered the nurse's suite. There was a large window with sunlight streaming over a desk covered with papers, brown folders, and a flip-page calendar. The black metal nameplate on the desk read, "Joyce Brooks, School Nurse." The two cushioned chairs next to the desk were bathed in sunlight. There were four cubicles with beds along one wall. Joyce walked in and stared at Matt's bandage. When Gene made the introductions, Matt sat in the chair by her desk and took out the M&M's. He offered the bag to Joyce; she smiled and shook her head. Gene walked to the door.

"Take good care of my friend, Joyce."

"I will," Joyce said, turning her attention to the boy.

Gene left the room. He was halfway down the hall when the door to the assistant principal's office opened. Charlie Hesston stepped out. After shaking hands with Mr. Stedman, Charlie turned and stopped quickly, almost bumping into Gene.

"Excuse me, Gene. I didn't see you. Do you have a minute?"

"Sure." Gene followed Charlie up the steps and across the hall to his room. The classroom was empty. The walls in the room were lined with portraits of the presidents. Next to the portrait of Jimmy Carter, the current president, was a poster of a colonial soldier. His young face angry and determined, he aimed his modern, over-sized M16 at the forehead of King George. "Protect the Second Amendment— Friends of NRA" was printed at the bottom of the poster.

The largest poster was on the bulletin board behind the teacher's desk. It portrayed the monumental Memorial Arch at Valley Forge. A brisk wind straightened the colonial flag; deep snowdrifts covered the cobblestones leading to the arch.

"Ever been there?" Charlie asked, pointing at the poster. "Valley Forge."

"A few times."

"Our history began in Valley Forge," Charlie boasted. "The Continental Army marched there on December 19, 1777. Those ragtag, shoeless soldiers fought and died to give us what we have today. I take my classes to Valley Forge every December during Christmas vacation. It's the exact same time the army was there." Charlie smiled, noticing the expression on Gene's face. "Oh, I know what you're thinking. Why go in the winter when it's miserable?"

"You want the students to experience the cold weather," Gene guessed. "Maybe get a feeling for the soldiers, how much they suffered."

"That's precisely what I want."

"In one day?"

"I wish I could keep the students there longer. I would make them sleep in those log cabins overnight. Put the big freeze on their spoiled asses. See what they're made of. But you know how it is. There are safety issues, liability issues, and, of course, expense issues."

"There are always issues," Gene said. "What is it you wanted, Charlie?"

"I'm looking for support, Gene. There's a group of us organizing a school security committee. At first, it was because of the kidnappings. Now because of the massacre at the Mennonite school, I don't think we can depend on the local police. We have to protect ourselves. We need to alert the community that the students at Twin River are in danger."

"Is that why you took a shot at Shakespeare?"

"What makes you think I did that?" Charlie asked, a puzzled expression on his face. "Oh, all right. There was no harm done. Maybe I did shoot through the window."

"Why Shakespeare?"

"To thy own self be true," Charlie quoted. "I hated *Hamlet* in high school."

"It's too bad you feel that way. I think you learned something from Shakespeare."

"What are you talking about?"

"You're being true to yourself. You feel the need to kill someone."

"You're exactly right, Gene." Pulling at his beard, Charlie straightened and spoke in a strong voice. "You bet I'll kill someone if I'm forced to. Like I said, we're forming this security committee. We would like you to join us."

"Why me?"

"Because you served in Vietnam like I did. You know guns and how to use them. My idea is to have an armed volunteer on each floor. I'll handle the second floor, and you can secure the first. Then if some crazed killer got loose in the building, we wouldn't have to wait for the police. We could take him out ourselves."

"Like we did in Nam?"

"Yes, just like we did in Nam."

"Can I ask you something, Charlie? How close were you to real combat over there?"

"I worked at Ton Son Nhat. Some shells hit the air base during Tet."

"But you were safe most of the time?"

"No one was safe in Nam, Gene. You know that. But back to what we were discussing. The school security committee is meeting at the bank at nine o'clock. I'm driving with Mr. Stedman. Sheriff Parks and the Reverend Towers will be there. And Mr. Henry."

"The bank manager?"

"Yes, the bank manager. Mr. Henry's very concerned about protecting the kids. Can you attend?"

"No, I can't. I have important plans tonight."

"But you're interested in keeping the students safe?"

"Yes, I'll stop anyone from hurting them."

"That's how we all feel." Charlie smiled confidently. "I just discussed everything with Mr. Stedman. He agrees that we should secure the building. I'm thinking of purchasing a SIG 540. I saw a great price on Gun Net."

"I wouldn't do that, Charlie. I wouldn't bring an assault rifle into Twin River."

"Why?"

"My son, Conner, attends this school," Gene answered tersely. "I'd probably kill you." Gene opened the door, crossed the hall, and went down the steps. When he walked past the nurse's office, Gene observed Matt sitting on the chair eating M&M's. Joyce had a serious expression on her face. Doors banged open, spilling students into the hall. Gene hurried to the parking lot, got into the jeep, and drove to the house. When he entered the bedroom, he dropped heavily on the mattress.

"That was a great assembly today," Abel said, standing on the dock below the estate.

"Frankly, I was disappointed." Cain slid the Sharpfinger under his belt and grabbed the rope tied to a wide sixteen-foot canoe.

"Why?" Abel asked, getting into the canoe.

"That crazy vet only killed one of those Mennonites." Loosening the rope, Cain got in and started the four-horsepower motor, and the canoe raced downriver. After a few minutes, Cain steered the canoe across the deep pool at Twin River High School. Blood Mountain slanted out of the rapids below the pool. The island dividing the rapids was shrouded in shadows. A vulture soared out of the shadows, and talons spread wide, it swooped low over their heads. Laughing, Cain angled the canoe toward the still channel.

"This is a real cool place," Abel said. "Maybe we should set traps on the mountain."

"We've already got enough traps set. I'll bet we get our wolf tonight." Looking past Abel, Cain pointed at a form that made jerking movements in the water. "What's that?"

"Those are antlers," Abel answered, sitting up. "I'm seeing eight, maybe ten points."

"Let's go hunting," Cain said. He swung the canoe in a half circle and sent it racing over the water. A short distance from the buck, Cain cut the motor. The canoe drifted into the antlers with a scraping sound and stopped. A stream of mist exploded from the buck's nostrils. Droplets of water rolled down the silken fur of its neck.

"Biggest one I've ever seen," Abel trumpeted.

"Hunters dream of a trophy like this." Cain grabbed the antlers, and shoving hard, he pushed the head underwater. The buck kicked; a profusion of bubbles boiled to the surface. Low in the water, the canoe drifted slowly; the bubbles popped lightly and ceased. Releasing his grip on the antlers, Cain was jubilant. "What a rush! Now I know why hunters feel so good."

"I don't feel too much of anything. This wasn't what you'd call real hunting."

"What are you talking about? We killed us a trophy, didn't we?"

"Yeah, we did."

"Then shut up and enjoy it," Cain advised. "I can't wait to tell the reverend how good we did." He started the motor and angled the canoe toward the bank. When the canoe slid onto the sand, Abel got out and pulled them out of the water. Unsheathing the Sharpfinger, Cain tramped into the woods. Abel followed him down a narrow animal trail. After a few minutes, Cain lifted his hand and stopped. There was a low growling sound. Crouching low, moving slowly, Cain crept into a small clearing. The cage at the edge of the clearing was covered with branches. The growling grew louder.

"We caught us something," Cain broadcast excitedly. Pushing the branches aside, he looked inside the cage. "Bullshit!"

"What is it?" Abel asked, stepping closer.

"A fuckin' dog!" Cain exclaimed, and he hit the side of the cage with the Sharpfinger. Making a whimpering noise, the black Labrador retriever crouched in the corner. Cain flipped open the hinge at the top of the cage. Ears drooping low, the dog raised its head. Its tail moved back and forth; its eyes glistened in the fading light.

"Look at those angel eyes," Cain said. With a powerful thrust, he stuck the Sharpfinger deep into the Lab's forehead. There was a shrill yelp, and the dog collapsed. Cain pulled out the knife and scraped the blade clean on the shiny black coat.

"Why'd you have to kill it?"

"Because I'm gonna cut it up and leave pieces of meat around the cage so we can lure us the wolf we need to finish the ceremony. You got any more stupid questions?"

"No, let's get started so we can make it home in time for dinner."

"You're always thinking about food." Cain grabbed the Lab by the neck and yanked it out of the cage. Abel spread the lab's hind legs and watched as Cain sliced the knife the length of the belly. Intestines and a dark fluid spilled over the ground. "Our wolf will find this carcass in no time." Cain sliced off sections of rib and gave them to Abel. "Leave these on the trail. I'll catch up to you."

After Abel left, Cain dropped the dog's head and hind legs into the cage. Latching the door securely, he picked up a handful of intestines, spattered the bloody glob against the nearest tree, and walked down the trail. Abel was waiting for him at the canoe. Cain waded into the river and splashed water over his arms and face. Then he pushed the canoe away from the bank and crawled inside. The motor started on the first pull of the rope.

"Cain." Abel turned and shouted above the noise. "I was thinking about Becky."

"Becky's my sweetheart. What about her?"

"Is she prepared for the ceremony?"

"You bet she's prepared. When we were swimming at the cliffs, she told me she's having problems with her period."

"What's that mean?"

"It means she's got herself pregnant. And when I felt her, I saw she was big inside. She could give birth to twins. That would make for a perfect ceremony."

"It sure would," Abel agreed, a smile forming on his face. "It would be real special. We ain't never done twins before." The canoe knifed through the water; the roar of the rapids grew louder. Blood Mountain was a dark silhouette looming over the river. The Flaming Cross filled the evening sky with a bright glow.

That evening Conner had dinner at Cindy's house. The table was set with dishes of green beans, mashed potatoes, stuffed pork chops, and a loaf of Italian bread. As soon as the family sat down, Mrs. Hoover began talking about the shooting at the Mennonite school. She insisted that Cindy stay home from school, but Mr. Hoover said Cindy shouldn't ruin her three-year attendance record because of one maniac.

"And besides," Mr. Hoover concluded, "the killer's dead."

"He got what he deserved," Mrs. Hoover added, spooning mashed potatoes onto her plate. "The TV 10 reporter said the killer was a Vietnam vet. That doesn't surprise me." She looked across the table. "Your dad was in the war, Conner. I was thinking maybe he knew the killer."

"Mom," Cindy interjected, "there were thousands of soldiers in Vietnam."

"More than five hundred thousand," Conner stated.

"Well, I was just saying, your dad and the killer could have accidentally bumped into each other at the American Legion or the VFW."

"My dad never goes to those clubs," Conner said, stabbing a section of pork chop. He took a bite, placed the fork on the plate, and stood up. "It's late. I should go home."

"But you haven't eaten much at all," Mrs. Hoover complained.

"I'm not very hungry," Conner said. "Good night." He walked around the table to the door. Cindy followed him.

"I'm sorry, Conner. My parents didn't mean anything with all those questions."

"It's not that. Dad wasn't at school this morning. When I heard that a veteran was involved in the shooting, I went home right away. Dad's jeep was there, but I didn't see him. I want to check the house again."

"Be careful."

"I'll be fine," Conner said. He kissed Cindy. Conner got on the bicycle, flicked on the light, and pedaled down the deserted street. The air was cool, and a breeze blew off the river. When Conner crossed the Barree bridge, he began to pedal faster. There was a squealing noise, and a black cat raced across the road. In the bouncing light of the bicycle, Conner saw a mouse protruding sideways from its mouth.

It took Conner five minutes to reach the house. There were no porch lights; the jeep was parked in the drive. Conner dropped the bicycle on the ground and climbed the steps. Entering the living room, he switched on the table lamp. The wall of antlers jumped into view. Balanced in the center rack, the wooden cabinet tilted, the door swayed open, and the Arkansas Toothpicks gleamed in the light. A stuffed military backpack was on the floor under the cabinet.

Conner walked to his dad's bedroom and looked inside. Shirtless, his face and upper body wet with perspiration, Gene lay motionless on the mattress. There was a thick bandage around his shoulder. Stepping closer to the bed, Conner pulled the sheet higher, tucking it under his dad's chin. Suddenly, Gene's eyes opened; his face darkened. Taking deep breaths, he stared at Conner. Moments passed; Conner didn't move. Then groaning loudly, his dad collapsed. Conner backed away and closed the door without making a sound.

I love this car! Jeffery thought. The setting sun reflected a silver glow off the immaculately polished hood. Spinning gravel, he raced the Porsche up the dirt road to the cabin. The security gate was open, and Jeffery saw a black BMW parked at the steps. A Green Hollow Correctional Camp vehicle was next to the BMW.

"Shit," Jeffery said. He parked, got out of the car, and climbed the steps to the porch. When he reached the top step, the door opened. Luther stood there, his muscular frame filling the entrance, a Marlboro dangling from his lips.

"We've been waiting." Luther stepped aside, and Jeffery entered the room. Max was behind the bar mixing drinks; Nathaniel sat on the sofa.

"We're very disappointed, Jeffery," Nathaniel stated in an abrasive tone.

"I'm sorry I'm late."

"I don't mean that. I mean progress on the video. What happened on Sunday?"

"Everything went smoothly. I brought Sally in as planned."

"We saw that on the video," Max verified. "It was getting real hot. Sally spread her legs wide open for you. You had this nice-sized lump in your jeans. And then what did you do, Jeffery? You ran out of the room, asshole."

"Sally was frightened. She screamed."

"She screamed because she was happy to see you," Luther said. "Turning shit-faced and running out of the room won't sell any videos."

"Wait a minute," Nathaniel said. "Jeffery has a point. If we wanted to scare the girls, we could use Max here."

"Can I?" Max asked, bringing Nathaniel a glass. "Can I be in Sally's video?"

"Hell, no," Nathaniel said. "You stay away from her." Nathaniel lifted the glass and drained the Manhattan. "Jeffery, just so you know.

Max called his brother, the deputy sheriff. He gave him a tip about the FritoLay van."

"What about the van? It's parked in the garage."

"Not yours, Jeffery. The local delivery van. Max put some of Sally's clothing behind the snack boxes. That way, when the sheriff searches around, he'll have the evidence to arrest the driver."

"You never said anything about that. The driver had nothing to do with the girls."

"What's better, Jeffery? Should you be arrested, or some stranger?"

"I don't want to go to jail."

"And neither do we," Nathaniel said. He stood and gave Jeffery a plastic pillbox. "I want you to use these in the next video."

"What are they?" Jeffery asked, taking the circular container.

"The best boner pills money can buy. They'll make your dick big and hard."

"I don't need pills to have sex." Jeffery looked at the label. Luther and Max stepped directly in front of him.

"Jeffery," Nathaniel said, his voice irritable and menacing. "Just take the pills. I don't like to keep our clients waiting. Every day we lose money. Do you understand?"

"Yes, but—"

"No buts, Jeffery." Nathaniel spoke in a soft voice. "Luther's going to give you a reason to work harder on the video. Aren't you, Luther?"

"Copy that," Luther answered, and moving quickly, he swung his fist into Jeffrey's abdomen. A blast of moist air sprayed from Jeffery's mouth. "Hold him steady."

"I've got him," Max said, grabbing Jeffery by the shoulders. He straightened Jeffery's body, and Luther crushed his fist lower and harder into the abdomen. Jeffery hit the floor in a crumpled position. Luther stood over the body, fists clenched.

"Pick him up," Nathaniel ordered. "The floor's no place for a movie star." When Max lifted Jeffery, some Pump House tokens fell from Jeffery's pocket and rolled under the sofa. Max lowered the body onto the cushions. Jeffery's watery eyes blinked open.

"We expect results this weekend, Jeffery," Nathaniel said. He walked out the door and down the steps to the BMW. As Nathaniel drove away, Jeffery pulled himself off the sofa. With his head lowered, he stumbled past Luther and Max to the porch.

"You'd better make an entertaining and sexy video," Luther advised. "Next time we won't be so nice." Luther laughed and nudged Max in the shoulder. In the darkness, the security lights clicked on, blinding Jeffery. Covering his eyes, he tripped clumsily on the bottom step and hit the ground hard. Jeffery grabbed his side, got to his feet, and walked slowly to the Porsche.

Gene heard the howling noise and woke at midnight. The wolf howled again and was quiet. Gene crawled out of bed. Reaching for the bottle of aspirin on the table, he lifted it to his mouth and gulped down some tablets. Then he went to the living room and grabbed the Arkansas Toothpick and harness. The backpack on the floor held a body bag, a roll of wire, and packing tape. Gene took a plastic storage bag filled with hamburger out of the refrigerator, and stuffing it into the backpack, he walked to the jeep.

A cool wind blew from the river; a bright crescent moon reflected off the water. Gene drove to Barree, crossed the railroad tracks, and accelerated up the hill to the mansion. Stopping at the gate, Gene took out the piece of paper from Matthew's locker. Checking the numbers, he punched them in the security panel, and the door squeaked open.

Driving slowly down the entrance road, Gene saw the portico and the white Cadillac parked under it. As he approached, a collie growled and moved out of the shadows. Gene unzipped the storage bag and threw the hamburger. The dog jumped, caught it in midair, and swallowed in the same motion. Then the dog whimpered and rolled onto its side.

Gene parked the jeep next to the white Cadillac. After brushing his hand over the hood, which was hot, Gene climbed the porch steps, pushed the door open, and walked into a large living room. The only light was from a half-open door off to the side. A gigantic chandelier filled the center of the room. An oil painting of a young boy dressed in elegant blue clothes was on the wall. There was a sofa, plush chairs, an entertainment center, and a spiral staircase that led to the second floor. A belt hung from the intricately curved fleur-de-lis ornament at the end of the railing. Gene noticed the dark stains on the leather.

"Blood," he whispered. Gene crept silently up the steps and pushed open the doors until he found Matt's bedroom. Looking inside, he saw a wall-sized Peter Pan mural. Brandishing a sword, Captain Hook stood in the center of the mural. His eyes had been scratched out. Wearing only shorts, Matt lay on his stomach on a king-sized bed. Wide, dark welts, some disappearing under the shorts, crossed his shoulders and back.

"Son of a bitch," Gene muttered fiercely. He retraced his steps, walked across the living room, and peered through the half-open door. Sitting in front of a computer, Mr. Henry had his hand on the mouse. The bank's homepage was on the screen. Gene slid out the Arkansas Toothpick, walked to the chair, and grabbed Mr. Henry's shoulder.

"Just keep on doing what you're doing, Mr. Henry." Gene positioned the Arkansas Toothpick under his chin. "And don't talk. Just listen."

"What's going on? What do you want?"

"I said don't talk." Gene twisted the Toothpick, slicing a thin line on the banker's neck. Blood dripped down the front of his shirt. Mr. Henry made a whimpering noise.

"I want you to bring up the bank mortgages," Gene requested. Nodding his head, Mr. Henry highlighted an icon, and the list of mortgages appeared on the screen. Gene glanced at the properties and saw the amount due on Holy Waters Church.

"Listen to my directions, Mr. Henry. Write a check to the bank for $55,000."

"So that's it. This is a robbery." Registering a sigh of relief, Mr. Henry took a checkbook from the drawer, filled in the amount, and signed it. "Is that all you want?"

"Write on the memo line, 'Mortgage Balance Holy Waters Church.' Then put the check in a stamped envelope and address it to the loan officer at the bank." After Mr. Henry finished writing, Gene took the envelope and slid it into his pocket.

"What's to prevent me from voiding this tomorrow?"

"Be quiet, and shut off the computer." Gene waited, and when the computer screen turned black, he lifted the Arkansas Toothpick and swung the handle into Mr. Henry's head. Mr. Henry slumped forward; his body hit the desk and then the floor.

Gene unzipped the black body bag and slid Mr. Henry inside. Lifting the bag over his shoulder, he walked to the jeep. When he shoved the body bag into the backseat, Gene saw the shadow of a figure at the upstairs window. The shadow quickly dropped out of sight.

"Matthew," Gene whispered, and he drove down the road.

Stopping in Barree, Gene dropped the envelope into a blue postal box. Then he went to Blood Mountain. Pulling at the tightness in his shoulder, Gene got out of the jeep. An owl sounded from a nearby tree; a wolf howled in the darkness. Dragging the body bag from the backseat, he momentarily lost his footing when Mr. Henry began kicking at the thick fabric. Gene took a deep breath, swallowed a handful of aspirin, and picked up the body bag.

Two hours later, Gene returned to the jeep. Dark shadows fell from the trees. Fresh blood seeped through the bandage on his shoulder. When Gene reached the house, he went to the living room and placed the Arkansas Toothpick securely in the cabinet. Then he walked to the porch and collapsed on the hammock. Clouds moved across the crescent moon. Frogs croaked from the riverbank. Raindrops began to patter off the roof. Soon there was a steady downpour that silenced the frogs. The gentle rocking motion of the hammock put Gene into a deep sleep.

Chapter Twelve

Ho Chi Minh Trail

1972

Propelled by the wind, fast-moving storm clouds covered the jungle and the river that wound through it. At one point, the river dropped sharply into a stretch of turbulent rapids. As the wind became stronger, clusters of bamboo swayed low over the river. Gene jumped into the water and pulled the dugout to a sandy section of bank.

Gene removed his shirt and wrapped the two Arkansas Toothpicks into a bundle. Walking to a nearby tree, he climbed through the branches. A gecko opened its jaws, hissed loudly, showing a blood-red tongue, and raced up the bark. Gene followed it. When he was high in the tree, Gene secured the harness, dropped to the ground, and returned to the bank.

Pushing the dugout in the current, Gene saw three large boulders downriver. With the rapids raging past them, the boulders created an inner pool of still water. A few yards from the boulder, there was a dark crevice in the side of a mountain. Before he died, the VC tracker Somchai had told Gene about the rocks and the entrance to the Buddhist sanctuary.

"The rocks in front of the cave are big like turtle shells," Somchai said, his hands bound behind him, his voice unsteady. "There is one rock in the shape of a turtle head protruding from one of the shells. Go directly there. It is the only place to safely land the dugout." Somchai hesitated and shifted his position. The giant tree cast dark shadows over his body. His face serene, Somchai stared at Gene. "You will place my body in the branches with the others?"

"Yes, but before I do, I have to ask you something. How did you track me here?"

"It was not by any skill. I climbed the tree to search the jungle for any sign of you. Then I saw where the bark was rubbed smooth."

"I'm sorry you climbed the tree."

"Karma," Somchai whispered. "You are not what I expected, Jungle Ghost. You are not a spirit. You are a soldier like me. You must do what a soldier does. And yet I fear being tied to the tree like the others. I fear a slow death of many days."

"You will not suffer. None of them suffered."

"It is a comfort to hear that." Somchai breathed deeply. When the sun broke through the branches of the tree, the beads of perspiration on his face gleamed in the light. His lips barely moved.

"You will return the amulet to the priest?"

"Yes," Gene answered, clutching the stone and golden chain in his fist.

"Then I am ready." Somchai closed his eyes. Not making a sound, Gene buried the Arkansas Toothpick powerfully and deeply into his skull.

Just where Somchai said it would be, Gene thought, studying the turtle rocks and the entrance to the cave. There was a bright flash of lightning, and thunder cracked. The sky darkened, and a heavy, vertical deluge cut off his view of the rocks. Gene paddled furiously;

the rain spattered against his face and shoulders. Blinking away the water, he saw the head of the turtle, the rounded empty eyes, and the beaked mouth. The mouth opened and closed with the rocking motion of the waves.

It's laughing at me, Gene thought.

The dugout hit the turtle, turned sideways, and sank. Gene lunged and wrapped his hand around the grainy turtle's neck. Pulling himself to the inner pool, he sat in the waist-deep water, rain pelting his body. Within minutes, the rain slackened and stopped. Thunder cracked weakly in the distance. Black, turbulent clouds raced downriver, and the sky opened to a deep blue; the air was moist and heavy. Steam lifted from the turtle-shell rocks.

Dripping water, Gene waded out of the pool and walked up a steep incline to the cave. The entrance was narrow. Gene turned sideways and slid his body against the rock surface. As he moved deeper into the entrance, the trail curved, and the ceiling dropped. There was a dim glow in front of him. Falling to his hands and knees, Gene crawled forward. He felt a cool draft against his face, and after a short distance, he entered a cavernous room. Twenty stone steps, worn smooth by use, led to a squared platform where a massive golden Buddha stared down at him. Thousands of candle lights flickered from cracks in the wall.

"Incredible," Gene whispered. He heard a soft brushing noise, and when he turned, he was struck on the back of the head, his body falling on the bottom step.

When Gene regained consciousness, he was lying on a cot in a small rectangular room. A single candle cast a flickering light on the thick wooden door. Gene walked over and was reaching for the handle when the door opened. Two boys dressed in the orange robes of Buddhist monks stood there.

The taller of the two boys motioned to Gene. Stepping outside, Gene followed the boys down a passageway that was lined with closed doors. There were low chanting sounds from behind some of the doors. The passageway led directly to the platform and the sitting Buddha. The candles reflected flames of light that danced on the surface of the golden statue. Looking through the glare, Gene saw an aged Buddhist priest in a tattered, dull-orange robe. Gene brought his hands forward in the prayer position and lowered his head.

"Please, sit," the priest said in English.

Crossing his legs under him, Gene sat opposite the priest. The priest had a slight body and a shiny, hairless head. Thin silver-framed glasses sat low on his nose. His face was lined with deep creases that moved when he spoke.

"You are the soldier called the Jungle Ghost?"

"Yes."

"You come to the temple without any weapons?"

"Yes. I made a promise to return this." Reaching into his shirt pocket, Gene removed the golden chain. A stone amulet shaped in the form of a triangle dangled from the end of the chain. Folding his hands again in the prayer position, Gene extended the chain to the priest. Barely glancing at the amulet, the priest scrutinized Gene's face.

"Somchai died quickly and with the honor due to a soldier?"

"Yes."

"The bodies of the dead should be covered. They should be cared for."

"In time," Gene whispered.

"Yes, all will be done in its proper time. Knowing this, I accept the return of the amulet." The priest took the amulet from Gene's hand and held it glistening in the light. There was movement below. Carrying an ornate silver tray, an elderly disciple appeared on the steps. His face was gaunt; thick black eyebrows covered his forehead. The disciple used a bowed crutch and struggled with his balance. When he reached the platform, he dropped with difficulty to his knees. The Buddhist priest addressed Gene in a clear voice.

"This is Pradit, Somchai's older brother," he said.

Gene felt the muscles in his body tighten. He looked furtively at the disciple and saw a vacant, lost expression. The priest dropped the golden chain. It made a sharp sound striking the tray. Still on his knees, the disciple backed down the steps and disappeared in the shadows. Gene found it difficult to speak.

"You called me the Jungle Ghost. How do you know who I am?"

"Everyone knows about the Jungle Ghost. Pradit was very keen to meet you. After meditation, he will begin to search for his brother. Is the body nearby?"

"Yes, it is near, but he will never find it." Gene studied the flames and the flickering shadows on the wall. The chanting from the passageway leveled to a monotonous hum. "I have killed many soldiers in this area. Is there danger here?"

"Do you feel danger?"

"No."

"Then there is none. I do not mean there is the complete absence of danger. I mean that you face no outward danger. The real threat to your safety comes from within."

"I don't understand."

"The demons within us fight for mastery. Until a person controls these forces, he will never be safe. And you are beset with demons, Jungle Ghost. You are consumed with anger, are you not?"

"Yes, but I have a reason for my anger. I have vowed to kill a traitor."

"Buddha teaches that holding onto anger is like grasping a hot coal. You intend to throw it at your enemy, but you are the one who gets most horribly burned."

"I am a soldier. I am already, as you say, horribly burned."

"We all are soldiers. How we fight, all our actions, will determine our proximity to the ultimate goal, nirvana." The priest raised a steady hand, straightened his glasses, and stared at Gene. "Supplicants have made comments about this *farang* you are hunting. Karma is the spring that we all drink from. Generation after generation, it shapes our lives. So it is with the American who now travels with the VC.

His spring has been poisoned by his past actions. He has killed as you have, but, unlike you, he kills for joy. And to our disgust, he carries *souvenirs militaire* of the dead. The Jungle Ghost has no such souvenirs?"

"No."

"The Jungle Ghost is a complex person. You are troubled by demons. Yet your time on the Trail has been valuable. It has exposed these demons to you and given you a glimpse of absolute truth. Buddha has written that there are two mistakes you must avoid if you are to find absolute truth. You will encounter pain and unbearable suffering. Thus you will be tempted to stop. The first mistake is not going all the way."

"What is the second mistake?"

"Not starting," the priest said. The chanting from the passageway ceased; the silence in the cavern was complete. "Know this, Jungle Ghost. By coming here and returning the amulet, you have started the journey to absolute truth. You, and only you, will determine how you finish the journey." The priest stood, his robes aglow from the burning candles.

Extending his hands in a prayer position and bowing his head, Gene stared at the stone floor. When he looked up, the priest was gone. Gene rose to his feet. As he walked, his body cast a gray, ghostly shadow on the side of the Buddha. Gene descended the steps, knelt down, and crawled into the passageway.

Minutes later, Gene walked into bright sunlight. Lifting his hand over his eyes, he saw the three large rocks in the water and the dugout bobbing next to them. A golden light flashed from the dugout. Gene maneuvered down the stone incline and waded into the pool. As he approached the dugout, he saw Somchai's golden chain and stone amulet hanging over the flat bow. Gene put the amulet around his neck, climbed on the rock, and leveled the dugout in the water. Getting inside, his foot brushed the bundled shirt. The ivory handles of the Arkansas Toothpicks protruded from the cloth.

Pushing away from the turtle-shell rock, Gene swung the paddle through the water. Almost instantly, the rapids slammed against the dugout. As he was propelled downriver, Gene glanced at the line of Buddhist priests watching him from the entrance of the cave. Propped on his bowed crutch, Somchai's brother stood in the shadows at the end of the line. Whitewater sprayed the dugout, clouding his vision. Gene felt the singular weight of the golden chain around his neck.

Chapter Thirteen

On Wednesday morning, the sun shone bright and warm. Gene met JJ Jackson at Miller's Diner on Route 22. While JJ labored over steak and eggs, Gene ate a tall stack of pancakes. Walking to the table, the waitress refilled their cups with coffee. Gene finished the pancakes and asked the waitress for an omelet with ham on the side. JJ cut into the steak and watched Gene across the table.

"You're really hungry today?'

"I was out late last night. I worked up an appetite."

"How's your shoulder?"

"It feels better now. I'm fortunate Leroy didn't kill me. What the hell was wrong with him, JJ? Did he have a rotten childhood? Was he a molested kid?"

"None of that. Leroy came from a rich family on the Philadelphia Main Line. He lived a normal life until his mom got thrown from a horse and broke her neck. The dad remarried a year later. Leroy's new mom had two clumsy, overweight boys, Roger and Simon. They were spoiled thugs, but she loved them to death and pretty much ignored Leroy. The family situation turned hostile on Christmas Day. The most popular toy in 1956 was the Daisy BB gun. That's what the loving mom bought for Roger and Simon. As for her stepson, she gave him the second most popular toy that year."

"How do you know this stuff?"

"Just like I knew about you, Gene. I read Leroy's file. Take a guess. What was the second most popular Christmas gift that year?"

"I have no idea. Maybe it was a stocking filled with M&M's. That's what I got every year."

"No, it wasn't candy. Leroy got a package of Play-Doh. It made him furious. While Mom and Dad were out visiting friends, Leroy confiscated the BB guns, tied Roger and Simon to a tree in the backyard, and peppered their bodies with about fifty BBs. Mom's reaction was immediate. She committed Leroy to Berks Mountain Christian Reform Camp. On the first night, some of the older kids roughed Leroy up. The next morning, Leroy roughed them up in a worse way. He broke bones and smashed faces. The counselors were too afraid to report him. At the Christian reform camp, Leroy became a serious head-case."

"The army knew his background and took him anyway?"

"Recruiters favor tough personalities. The army put Leroy on the fast track. They eliminated psychology and sensitivity training and got him in the war killing Viet Cong way ahead of schedule. Leroy was good at it. He just didn't know when to stop." JJ glanced out the window. There was a line of Mennonite horses and buggies moving down Route 22. The buggies, horses dropping piles of excrement on the asphalt, backed up traffic for miles. "Where are the Mennonites going?"

"The same place we are," Gene said. "The train station."

"We'd better get there first," JJ said, getting up. "I'll take care of the bill."

After the stop at the cash register, Gene and JJ went outside and got into the jeep. Turning onto Route 22, Gene drove with caution past the horses and buggies. When he approached the bridge over the Juniata River, traffic was moving very slowly. Gene nudged JJ in the shoulder and pointed to the black-and-white POW-MIA flag.

"The bridge is named after a Twin River graduate. I was here when State Senator Sam Hayes made the dedication to Sergeant Port."

"I heard about him, Gene. He was First Cav. A grenade landed in the middle of his men. He fell on it."

"Yeah," Gene said. "The grenade ripped open his side. Somehow he survived. When the position was overrun, the VC carried him out, gave him medical attention, and fed him monkey meat to get his strength back. He died in a POW camp ten months later. President Nixon awarded him the Congressional Medal of Honor posthumously in 1970."

"Did you know him?"

"Twin River is a small school. Everyone knows everyone else. Sergeant Port was just like the rest of us. You would never have known that he had that something extra in him. He saw the danger to his friends and jumped on the grenade. That was real courage."

"I have a theory about courage, Gene. I think it's in the genes passed on from generation to generation. Coming out here in the wilderness like they did, the first settlers had to be brave. It was an act of courage to find food, to carry water from the spring, just to stay alive and protect the family. Only heroes survive the wilderness, Gene. Were Port's ancestors from this area?"

"The name's on some markers in the Hartslog Cemetery. But the dates are worn off."

"I figured as much," JJ said with confidence.

A loud horn sounded from the line of traffic. The horses and buggies began moving. Gene drove across the bridge, bumped the jeep over the railroad tracks, and parked along the side of the road. He and JJ stepped out into bright sunshine. There was a crowd of people around the train station. A reporter pushed his way through the crowd and focused his camera on a horse and buggy. When the Mennonite couple covered their faces and turned away, Gene walked to the reporter.

"These people have been through a lot," Gene said, positioning himself in front of the camera. "I wouldn't be taking any pictures right now." Gene put his hands on his hips and stood there. After the reporter reluctantly lowered the camera, Gene returned to JJ.

"What was that about?"

"The Mennonites don't like having their pictures taken," Gene said. He watched the driver and the woman step down from the buggy and walk toward them.

"Now what?" JJ whispered. "She's the teacher. She was in the classroom when you killed Leroy." The woman, dressed in a dark bonnet and long dark dress, stopped in front of Gene. She spoke in a soft voice.

"We live our own lives. We don't understand your ways." Gene didn't say anything. His hands low at his side, he stood at attention. His shoulder began to throb; the Mennonite teacher stared at him. "I saw what you did to that intruder in our school. I talked to the community, and we discussed it for a long time. They agreed to come here to say prayers."

"For the dead man?" Gene asked.

"No, not the dead man. We came to pray for you." The woman straightened her shoulders and stared at Gene's face, her eyes meeting and locking onto his. She held the gaze for a few moments, and then she turned and walked back to the buggy.

"The Mennonites are praying for you," JJ commented. "I guess that's a good thing."

Gene and JJ walked to the train station. It was ten twenty. There were six people waiting on the platform. Three of them were students from Juniata College. A horn sounded, and a dusty black car, Green Hollow Correctional Camp stenciled on the door, stopped in a no parking zone. Luther Cicconi and Max Wright stepped out. Pulling up his pants, a leather blackjack protruding from under the belt, Luther scoped the people on the platform. He saw Gene and walked over. Max followed closely behind.

"Leaving town, are you, Gene?" Luther said.

"No, what about you?"

"I'm not going anywhere, Gene. Unlike some people, I work for a living."

"Keeping track of juvenile delinquents inside a chain fence—that takes real skill."

"You bet it does. And you can also bet I don't need a broom or mop when I do my job." The train horn sounded in the distance. Grabbing Max by the arm, Luther pulled him to the edge of the platform. JJ nodded in their direction and nudged Gene in the shoulder.

"Who's your friend?"

"He's not my friend. Never was. We graduated high school together. His wife, Ann, and my wife were neighbors. I was obligated to go to their wedding."

The Amtrak train screeched to a stop, and the metal door swung open. After dropping the steps, the conductor helped an elderly couple to the platform. Standing at the bottom of the steps and looking irritated, Luther didn't move. The couple detoured around him. Holding a folder in his hand, pushing a teenage boy, a man in a blue suit and tie came down the steps. Max took the folder; Luther removed the handcuffs from his belt.

The teenager was wearing faded jeans, a black-and-white Pittsburgh Penguins T-shirt, a Penguins cap, and sunglasses. His shoulder and chest muscles stretched through the T-shirt. He had a light complexion, handsome features. Luther grabbed him by the arm. Cuffing one wrist and then the other, he pushed the boy past Gene. When they reached the car, Luther removed the boy's sunglasses and smashed them on the asphalt.

"I feel sorry for that kid," JJ said. The train whistle sounded.

"Luther's a certified jerk," Gene remarked. He shook JJ's hand. JJ climbed the metal steps and disappeared behind the closing door. As the train left the station, crossing bells clanged. The pole lifted in the air; horses and buggies began moving across the tracks.

The radio was loud. The announcer talked enthusiastically about the weather—nothing but sunshine for the rest of the week. Luther Cicconi drove through Huntingdon, past the campus of Juniata College, and turned onto the Petersburg Pike. Ten minutes later, he spun the wheel sharply and turned off the pike onto a dirt road. Looking through the rearview mirror, he laughed when the boy slid across the backseat and cracked his head on the window. Luther stopped the car, opened the back door, and pulled the boy off the seat.

"Who is he?" Luther asked. Max opened the folder and looked at the papers.

"Ira Hayes," Max said. "He's named after the famous Indian Johnny Cash sang about. He helped raise the flag on some Japanese island. I guess the Indian drank too much whiskey and fell and drowned in a puddle of water. I liked listening to the story."

"Quit with the dead Indian lesson," Luther growled. "What else you got?"

"Okay," Max said, glancing back at the paper. "He's sixteen years old. He punched a Pittsburgh police officer and broke his nose."

"You fuckin' city kids!" Luther took the blackjack from his pocket. "You're not in Pittsburgh anymore. We need to educate you to your new home. First, we'll show you who's boss-man." Luther swung the blackjack across Ira's shoulder, knocking him against the car. "And we don't like these pussy Penguins shirts."

Luther stuffed the blackjack into his pocket and held Ira by the neck. Ripping off the shirt, he threw it in the trees. The shirt caught on a branch; the Penguin and hockey stick swung loosely in the air.

"Here's your new uniform." Max laughed and threw out a brown shirt. Luther caught the shirt, and releasing his grip on the boy's neck, he draped the shirt around Ira's shoulders. "This will do for now, Penguin. We'll continue your education at the Hollow."

Luther pushed the boy into the backseat and slammed the door shut. Getting inside, he put in a cassette, turned up the volume, and drove to the pike. The sounds of *Another One Bites the Dust* filled the vehicle. Listening to the blast of bombastic music, Ira Hayes was quiet. The handcuffs were tight on his wrists. He closed his eyes, and in the bumping movement of the car, he thought about Lisa and her dad, Officer Hendricks.

Ira and Lisa sat together on her porch. Lisa was seventeen years old. She had black hair, long smooth legs, and breasts that felt firm as she pressed against his body. It was eleven thirty, and there were no lights in any of the neighbors' houses. Gliding back and forth on the porch swing, Lisa was laughing and holding him tightly.

"You know my dad don't allow you here after ten o'clock."

"I don't care about your dad," Ira said. "I care about you." He felt the warmth of her body. He kissed her and placed his hand on her breast. A patrol car screeched to a stop; the door slammed open. Dressed in a wrinkled blue uniform, Officer Hendricks ran across the sidewalk and up the steps.

"I told you to be off my property by dark!" he roared.

As Ira got to his feet, Hendricks punched him in the neck. The force of the blow knocked Ira into Lisa, and they both flipped over the back of the swing. Lisa hit her head on the wall and dropped to the floor. Bellowing loudly, Officer Hendricks threw another wild punch at Ira, which hit against the chain, jerking the swing high in the air. While Hendricks pulled his bleeding knuckles back, Ira smashed him in the face. The police officer rolled down the steps, hit the cement, and didn't move. After checking Lisa, Ira ran into the house and called 911. The ambulance arrived and took Lisa to Allegheny General Hospital; Ira was handcuffed and taken to jail.

The judge called it aggravated assault and committed Ira Hayes to the Green Hollow Correctional Camp. Early that morning, Lisa skipped school and waited for Ira at the train station. The officer in the blue suit left them alone for ten minutes. Then he walked over and grabbed Ira by the arm, and they boarded the train.

Luther braked as he approached the camp entrance. The large wooden sign, "Green Hollow Correctional Camp," was attached to the fence with barbed wire. An air-conditioned security building sat next to the gate. The guard hit a button, and the entrance gate swung open. After going over a speed bump, Luther drove past the football field, past two basketball courts, and stopped in front of a yellow cement building. Luther got outside and opened the door for Ira. When Ira stepped out, Luther took off the handcuffs and pushed him to the side of the building, where a hose was coiled on a circular support.

"You smell bad, like a penguin, Ira. Before we start the tour, we have to clean you up a little. Take off those clothes."

Ira removed his brown shirt, shoes, and socks; slid off his jeans; and placed everything neatly on the ground. Max walked over with an open box of heavy-duty cleanser.

"You may be tough in Pittsburgh," Luther said, pulling out the hose and turning the nozzle. "But at the Hollow, you're just a number." The hose bloated and began to spurt water. Luther pointed the blasting spray at Ira. When the pale skin was peppered with red welts, Max moved closer and dumped the white-and-green powder over Ira's head.

"It kills all bacteria, like E. colee and Strepto-coccus." Howling the word *Coccus*, Luther turned the nozzle on high; the burst of water slammed into Ira's crotch. Ira grimaced and fell to the ground. Luther sprayed the withering body for a few minutes. Ira's face lay in foaming bubbles of soap.

"Don't be drowning like that crazy Indian," Max cautioned, and he pulled Ira to his feet.

"You're gonna love this next part of your education," Luther said. He grabbed Ira by the wrist and pulled him around the side of the building to a caged pen. The pit bulls began growling as soon as they saw Luther. Removing the electric prod from the holder, Luther unlocked the gate, and they stepped inside.

Three dogs charged up and stopped directly in front of Ira. They sat there, teeth bared, dripping froth on Ira's feet. Luther touched the nearest one with the prod. It yelped and spun around, biting at its tail.

"Here at our camp, we keep things simple!" Luther shouted above the noise of the squealing dog. "You follow the program, or you feel pain. If I can teach these pit bulls how to behave, I can surely teach a dumb Penguin. I'll give you a demonstration."

Luther stuck the prod in Ira's side. Ira's abdominal muscles contracted; his legs weakened, and he fell to the ground. The dogs circled, their jaws snapping within inches of his body. The largest dog bit into Ira's calf; a curved line of holes appeared on his skin. Luther jolted the dog with the prod; it howled and fell back.

"You ain't hurt none," Luther said, tossing Ira his clothes. "Get dressed, and we'll finish the tour. The dormitory's your last stop." Luther held the dogs back as Ira slid on his jeans and shirt. "This training is 100 percent effective," Luther boasted. "It works with dogs; it works with prisoners, and it does wonders at home. Ann does exactly as ordered. The house is clean. Dinner is ready on time. My kids, Lilly and Jack, don't make a sound, except when I have to train them. And that's only a few times a week!"

They walked past the administration building. Two boys, shirtless, dripping perspiration, were painting the wall with a white gloss that glowed in the afternoon sun. A guard sat in the shade of a tree. One boy lowered his brush and picked up a bottle of water.

"Quit wasting time!" the guard shouted. The boy dropped the bottle on the ground. There was no wind; the blue-and-gold Pennsylvania State flag—"Virtue, Liberty and Independence" embroidered in bold letters—hung loosely against the metal pole.

Chapter Fourteen

After the last horse and buggy crossed the railroad tracks, Gene walked to his jeep. He was reaching for the door handle when he saw Sergeant Delaware Smith approach.

"You've got that sleepless expression on your face," Del observed, shaking Gene's hand. "What's wrong, Gene?"

"Nothing. I was up late."

"Did you hear about the boy getting killed at the Mennonite school?"

"Sure, I heard about it."

"The man who did the killing, Leroy Watkins, was a Vietnam veteran. Being over there for so long a time, I guess you've seen your share of dead bodies."

"You're right. I've seen my share."

"Even with all your war experience, I'll bet you've never seen anything like Leroy."

"What do you mean?"

"He was shot two times up close, but that ain't what killed him."

"What killed him, Del?"

"I know a knife wound when I see one, Gene. It had to be a big knife, like the kind you've got in your living room." A horn blew, and Del looked up at a passing car. A lady waved through the open window, and Sergeant Del waved back. "But that's not all. I know Leroy fired two shots. One bullet killed the boy. We dug the other bullet out of the wall by the door. Leroy saw someone there. Saw him as a threat." Del looked at the wet smear on Gene's shirt. "So he shot him. There was blood on the floor. We don't know who the man was. A teacher witnessed everything. But she won't say a word."

"The Mennonites are that way."

"I understand that," Del said. He brushed his hand over his chin, a puzzled look on his face. "Then I saw the strangest thing this morning."

"What was so strange?"

"I watched this same Mennonite teacher who never said a word to anyone get out of her buggy and talk to you. What was that about?"

"The *Daily News* reporter was taking pictures. I told him to stop. The teacher came over and thanked me."

"Well, I guess you did your good deed for the day."

"I guess I did."

"That Leroy guy. Did you know him?"

"Yes, I knew him. We were on the same base together."

"That's quite a coincidence … you knowing him in Vietnam, and then he comes into your backyard, commits a murder, and gets himself killed with a big knife."

"He deserved to die, Del."

"I guess you could say that."

"Then why all the questions, Del? Do you think Leroy was treated unfairly, that no one read him his constitutional rights? You have the right to remain silent. You have the right to an attorney. I'm asking you, Del? Do you think Leroy got cheated?"

"No, I don't think that. That bastard lost all his rights when he shot that boy in the head. The person who killed him did us all a service."

"That's quite a statement coming from a state police sergeant."

"It's not coming from no police sergeant, Gene. It's coming from Vincent Delaware Smith." Del turned and motioned to the patrol car. Then, shaking Gene's hand again, he focused his gaze on the dark stain on Gene's shirt. "Looks like you've got a wound there. You should get that checked." The patrol car stopped at the curb.

"Ready when you are, Sergeant," the driver said. Getting into the car, Del closed the door and clicked on his seat belt.

After the patrol car pulled away, Gene got into his jeep, turned on the radio, and drove down Penn Street. The radio weather reporter called for a week of warm Indian summer weather. Then the news reporter gave a dismal assessment of the situation in Iran:

President Carter's rescue attempt of the fifty-one American hostages held in Iran ended in disaster. During a haboon, which the locals call a fierce sandstorm, in the Great Salt Desert 50 miles outside of Teheran, eight Americans were killed when a helicopter crashed into a C-130 refueling aircraft. The exploding munitions from the massive fire caused the helicopter aircrews to believe they were under attack, and in their haste to evacuate, they left behind six helicopters in the Iranian desert. They also left behind the bodies of eight American servicemen. Ayatollah Khomeini called for nation-wide celebration for this victory over the Great Satan. Two of the abandoned US helicopters are now being used by the Iranian Navy.

"Haboon," Gene muttered. "Alpha Dumb ..."

It was one thirty when Gene reached Twin River High School. After checking the maintenance room, he walked to the main office. Mr. Port glanced up from the counter.

"You look all beat up. I hope the other guy is worse off than you."

"He is."

"Thanks for cleaning up Mrs. Walters's room."

"It's my job. Did she get a new Shakespeare?"

"Will was too expensive. She's got a cheap John Milton on her desk now. The kids don't know the difference." The phone rang, and the principal picked it up. Gene nodded to him and left the office. Climbing the steps to the second floor, he saw Matt standing in front of the display case. Matt's hands were straight at his side, and his hair was disheveled, drooping loosely over the bandage on his forehead. The cut on his lip was cracked and red.

"You hungry today?" Gene asked.

"A little."

"How about more of those M&M's?"

"Sure," Matt said. On the way to the exit, Gene stopped in the maintenance room and got a package. He gave the M&M's to Matt. They went outside and sat on the top step overlooking the river. Matt opened the package, and after separating the colors, he began eating the green ones.

Blood Mountain and the bottom half of the pine trees at the summit were covered by gray, voluminous shadows. Alighting on the branches of the tallest pine tree, vultures formed black clusters that thrashed about before dropping away in smooth, circular patterns of flight. Watching them closely, Matt spoke in a clear, respectful voice.

"Mr. Brooks, I saw you last night from my window."

"What exactly did you see, Matt?"

"I heard noise downstairs. I got up and saw you leave the house. You had something over your shoulder."

"Do you know what it was?"

"A black bag."

"Do you know what was in the bag?"

"In the dark I wasn't sure. I took my time and looked through the whole house. The only thing missing was Mr. Henry." Matt swallowed some chocolate and stared at Gene. "I'm glad you took him away. I hate Mr. Henry."

"Why?"

"Because …" Matt began, and then he lowered his head. He reached into the bag and began picking out the red M&M's.

"Because he hit you with the belt?"

"Yes, I hated him for that. And I hated him for what he said to me."

"What did Mr. Henry say?"

"He said I was evil. Fourteen years ago, Mom died in childbirth, but I lived. Mr. Henry said I was the one who killed her. He said I must be punished. He was swearing and spitting when he hit me."

"Why didn't you tell anyone?"

"I told Conner."

"I mean, when he first started to hit you."

Matthew's lips closed tightly. Bright sunlight swept across his face and magnified the swelling under his eye. Matt's gaze moved from the river to the mountain and then higher to the Flaming Cross on the summit.

"I did tell someone," Matt said. "I told the Reverend Jeremiah Towers. Mr. Henry took me to his new church on the mountain. He planned to move Mom from the cemetery and place her in the Catacombs of Rapture. When Mr. Henry left to look at the catacombs, the reverend asked me why I was sad. At first I didn't want to say anything, but the church was beautiful, and I saw Jesus on the cross. So I told him about the beatings. The Reverend Towers told me to 'Shut up.' He said Mr. Henry was a good man and that I was lying."

"The reverend was wrong. Mr. Henry was not a good man. He was a son of a bitch."

"I know." Matt crunched his shoulders. "That's what I called him, too." Lifting the bag, he poured M&M's into his mouth; chocolate smeared into the cut on his lip.

"What did he do, Matt?"

"I can't …" Matt began. His eyes reddened; tears streaked down his face. Wiping at his eyes with his forearm, he spoke in a whisper. "Mr. Henry would come for me at night. He would hit me and take off my pajamas and throw me in the bed. He said that since I killed Mom, I would have to take her place." Matt's chest heaved. Sobbing, he lowered his head. "Mr. Henry did things to me. Captain Hook stared from the wall."

Gene turned suddenly and looked at the vultures circling Blood Mountain. He closed his eyes and saw the darkness of the previous night: *Mr. Henry was strapped to the branch; wires cut deep grooves into his flesh. Muffled, pleading sounds emanated from the taped mouth. Swinging out of the darkness, the silver blade sliced across Mr. Henry's throat; all sound and movement stopped.* Gene opened his eyes and spoke in a soft voice.

"I'm sorry, Matt. I'm sorry I didn't come for Mr. Henry sooner."

"When Mr. Henry was done with me, I saw his eye. It was streaked with blood. I never understood how a fake eye could bleed. Then I realized it was my blood." Matt sat motionless; he wiped at the tears. "What did you do with Mr. Henry?"

"Wait here, Matt." Gene stood and walked to his jeep. Moments later he returned with the binoculars. After zooming in on Blood Mountain, he gave the binoculars to Matt.

"Focus on the pine tree on top of the mountain."

Matt looked through the binoculars. First, he saw the infinite blue sky. His back and shoulders tightening, Matt saw the top green branches of the pine tree and how the vultures lowered their beaks into a cream-colored figure. Black wings flogging the air, they pulled and devoured long stringy organs. Zooming in closer, his chest rising and contracting in quick breaths of air, he saw the skeletal head and the red glow off the artificial eye. Matt's shoulders relaxed; a calm expression spread over his face. Lowering the binoculars, Matt looked at Gene. "What's going to happen to me?"

"I'll talk to the principal. I'll arrange for you to stay at the house with Conner until things are straightened out."

"And what about SenSay? You put him to sleep, but he's running around now. Next to Conner, he's my best friend."

"SenSay can stay with us, too."

"That's great," Matt said, a big smile on his face. He gave the binoculars to Gene. "Can you take me to Blood Mountain?"

"Why?"

"I need to see Mr. Henry up close."

"Then let's do it now while there's still something left to see." Gene took Matt's hand, pulling him off the step, and they walked to the jeep. It was a short ride to the base of the mountain. Matt started for the trail, but Gene led him down a narrow path to a small utility shed. Gene took a key from under a rock, unlocked the door, and went inside. When he came out, he was pushing a bright red four-wheeler. Dark circles smeared the paint.

"Get on, Matt. You didn't think I carried Mr. Henry up the mountain, did you?"

"This is cool, Mr. Brooks. This is so cool," Matt said, getting on the backseat.

Gene maneuvered the four-wheeler down the path, drove a short distance on the gravel road, and then turned onto the mountain trail. He went fast, spinning around boulders and trees. Feeling the wind in his face, Matt held on with both hands. When they reached the summit, Matt jumped off at the towering pine tree. Large coned ant mounds spilled over the gnarled roots.

"Wait here." Gene walked to the pine tree, jumped for the low-hanging branch, and began climbing. Pine needles spiraled down, landing on the ant mound. An army of red-and-black ants streamed out of the opening at the top. Making a steady clicking noise, the ants crossed to the tree and formed lines that moved up the bark.

"Matt," Gene called from above. "Catch." A rope fell through the branches. Matt grabbed it and saw the harness. "Strap yourself in."

"Okay," Matt said after securing the harness around his shoulders. "I'm ready."

"Are you sure?"

"No."

"Let me know if you fall off," Gene cautioned, and he jerked on the rope. The air left Matt's lungs. Spinning upward, Matt frantically pushed the branches out of the way. Halfway up the tree, he cracked his shoulder against the rough bark.

"Did you hit your head?" Gene asked.

"No, just my shoulder. It doesn't hurt much."

"Don't worry. You're almost here." Gene pulled Matt through the remaining branches and hoisted him onto a wide platform that was hammered solidly in the tree. Gene removed the harness, and Matt sat down.

"Wow!" he whispered, his eyes opening wide.

The sky was blue to the horizon, and below it, the river flowed a glistening, winding course through woods and farmland. Matt saw Twin River High School. Across from the school, the Flaming Cross was bright in the afternoon sky. There was noise overhead, and a thick liquid substance spattered against the branches on the other side of the tree.

"What's that, Mr. Brooks?"

"The vultures. They gorge themselves and then excrete huge volumes of stuff. That's why I built the platform on this side."

"Is Mr. Henry very far up?"

"He's at the top. Start with that branch over your head. Then just follow your nose."

Matt didn't say anything. He grabbed onto the branch with both hands and began to climb. A cool wind blew over his body. Then he began to smell the stench. Looking up, he saw the vultures bunched together, flapping wings, burying their beaks in the mutilated remains. Reflecting bright sunlight, the silver wire securing Mr. Henry to the branch was buried deep to the bone.

"You son of a bitch!" Matt shrieked. "You son of a bitch!"

The sudden noise sent the vultures thrashing wildly in flight. Leery of their erratic movements, Matt pulled his sweatshirt over his nose, crawled to the body, and reached a trembling hand toward the skeletal head.

Gene sat on the platform and watched the startled vultures. Soon he heard noise on the branches, and Matt dropped down. Pine needles stuck in his sweatshirt; his face was pale. When he collapsed on the platform, Gene noticed the closed hand.

"Matt, what's that in your fist? You brought something with you, didn't you?"

"I …" Matt hesitated a moment. "I took Mr. Henry's glass eye."

"Matt, you can't do that!" Gene snapped. "You can't desecrate the dead."

"I didn't desecrate anyone," Matt said, his lips quivering. His shoulders heaved, and he lowered his head.

"I'm sorry I shouted," Gene said, a note of exasperation in his voice. "I saw this happen in Vietnam. Some soldiers kept souvenirs."

"I didn't take the eye for a souvenir. I took it because of what Mr. Henry said. When he did things to me, he would lean close to my face so I could see his eye. He shouted that he would always be watching me. I want to go in the Shadows of Death. I want to throw his eye in the rapids."

"You can't do that," Gene said, shaking his head. "The rapids are too dangerous."

"I don't care," Matt said. He stood and looked at the river. The shadows were wispy puffs of white cloud. Matt slid his feet closer to the edge of the platform.

"That's far enough."

"I'm not afraid of the Shadows of Death," Matt said, but his body trembled.

"I know that." Gene placed his hand on Matt's shoulder and moved him back from the edge. "Let me think about this for a while."

Matt was quiet. A dark shadow moved across his face. The vulture circled close before soaring upward with a loud hissing sound. Listening to the sound, Matt smiled.

"Those who receive the mark of the beast," he whispered. Matt noticed the confused expression on Gene's face. "In the time of the Apocalypse, four horsemen galloped down from the heavens. The rider on the red horse had a gigantic sword, and he slew the wicked."

"What are you saying, Matt?"

"The wicked 'were killed by the sword and all the birds were filled with their flesh.' It's from the book of Revelation. I think you are the rider on the red horse, Mr. Brooks. You killed Mr. Henry with your sword, and the birds are devouring his flesh." Matt stared at Gene, who gave him a hard stare back.

"I have an orange jeep, not a red horse."

'You have a red 4-wheeler. You use it to transport the wicked." Matt spoke with conviction. "Can I ask you something, Mr. Brooks? When Conner and I camped on Blood Mountain, skeletons fell from this tree. One skeleton was missing a head. The other was missing both legs. Who were they?"

"Why do you need to know their names?"

"I want to know the company Mr. Henry will have for eternity."

"For eternity?"

"I mean in hell, Mr. Brooks."

"Oh, of course … hell," Gene said. "The two skeletons belonged to the Calvin boys."

"Were they bad like Mr. Henry?"

"Why all the questions, Matt?"

"I want to understand you, Mr. Brooks. You pretend to be a janitor, but you're more than a janitor. You take away bad people. I know what Mr. Henry did. What did the Calvins do that was so bad?" Matt stared at Gene, who shrugged his shoulders and motioned to the platform.

"Sit down, Matt. You don't want to be on your feet when you hear this."

The setting sun cast a glow across Matt's face. The bandage on his forehead was spotted with dirt; green pine needles slanted out of the cloth. Vultures shook the branches overhead; a few winged bodies circled lazily in front of the platform.

Chapter Fifteen

"I think I'm ready, Mr. Brooks." Matt crossed his legs one way, changed his mind, and then threw them straight out in front of him.

"I hope you're ready," Gene remarked. "This all began on one of the best days of the year, Matt. What day is that?"

"Christmas?"

"No."

"Thanksgiving."

"Hell, no, Matt. Get a life. The best day of the year is the first day of buck season."

"Oh, I knew that."

"Two friends, Sam and Robert, moved to Pittsburgh, but they always returned for deer season. I talked to Mr. Wilson, and he said they could hunt in Polecat Hollow. Mr. Wilson warned them not to go past the first hill. All that land past the hill was Calvin property."

"Mr. Brooks, I read in the newspaper that your friends died."

"Yes, they died. I left school at noon and went to the Hollow to check on them. Their truck wasn't there. Mr. Wilson said there were shots early that morning. Hours later he heard the truck start up, but it never went past his house."

"The Calvins stole it, didn't they, Mr. Brooks?"

"Please don't interrupt," Gene advised. "I went to where Sam and Robert had set up. I saw they had shot something and followed the blood trail. It led over the second hill."

"They went on Calvin land?"

"Matt, will you quit with the questions?"

"I'm sorry. It's just that …" Matt began; Gene glared at him until he was quiet.

"I found the pools of blood and entrails. I don't know who gutted the deer. But it was easy to see that the Calvin boys had been there. They never wore shoes. When they left, Sam and Robert carried the deer. One Calvin boy was in front, and one was behind.

"I thought about going back to the jeep for my gun. But then I heard screaming in the distance and immediately took off running. As I got closer to the farm, I heard loud grunting. I knew right away what the noise was. The Calvins had these four hogs; they fed them garbage and any animals they trapped."

Matt sat perfectly still. He squinted nervously; furrows formed on his forehead. Lifting his hand, he began to rub his neck. Wind rustled through the pine branches. The light of the setting sun formed a misty rainbow in the Shadows of Death. Listening intently, Matt stared into the bands of color, which glowed brighter as the sun descended.

"The screaming and grunting were deafening when I broke clear of the woods. Right away I saw Sam's and Robert's clothes stacked in a neat pile. I saw their guns next to the clothes. I saw the Calvin boys standing in front of the wooden pen.

"At first I wasn't sure what was happening. Then a naked man jumped out of the mud and pulled himself to the top of the pen. I saw the bloodied face; it was Sam. His one hand gripped the log, but the other hand had been chewed off at the shoulder and was gushing blood. The blood sprayed in the air. The Calvin boys were dancing around with their mouths open. The blood hit their lips. They drank it."

With a fading glow of brilliance, the sun dropped behind the mountain. Breathing deeply, his face wet with perspiration, Matt watched the blue-and-red bands of the rainbow expand, lose color, and fuse with the shadows.

"The bigger Calvin stepped on the bottom log of the pen. He pulled Sam's hand away and pushed him back inside. The hogs attacked the body, and their squealing and Sam's screams increased. I began screaming, too, but the Calvins never heard me. I grabbed the closer Calvin and smashed his head into the side of the pen.

"The bigger Calvin turned and tackled me. We rolled around in the mud. I got a strong grip on his throat. His body was squirming all over the place, but he wasn't going anywhere. When he stopped moving, I pulled him over to his brother.

"There were just grunting sounds now. A hog brushed against the side of the pen, and the logs bent outward. One log was warped. I noticed this gap under it." Gene hesitated, staring across the platform. Matt's sweatshirt was damp. His face was pale. With a trembling hand, Matt wiped at the perspiration on his face.

"Are you cold?" Gene asked.

"I don't know what's wrong. I can't stop shaking."

"Maybe we should go home."

"No, Mr. Brooks. I want to hear all of it."

"There's not much left. I dragged the bigger Calvin over and shoved his feet through that gap in the logs. When the hogs started crunching and chewing on Big Calvin, he came back to life real fast. His screaming woke his brother. Little Calvin tried to get away, but I grabbed him in a headlock and held him tight so he could watch.

"Big Calvin fought like hell, but starving hogs don't let go that easy. And there were four of them chomping on his legs. Big Calvin sat straight up and began clawing the logs with his fingers and then biting into the logs. His front teeth broke off and stuck in the wood. When his legs were chewed to the knees, his torso dropped. It was strange how his hands spread out in the mud, like he was on a cross."

There was a squawk from above and a loud ruffling of wings. A strip of flesh fell through the pine needles and landed on the edge of the platform. Matt jumped as a vulture swooped down and deftly picked up the skin. Wings flogging waves of stench through the night air, the vulture flew into the shadows. Matt pinched his nose with his fingers.

"That was a terrible story," Matt said, releasing his nostrils.

"I warned you. You're just like Conner. You have to know everything."

"I know how Big Calvin lost his legs. I know Little Calvin was missing his head. I'll bet you stuck it in that same gap."

"You're right, Matt. Little Calvin was crying and praying to Jesus when I shoved his head into the pen. He put up a fierce struggle, but it didn't last long. The hogs crushed his skull like it was a melon. I bagged their remains and carried them to Blood Mountain. It was a freak accident that the storm dropped the skeletons into your tent." Moonlight flooded the platform; Gene's face was in shadow. "Any more questions?"

"Did you kill the hogs, too?"

"No, I didn't. Unlike the Calvins, who should have known right from wrong, the hogs were just doing what hogs do. I opened the pen. The hogs were slow coming out. The last one, the biggest one, stopped right in front of me. I'll never forget that. The hog rubbed its bloody snout against my leg. I was expecting something bad to happen. But that hog just snorted and waddled away." Gene got to his feet, but Matt didn't move. He sat there motionless on the platform. After a moment, he stood.

"Mr. Brooks, I'm sorry. But I have another question. What you did to the Calvins—was it worse in Vietnam?"

"Damn it. Where do you get these questions?" Gene was quiet for a moment, studying Matt's upturned face. "I'll make this very clear, Matt. What happened to the Calvins might happen once in a hundred years. In Vietnam, that kind of killing happened on a regular basis."

"Did you tell Conner about Vietnam?"

"No, I didn't tell him."

"You should tell him, Mr. Brooks. He's your son. He deserves to know."

"Sometimes it's better not knowing," Gene said. Stars lit up the night sky. "It's late. Let's get off this tree." He reached down and picked up the harness.

"I don't need it, Mr. Brooks. I can climb down myself."

———

On the ride home, Matt sat stiffly in the seat. The truck thumped over a pothole, lifting him in the air. Holding the glass eye firmly in his fist, he looked at Gene.

"Mr. Brooks, can you teach me how to remove the wicked like you did with Mr. Henry and the Calvins?"

"No, that's something you should never think about. You were shaking back there."

"Maybe I was shaking, but I wasn't scared. I was more excited than scared."

"If you need excitement in your life, I can teach you how to be a good hunter."

"Great. That would be the best way to start." The headlights flashed on a possum in the middle of the road. Gene slowed and swerved around the animal. Pointing a finger through the window, Matt made a spitting sound through his lips.

"Bang. You're dead," Matt said with satisfaction. "Mr. Brooks, I'm almost finished with my project for woodshop. It's a model Colt .45, the Peacemaker. Buffalo Bill had one. And Billy the Kid had one, too. Mr. Gates said it was perfect in every detail. I want to know everything about guns. Will you teach me how to shoot like you did Conner?"

"Conner's pretty good."

"He told me that when he started, you said, 'If you want to shoot a gun, soldier, you'd better be damn good at it.' He said he had to practice for months before you would take him hunting. He killed a trophy buck with his first shot. I saw the antlers on the wall."

"Conner surprised me. He learned real fast."

"I'll be better," Matt said. "You'll see, Mr. Brooks. I'll be better."

Chapter Sixteen

Early Thursday morning, Sheriff Parks waited patiently in the QuikStop parking lot. The sheriff's car had a prominent badge-shaped "NRA Law Enforcement" insignia on the side window. Staring through the tinted glass, Parks and Deputy Oliver Wright watched Pete Rogers remove boxes from the FritoLay van.

"Shouldn't we have cuffed him as soon as we got here?" Oliver asked.

"No," Sheriff Parks answered, following Pete's progress to the QuikStop entrance. "It'll be easier to search the truck with those boxes out of the way."

"What if Pete found the pink panties?"

"Then we'd have his fingerprints." The door to the QuikStop opened, and holding a cup of coffee, Pete approached the van. Sheriff Parks slammed the car door open and stepped out. Deputy Oliver hurried out the other side.

"Good morning, Sheriff," Pete said.

"Not so good for you," Parks stated in a gruff voice, and he waved a brown courthouse envelope in Pete's face. "We have a warrant to search your van."

"What are you talking about?"

"Just step away," Deputy Oliver advised. Carrying a Polaroid camera in one hand, he pushed Pete to the side and climbed inside the van. He kicked a box and then another one. There was a scraping noise; Deputy Oliver laughed. "Hello!" he proclaimed. Stepping to the door with a big smile on his face, he twirled pink panties on his finger. The sheriff glared at him.

"You dumb-ass. I told you to take pictures, not tamper with the evidence. Now put them panties back where you found them. Where's the sock?"

"I've got it here." Oliver reached into his back pocket and pulled out a white sock. A line of red roses was stitched around the top.

"Put the sock back, too," Parks ordered. "And take a lot of pictures so the judge knows where you found the evidence."

"No need for concern, Sheriff. I remember exactly where I found them." Oliver backed inside the van. After a few moments, a series of bright flashes lit up the van's interior. Sheriff Parks took out his handcuffs and approached Pete.

"You're under arrest for kidnapping those two girls," the sheriff said. He knocked the coffee cup out of Pete's hands and cuffed him.

"I didn't kidnap—"

"Save all your bullshit for the judge," Sheriff Parks interrupted. "I need to read you your rights. You have the right to an attorney." The sheriff paused. "No, that's not first." Sheriff Parks was thinking hard when Oliver called down from the van.

"Got me four good pictures," he said. Sheriff Parks ignored the deputy, his eyes focused on Pete.

"The hell with your rights!" he proclaimed, and he pushed Pete toward the patrol car. "Where's the key to the van?"

"In the ignition."

"Hear that, Oliver? Get in the van and follow me to the jail."

"Sure thing, Sheriff." Oliver jumped to the pavement, shoved his way through the crowd, and got into the van. After locking Pete in the patrol car, Sheriff Parks turned on the flashing lights and pulled onto Route 22. Blowing the horn, Oliver parted the bystanders and pulled up behind the patrol car, and the two-vehicle procession raced toward Huntingdon.

During the second period, Wayne raised his hand and asked to be excused. The teacher nodded his head. Wayne took the hall pass and walked to the restroom. When he pushed open the door and stepped inside, he saw Cain and Abel standing there.

"Hey, Wayne," Abel said, grabbing his shoulder. Cain grabbed the other shoulder, and they threw Wayne against the wall.

"We got us a problem, Wayne," Cain said. "I hear you've been telling my girlfriend Becky that we're lowlife. Is that true?"

"I told her to stay away from you."

"That's not neighborly," Cain said. He punched Wayne in the stomach, knocking him to his knees. The door opened; a startled boy looked in and quickly disappeared.

"We want you to stop that kind of talk." Abel pulled Wayne to his feet; Cain gripped his neck. They pinned him against the wall again. "Do you understand?"

"Yes." Wayne coughed and struggled to move.

"I'm glad you understand." Cain relaxed his grip. "Now, what brought you in here?"

"I have to go to the bathroom. I have to go real bad."

"That's fine, but it costs money to take a piss in here. It costs five dollars. And that's a real bargain when you've got to go bad."

"I don't have five dollars."

"That's not good, not good at all, Wayne. We're just starting a business, and we need our customers to cooperate. That way the word gets out, and everyone comes here with the correct change. Ain't that right, Abel?"

"That's the only way to run a profitable business." Abel crushed Wayne in a headlock and kicked his legs apart. "We'd better teach Wayne a lesson."

Cain pulled a lighter out of his pocket. Flicking the top open, he leaned forward and lowered it between Wayne's legs. After the second click with his thumb, the wick burst into fire. The flames brightened and scorched the crotch area. Wayne's face reddened;

he began to scream. Cain shoved paper towels into his mouth; tears rolled down Wayne's face. Dark stains appeared along the crotch, and yellow liquid began to drip to the floor.

"Well, lookee here." Abel laughed. "Wayne didn't need to use the urinal at all. I guess this piss is for free."

"We'll have to charge him double next time," Cain said, closing the lighter.

"You hear that, Wayne? It's ten dollars next time," Abel stated. They released his shoulders, and Wayne dropped in the pool of urine. The bell rang. Cain and Abel washed their hands and left the restroom.

Tears in his eyes, Wayne struggled to his feet. He opened the door to the toilet stall, lowered his jeans, and sat down. Wayne's legs quivered uncontrollably as the remaining urine gushed into the bowl. A mob of students entered the restroom. The sounds of laughing voices, toilets flushing, and running water echoed inside the stall. When the bell rang again, the room emptied quickly. Wayne pulled up his jeans, went to his locker for his jacket, and walked to the front entrance. After grabbing his bicycle from the rack, he pedaled across the parking lot, weaving his way clumsily around the cars, and turned onto Route 305.

Halfway down Polecat Hollow Road, Wayne pulled the bicycle off the road. Loosening his jeans and leaning against a tree, he took a box of matches and a pack of cigarettes from his pocket. He lit a cigarette, and through clenched teeth, he inhaled deeply, the smoke clouding his vision. After two cigarettes, he pushed the bicycle back to the road.

When Wayne reached the house, he went to the small workroom in the back of the barn. Entering the room, Wayne clicked on the overhead light and walked to the wall cabinet in the corner. Lifting the loose floorboard, he grabbed the key and unlocked the cabinet. His dad's military Smith & Wesson Victory Model was on the top shelf. Picking up the gun, feeling its weight, Wayne checked the cylinder, which held six bullets.

"I'll only need two," Wayne said, and he placed the Victory Model back on the shelf.

"Mr. Gates," Gene said, stepping into the empty wood shop classroom, "Matt Henry was excited about his project. Would you have time to show it to me?"

"Sure." Mr. Gates walked to the display case along the wall, took out the model Colt .45, and handed it to Gene.

"It feels good." Gene lifted the gun and pointed at the deer mount across the room. "The balance and weight are perfect." Clicking open the cylinder, he saw the lead slugs and brass casings.

"Don't worry, Mr. Brooks. They're exact replicas but without the powder. Matt worked endless hours until they fit perfectly. Did you count them?"

"There are five rounds," Gene observed, nodding his head in approval. "Matt left an empty chamber. He knew there was no safety on this model, so he left the chamber under the hammer empty."

"Exactly right, Mr. Brooks. Matt pays attention to every detail. In fact, he's very precise in everything he does. When he sets his mind on something, he goes all the way. I don't know where he got the idea for the gun. John Wayne used the Colt in all his westerns. And Billy the Kid started killing with it when he was a boy."

"Matt might be a mixture of both," Gene said, handing Mr. Gates the Colt. "I hope he's more like the Duke than the Kid."

"Me, too," Mr. Gates agreed.

Gene left the room, stopping to pick up a wad of paper off the floor. As he dropped it into the trash can, the bell rang and students burst through the doors. Gene watched Cain and Abel stride down the hall. The crowd of students moved quickly out of their way.

"Get in," Andrew Brooks said, blowing the horn and stopping the truck next to Conner. "I'm going to Huntingdon. I'll buy you a burger."

"Great," Conner said. "I'm starved!" Dropping the bicycle in the back, Conner got in the front seat. There was a bundle of freshly cut violets mixed with red roses, and he pushed it to the middle.

"You're late today," Andrew said, driving past the school.

"I was shooting baskets."

"It's football season, Conner. Why are you practicing basketball?"

"I scored eleven points all of last year. Coach Eckin says he'll cut me from the team if I don't double that total."

"Eckin's a jerk."

"It don't matter. He blows the whistle and decides who's playing."

"He's still a jerk," Andrew said, turning onto Route 22.

When Andrew reached Huntingdon, he drove by the fast-food places and veered onto Snyders Run Road. Stopping at an intersection at the bottom of a steep hill, Andrew parked the truck in a cleared gravel area next to a small stream. He picked up the flowers, got out, and walked to an oak tree. A wooden cross was nailed to the tree. Below the cross was a tin cup with flower stems sticking over the edge. Andrew removed the dried flowers and placed the bright violets and roses in the cup.

"I visit here often, Conner. I'll never forget that day."

"I was young, Uncle Andrew. We were on our way to Corbin's Island for a picnic."

"Joyce and I were right behind your dad. The light on 22 turned yellow, and your dad drove through it. I could have made the light, too, but Joyce grabbed my hand. She was eight months pregnant. So I stopped and waited." Andrew was quiet, staring at the red stop sign at the bottom of the hill.

"Dad never said much about the accident."

"We just got to this intersection. This tourist was driving down that hill in his new Winnebago. His pontoon boat broke loose on that horseshoe turn up there. He slammed on the brakes, but the pontoon boat kept moving. There was no reason for it to stay straight on the road, but it did. The boat picked up speed, went through the stop sign, and crushed the passenger door. Our car landed on its roof in the stream. Joyce was trapped. She couldn't move. I put my arm around her. She was very quiet. I think she knew."

Conner looked at the stream. Sleek minnow bodies flashed silver in the light. Wrens dropped from tree branches and splashed wings in the water.

"We set up the picnic table and were waiting," Conner said. "Then Dad went looking for you. He thought you had a flat tire or something."

"I saw Gene running down the bank. He and the tourist finally got the door open and pulled me out. The ambulance and fire truck arrived. The firemen worked quickly. They removed the passenger door and put Joyce on a stretcher. The emergency people wanted to examine me, but I was fine. Later the doctor called me to his office. He told me that we had lost the baby. He also told me Joyce wouldn't be able to have children."

"I remember going to the waiting room with Mom. She was real distressed. She didn't understand how hurting Joyce and the baby could be part of God's plan. She was praying and crying at the same time."

"I didn't say any prayers. I didn't look for God that day."

"But you're a pastor."

"Yes, Conner, I'm a pastor. But I love God too much to think he was responsible for the accident. I don't think God plans how each human being dies. We do that. We do it ourselves, sometimes in the most horrible way."

The sky was a light blue; wrens chirped from the stream. Andrew and Conner got into the truck. At the intersection on Route 22, the signal light was yellow. Andrew accelerated through it and turned into the Golden Arches.

"I'm not that hungry," Conner said.

"Just a cold drink then." Andrew ordered at the drive-in window. Paying the cashier, he gave a strawberry milk shake to Conner and turned onto Route 22. He was quiet for a moment; then he spoke with a degree of satisfaction.

"Joyce and I got some good news today. I went to the bank to pay the mortgage on the church, and the cashier said we didn't owe anything. I don't know what happened with the account. Did you talk to your dad about the mortgage?"

"I mentioned it, but he didn't seem very interested in helping."

"No matter. It's not a problem anymore. Things are definitely getting better."

Chapter Seventeen

Lisa Hendricks walked to the dresser and picked up the picture of Ira Hayes. She looked at his smile, and her hand began to tremble; tears formed in her eyes. Wiping her face with a tissue, Lisa replaced the picture and sat on the bed. When her mom arrived home, Lisa stood nervously behind the door.

Ten minutes later, Lisa glanced into the darkened room and saw her mom sprawled on the bed. Closing the door, Lisa went downstairs, took the car keys from the table, and ran out the door to the black Ford parked in the driveway. When Lisa saw the school bus turn the corner, she jumped inside the car. Ducking behind the steering wheel, Lisa watched the bus slow down. The driver momentarily looked toward the porch. Then there was a grating noise from the engine, and the bus pulled away.

Holding her breath, Lisa started the car, backed out of the driveway, and cruised down the middle of the street. When Lisa reached the 376 Expressway, she drove at a steady, slow speed. Turning on the radio, she heard the weatherman call for showers; Lisa saw nothing but blue sky through the window. She laughed and drove faster. Approaching the Turtle Hill Tunnel, she glanced at the exit sign for Kennywood Park, and her heart began to beat rapidly.

"Ira," she whispered.

As she headed into the dark tunnel, a FedEx truck thundered

past. Vibrations shook the Ford. Lisa turned on the headlights, and staring at the double white line, she watched the curved walls of the tunnel close around the Ford. Leaning against the steering wheel and listening to the static hum of the radio, she remembered her last trip to Kennywood.

Watching each other behind the heavy glass divider, Ira and Lisa sat at opposite ends of the backseat. There were no handles on the doors of the patrol car. The air in the confined space reeked of detergent. Lisa knocked on the glass.

"Dad, why's it smell so bad back here?"

"A hooker …" he began. "I mean, a lady got angry and urinated on the floor."

"Nice," Ira said. "Real nice."

Officer Hendricks spun the patrol car off the Kennywood exit and made a series of quick turns. Switching on his flashing lights, he sped by a line of backed-up vehicles and screeched to a stop at the entrance to the park. There was a sharp clicking sound. The doors opened, and Lisa and Ira stepped outside. With the engine idling, her dad shouted through the open window.

"I'll pick you up at nine o'clock."

"But, Dad, that's so early."

"It's past dark. That's when all the trouble starts. So when I say nine o'clock, I mean nine o'clock. You hear me? I don't want to come looking for you. Because if I do, this will be your last date."

"We won't be late, Dad. Thanks for the ride."

"Don't forget the time!"

"We won't, sir," Ira said in a reassuring tone.

Lisa's dad watched them for a moment. Then he bumped the patrol car off the curb and drove down the street. Ira took Lisa's hand, and they walked through the crowd. There were six ticket lines. Stopping at the end of the shortest one, Ira pulled Lisa closer.

"I think your dad arrested one of my girls last night."

"The hooker?"

"Yeah, I have ten on call, and they're all drop-dead beautiful. But I prefer you."

"You're sure of that?"

"I can't think of anyone I want more than you. You're all I think about." Ira paused, shrugging his shoulders. "What is it with your dad? He's always angry with me."

"He thinks you're a criminal. He thinks you're trying to kidnap his daughter."

"Your dad drinks too much. And I think he needs a seeing-eye dog."

"He does drink too much, but he's not blind."

"Yes, he is, Lisa. He didn't notice that I kidnapped his daughter two years ago."

"I think he did."

"Then why wasn't he angry back then? Wait a minute," Ira said. Standing there in the middle of the ticket line, he looked at her face, the sharp profile of her body, the tight slacks. "I know why he's angry now. You weren't so sexy two years ago. Your dad's worried that I want your body."

"You do, don't you?"

"No," Ira said. Taking off his Pittsburgh Penguins cap, his hair falling over his forehead, he pulled her closer. "I want all of you."

"Not here," she whispered, smiling.

"You're beautiful when you smile," Ira said. "I can't resist you." His hand around her waist, Ira maneuvered Lisa out of the line. The crowd rushed by.

"But the tickets!"

"They don't sell the ticket I want."

"What ticket is that?"

"The one that says I can kiss the life out of you."

"Nine o'clock doesn't give us much time," Lisa said provocatively. Brushing against his body, she whispered softly, "You didn't kidnap me two years ago, Ira. I came willingly."

The loud sound of a car horn cracked against the window. Startled, Lisa blinked at the narrow confines of the tunnel. She saw the bright sunlight ahead and drove out of the tunnel at twenty miles an hour. Lisa gradually accelerated to thirty-five and then forty-five miles an hour.

Four and a half hours later, Lisa pulled into the Route 22 QuikStop and filled up the gas tank. As she handed the twenty-dollar bill to the cashier, she asked for directions to the Green Hollow Correctional Camp. The young lady handed Lisa the change and smiled.

"You don't want to go there, honey. That place is worse than the state institution in Huntingdon. At least at HCI, the prisoners got some rights. Out there at the Hollow, the kids got no rights. They're treated like dirt."

"It can't be that bad," Lisa said, a worried expression on her face.

"My cousin from Harrisburg just got out. He was all bruised up. No one listened to our complaints. The sheriff don't care. He didn't even return our calls. And the camp's hard to find. It's way back in the woods." The cashier studied Lisa—the imploring eyes, the troubled expression on her face. "You sure you want to go out there?"

"I'm sure," Lisa said.

"Okay, then," the cashier said. Grabbing a pen and paper, she drew a map on a napkin and gave it to Lisa. "The camp's at the end of Green Hollow Pike. Right here." She pointed her finger to a red circle on the paper. "Good luck."

"Thanks," Lisa said. "Thanks a lot."

Walking to the car, Lisa studied the map. She pulled out on Route 22, crossed the bridge, and went through the small town of Alexandria. Going into Petersburg, she slowed down at the William Port War Memorial. After leaving Petersburg and driving another twenty minutes, she came to the intersection highlighted on the map. Putting the napkin aside, she turned onto Green Hollow Pike. The pike was gravel and covered with potholes. Some of the potholes were deep and bounced the Ford in the air; Lisa gripped the steering wheel with both hands. When Lisa noticed a hunting cabin with an empty driveway, she stopped the Ford and hurried to the outhouse in the back.

Later that afternoon Lisa bumped the car onto a straight stretch of asphalt and saw the iron fence. Sunlight reflected off the long, twisting coils of barbed wire at the top. The sign, "Green Hollow Correctional Camp," was attached in the middle of the fence. A black motorcycle was parked next to the sign. Stopping at the guard station, Lisa got out of the car and walked to the window; the guard stared at Lisa.

"What do you want?"

"I came to visit a prisoner, Ira Hayes."

"Visiting hours are on Monday," the guard said, pointing to the notice on the window. "You'll have to call and schedule an appointment."

"I've driven all day. I can't go back to Pittsburgh without seeing Ira."

"Miss, I'm sorry, but you need to schedule your visit on Monday." Shaking his head, the security guard sat back in the chair.

The youngest guard ever hired at Green Hollow, Dan Boonie was twenty years old. A week ago, after all the interviews were finished for the position, Dan was at the bottom of the list. The camp director, Stan Williams, and three other interviewers gave Dan low marks for his youthful disposition, soft voice, pleasant personality, and eagerness to help others. One official wrote he was "too friendly to deal with prisoners."

The decision to dismiss Dan was all but made when the director asked the applicants if they knew how to handle a gun. A cousin to Luther Cicconi, Earl James, an older man with a dark stubble of beard, complained in a loud voice.

"Why should we know that? The guards don't carry guns."

"The guns are right here." The director walked to the wall cabinet, unlocked the door, and pulled out a Winchester. "Let's go to the practice range out back."

Director Williams led the applicants outside. After he pulled a guard and two of the older prisoners off the football field, he led them through the woods to the shooting range. The oval bull's-eye target at the end was ripped and dropped low to the ground. The director scraped a line in the dirt with his shoe.

"You all get three shots," he instructed. "Don't cross this line."

The first applicants peppered the outer perimeters of the bull's-eye. When Earl James grabbed the Winchester, he gave everyone a confident thumbs-up. Leaning forward, Earl slid both shoes inches over the line, aimed casually, and fired, missing the target on all three attempts.

"This is bullshit," he blurted.

Dan had a smile on his face. He was a boy when his dad bought him a Winchester. Dan never stopped practicing, and through the years, he always brought turkey and deer down from the mountain. Dan walked over to Earl James and reached for the Winchester. Earl gripped it tightly and laughed before shoving it in Dan's chest. Dan didn't react. Stepping to the line, he shot without hesitation and blew out the center of the target. Noticing how the two prisoners jumped to attention, Stan Williams hired Dan on the spot.

"I don't think I can help you, Miss," Dan said, leaning forward in the chair. He heard the noise on the road and saw the Green Hollow Camp car stop at the guardhouse. Opening the door, Luther Cicconi stepped out and walked to the window.

"What's going on, Boonie?"

"She drove out here to see a prisoner."

"Which prisoner?"

"Ira Hayes," Lisa answered. "Do you know him?"

"Sure, I know him. We checked him in yesterday. He was a real stubborn kid." Luther turned and called to the car. "Hey, Max, what about that new kid, Ira Hayes?"

"Nothing but trouble," Max said, getting out of the car. He stared at Lisa's body, his eyes lingering on her breasts. "What's your name?"

"Lisa."

"What's your interest in Ira?"

"We're friends. Good friends."

"And you came from where?"

"Pittsburgh."

"I remember now," Luther said. "Ira was wearing this stupid Penguins shirt. Pittsburgh's a long drive. I guess we could take you inside for a few minutes. No one has to know. Would you like that, Lisa?"

"Oh, yes. Please."

"It's probably going against the rules, but just this one time won't hurt nothing," Luther said, glancing at Dan. "Boonie's new here. He stole this job from a good man. You can follow directions and keep your mouth shut, can't you, Boonie?"

"Yes, sir."

"Then why don't you do your job and get the gate for us?"

Dan didn't say anything. He hit the switch, and the gate swung open. Luther went to his car and motioned the girl inside. Max got into Lisa's car and started the engine. He followed Luther over the speed bump and through the gate. The two cars went around the corner of the football field, past the glistening-white administration building, and turned behind the two-story educational skills building.

The parking area behind the educational skills building was empty. Luther shut off the engine, stepped out of the car, and looked around. There were loud shouts from the basketball court. The sound of a guitar came from the dormitory across the field. Lisa opened her door and got out.

"Where's Ira?"

"This way," Luther said, pointing to a dirt road. "He's working at the storage building. We'll take you there."

When Lisa hesitated, Max pushed her roughly in the shoulder, and she stumbled forward. As they approached a wooden bridge, the sounds of croaking frogs filled the air. The stream of water under the bridge was crystal clear. Lisa looked at the field of tall grass and wildflowers beyond the bridge.

"I don't see anything."

"Just a few more minutes," Max said. They started across the field. Luther pointed to the shadows in the far corner; two deer lifted their heads. Their ears twitching, they jumped and disappeared in the woods.

"I'll bet you don't see any wild animals in Pittsburgh, Lisa."

"Maybe in the zoo," Max said, laughing.

Lisa was quiet. After they crossed the field, Lisa saw a large log building. A truck and backhoe were parked at the side. Narrow windows were set high in the wall. A path of flat yellow rocks led to the front door.

"Follow the yellow brick road." Luther laughed. They walked down the rock path. When they reached the steps, Luther pulled a ring of keys from his pocket.

"Why's he locked inside?" Lisa asked.

"Because he's a prisoner," Luther answered in a sarcastic tone. Climbing the steps, he turned the key in the lock and pushed the door open. Lisa didn't move. Max grabbed her by the arm and shoved her inside. The room was empty.

"Ira's not here," Lisa said, her voice cracking.

"Don't worry," Luther said. "We're going to bring him here. You have to understand, Lisa. It's not like visiting hours when you meet in the reception room."

Luther hit the wall switch. Four rows of fluorescent tubes covered the room in bright light. There was a circular support beam in the center. A cracked mirror was on one wall. A cabinet and sink were under it. Water dripped from the rusty faucet. Some folding tables and rows of student desks lined the back wall.

"We want you to be comfortable while you wait," Max said. Walking to the back of the room, he pulled out two student desks and dragged them to the support beam. "One for you, and one for Ira." He pushed the back of the desk against the beam. "Sit down, Lisa."

"I don't like being here," Lisa said, stepping away from the desk. "I can come back on Monday."

"It's too late for that, Lisa. We've gone to all this trouble so you can see your Penguin boyfriend." Luther raised his voice. "So just sit down!" When she didn't move, Luther grabbed her, ripping her blouse, and shoved her in the seat. Her knees scraped against the metal support under the desk, and she cried out. He slapped her across the face.

"We don't need any noise," Luther said, nodding to Max. Max went to the cabinet and pulled out rope and tape. He gave the tape to Luther. While Max roped Lisa's legs and arms to the desk, Luther taped her mouth shut.

"That should keep you quiet. Don't worry, Lisa. We won't forget about you. We'll be back tonight." Leaning forward, Luther wiped the tears from her face and kissed her on the forehead. Then he walked across the floor, switched off the light, and locked the door. When they got to the parking area, Luther got into the camp vehicle and Max got into the Ford. They drove slowly over the speed bump at the exit. Giving a quick glance at Boonie in the guardhouse, Luther accelerated down the empty road.

Thirty minutes later, Luther turned onto a weed-covered road. It went through the forest in a straight line and ended at the Brick Yard, an abandoned gravel pit. The water in the pit was green with mats of vegetation floating on the surface. Luther parked next to a two-story wooden platform painted with graffiti. Max drove the Ford to the edge of the pit and put it in neutral. Jumping out, bracing his feet solidly on the ground, Max pushed the car down the slope. It hit the water, bobbed in the air, and then in a cascade of exploding bubbles, sank below the surface. Max walked to the platform and got into Luther's car.

"What time does the show begin tonight?"

"Ten o'clock should be about right, Max. All the prisoners will be locked in, and our new security guard, Boonie, should be asleep by then."

"I was checking her out the whole time," Max said. "She's real pretty. I hope the Penguin ain't fucked her yet. I never had a virgin before."

"And you won't have a virgin tonight, Max."

"What do you mean, I won't have a virgin?"

"Because I get her first." Luther laughed. A grin on his face, he lit a Marlboro and blew a circle of smoke toward Max.

Walking into the camp, Boonie saw a guard on the steps of the administration building. On the center athletic field, two boys were throwing a football. A larger, vocal group of boys was playing on the basketball court. Dan watched Ira Hayes shoot the ball and head toward the dormitory. Dan hurried to cut him off.

"Ira," he called, "were you surprised?"

"Surprised at what?"

"A girl named Lisa came to the camp. Didn't Mr. Cicconi and Max find you?"

"No." Ira's face reddened. "What's going on? Where's Lisa?"

"I don't know. When Luther and Max left, she wasn't with them."

"Then she's still in the camp?"

"She has to be," Dan said. "Luther took Lisa behind the education building. We can look there." With Ira at his side, Dan walked quickly to the parking area and pointed to a road through the trees.

"There's a storage building at the end of the road."

Not saying anything, Ira took off running; Dan sprinted after him. They ran down the road and across the bridge. When Ira saw the log building, he ran faster. Sprinting down the path of yellow rocks, Ira jumped up the steps and began twisting the doorknob.

"Lisa!" he shouted. "Lisa!" There was a shuffling noise inside. Ira turned and faced Dan. "I heard something."

"I can't open the door now. The key's in the director's office. I'll get it tomorrow."

"She could be injured."

"There's no way in without the key," Dan repeated. A whistle sounded from the camp. "The guards are checking the dormitory. We have to go back now."

The whistle sounded again. Ira hesitated; he put his ear to the door. Hearing nothing, wiping the perspiration from his face, he followed Dan down the steps. Minutes later at the dormitory, Dan talked to the guard. The guard motioned Ira inside; Ira didn't move, his eyes focused on Dan.

"I'll search the cabin in the morning," Dan said. "I promise."

"Please find her," Ira implored. Walking slowly, shuffling his feet, Ira went inside the dormitory. The prisoners were in groups laughing and talking. One prisoner lowered his guitar and fired a question at Ira, but Ira walked past without answering. Reaching his cot, he sat down, dropped his head in his hands, and stared at the floor.

Hours later Ira was wide awake. Although the night air was chilly, perspiration covered his face and chest. The door opened, and Ira heard footsteps move across the floor. Leaning forward on his elbows, he watched two bodies grow larger and stop at his cot.

"Mr. Penguin," Luther said. "Boy, do we have a surprise for you." Max pulled Ira off the cot and secured his hands with plastic cuffs. Standing barefoot in his shorts, Ira stared fiercely at Luther.

"I know you took Lisa."

"Doesn't matter what you know," Luther said, pushing Ira toward the door. "You're still in for a big surprise."

Walking in a line with Ira pressed between them, they made their way behind the dormitory. Luther clicked on a flashlight, and they followed the beam of light down the dirt road. When they reached the storage building, Luther unlocked the door.

"Here's your surprise," Luther said, pushing Ira inside and flicking on the fluorescent lights. Tied to the chair, Lisa made muffled cries and struggled with the ropes.

"You bastards!" Ira shouted. Rushing toward Lisa, he saw the tears and the torn blouse. Then stopping suddenly, Ira pivoted, lowered his shoulders, and charged wildly.

"What the hell!" Max muttered.

Ira smashed Max in the ribs. Max fell backward against the door. Luther moved quickly and swung his blackjack, hitting Ira on the forehead. Ira collapsed to the floor.

"The fucker almost killed me." Max straightened painfully, his hand holding his ribs.

"The boy's going to miss all the fun," Luther said, putting the blackjack into his pocket. "Let's sit him next to his girlfriend." They lifted Ira and dropped him in the chair. When the boy's head fell on his chest, Max smashed it against the center post, where it stuck.

"Now Ira can enjoy the show, if he wakes up."

"And what a show it will be," Luther bragged, loosening his belt and dropping his trousers to the floor. "I'll let you know shortly."

"Let me know what, Luther?"

"Whether this Pittsburgh bitch is a virgin or not." Chest heaving, bubbles of spit breaking on his lips, Luther advanced toward the girl.

It was past midnight when Luther and Max took Ira back to the dormitory. They threw him on the cot and removed the plastic cuffs. Turning Ira's head, Luther bent down within inches of his ear.

"Remember one thing, Ira. We have Lisa now. If you say anything about tonight, she'll just plain disappear. I promise you'll never see your girlfriend again." Luther patted Ira on the cheek a few times. Then he and Max left the dormitory. The prisoner in the cot next to Ira coughed. Ira closed his eyes and lay perfectly still.

Leaning back on the swivel chair, his head lowered, Dan watched Luther and Max drive through the gate. When the car lights were far down the road, he left the guard station and hurried to the dormitory. Approaching the cot, he saw the dark bruise on Ira's forehead.

"What happened?" Eyes glaring at Boonie, Ira didn't move. Dan nudged him in the shoulder. "Did Luther and Max threaten you?"

"Not me," Ira whispered. "They said they would kill Lisa. She's tied up in the storage building. But you can't tell anyone. They'll hurt her. I know they will."

"Trust me, Ira. I'll get help." Boonie left the dormitory and ran to the administration building. Using the secretary's phone, he called Director Williams. After a long series of rings, the director picked up the phone.

"Who is this?" he asked in a tired voice.

"It's Dan Boonie."

"Who?"

"Dan Boonie. I'm the new security guard."

"Do you know what time it is, Mr. Boonie?"

"I'm sorry, but we have a problem. There's a girl locked in the storage building."

"That's impossible."

"I'm sure she's in there. She may be hurt."

"I'll drive over now. You'd better be right about this, Mr. Boonie." Hanging up and then redialing, Director Williams called Luther Cicconi.

Dan paced nervously in front of the administration building. Director Williams was coming out of his office with the key to the storage building when Luther parked his car. The security lights cast a dark shadow across Luther's face.

"What's going on?"

"Boonie claims there's a girl locked in the storage building," Director Williams explained in a tired voice. Luther turned and faced Boonie.

"What the hell are you talking about? I was there today. The place was empty."

"What about that, Mr. Boonie?" the director asked.

"I heard something."

"Since we're all wide awake, let's check it out." Director Williams walked around the side of the building. Luther grabbed Boonie roughly by the arm.

"You're going to regret this," he whispered.

Ignoring Luther, Dan caught up to the director. There was one spotlight behind the education building. Its bright glow faded as they walked down the dirt road. Director Williams had a small flashlight, but Luther had a brighter one, and he took the lead. They walked over the wooden bridge, spooking two deer at the water's edge, and continued to the storage building.

Director Williams climbed the steps, unlocked the door, and stepped inside. Luther clicked the wall switch; the fluorescent tubes pulsated erratically, darkened, and then filled the room with a bright glow. Except for the folding tables and rows of desks, the room was empty. The only sound came from the leaky faucet.

"Luther, get the damn plumbing fixed," Director Williams instructed. Luther nodded; the director fixed his gaze on Dan. "Where's the girl, Mr. Boonie?"

"I don't know," he said, walking to the center post.

"It's just like I said all along." Luther had a smile on his face.

"The kid's too young for the job. Cousin Earl would never make up phony girl stories."

"Over here," Boonie said, pointing to the dark marks on the floor. "It's blood."

"Probably a squirrel," Luther explained quickly. "There's no girl in here."

"No, there sure isn't. What a waste of time!" The director turned and faced Dan. "Mr. Boonie, I'll see you in my office first thing in the morning. And, Luther, I'm sorry for dragging you out here."

"So am I," Luther said gruffly, glaring at Dan.

When Luther Cicconi got home, he woke his wife and ordered her to get him a Heineken and make a hot meatball sandwich. Lighting up a Marlboro, he picked up the telephone and called Max.

"What?" Max asked, a note of irritation in his voice.

"You had a good idea taking Lisa to Muddy Run hunting camp. Dan Boonie called Director Williams and fed him this story about a girl being locked in the storage building. When we went inside, the director saw it was empty."

"Good," Max said. "What are we gonna do about Boonie?"

"We'll take him to the Brick Yard. Cousin Earl should have had the job in the first place. How are your ribs?"

"They hurt like hell. I missed all the fun. When are we going back to Muddy Run?"

"Saturday night?"

"Remember, it's my turn," Max said, his hand falling to his crotch. "I'll call my brother, Oliver. He's been promoted to Chief Deputy Oliver. He'll want to meet Lisa. Tell me, Luther. Do you think Lisa's as pretty as Brenda? What if I borrow our equipment? You could videotape me and Lisa. Then Nathaniel would see how good I am."

"That's a bad idea. A very bad idea. Go to bed, Max," Luther said, and he hung up.

Max replaced the phone on the receiver. The bag of ice on his ribs was covered with moisture; a stream of water rolled down his stomach, saturating his shorts.

"That damn fucken' Ira," Max swore, and he limped to the bedroom.

Chapter Eighteen

Early Friday morning, Officer Hendricks watched his wife, Pam, pull into the driveway. Grabbing the bulletproof vest, he hurried down the steps and opened the door for her. When she stepped out, he tossed the vest on the seat. His wife had a worried look on her face.

"Did you find out anything at the station?"

"No, I wasted too much time there. Then I went to the hospitals. There's no record of a Lisa Hendricks."

"What about the school?"

"Their daily procedures are criminal," Hendricks said bitterly. "Her homeroom teacher never reported her absent. It wasn't until sixth period that her physical education teacher turned her name into the office."

"Where are you going now?"

"Huntingdon County. I've got my map. I've got my route planned out. I'm going to the Green Hollow juvenile detention camp where Ira is. Because that's where she is."

"You should stay here."

"Nothing's happening here, Pam. I know the damn system too well. The missing kid either returns home in a few days, or the picture goes on the milk carton."

"Lisa can't be far. She doesn't even have a driver's license."

"What does she care about a license? She's chasing after that bastard."

"Maybe you've been too hard on Ira."

"You're on his side now?"

"All I know is that our daughter loves him," Pam said. She saw his gun and the vest on the seat. "You expecting trouble?"

"I'm always expecting trouble. But don't worry. I'll find Lisa and bring her home." Officer Hendricks kissed his wife and got into the car. Turning on the engine, Hendricks backed out of the driveway, waved to his wife, and raced down the street. At the stop sign, he accelerated, and tires screeching, he spun the car toward the expressway.

Three hours later, Hendricks was driving at a high rate of speed on a dirt road in a heavily wooded area in Huntingdon County. He bumped over a narrow wooden bridge and saw the shelters and picnic tables.

"Shit!" he exclaimed. "It's the same damn bridge I passed earlier!" Hendricks pulled to the side of the road, grabbed the Pennsylvania map, and traced his finger along the network of unmarked back roads. There was a loud noise behind him, and looking through the rearview mirror, Hendricks saw a flash of orange color. Then the FritoLay van drove past him, leaving a cloud of dust over the road.

Finally, a break, Hendricks thought. *They're making deliveries to the camp.* Throwing the map on the seat, he turned the wheel and drove into the cloud of dust. At times the driver would race the van forward, and then, braking suddenly, he would slow down, the van barely moving. Hendricks glared through the dust.

"I should arrest your ass for driving like that," Hendricks whispered. Then his anger subsided. *This isn't Pittsburgh. I'm nobody in these mountains.*

"The bastard's been behind us for ten minutes," Max said. "Who the hell is he?"

"How should I know?" Luther turned onto an old logging road and stopped the van at the pole barrier. Max got out, unlocked it, and swung the pole to the side.

"Keep it open, Max."

"He'll follow us to the cabin." Max got into the van. "Is that a good idea?"

"How else are we going to find out who he is?" Luther answered.

Driving past the pole barrier, straining his eyes, Hendricks drove at the edge of the cloud of dust. The FritoLay van was moving faster now. Clouds of dust mushroomed in the air. When Hendricks saw the fence, open gate, and cabin, he pulled to the side of the road and looked inside the compound. The dust settled; two men stepped out of the van and climbed the steps of the cabin.

"Damn it!" Hendricks grunted. "What a waste of time!" He started to turn the wheel and stopped. *Get directions*, he thought. Hendricks drove through the gate and parked next to the van. After climbing the porch steps, he knocked. The door opened immediately.

"What the hell you want?" Max asked, noticing the bulge under Hendricks's jacket.

"I need to find someone. I need directions."

"Directions to where?" Luther asked, stepping next to Max. Luther had a smirk on his face; he gripped a revolver in his right hand.

"Green Hollow."

"Why you packing a gun?" Max asked.

"Let me explain."

"You don't need to explain anything," Luther said, aiming the revolver at Hendricks. "Hand it over."

"You're making a big mistake," Hendricks said. Reaching under his jacket, he removed the gun with his fingertips and gave it to Max. "I said I can explain everything."

"Just be quiet. Get out your wallet," Luther ordered. Hendricks removed his wallet and gave it to Luther, who flipped it open to the driver's license.

"Albert Hendricks," he read. Opposite the license he saw the blue-and-gold logo of the Pittsburgh Police. "You're way out of your jurisdiction, Officer Hendricks. What the hell are you doing in these mountains?"

"Like I said, I'm looking for someone."

"Who?"

"A girl."

"That's the wrong answer!" Swinging the gun with sudden quickness, Luther bashed Hendricks in the head. The police officer collapsed on the floor.

"You can bet he's looking for Lisa," Max said. "How the hell did he find us?"

"I don't know."

"Maybe you should have asked him."

"Maybe you should let me do the thinking."

"I was just saying—" Max stopped speaking when Hendricks grabbed onto the porch railing and pulled himself to his feet. "Damn. They make 'em tough in Pittsburgh."

"Tough and stupid." Luther raised the gun. Hendricks lunged, and Luther shot him in the chest.

"Shit!" Max exclaimed at the explosion of noise. Watching the body topple over the railing, he shook his head. "You can't shoot a police officer like that, Luther. That's all wrong. You never read him his rights like the law says you should." Looking over the railing, Max saw Hendricks struggling to sit up. "What the hell! You missed him!"

"No, I didn't," Luther said, noticing the vest. "But I can do this all legal now." He leveled the gun at Hendricks. "You have the right to remain silent. You have the right to an attorney. If you can't afford an attorney, one will be provided for you. That's all the rights you get, Officer." Luther laughed and fired two shots in Hendricks's face. Blood spurted in the air; the body flattened on the ground. "There, I read him his constitutional rights. You happy now, Max?"

"Yeah, you shot him all legal and proper," Max said, a big smile on his face. "What should we do with him?"

"He'll most likely end up in the Brick Yard with the others. But for now, we'll keep the body in the freezer. Go get some of those heavy trash bags."

Max went inside the cabin and returned with two trash bags. They wrapped the bags around Hendricks's head and body. After winding tape around the bags, they took the body to the basement and dropped it into the freezer. The two puppies came running across the floor.

"You want to play, Skippy?" Max said, kicking the dog. Tapping Luther on the shoulder, he stopped in front of the Shangri-la Room. "Maybe I should check on Brenda."

"Maybe you should forget about the girls."

"I'm just saying that asshole Jeffery hasn't done nothing yet."

"He's scheduled for a session tonight. If he doesn't do this video soon … I heard Nathaniel mention the Brick Yard."

"It's going to get real crowded in the Yard," Max reasoned. "Before we kill Jeffery, maybe I could smash his pretty face a little. Maybe cripple him, too. We could video the whole thing. Then I could fuck Brenda with Jeffery on the floor right next to us. That would add an unusual twist to the story."

"That would be an unusual twist, Max. Some sick viewers might enjoy it."

"Don't call them sick," Max grumbled. "I don't think they're sick at all."

"If they're not sick, what are they?"

"I think they enjoy having a good time, that's all."

"Right," Luther said. "You just keep thinking that." He brushed past Max and started up the steps. Skippy and Tippy were whimpering in the corner.

"You'd better feed the dogs," Luther said, and he continued up the steps. When he got to the living room, he went to the bar and pulled an ice-cold Heineken from the refrigerator.

Chapter Nineteen

After school on Friday, an Arkansas Toothpick strapped on his back, Gene called Conner and Matt in a loud voice. The door slamming open, the boys hurried down the steps to the front yard.

"What's going on, Dad?"

"I promised to teach Matt how to be a good hunter. We start the lessons today. Look over there, Matt." Gene pointed to the rows of dark shells that covered the side of the garage. "Do you know what kind of turtles those are?"

"Snapping turtles. They've been around forever. They're prehistoric."

"They've survived because they're excellent predators," Gene said. "Some people kill snappers on land, where they're slow-moving and helpless. But not you, Matt. You're going after them in the river, where they have no equal. First, you locate the den. Then the turtle."

"How?"

"With your hands."

"Hands!" Matt exclaimed. "That sounds kind of dangerous."

"It *is* dangerous," Conner volunteered. "A snapper would clamp down on your finger and bite through the bone. Then he would go after the next one."

"Be quiet, soldier. Quit filling Matt's head with all that fear talk."

"But it's the truth!"

"Matt," Gene said, ignoring Conner, "come over here." They walked to the barn. Gene pointed to the largest shell. "Notice how one end of the shell is rounded, but the other end has these jagged points. The snapper's head and jaws are at the rounded end. You don't want to go there. Search around with your fingers until you find the jagged end. That's where the tail is. Just reach under the jagged points and grab the tail."

"Then what?"

"You grip the tail tightly, jerk the snapper out of the water, and toss it on the bank." Gene gripped the Arkansas Toothpick. "I'll do the rest. It's a great adventure getting one of these. Ask Conner how many of these shells are his."

"Not a damn one," Conner said quickly. "I wasn't born stupid. I would never go into the water after a snapper. Even Mom said it was crazy."

"Your mom spoiled you with all her worries. You could never be a soldier with her around." Gene stared at his son. "I caught every one of those with you watching and pissing your pants on the riverbank. Yet you and your mom ate the snapper soup, didn't you?"

"Yeah, it was good. Chili dogs are good, too. And guess what, Dad? You can eat them with all your fingers intact." Conner was quiet for a moment, his eyes moving from Matt to his dad. "I don't like this. Can't we start with something easy, like a rabbit?"

"No, you never want to start easy, soldier. We need to find out who Matt really is."

"I know who I am, Mr. Brooks."

"You don't know anything yet, Matt. Except for man, the snapper has no natural enemies. It has fought its way to the top of the food chain. And it will fight you. The fight will tell us what you're made of, Matt—whether you've got the genuine stuff to be a real hunter, or you're nothing but talk, like most people. Do you understand what I'm saying?"

"Kind of," Matt answered. "Should I bring my Roman death hammer?"

"No, Matt. You'd sink to the bottom of the river with that around your waist."

Gene turned and started walking down the road. The boys followed. They entered a shaded trail that skirted the Little Juniata. After fifteen minutes, Gene stopped at a path that angled down a steep incline of rocks and gravel. A railroad trestle was at the end of the path. Its black girders threw shadows over the river. The current under the trestle moved slowly, lapping against the wide cement platform.

"Matt, come here."

"What, Mr. Brooks?" Matt asked, stepping next to him.

"Notice how the river reflects the trees … the bridge … the sky? The river's a mirror, Matt. You'll see your face in the water. When you jump into the river and fight a snapper, you'll discover who's really behind that face."

"What do you mean?" Gene didn't answer. Planting his feet firmly, he made his way down the path. Conner came up to Matt.

"Did he tell you about the river being a mirror to the soul?"

"Something like that."

"He tried that line on me years ago. I didn't buy it. You don't have to do this."

"But I want to do it," Matt said, starting down the path. He and Conner caught up to Gene. When they reached the river, Gene pointed to the eroded section of bank at his feet.

"The snappers love these big holes because food drifts right into their jaws. Right here, under this bank, there's a snapper's den."

"Jeez, Dad. It's too deep here."

"Be quiet, soldier. Are you ready, Matt?"

"What should I do?"

"Just do like I explained at the barn. Jump into the river, put your hand into the den, and search around until you find the jagged end of the shell." Matt hesitated. The current splashed foam and debris against the bank. "What are you waiting for?" Gene asked.

"Nothing," Matt said, and he began to remove his shirt.

"Leave your clothes on," Gene advised. "And leave your tennis shoes on, too."

"They'll be ruined. Why can't I take them off?"

"So you won't lose a toe, that's why," Conner answered.

"I told you to be quiet," Gene said sharply. A breeze blew under the trestle. There were cooing sounds from the pigeons perched on the steel beams. Gene nodded to Matt. "Just get into the water."

"Okay," Matt said. When he slid into the river, mud broke away from the bank, turning the water brown. Pigeon droppings splashed in the water and sank; some buoyant particles floated past him. His brow furrowed, Matt lowered his hand into the murky depths. Watching him closely, Gene pulled the Arkansas Toothpick from the harness. Seeing the knife, Conner shook his head.

"Dad ..."

"Not now, soldier."

Sinking deeper into the pool, Matt steadied his feet on the slippery bottom and inched his hand into the den. When his fingers scraped a hard surface, Matt felt the muscles in his back tighten.

"I found the shell," Matt whispered.

There was a deafening rumble, and directly overhead, the trestle vibrated. The Amtrak horn blasted; the train screeched across the bridge. Flapping wings wildly, pigeons scattered in all directions. In the thunder of shadow and light, Matt spread his fingers and found the jagged edge of the shell. His eyes expanded wide; his face turned pale. He froze motionless in the swirling current.

"Don't quit now!" Gene shouted.

"I'm not quitting!" Matt shouted back. Lowering his hand, he gripped the thick girth of the tail. The snapper lurched sideways; claws ripped into Matt's forearm.

The noise of the train drowned out Matt's scream. Matt lost his footing, and his face slammed into the wall of mud. Sharp needles raked the length of Matt's arm; red stains appeared on the surface of the water. The rattling echo of the train drifted down the tracks. As Matt lifted his face out of the mud, Gene readied the Arkansas Toothpick.

Using all his strength, Matt pulled the snapper out of the den. The shell slid smoothly, buoyantly through the water. When Matt raised the turtle in the air, his bloody forearm bent under the weight, and the snapper's head swung in front of his face. Its eyes blinking open, the turtle made a horrific hissing noise. The neck contracted, and deep, wrinkled lines formed on the skin. Then the lines disappeared in a blur, and the jaws struck forward.

"Throw the fucker!" Conner screamed. Astounded, Conner saw the silver flash of the knife slice through the snapper's outstretched neck. The head hit Matt's chest and stuck there, the beaked jaws clamping shut on Matt's T-shirt.

"Son of a bitch!" Matt hollered. Twisting his body, he spun in a half circle and tossed the turtle on the bank. The shell rolled over once, twice, and with blood spurting from the severed neck, the turtle lay still.

"Great job, Matt," Gene said, putting the Arkansas Toothpick into the harness. He and Conner pulled Matt out of the river. Clinging to the T-shirt, the snapper's head swung back and forth.

"I think I pissed my pants," Matt said weakly. He smiled and wiped mud off his face. "Everything was in slow motion. I saw it strike out. Its jaws were aiming at my nose!"

"I warned you not to mess with snappers," Conner reminded everyone. He pulled off his T-shirt and wrapped it around the bloody claw marks on Matt's forearm. Then, stretching Matt's T-shirt, he grabbed the snapper's head with both hands.

"Leave the head alone," Gene said.

"What?" both Matt and Conner asked simultaneously.

"You heard me. Leave it right where it is. Let's go back. It was a good hunt. We'll eat fresh turtle tonight." Gene picked up the snapper by the tail and began climbing the steep bank. The boys followed. When they reached the river trail, Matt pulled Gene's sleeve.

"Can I carry it?"

"Sure, but I think it weighs more than you do." Gene handed the tail to Matt. Matt struggled with the weight and began dragging the shell in the dirt. Conner reached over, and they carried it together.

At times, the rocking motion swung the snapper's head against Matt's chest. When he looked down, two smoky-gray eyes met his gaze; blood from the severed neck formed red smears the length of his T-shirt.

———

At the house, Gene placed a flattened board on the grass. Dropping the snapper on top, he began cutting around the shell. When he finished, he gave the shell, wet and dripping blood, to Matt. Swinging a hammer, Conner rushed over.

"I know my job," Conner said.

"You should. You've done it often enough. Matt, you hold the shell in place, and Conner can nail it to the garage."

"What about the head?" Matt asked tentatively.

"Oh, that. Come closer, Matt." Taking the Arkansas Toothpick, Gene gripped the snapper's head, pulled it away from Matt's body, and with a quick motion, sliced the blade through the T-shirt. Matt tripped backward. Peering down at the hole in the middle of his shirt, he looked helplessly at Conner. Conner's mouth dropped open.

"Here." Gene gave Matt the head, the shredded piece of shirt hanging loosely from its clamped jaws. "Nail the head under the shell so the eyes are staring toward the road. It'll scare the hell out of any trespassers."

"It sure will," Matt agreed. He and Conner ran to the garage. They nailed the head to the wall and slid the shell over the neck. When Conner hammered the nail into the wood, the shell vibrated. Drops of blood spattered a jagged line across Matt's forehead.

"Damn," Matt said. "This is a bloody war."

Racing each other to the porch, jumping the steps, Matt and Conner rushed into the kitchen. Three soup dishes, spoons, a stack of napkins, and nine empty Iron City bottles littered the table. Holding a long wooden ladle, Gene stood over the stove stirring liquid in a large crock pot. When he looked up and saw Matt, he dropped the ladle on the stove.

"Matt, get that face washed!" he ordered in a brusque voice.

"What?"

"Get that damn blood off your forehead!"

"Jeez, Dad, it's nothing," Conner said. Matt walked to the sink and washed water over his face. Gene picked up the ladle and began stirring the liquid in the crock pot again.

"Conner, you and Matt get those oyster mushrooms and some corn from the freezer."

The boys went to the basement, and Conner opened the freezer. Deer steaks and sausage filled one side. The fish in the middle section were frozen in bags of ice. Conner saw the container of mushrooms and pulled it out.

"Matt, there's a problem. You're a vegetarian. You can't eat turtle meat?"

"It's no problem. I have this exemption. I'm permitted to eat anything I kill."

"That's very convenient, Matt. I got the mushrooms. You get the corn."

"How can you find anything in here?" Matt asked. When he overturned some packages of venison steaks, the black plastic bag under them ripped; icy fingers protruded through the opening.

"Ahhhhh!" Matt screamed.

"What?"

"That damn hand's still in your freezer!"

"So, I forgot about it. Remind me to throw it into the river tomorrow. Just put the bag away and get the corn. It's not a good idea to keep Dad waiting too long."

"This is crazy." Making a face, Matt twisted the frozen fingers back into the garbage bag and buried it under the packages of venison. Shaking his head, he grabbed a container of corn and followed Conner up the steps.

In the kitchen, Gene removed the lid from the crock pot and dropped the corn and mushrooms into the steaming liquid. Then he grabbed the black iron skillet off the burner and scraped garlic, chopped onion, and cubes of seared turtle into the pot. An intoxicating aroma filled the kitchen. Matt moved closer, but Gene slammed the lid down.

"You can't look in there."

"Why?"

"It's a secret recipe. Only us river folk know it."

"Does Conner know?"

"I won't tell him 'til he kills a snapper."

"Don't worry, Dad. That'll never happen."

"Don't be so sure. You may grow up sooner than you think. This soup has to simmer for a few hours. Come on, you two. I want to show you something."

"What?"

"You'll see when we get there." Gene walked out the door and down the steps to the jeep. The boys jumped into the back, and Gene drove out of the driveway. After ten minutes, he turned onto a dirt road that was rocky and filled with ruts.

"It's the old pike," Gene said. The road narrowed, and low-hanging branches scraped across the roof. After a bumpy ride, Gene pulled the jeep to the side of the road and got out. Conner and Matt followed him down a path to a large squared foundation. Black charred pieces of wood protruded through the dirt and weeds. There was a row of apple trees behind the foundation.

"What was here, Dad?"

"A cabin," Gene said, and he kept walking. "Two hundred years ago, Indians and Tories burned it to the ground."

They crossed an open area and stopped in front of a large spring. The wooden sluice had warped, moss-covered sides. The flowing water was swift and glistened in the sunlight. Frogs croaked and jumped in the stream; a cloud of yellow butterflies circled over damp ferns. Blue violets grew wild to the edge of the trees.

Taking a leather flask from his pocket, Gene filled it with spring water and gave it to Conner. Reaching for the bottle, Conner saw his dad's hand was a bright red. Drinking the water, Conner laughed.

"It's ice-cold! Try some, Matt." Conner held out the flask, but Matt didn't move.

"What's wrong, Matt?"

"Nothing's wrong," Matt said. He stared at the glistening pool of water, which reflected a blue sky. Leaning closer, seeing his face sparkling with light and energy, Matt laughed and buried his head in the spring. The icy rush made his body tremble. Vast quantities of air escaped from his lungs and boiled to the surface. A loud ringing sound pummeled his ears. Matt lifted his head in a quick motion, water spraying in all directions.

"Wow!" he exclaimed, breathing deeply. "I heard a popping noise."

"Just your ears freezing up," Conner said. "Why'd you put your head in?"

"I just felt the urge to. I saw a strange face"

"You saw yourself, Matt. You're changing. You're stronger than the shit-faced boy you saw at the river this morning." Gene motioned to Matt. "Put your forearm into the spring. See if it helps with the swelling."

"Sure, Mr. Brooks." Matt pulled off the T-shirt bandage and lowered his arm into the water. "Wow!" he exclaimed again, his whole body shaking. Gene studied Matt's face … the ragged hole in the center of his T-shirt … the streaks of blood.

"Matt, I have a question. Is your family from this area?"

"What do you mean?"

"Are your ancestors from Hartslog Valley?"

"I think so. Mr. Henry has a picture in the bank. It shows my great-great-grandfather standing in front of a cabin next to Standing Stone Creek. Why do you ask?"

"I was just curious about some theory I heard," Gene said. After a few moments, he lifted Matt's arm out of the spring. The skin was painted crimson to the elbow; the jagged line of cuts across the forearm was closed tight.

"My whole arm's numb." Matt opened and closed his hand. "Who built this spring, Mr. Brooks?"

"The Dean family built it. Mr. Dean and his friend Captain Simonton were killed here. The captain's son, Matthew, was taken prisoner. The Indians and Tories tracked Dean's wife and children to Blood Mountain."

"In his sermon, the Reverend Towers said Matthew was the only survivor."

"He did survive. The journals say Matthew watched his sister Beatrice die in the Shadows of Death. He carved her name in a cave at the cliffs as a memorial. Soon after the massacre, Matthew tracked down a wealthy Tory landowner named Jacob Hare. Matthew gutted him."

"What happened to Matthew?"

"He hunted Indians, mostly Shawnee, for years. No one knows how many he killed. Eventually, he was jailed. But they couldn't keep him locked up. He escaped. They chased him to Blood Mountain. He was never seen again. Some say he jumped into the Shadows."

"That's not right," Conner stated. "Why would the authorities put Matthew in jail?"

"He was a killer."

"If you call killing Indians killing ..."

"That's exactly what you call it, soldier. Killing anyone makes you a killer."

"What about you, Dad?"

"What about me?"

"You've done some killing in Vietnam."

"That was war!" Gene shouted loudly, caustically. There was an awkward silence. Gene lowered his hands into the spring and splashed water on his face. "Why don't you and Matt pick some apples for dinner?"

"Good idea," Matt said. As he and Conner walked around the ruined foundation, Matt nudged Conner on the shoulder. "I agree with you. I agree with everything you said."

"About what?"

"About Matthew killing the people who hurt him. He did the right thing. He should never have been imprisoned."

"It's fine you think like that, but I wouldn't talk about it too much. For some reason, Dad got real testy." Conner stopped at the first tree. After selecting some of the bigger apples, he and Matt returned to the jeep.

"How's your turtle soup?" Gene asked, looking across the table at Matt.

"Delicious," Matt said. Swiping bread across the bottom of his dish, he lifted it dripping to his mouth. "This soup is absolutely delicious."

"Matt, I know one of Dad's secret ingredients. It's Iron City."

"There's beer in the soup?"

"Yeah, Matt, lots of it."

"I didn't know beer tasted so good. I think I'll enjoy becoming an alcoholic." Matt lifted the bowl to his mouth, drank the remaining soup, and gave a loud burp. "It's the best soup I've ever had."

"It's not just the Iron City that makes it taste so good, Matt," Gene explained. "It's everything you did to get the snapper out of the den and onto the bank. It's the way any hunter feels after a kill."

"I do feel good about that, real good."

"Since you did so well today, I think you're ready for your second test. We'll be going to the Jersey shore tomorrow. We can stay with an old army friend. He has a house right there on the beach."

"Is this the Vietnam veteran, JJ, who I met on the porch at three in the morning?"

"No, Conner, this is Lieutenant Chase Butler. He's much younger than JJ."

"Why go to the shore, Dad? What's Matt going to learn there?"

"He'll learn plenty. You boys are going blue fishing in Wildwood first thing tomorrow morning. Matt, you're in for a major challenge. Bluefish got attitude and will fight you to the death. Plus, they have razor-sharp choppers."

"What's a chopper?"

"Choppers are their jagged rows of teeth. It's a struggle to get a bluefish into the boat. Then you have to be careful because bluefish can see out of water. Once they clamp down on any part of you, they don't let go. Even after they're dead, they don't let go."

"You're kidding me?"

"No, Dad's saying the way it is. I've gone twice, and I was dead tired and stinking of blood and fish guts both times." Conner looked across the table. "Dad, Cindy's family has a place in Wildwood. Can I call her?" Gene nodded. "I'll do it right now." Conner jumped out of his chair and rushed to the living room. After a few minutes, he returned with a big smile on his face.

"It's all set," Conner said. "Her dad wasn't sure at first. Then I heard Cindy shouting at him like she does at me, and he changed his mind. They're driving down after breakfast. And Alice is going, too. I heard her telling Cindy she was all excited to be with Matt on the boardwalk."

"I don't know Alice that well," Matt said. "Why would she be excited?"

"Because she likes you, Matt. Don't look so worried."

"But I *am* worried," Matt said, walking inside the house.

Later that night, Gene sat on the sofa watching TV. There were four vehicles zigging and zagging on the narrow country road trying to pass each other. Shouting out the truck's window, Crazy Cooter rammed his bumper into the back of the orange Dodge Charger. Bo Duke yelped a loud, "Hee haw!" The roar of engines and squealing tires filled the living room. When the episode ended with Waylon Jennings singing *Good Ole Boys*, Gene grabbed a bottle of Iron City, went to the porch, and flopped on the hammock.

After a few minutes, Conner walked out with a Mountain Dew in his hand. Matt slammed the door to the bathroom, and soon there was the noise of splashing water from the shower. Sitting across from his dad, Conner took a drink of Dew.

"Why do you keep watching the *The Dukes of Hazzard*? There's not much story."

"I don't care about the story. I love the racing, and I love that Dodge Charger."

"That's why you painted the jeep orange?"

"Yeah. When I was growing up, I wanted a car more than anything else in the world. That's all I could think about. I kept hinting to Dad I wanted a car to pick up the local girls."

"Did he get you a car?"

"No," Gene said, taking a drink. "He couldn't afford a car for himself. On my birthday, do you know what he got me? He got me a secondhand Radio Flyer."

"The wagon!" Conner exclaimed, glancing at the roof of the garage. "I love the Flyer, Dad. I think it was a perfect gift for you. I can see you pulling it around Hartslog. How many girls did you pick up?"

"Only one." Gene laughed. "Your mom." Finishing the beer, Gene bent down to put the empty bottle on the floor. A gold chain holding a stone amulet and green medallion slid out from under his shirt. The green medallion spun in a slow circle. Conner looked at the medallion and sat up straight.

"Dad, the Batman medallion on your chain."

"What Batman …" Gene began. Straightening, he grabbed the chain and shoved the amulet and medallion under his shirt.

"Dad, you never said you had the medallion."

The night was black; tree frogs filled the yard with their back-and-forth piercing croaks. The screen door swung open, and rubbing a towel across his chest, Matt came onto the porch. He saw Conner sitting across from his dad. Conner's face was drained of color.

"What's wrong?" Matt asked. Conner didn't take his gaze off his dad.

"Dad, the medallion—you got it from Wally?"

"Yes."

"We were at the train station," Conner said. "I put the medallion in Wally's hand. I told him to give it to my dad and tell him …"

"That you wanted your dad to come home." Gene spoke tentatively. "I was on Hill 101. Wally showed up out of nowhere. He surprised the hell out of me." Looking at Conner, Gene began to rock slowly on the hammock. A train whistle sounded across the river, and soon the dark shadows of the engine and boxcars moved with a rhythmic clanking sound. When Conner spoke, there was a crack in his voice.

"What happened to Wally, Dad?"

"He was killed on Hill 101. You know that."

"Why was the coffin closed?" There was a moment of silence, punctuated only by Conner's heavy breathing.

"What do you mean, why was the coffin closed?"

"At the viewing, Dad, everyone was asking that question. Mom wanted to know, too. You never told her. You never said anything."

"You're just like her," Gene snapped, jumping to his feet, the hammock swinging high in the air. "You have all these questions. You can't leave things alone. Wally was killed in the war. Answering your stupid questions won't change that."

"They're not stupid questions, Dad!"

"That's enough talk about Wally!" Gene blurted. "We're leaving for Jersey in a few hours. Get packed, and be ready when I get back." Gene stomped down the steps and walked across the yard. When he disappeared in the dark shadows along the riverbank, Conner and Matt went inside the house. Matt went to the bedroom and started throwing clothes into a gym bag. He slid the death hammer next to his extra pair of sneakers. After they finished packing, they carried the gym bags to the porch.

Conner heard a splash near the bank and began walking toward the river. Matt followed him. They came to a line of fallen trees. Three trees had landed in the river, their branches thrashing against the current. The trunks had been nicked away neatly in the same circular pattern. Some of the trunks were snapped five feet off the ground; others were snapped one or two feet higher.

"Boy, do you have some big beavers around here."

"They're not beavers, Matt. Dad practices here with those

Toothpicks … sometimes for hours. And all the trees aren't cut the same. The higher stumps are cut where a man's throat would be."

"I'll be damned," Matt said in amazement. "So that's why he never uses a gun."

"Oh, he has guns, Matt. He's got that revolver in the truck. He's got a rifle, and he's got a shotgun for the porch. But he won't have anything to do with assault rifles."

"Why?"

"He believes a gun is necessary for hunting or protecting your home. All you need is one, maybe two shots to kill a deer or stop an intruder. Dad says if you possess an assault rifle to blast away at someone, you're incompetent and probably should be arrested for carrying any kind of weapon." There was noise on the trail. The footsteps moved closer.

"Dad's back. Let's put our stuff into the jeep and get ready for this fishing trip." Conner pushed Matt in the shoulder, and they took off running toward the house. As they neared the porch, Matt grabbed Conner by the arm, slowing him down.

"You're not going to bring up the subject of Wally anymore, are you?"

"I might bring it up," Conner answered. "How else can I find out the truth?"

Chapter Twenty

On Friday night the Pump House was packed with Penn State students and alumni. A local band blasted music from the stage. Sitting at the bar, Jeffery shoved his hand into his pocket. He felt the circular pill container and Pump House tokens. Grabbing one of the tokens, he dropped it on the bar.

"The usual?" Josh asked.

"Yes," Jeffery said. After a few minutes, Josh returned and set the rum and Coke on the bar. Jeffery took a quick drink. "You've got a great crowd tonight."

"Everyone's excited about the Nebraska game tomorrow. We're both ranked in the Top 10. You going to the game, Jeffery?"

"I can't make it."

"Then stop in afterward for the celebration."

"I will. Is that upstairs apartment still vacant?"

"Yes. The manager had the rugs shampooed today."

"I'm looking for a new place. Can I rent it?"

"Sure." Josh reached under the counter, grabbed a key, and gave it to Jeffery. "I'll tell the manager tonight. On the way out, just take down the vacancy sign."

"I will. Thanks a lot."

Taking a drink, Jeffery turned and looked at the dance floor. The door burst open, and a noisy group of students waving blue-and-white banners charged inside. As the group moved past the bar, a tall girl wearing a Penn State sweatshirt and tight jeans was pushed into Jeffery. She bumped his elbow; a stream of rum and Coke splashed on his chin.

"Sorry," she said. Laughing, her face flushed, she showed pink lips and white, perfectly straight teeth. As the crush of students moved past them, her body pressed tightly against Jeffery. She lifted her hand, and gently moving her fingers across his chin, she wiped away the Coke stains. Then smiling, she slid the fingers into her mouth.

"You have this sweet taste of the islands. My name's Mindy. What do I taste like?" She removed the lubricated fingers from her mouth and slid them across Jeffery's lips.

"Like rum and Coke but much sweeter."

"I can be very sweet," she admitted in a soft voice. "What's your name?"

"Jeffery."

"Well, Jeffery, I hope you're alone tonight." Her face stopped inches from his. She lowered her hand, her fingers sliding down the side of his leg. She smiled when she felt a round, hard object. "That's a good sign."

"What's a good sign?"

"You're already excited." Mindy began to stroke the object. When the pills inside the container made a light rattling noise, she pulled her hand back.

"That's not what I thought it was," she said, a surprised look on her face.

"No, it's not," Jeffery said, putting his glass on the counter and moving off the stool. "I'm sorry. I don't have time to talk. I'm supposed to meet someone." Without waiting for Mindy's reaction, Jeffery squeezed by her body. When he reached the exit, the door flew open, and a mob of older alumni pushed their way past him.

Outside, Jeffery took down the "Apartment for Rent" sign and dropped it behind the staircase. Headlights flashing in his face, Jeffery watched the cars maneuver through the parking lot. He started walking, and a yellow Mustang, radio blaring loudly, followed him to the Porsche. Jeffery got into the Porsche and backed out. Squealing tires, the Mustang filled the vacant space.

It was eleven o'clock when Jeffery parked the Porsche next to the FritoLay van. Climbing the steps to the cabin, he unlocked the door, headed straight to the refrigerator, and grabbed one of Luther's Heinekens. Walking to the window, Jeffery opened the pillbox and dropped two large yellow tablets into his mouth, swallowing them with a long swig of beer. Outside, under the glare of the security light, the Porsche gleamed silver next to the van. His eyes turning bright, glazed over by the silver glow, Jeffery admired the sharp, smooth lines of the car.

"I love that Porsche!" He laughed, finishing the Heineken. His body was suddenly hot, and a strong arousal pushed against his shorts. "It's time to make my first payment."

Jeffery inserted a Michael Jackson cassette into the player, went to the bathroom, and undressed. After he showered and shaved, he put on a blue silk bathrobe. The notes of Michael Jackson's *Off the Wall* drifted into the bathroom. Listening to the lyrics, Jeffery walked across the living room to the staircase. The phone rang, but Jeffery didn't answer it.

> C'mon and groove …
> Life ain't so bad at all if you live it Off the Wall.
> Do what you want to do.
> There ain't no rules; it's up to you.

"There ain't no rules," Jeffery half-shouted. When he walked down the steps to the basement, the sensor tracked his movements; the video camera began to record. Skippy and Tippy ran barking across the floor. They licked Jeffery's face, and he hugged them. Picking up both puppies and holding them against his chest, Jeffery carried them to the cage and put them inside. After dropping in some biscuits, he walked to the Shangri-la Room, unlocked the door, and went inside. Reclining on the bed, Brenda sat up; the strobe light flashed across her nude body. Music filtered into the room: *Do what you want to do. There ain't no rules; it's up to you.*

Brenda had a blank expression on her face. Her eyes were moist; her skin was clear and smooth. Jeffery took off his bathrobe. The strobe cast a pulsating light over his body. It clearly illuminated the black-and-blue lump below his ribs.

"That's grotesque," he muttered. Staring at his reflection in the wall mirror, Jeffery saw the disgusted expression on his face. Then Brenda made a moaning sound, and Jeffery glanced furtively in her direction, taking in the soft curves of her body. Suddenly, he experienced a hot flash, and his face blushed. A tingling sensation shot through his groin; the strength of his erection slanted upward. Jeffery stepped toward the bed. The bruise turned a deep purple and throbbed; sharp pains dug into his ribs. Brenda put her hands to her face and began to cry.

"I can't," Jeffery said, stopping next to the bed and covering his erection. "Porsche or no Porsche, I can't do this." Jeffery put on the bathrobe, pulled the cord tightly around his waist, and walked away. Locking the door behind him, Jeffery went upstairs. After getting dressed, he took the plastic pillbox from his pants, ripped off the cap, and flushed the tablets down the toilet. As Jeffery dropped the empty container into the waste can, the phone rang. Hesitating for a moment, he picked up the receiver.

"Hello, Jeffery. How's the video going tonight?" Nathaniel asked.

"I didn't do any video. And it wasn't my fault. It was Max and Luther's fault."

"You're not making any sense, Jeffery."

"Let me explain. I was in the Shangri-la Room, and Brenda was ready."

"So what's the problem?"

"When I took off my bathrobe, I saw those black-and-blue marks that Luther gave me. They're ugly, and they still hurt. So I can't do the video until the bruises clear up. Probably in a couple of days."

"You're running out of time, Jeffery."

"Like I said, it's not my fault." Jeffery heard a click on the other end of the line. He replaced the phone, turned off the lights, and walked out into the cold night air.

Thirty minutes later, Jeffery parked the Porsche at the entrance to the Pump House. Rushing inside, he saw Mindy at the bar. Jeffery circumvented the couples on the floor and stepped behind her, brushing his body tightly against hers.

"Jeffery," she said, turning to face him. "You're back so soon."

"I'm sorry I left earlier. I apologize." He kissed Mindy on the cheek. "I just rented the apartment upstairs. Would you like to get out of this noise?"

"Sure, Jeffery."

They exited the Pump House and climbed the stairs to the apartment. Taking the key, Jeffery unlocked the door, went inside, and hit the wall switch. As the living room flooded with light, he began unbuttoning his shirt.

"You're in a hurry," Mindy said, helping him with the buttons. When she removed his shirt, she saw the coloration. "Ouch," she said, sliding her hand over the bruise.

"It's nothing."

"It's got to hurt."

"It hurts now. It'll hurt more later. I can't wait." Sliding off his shoes, Jeffery felt the moisture seep into his socks. "Damn it. The carpet's just been shampooed." Jeffery saw cushions stacked in the corner, and picking them up, he spread them evenly on the carpet.

"Nothing but the best for you," he said, removing his pants and shorts. Mindy pulled the sweatshirt over her head, dropped her jeans, and stretched out enticingly on the cushions. Jeffery had the biggest smile on his face.

"Why so happy?"

"I'm excited about being with you tonight."

"Jeffery, you could have any girl."

"After I left you at the bar, I found out something very important about myself."

"What, Jeffery?"

"I don't want just any girl," he said, and he lowered his body over hers. When the Pump House band kicked up the volume, the walls of the apartment vibrated with a booming bass sound that echoed through the floorboards.

Early Saturday morning, Dan Boonie rushed up the steps of the administration building, and seeing the secretary's empty chair, he knocked on the door to the director's office. The door opened, and the secretary stepped out. Dan went inside, and Director Williams motioned to an empty chair. Sitting down, Dan stared at Mr. Williams.

"Don't worry, Mr. Boonie. You're not in any trouble. You thought a girl was in trouble, and your choice was to find help. You were doing your job. But Mr. Cicconi was really concerned. He manages things in the yard. Now and then there's a fight, and the boys beat up on each other. But for the most part, we have good control of this camp. Wouldn't you agree with that?"

"Yes, sir."

"You really heard a girl's voice?"

"I heard something."

"Well, I hope we can get to the bottom of this." The director stood and shook Boonie's hand. "You have good judgment. Just keep doing your job."

"Yes, thank you, sir," Dan said, and he left the office.

It was noon when Luther and Max went through the security gate. Ignoring their hostile stares, Dan watched them drive the car behind the cafeteria. Seeing his replacement coming up the road, Dan left the security station and walked quickly to the cafeteria. From the shadows, he watched Luther and Max put a box of canned food and large water bottles in the backseat of the car.

It's for the girl, Dan thought. *They have to feed her.*

After Luther and Max drove back through the security gate, Dan got on his motorcycle, and accelerating fast, he soon saw the Green Hollow car spinning dust in the air. Maintaining a safe distance behind the cloud of dust, Dan sped past hunting cabins and rumbled over rickety wooden bridges. The road narrowed through a section of dense forest and then angled sharply up the side of a mountain. A wall of rock was on one side of the road. On the other side, there was a steep cliff strewn with boulders and blackened tree stumps split by lightning.

Reaching the top of the mountain, the car moved slowly on a level stretch of road and turned onto a grass-covered driveway. Dan stopped and pushed the motorcycle into the pine trees. Removing his helmet, he heard the car door slam and the sound of voices. Dan began walking toward the noise. It was moist and cool in the woods; pine needles cracked under his feet. Forming thin clouds, mosquitoes swarmed out of the shadows.

Taking long strides, Dan came to the edge of a large pond. The water was clear; dragonflies skimmed the surface. The road circled around the pond and ended at a two-story log cabin. "Muddy Run Camp" was etched on the wooden sign hanging from the porch.

Crouching in the bushes, Dan glanced at the cabin and the slanting roof of the outhouse next to it. Suddenly, there was an explosion of noise from the pond. Dropping clumsily to the ground, Dan watched a large rainbow trout twist in the air and splash back into the water. He laughed nervously, and staying low to the ground, he approached the cabin. Tall weeds grew along the wall. Brushing through them, Dan stepped next to the window. The glass was smeared with dirt; a wasp buzzed around a nest in the corner. Another wasp crawled out of the cone, and both black bodies dropped angrily toward Dan.

Listening to the buzzing noise, Dan looked inside and saw Luther take a can of beer from the refrigerator. Lisa sat on a sofa in the corner of the room. Wearing only a brown corrections shirt, she had dark bruises on her face. Her hands and feet were tied. Struggling to sit up, she glanced toward the window; her eyes locked on his. There was an instant moment of recognition. Luther laughed loudly and walked toward the sofa.

I wish I had my gun, Dan thought. Then directly behind him there was the sharp snap of a breaking branch, and Dan couldn't move his arms or legs. The buzzing noise of the wasps grew louder.

"What the hell you doing, Boonie?" a voice bellowed.

Dan spun around and saw Max standing there pulling up his pants. Not hesitating, Dan charged at the bigger man. Before Max could get his hand free, Dan bludgeoned him in the chest, knocking him backward. Bellowing in pain, his pants dropping to his knees, Max hit the ground. Dan ran past him; the cabin door banged open, and Luther rushed toward Max, who was cradling his ribs.

Dan was breathing heavily when he reached the motorcycle. He slid on his helmet, bent low over the cycle, and twisted the handgrip to full throttle. Dirt and pieces of stone spun away from the tires. As Dan descended the steep grade of the mountain, he heard the car engine. The horn sounded, each staccato blast echoing louder. Looking in the mirror, Dan saw the headlights through the cloud of dust. The Green Hollow car roared closer; Luther's forehead was pressed against the windshield.

Dan accelerated, but when he braked for a sharp curve, the front bumper of the car banged against his rear tire. The impact sent the motorcycle flying off the side of the mountain. Dan clung to the handlebars. Wind roaring through the helmet, he saw blue sky and white clouds. Then the cycle angled downward. It crashed through the outer branches of a pine tree into a deep area of open space. Dan clearly saw the jagged pattern of rocks that rose to meet him. When the motorcycle smashed into the earth, the front tire broke away, and Dan's body was thrown against the rocks. A heavy weight crushed his leg. There was a brief moment of blinding red flashes and then total darkness.

Standing on the edge of the road, Luther and Max watched Boonie's body disappear in the dark rock shadows. A tire bounced high in the air and spun out of sight. Luther clapped his hands and nodded to Max, who had his arms wrapped around his ribs, and they walked back to the car.

Chapter Twenty-One

It was six thirty Saturday morning when Gene crossed the drawbridge into Wildwood and turned into the spacious parking area reserved for the fishing fleet. The sun was rising through the haze; seagulls squawked noisily overhead. Taking the cooler full of ice and Mountain Dew, Gene handed the heavy-duty spinning rods to the boys. They followed him to the Rainbow, one of the smallest in the line of six party boats. Gene went to the stern and told the boys to place the poles in the metal rod holders.

"Why here?" Matt asked. "No one's in the front of the boat."

"That's the bow," Gene instructed.

"Well, no one's at the bow. We could sit there, and I could see where we're going."

"What's there to see? There's water in every direction."

"Then why not sit in the shade?" Matt pointed to benches on the side where the roof jutted over the deck.

"Because fishermen who know what they're doing set up here in the stern. The mate throws chum into the water, and it drifts to the back of the boat."

"What's chum?"

"Ground-up fish and slime," Gene answered. "Bluefish school up and feed on the chum. If you toss your bait in the middle of it, you'll catch bluefish."

"The deadly bluefish." A confident smile on his face, Matt placed his hand on the Roman death hammer under his belt. "Last night, you made it sound like a big deal, but those choppers don't frighten me."

"It is a big deal," Conner said. "Dad and I were at Fortescue last summer. There was a family swimming right off the beach. A fat lady sat in an inner tube laughing and slapping her feet in the water. She had this luminous silver paint on her toenails."

"It sounds like a good time."

"It was a good time, Matt, until a school of bluefish chased these baitfish into the shallows. Of course, all the baitfish darted for the safety of the inner tube. When the lady saw them, she began shrieking and splashing around. The bluefish attacked everything. Dad and I ran over and helped the lady to the beach."

"What happened to her?" Matt asked.

"You sure you want to know?"

"This ain't *Jaws* here. Sure, I want to know."

"It wasn't pretty, Matt. With that silver glow on her feet looking like bait, the lady didn't have a chance. The bluefish chewed off her toenails and both baby toes."

"Bullshit!" Matt exclaimed.

"Conner described it just the way it happened," Gene verified.

"Thanks for telling me. I feel great now. Like, I'm scared shitless."

"Why be scared, Matt? Did you paint your toenails this morning?"

"No, Mr. Brooks, I didn't."

"Then relax. And besides, you have your Roman death hammer."

"That's right," Matt said, slapping the handle inside his belt. "No bluefish is gonna mess with Dis Pater."

A truck backed up to the dock, and a school-aged boy got out. Quick and agile in his movements, he had a tanned face, thin patches of skin peeling on his forehead. He wore sunglasses and a

Philadelphia Phillies red-and-white T-shirt. Dropping the gate, he unloaded brown boxes and carried them to the Rainbow.

"That's frozen chum," Gene said. After storing the boxes, the boy pulled on yellow deck pants. Gene walked over, introduced himself, and paid for Conner and Matt.

"Are they in the pool?" the boy asked. Gene nodded, and after he gave the boy twenty dollars and an additional two dollars for a burlap sack, they walked to Matt and Conner.

"This is Robby, the first mate," Gene said, tying the sack under the rod holders. "I put you both in the pool, so try to catch at least one fish. And pay attention to Robby. The boat's going to be packed. Just keep your mouths shut and don't annoy the real fishermen." Gene stared directly in the faces of the two boys. "You hear me?" Gene turned, stepped on the ladder, and climbed down to the dock.

"Yes," Conner shouted after him, "I hear you! Everyone on the dock heard you!"

"What's the pool?" Matt asked.

"It's the money that goes to whoever catches the biggest fish. Sometimes it's hundreds of dollars."

Cars and trucks began racing into the parking lot. Slamming doors, the passengers got out quickly and rushed to board the Rainbow. Soon all the spots on the stern and along the sides were taken. Some of the rods jutting out of the holders were six feet long; others were over ten feet.

A station wagon drove up and stopped in front of the Rainbow. The driver was a slight middle-aged woman dressed in slacks and a yellow blouse. Opening the back door of the wagon, she slid out a wheelchair. A veteran dressed in a brown military uniform struggled out of the wagon. He was medium build and had muscular arms and shoulders. His face was clear, showing handsome features mixed with a deep sense of gloom. Leaning on the woman's shoulder, he limped to the Rainbow.

Wearing a white cap, the captain appeared out of nowhere. He was big-chested and had a neatly trimmed mustache and beard. The captain and Robby helped the crippled veteran get into the boat.

Robby set up the wheelchair and fishing gear next to the cabin door. The woman kissed the man on the forehead and went back to the wagon.

At a few minutes to eight, the captain started the engine, sending vibrations the length of the boat. Horn blasting loudly, a mud-crusted white van careened to a stop and double-parked. An unshaven and overweight man burst from the door.

"Get us a good spot, Ike!" the driver shouted.

"Don't worry," Ike said, and he rushed to the ramp. Dragging a cooler and wearing a white wife-beaters shirt, Ike was sweating profusely. He kicked gear out of the way and squeezed into a small space along the side.

The driver, who was extremely thin, locked the van's door, grabbed a plastic tackle box, and hurried to the Rainbow. He was dressed in red Bermuda shorts, red tennis shoes, and a red cap. His eyes were narrow slits under the cap.

"He looks like a weasel," Matt said.

"His friend Ike is huge, maybe two tons," Conner observed.

"Let's go fishing!" Ike shouted. He removed a bottle of Jack Daniels from the cooler, unscrewed the cap, and taking a drink, he burped spray over the railing.

With the motor chugging and clouds of gray smoke covering the stern, the Rainbow left the dock, drifted under the elevated drawbridge, and entered the main channel. After a fifteen-minute ride in the placid calm of the channel, the Rainbow crashed against the ocean surf. The boat lifted high in the air and slammed into the first series of waves.

Suddenly, the cabin door burst open, and a man, with a young boy holding onto his shirt, ran to the railing and threw up over the side. Legs wobbly, ocean spray showering his body, the man dropped to the deck and burped a stream of yellow-and-brown liquid that flowed down his chin. The man lifted his hand and wiped at the mess, spreading it over his face. The boy started to cry.

"Conner, did your dad ever get sick like that?"

"No," Conner answered. "My dad never gets sick."

When the Rainbow anchored over the Coral Beds, Robby began spooning chum over the side. The fishermen stuck chunks of mackerel on their hooks and dropped them into the water. The current slowly pulled the bait toward the oily slick. Birds dropped out of the sky; dark fins sliced through the water, and the ocean began to boil in the morning sun.

Using an underhand flipping technique, Conner showed Matt how to cast the bait. Within seconds after the mackerel hit the slick, Matt's rod bent, the sudden force knocking him against the railing.

"Oh, no!" he shouted. The fish pulled him around the corner and up the side of the boat. Robby rushed over and showed him how to keep clear of the other lines.

"Oh, yes!" Conner shouted. His rod bent, and line began zinging off the spool. Grasping the rod with both hands, he followed a few yards behind Matt.

"You, too?!" Matt shouted when he saw Conner approaching.

"Me, too!"

Matt and Conner stood shoulder-to-shoulder at the bow. Their rods bent sharply, and when the boat lifted and fell with the waves, their bodies slammed against the railing. As the fish ripped out line, Matt struggled to get the rod straight in the air. At times the rod twisted clumsily in his grip, the rounded handle sinking deeply into his abdomen.

"This is hard work!" Matt shouted. "He's damn big!"

"Not as big as mine," Conner bragged, bringing his fish near the boat. Robby rushed over and gaffed it. Minutes later he gaffed Matt's fish and dropped the body on the deck.

"About fifteen pounds," he said. "Nice catch."

"My first bluefish." Matt looked at the slick dark body slapping against the deck. Luminous eyes stared upward; Matt stepped closer.

"I wouldn't do that," Conner warned.

"Do what?" Just as Matt asked the question, the bluefish clamped down on his sneaker. Matt screamed, losing his balance; Conner grabbed him.

"I tried to warn you."

"Damn *Jaws* got me!" Matt grimaced. The bluefish tail pounded on the deck, and with each motion, it crunched harder on the sneaker. Matt's leg was shaking.

"Holy shit!" Matt grabbed the death hammer from under his belt and brought it down with all his strength on the skull of the bluefish. The metal sliced through the skin, flattened the gills, red filaments sticking straight in the air. Slapping its tail, the sleek body shivered and then lay motionless on the deck. Matt tried to jiggle his toes but couldn't.

"The son of a bitch isn't letting go!" In a frenzied motion, Matt began slamming the hammer into the bluefish. Pieces of bone and bloodied skin flew in the air. Finally, crushing the choppers to small fragments, Matt forced the jaws open and pulled his sneaker free. Conner came over and grabbed the bluefish by the tail.

"Good job, Matt. You and Dis Pater are a deadly team." Conner smiled and threw the bloodied remains over the railing. Shrieking seagulls splashed into the water. The boys walked back to the stern; Matt had a slight limp.

"How's your foot?"

"Mangled, but fine," Matt answered. He picked up a mackerel head, stuck the barb of the hook through its eyes, and flipped the bait far into the chum slick. "Conner …"

"What?"

"Don't tell Mr. Brooks about my sneaker. If he asks about it, tell him anything you want. Tell him a pit bull chewed on it. But don't mention anything about the bluefish."

"I won't say anything. Dad probably won't even notice it."

"Your dad notices everything."

Conner and Matt caught bluefish after bluefish. The deck of the

Rainbow was covered with blood and tubes of excrement. A squid with long, stringy tentacles clogged a drainage hole. The stench of rotten bait and dead fish lingered in the air. By noon, Conner's burlap sack was filled with bluefish. He reached into the cooler, pulled out two cans of Dew, and gave one to Matt.

"Did you see the soldier in the wheelchair?" Matt asked. "He's clueless. He hasn't caught anything."

"There's a reason for that, Matt. He's got that boat rod, and he's using a heavy sinker. His bait drops below the chum. There's no fish down there."

"We caught so many. Let's give him some of ours."

"I have a better idea. Let's give him our spot and my spinning rod. Then he can catch his own fish." Conner stuffed his rod in the holder, and the boys walked up the side of the boat. The veteran was sitting in the wheelchair, the rod balanced on the railing.

"How're you doing?" Conner asked, moving next to the wheelchair.

"I haven't caught one fish," the man said, a dismal expression on his face. "The only person worse off than me is that guy sleeping in the cabin."

"He's seasick," Matt said.

"You guys are doing great. I see your bag is full."

"That's because we're in the stern," Matt said knowingly. "That's where you should be. We're taking a break now, so you can use our spot. What do you say? Do you want to catch some monster bluefish?"

"Damn right, I do." He began reeling in his line. "It's really important that I catch something."

"Why?" Matt asked.

"I promised my wife fresh fish for dinner. My big-mouthed neighbor Goofus was there. Goofus was a peacenik. We don't get along. He said I was too crippled to go fishing. I have to show them. I have to show them both. Thanks for helping. What's your name?"

"My name's Matt, and this is my best friend, Conner."

"I'm Tom Rawlings," the man said, shaking hands with the boys.

"What's your rank, soldier?" Conner asked.

"Sergeant."

"Were you in Vietnam?"

"For a few months," Rawlings answered, nodding at his legs. "Then this happened."

"I'm sorry," Conner said.

"It's taken a while, but I've adjusted. I'm ready to fish. I sure hope I catch some."

"I guarantee you'll catch enough fish to feed your neighbors, even that damn Goober," Matt announced confidently.

"Goofus," Rawlings corrected.

"Goofus it is." Matt spun the wheelchair around and pushed it down the deck. "Coming through!" he shouted. "Coming through!"

Squeezing next to the fishermen, reclaiming his space, Conner secured the wheelchair against the railing. Matt twisted a hunk of mackerel on the hook and cast it into the chum. As soon as he gave the rod to Sergeant Rawlings, line began peeling off the reel.

"Fish on!" Conner shouted.

"What the hell!" Rawlings exclaimed. Leaning forward and gripping the rod with both hands, he was lifted in the air. Conner and Matt caught him by the shoulders and pushed him back into the wheelchair. The fish changed direction, ripping the line through the water. Robby rushed over and moved people out of the way.

"It's moving fast," he said, almost apologetically. "You'll have to follow it, or you'll tangle everyone."

Conner released the lock and turned the wheelchair around. Shouting "over" and "under," he maneuvered the wheelchair cleanly through the jumble of lines. One fisherman in a red flannel shirt got out of the way and broadcast in a loud voice.

"You got 'em, General! You done caught Moby Dick!"

Reaching the bow, Conner secured the wheelchair; Rawlings was pulled against the metal railing. Suddenly the fish dived. The taut line stretched and vibrated, sending droplets of water in the air. Grunting loudly, red veins appearing the length of his neck, the sergeant had difficulty holding the rod.

"Are you tired?" Conner asked.

"No, but I sure could use something to drink."

"I'll get it," Conner said. Giving control of the wheelchair to Matt, Conner ran, slipping and sliding, to the stern. He pulled a Mountain Dew from the cooler and raced back. Rawlings gulped down the Dew, grimaced, and began to pump the rod. Slowly, he gained line, and after ten minutes, he had half the spool filled. His chest heaved; Rawlings slumped back in the wheelchair.

"If you want, I can reel some," Conner said.

"Thanks, but I'm fine. I'm the one who has to feed the family."

Just then there was a whirring sound, and the line began to slant upward. Matt ran to the railing, shouted, and pointed at the water. Twenty yards away a dark form exploded vertically from the waves. Balanced on its tail, the giant bluefish shook its head, spewing chum in all directions.

"It's a monster!" Matt shouted.

"The biggest one I've seen this year!" Robby proclaimed. When Sergeant Rawlings lifted the rod high, line spiraled out of the reel, and the bluefish began moving back toward the stern.

"After him!" Conner shouted, and he spun the wheelchair around. Trying to avoid the careening wheelchair, the fishermen were shouting and laughing.

"You still playing with Moby?" the man in the red flannel shirt said with enthusiasm. "What's the problem, General. Didn't you bring no grenades wit' you?"

The laughter was loud, the shouts supportive. Conner reached the railing, and bracing his feet on the slippery deck, he locked the wheelchair into place. Robby told the other fishermen to bring their lines in. His shoulder and arm muscles bulging, Sergeant Rawlings brought the fish closer to the boat. Perspiration streamed down his face.

"Matt," Conner said quietly, "I'm worried. Sergeant Rawlings is exhausted."

"You already asked to help, and he said he was fine."

"I know. He's stubborn like Dad. Can you keep an eye on him?"

"Sure, Conner, I'll keep both eyes on him."

After another five minutes, Robby swung the gaff into the side of the bluefish. When he tried to lift the fish out of the water, the weight pinned him against the railing. The captain rushed over, and grabbing onto the gaff, he and Robby hoisted the giant bluefish over the railing and slammed it onto the deck. Blood spurted on Rawlings's shoes and pants. The captain walked to the wheelchair.

"Congratulations," he said, shaking the sergeant's hand. "It should win the pool."

"It's got to be the biggest fish on the boat," Conner affirmed.

"Thanks," Sergeant Rawlings said. His lips were pressed tightly together; his face was pale. "I need to rest," he said weakly. "Can you take me to the cabin?"

"Sure." Conner motioned to Matt, and they pushed the wheelchair through the door. The seasick man was sprawled on a bench. His son sat with him.

"Dad doesn't speak or do anything," the boy said nervously.

"He'll be fine," Conner assured him. He and Matt pushed the wheelchair to an empty booth, and Sergeant Rawlings pulled himself onto the cushioned seat. Taking a measured breath, he lowered his hands to the table and looked at the boys.

"I'm taking a nap. You two continue fishing." Conner didn't move; the sergeant looked at him. "Go on. Get out of here. That's an order, soldier." Sergeant Rawlings motioned to the door. After exchanging glances, Conner and Matt stepped outside the cabin.

"I don't like leaving him alone," Conner said. He and Matt jumped out of the way when Robby rushed by. Hearing loud shouts and whistles, they followed Robby to a crowd of fishermen surrounding Ike and Weasel.

"They've got themselves a trophy fish," the man next to Conner said. "But I don't know whose fish it is. They're both fighting over the rod."

Sweating profusely, the rod handle buried in his massive belly, Ike cranked on the reel. Assisting him, Weasel pulled on the rod with one hand and held the bottle of Jack Daniels with the other.

"I can't see *chit*!" Ike yelled, wiping at his eyes. "You take it!"

"Hold on a second," Weasel said. Handing the bottle to Ike, he grabbed the rod. Weasel's feet slid on the deck, and the fish surfed him down the railing.

"There it is!" Robby pointed to the line slicing through the rolling waves. A long dark shadow moved slowly upward, and the bluefish broke the surface.

"A fuckin' whopper!" Ike shouted. He drained the Jack Daniels and threw the bottle spinning at the bluefish.

"Damn it! Help me!"

"Don't worry, partner. I've got your back." Grabbing the rod with Weasel, Ike helped pull the bluefish next to the boat. Robby gaffed it on the first attempt and lifted the bluefish out of the water. Looking at the massive body, Weasel jumped in the air and bellowed.

"It's the pool fish! Whoopee, it's the pool fish!" Opening the cooler, Weasel pulled out another bottle of Jack Daniels and began strutting around. Ike grabbed the bluefish by the tail, and biceps bulging, he lifted it triumphantly in front of the other fishermen.

"Thanks for your contributions," Ike proclaimed. "The pool money is mine."

"Ours," Weasel corrected. He opened the burlap bag on the railing, but when Ike lowered the fish inside, the cord snapped, and the fish flopped to the deck.

"Holy chit!" he said. "It's too damn big!" Then kicking the fish under the bench, he turned to Weasel. "Keep that fish wet. We ain't losing the pool money on no dried-up fish."

"Sure thing," Weasel said. He began pouring Jack Daniels on the fish; Ike slapped him on the side of the head.

"Use water, you dumb-fuck," Ike instructed, and he sat down heavily on the bench. Matt nudged Conner in the shoulder.

"Do you think it's the pool winner?"

"It's gonna be close," Conner admitted.

A man turned the corner and shouted at him, "Hey, there's something wrong with your friend in the cabin."

"Jeez, no!" Conner grabbed Matt, and they rushed to the cabin. Looking through the salt-specked window, he saw the wheelchair jammed against the door. Rawlings was sprawled on the floor; Conner crashed his shoulder against the door. The wheelchair rattled loose and rolled the length of the cabin, stopping against the sergeant's outstretched hand. Conner, Robby, and Matt burst into the room. Making a whimpering noise, the boy on the bench held his father's head.

"He's dead," the boy said sadly. The sergeant's eyes were closed, and there was blood on his forehead. Robby knelt next to the body.

"Is he all right?" Conner asked, his legs wobbly.

"I don't know." Robby placed a hand over the sergeant's chest. "His heart's beating." Rawlings's bloodshot eyes opened, and his pupils stared at them. The sergeant's lips barely moved.

"What's up, soldier? I must have fallen asleep."

"On the floor?" Conner asked. He and Matt slid the sergeant back into the booth.

"I had this nightmare. I thought I was back in Vietnam." Rubbing his eyes, he looked at the mate. "Do you have coffee on the Rainbow?"

"Sure do," Robby said, and he left the cabin. Conner and Matt sat down opposite the sergeant. Conner studied the hard lines on Rawlings's face; the blood on his forehead; and the cracked, rough skin around the edges of his eyes.

"How old are you, Sergeant Rawlings?"

"Today, I'm not so sure. But yesterday, I was twenty-six."

"You remind me of my dad."

"Is that good?"

"I don't know. I think it's good, but I don't really know anything about you or Dad or the Vietnam War. I guess I'm just dumb."

"I don't think you're dumb. I'm glad I met you. I'm glad I met both of you. I'm glad we're friends."

Robby burst into the cabin and gave the sergeant a steaming cup of coffee. In his other hand, Robby was holding a blue pillow with a golden globe and an anchor sewed on the front. He fluffed it into position and placed it behind the sergeant's head.

"The captain wanted you to have his pillow. He said it would be better than sleeping on the floor. He said you should bring it on all your trips."

"You bet I'll bring it." Sergeant Rawlings finished drinking the coffee with a big gulp and placed the cup on the table. "That's just what I needed."

"We should go outside," Robby said. "It's time to weigh the fish for the pool."

"How much money's in it?" Matt asked.

"It's a Rainbow record," Robby said. "Four hundred and twenty dollars."

The scale was an iron bar hanging from the ceiling. It had a massive hook at each end. The weight of the sergeant's fish dropped the bar nearly vertical. A proud smile on his face, Sergeant Rawlings sat in the wheelchair next to the scale. Dragging all sizes of fish, a line of excited, quarrelsome pool members walked up, and as each entry lost to the monster fish, the smile on Sergeant Rawlings's face grew wider. Pulling his fish off the hook, the last contestant walked away.

"Get out of my way!" a voice shouted. "Get out of my way!"

"It's Two-Ton," Matt said, watching Ike push through the crowd. He was dragging a wet and bloodied bluefish along the deck. Weasel was a step behind him kicking at the tail.

"Here's the pool winner!" Ike proclaimed. He stuck the fish on the scale. The weight lifted the sergeant's fish in the air. When the bar steadied, both fish were parallel.

"It's a tie!" someone shouted.

"Come on!" Ike ordered. He slid his hand down the side of his bluefish. Rough waves rocked both fish back and forth. Then Ike's fish dropped slightly.

"Mine's heavier!" Ike shouted. "I've got the money fish!"

"We've got the money fish," Weasel corrected. "Whoopee!" he brayed, and he and Ike danced around the scale. "Whoopee!"

"Sorry," Robby said, glancing at the sergeant. He took the pool money from his pocket. Matt moved closer and studied the two bluefish.

"Wait!" Matt yelled. "Wait a minute!" He lifted Dis Pater and walked to the scale.

"Hey!" Weasel shouted. "What the fuck you doing?"

Matt didn't answer. With a quick motion, he sliced the pointed tip of Dis Pater through the belly of Ike's bluefish. Intestines, globs of blood, and thick slimy fluid spilled over Matt's sneakers. Then three lead sinkers fell out of the belly and hit the deck with loud thumps. The circle of fishermen grew silent; Ike's mouth dropped open. The fisherman in the red flannel shirt shouted loudly, "You cheatin' bastards!"

"Kick 'em off the boat!"

"Ike's fish is disqualified!" Robby announced in a loud voice. "The veteran wins the pool!" There were loud cheers and hand clapping.

"This is *bullchit*!" Ike shrieked. Red-faced and sweating profusely, Ike went to the scale, pulled the bluefish loose, and threw it over the railing. As soon as it hit the water, seagulls dove and began ripping away chunks of meat. Robby walked to the wheelchair and handed the thick wad of bills to Sergeant Rawlings.

"Thanks for helping," Sergeant Rawlings said. He peeled off some bills and gave them to Robby. Other fishermen came up and congratulated Rawlings.

"No doubt in my mind, General. You done caught Moby Dick," the man in the red flannel complimented.

"Conner and Matt," Robby called. He held a Polaroid camera in his hand. "Come and stand next to the sergeant." Robby took pictures of the three fishermen and the money bluefish hanging from the scales. He gave them each a copy.

"Thanks, Robby," Conner said. He and Matt walked to the bow. The anchor chain made a loud grinding noise.

"Holy *chit*, Matt, how the hell did you know about the sinkers?"

"I was outside when you were talking with Sergeant Rawlings. Ike was there gulping Jack Daniels. Weasel was next to him looking around with those shifty eyes of his. Then Weasel took those three sinkers out of his plastic box, bent low, and shoved them one at a time up the fish's anus."

Conner laughed and slapped Matt on the shoulder. The anchor chain rattled loudly and locked into place; the boat lurched forward. Conner and then Matt grabbed onto the railing with both hands. Mighty waves crashed across the bow of the Rainbow; wind and salt spray washed over their bodies.

It was low tide when the Rainbow reached the dock. Dragging coolers and burlap bags, some with tails hanging over the side, the fishermen stepped up to the platform. The captain and Robby helped Sergeant Rawlings carry his trophy fish to the station wagon. Waiting by the open door, his wife laughed and kissed her husband. Sergeant Rawlings saw Conner and Matt with their cooler and headed their way. Spinning the wheelchair to a stop, he spoke in a soft, clear voice.

"I really appreciate you two taking the time to help me. But I don't understand why."

"Why what, Sergeant?"

"Why you helped me. I've been on that boat three times. I've never caught any fish. Once the captain wanted to refund my money, but I refused. He was the only one who showed any interest. No one else cared. Why did you two care about me?"

"Oh, that's easy to answer," Conner said. "It's for what you did."

"What I did?"

"You're like Dad. You fought for my country." Conner jumped to attention and saluted. "Thanks."

"Yeah, thanks." Matt saluted also. Then he began pumping the sergeant's hand. "You're awesome! You won the pool! Whoopee!" They all began laughing; tears sparkled in the sergeant's eyes.

Gene parked the jeep at the end of the lot. He was walking toward the Rainbow when he heard the laughter and saw Conner and Matt and the veteran in the wheelchair. The veteran shook hands with the boys and returned to his car. The captain approached Gene and pointed to the boys.

"Do you know these two?"

"Yes, the taller one's my son."

"Can I talk to you for a minute?" The captain led him to the side of the dock. After a brief conversation, the captain's voice loud at times, Gene returned to the boys.

"Conner, what'd you and Matt do on the Rainbow?"

"We caught a lot of bluefish."

"Yeah, we caught a whole lot of bluefish," Matt affirmed, sliding his ripped sneaker out of sight.

"Why you asking, Dad? I saw you talking to the captain. What'd he say?"

"Is that all you did, catch fish?"

"No, Dad. We did a lot of things. We met this veteran, Sergeant Rawlings. He was handicapped. He was in a wheelchair."

"Did you annoy him?"

"No, he's our friend. What's wrong? What did the captain tell you?"

Gene didn't answer. He moved closer to the two boys. Cars started pulling out of the parking lot. Seagulls darted low over the cleaning stations. The imposing figure of the captain appeared at the railing and stared at them from the stern of the Rainbow.

"What'd he say?" Conner asked again.

"The captain said if you ever needed a job, you could work for him as first mate."

"Me, too?"

"You, too, Matt. The captain was impressed. He said you both went out of your way to help the veteran."

"The captain was so busy. He really noticed us?" Conner asked.

"He sure did." Gene turned his attention to Matt. "Yesterday you learned about toughness when you pulled the snapper out of the river. Today you learned something more important than being tough. You helped a stranger. You learned about compassion."

"What about me, Dad?"

"You've always had compassion, soldier. I'll talk to you about toughness after you nail your first turtle shell to the garage." A breeze blew across the parking lot, and Gene covered his nose. "You two smell like fish chum. Take those sneakers and socks off and throw them into the trash before you get into the jeep."

"What?" Conner asked.

"You heard me."

"But, Dad!"

"Take them off, or you can both walk back to the house."

"No way am I walking," Conner grumbled. He removed his sneakers and socks and threw them into the barrel. Matt removed his sneakers, and when he cautiously slipped off his socks, Gene looked at the cuts in the skin.

"What happened to your toes, Matt?"

"Nothing," Matt said. "Nothing happened."

"Yeah, nothing happened, Dad." Conner started to walk toward the jeep, but Gene stepped in front of him.

"Wait. You both still stink. You'd better throw away your shirts and jeans."

"Jeez ..."

"You heard me."

Conner looked at Matt. Shaking his head, he undressed quickly, retrieved the picture from his jeans pocket, and threw everything into the barrel. Matt did the same. Then clad in their boxer shorts, they ran across the parking lot. Conner had some tan, but Matt's body was pale. A horn sounded from the road, and two girls waved at them through the open window of their car. Conner waved back, and he and Matt jumped into the jeep.

"They think you're hot, Matt."

"They're right, Conner. I'm hot, and I smell real manly."

"You both smell like chum," Gene said. He got into the jeep, turned on the engine, and drove out of the parking lot. When they stopped at a red light, Conner showed him the Polaroid. The huge bluefish hung from the scale, and next to it the veteran held a wad of green bills in his hand. Their shirts smeared with blood, Conner and Matt stood on either side of the wheelchair. They had their hands solidly on the veteran's shoulders; they had exuberant smiles on their faces.

"You did well, soldier," Gene said. "You, too, Matt. I'm proud of both of you." The light turned green, and he drove through the intersection. "When are you meeting the girls?"

"Cindy said their house is a block off the boardwalk. Last night, Alice shouted in the phone that she couldn't wait. They're planning to meet us at Morey's Pier."

It was ten o'clock; the boardwalk was crowded with people. Conner and Cindy walked through the entrance of Morey's Pier, a brightly lit amusement park that extended far into the ocean. The Ferris wheel in the center rotated a shimmering circle of red-and-blue specks of light that reflected in the waves rolling against the pier.

Holding a yellow teddy bear, Matt waited with Alice at the entrance to the pier. Without saying a word, she took his hand and led him down the steps to the beach. Walking to a lifeguard station, Alice first, and then Matt climbed to the wooden platform. Matt placed the teddy bear between them. The moon was full; bright stars twinkled overhead.

"I love Mr. Teddy," she said, pushing it out of the way. "This is the best time I've ever had at Wildwood, and I've been coming here for years."

"I had fun, too."

"Matt, I really like you."

"I like you, too."

"Then kiss me." Alice spoke softly and positioned her body closer. Waves crested and rolled white lines of foam along the sand; a warm, moist wind blew over their bodies.

"Now?"

"Yes, I want you to kiss me now, Matt."

"If you're sure."

"Yes, I'm sure."

"Okay." Hesitating a moment, Matt stared at her mouth, the glistening curve of her lips. Then he kissed her on the cheek and jerked back quickly.

"Not like that, Matt. Not there."

"Where?"

"Here," Alice said, and she kissed him on both lips. She positioned her hand on his jeans. Her fingers massaged his groin. Shivers ripped through Matt's body; his heart pounded.

Alice smiled. Her lips opened against his, and she slid her tongue into his mouth. Matt struggled against the pressure. Gasping for air, he coughed and pushed Alice away. His leg hit Mr. Teddy and sent it spinning off the platform. Matt lowered his head, and holding back tears, he covered his face.

"I'm sorry. I can't."

"It's all right, Matt."

"No, it's not all right. I don't understand what I'm feeling now. I'm scared."

"There's nothing to be scared of."

"Then, maybe it's something else." Matt stood up and looked at the shadows on her face, the wind blowing through her hair. "Let's go back."

Matt waited for Alice to descend the steps, and they started walking across the beach. Turning quickly, Alice ran back to the lifeguard platform, grabbed the yellow teddy bear, and caught up to him. Matt's feet left deep prints in the sand. When they reached the boardwalk, he saw Conner and Cindy standing at the railing.

Chapter Twenty-Two

Gene and Lieutenant Chase Butler sat on the porch steps of the beachfront house. There were two glasses and a half-empty bottle of Johnnie Walker Black on the floor between them. The full moon was bright on the horizon, dropping rays of light that crashed with the waves and left receding lines of glitter on the sand. The boardwalk at the edge of the yard was deserted. Gene filled the glasses and handed one to the lieutenant.

"I expected to see your wife and two boys."

"Beth left years ago. The court gave her custody of my sons. But Beth does need her vacation time, so every year she sends them to Wildwood for a week."

"How have they handled it?"

"They've changed. They grew up here. They used to love the beach and the boardwalk." The lieutenant pointed to the bright glow of light over the ocean. "That's Morey's Pier. We spent so much time on the rides and the Ferris wheel. Most nights we'd be the last ones to leave the water slide. Being with my sons ... those were the best days of my life." Chase took a drink. His hand trembled, whiskey spilling over the side of the glass.

"I don't know my sons now. They come here for the week and disappear. I see them on the first and last day." Chase twisted the glass in his hand, took another drink, and gazed at the ocean. "I don't have a family anymore. I don't have a life. To be honest, Gene, you're the only friend I have. But I guess there's a reason for that."

"What do you mean?"

"I mean that I got my friends killed on Hill 101."

"I was there, too."

"I know that, Gene." Lieutenant Butler fingered the scar on his forehead. Leaning back on one elbow, he spoke cautiously. "I never explained what happened that night."

"You don't have to explain anything."

"I need to talk about the attack," Chase said. "Maybe it'll help."

"Maybe we're beyond help, Lieutenant." Gene filled his glass and took a drink. Holding hands and listening to rap music, a young couple walked by. The music moved slowly down the boardwalk; waves broke against the sand. Chase spoke in a subdued voice.

"When the attack began, the VC were easy targets on the hill. We killed so many of them, but they kept coming out of the jungle. The bugle blew, and the second and third waves came faster. They ran over the bodies caught in the barbed wire. Just as the first VC reached the perimeter, I got Wally, Junior, and Frank, and we headed for the escape tunnel." Lieutenant Chase sat up, raised his head, and looked at Gene. "Harry and the VC were waiting in Captain Din's room. They shot Junior and Frank. Nothing serious. Junior was hit in the shoulder and Frank in the leg. Then they tied the barbed wire around our bodies and threw us on the cot."

Flickering red and white on the horizon, a buoy marked the deep channel. The dark shadow of an oil tanker moved sluggishly toward Delaware Bay. Grabbing the Johnnie Walker, the lieutenant filled his glass.

"I watched Harry use his knife. My men were alive and screaming. They suffered greatly. Harry was laughing. He cut around the edge of the hairlines and ripped off their scalps. I was terrified. I pissed all over myself."

"Harry was plenty terrified himself. He pissed volumes of urine."

"Then you caught up to him? I was afraid Harry would return home."

"Harry will never return home," Gene commented. Looking at the solitary buoy in the deep channel, he took a drink. "It was strange, Lieutenant Chase. All that time I was looking for Harry. In the end, Harry came looking for me."

Thick clusters of bamboo grew around the tree on the edge of the clearing. Nestled in the branches, thirty feet above the jungle floor, Gene Brooks was motionless. Patches of bark and leaves were woven into his long-sleeved shirt and fatigues; brown-and-green tints smudged his face and hands. A red handle and a white handle Arkansas Toothpick were in the sheath secured tightly around his back. Gene focused his eyes on the trail that snaked through the clearing. Suddenly, a black monkey with large oval eyes jumped and landed on a branch in front of him. It sat there, bared its teeth, and emitted a slight farting sound.

"Fuck off, monkey," Gene snarled. Staring past the monkey, he watched the change in the color patterns at the edge of the clearing. Strands of blond color seemed to explode out of the darkness. A shadow moved along the edge of the jungle.

We meet again, Gene thought. *After all this time, we finally meet again.*

The shadow descended into the tall sawtooth blades of elephant grass, and the blond color disappeared. Gene didn't move. Bird and insect sounds pierced the air. As the cacophony of noise grew louder, the shadow elevated into full view. Carrying an AK-47 and dressed in VC black pajamas, Harry walked slowly into the clearing. He maneuvered around the thorn-laden brush on both sides of the trail. When the blond hair was directly below, Gene dropped from the bamboo.

Howling at the sudden movement, the monkey scampered away. Startled, Harry looked up at the noise just as Gene crushed him to the ground. Air exploded from Harry's lungs. Gene swung his fist twice into Harry's forehead, knocking him unconscious.

A hemp belt holding patches of scalp and hair was wrapped around Harry's waist. Seeing painful visions of Wally, finding it difficult to breathe, Gene grabbed a handful of scalp and stuffed it into Harry's mouth. When he ripped off Harry's shirt and VC pajama pants, Gene noticed the skinning knife lashed to Harry's calf.

"You bastard," Gene muttered. He removed the knife, slid it into his pocket, and peered down at Harry. The blond hair reached to his shoulders. Except for the tanned face and arms, the skin was pasty. Gene lashed Harry's wrists together with the belt. Then in a deft motion, he sliced the Arkansas Toothpick across Harry's right calf muscle. Harry's eyes blinked open; his body quivered violently.

"You can't be crawling away," Gene whispered. Lifting the Toothpick, he cut through the left calf muscle. As Harry's body arched upward, Gene struck him in the head. Harry's eyes rolled, and he lost consciousness. Gene sheathed the Arkansas Toothpick and moved down the trail, retracing Harry's steps in the jungle.

Thirty minutes later when Gene returned to the clearing, Harry was gone. Treading cautiously, Gene heard rapid breathing and scraping noises. Gene followed the sound into the jungle shadows.

"You're a tough little traitor," Gene said, approaching Harry's body. He grabbed Harry's shoulders and dragged him back to the clump of bamboo.

Picking up the black pajamas, Gene wrapped one end around Harry's neck. He tied the other end around stalks of bamboo. Harry sat there moaning, his back pinned against the bamboo, his blond hair plastered wet over his forehead. Bending down, Gene pulled Harry's legs straight and flat on the grass.

"I guess I have time to listen to your story—like how beautiful your wife is and how talented your kids are. You could even tell me all the good reasons you became a traitor and how many Americans you've killed. Stuff like that might be interesting to know. But ..." Gene grabbed Harry's right hand and placed it on Harry's outstretched leg. Holding the wrist steady, he took the white Arkansas Toothpick from the sheath.

"But I don't give a fuck about any of that!" Gene brought the knife down with considerable force. The blade sliced through the wrist, through the leg, and then sank deep into the ground. Harry was impaled. His body jerked violently. The pajama noose tightened around his throat. His face turning blood-red, Harry slobbered bubbles of foam through the strands of hair protruding from his mouth. Yellow liquid streamed down his leg.

"At first, Harry, I wondered why they sent you out here alone. So I went back and studied your trail. Oh, it was good. I mean, all the signs you left for the real trackers. How many VC are working with you, Harry?" There was a dull explosion in the jungle, followed by muted screams and shouts.

"No one can help you, Harry. I placed three claymores along your trail." Gene removed the red Arkansas Toothpick from the sheath. He grabbed Harry's left hand and laid it flat on the pale skin of leg.

"On Hill 101, you killed them all, Harry. I guess that's what traitors do. But you shouldn't have done the torture and the scalping. Because one of them was family." There was a second explosion in the jungle. It was closer; shrill cries echoed through the trees.

Holding Harry's hand in place, Gene raised the Toothpick. Harry's leg trembled spastically. Thrusting down, Gene drove the Toothpick through the wrist, the leg, and firmly into the ground. Blood spurted in the air and mixed with the hot urine on Harry's leg. Harry lurched forward. Knotted together by the black pajamas, the pliant bamboo shoots shook violently; slender leaves broke loose, spun downward, and stuck in the pools of blood.

A third explosion went off, followed by a sudden, brief scream. Gene could see smoke rising through the trees. An eerie silence descended over the clearing. Then, emitting a shrill cry, a green-and-white parrot flew from the trees at the opposite end of the clearing. Gene took a quick glance at Harry and crawled into the bamboo

A thin figure holding an AK-47 stepped casually out of the shadows. The VC soldier walked down the path, stopped in front of Harry's naked body, and stared at the red and white ivory handles protruding from the legs. Flies buzzed from the shadows; they flew in circles before settling on the ripped scalp and hair stuffed in Harry's mouth. Harry coughed; his right eye opened to a narrow slit.

"*Farang*," the VC soldier mumbled. Harry's chest heaved upward; the outline of the rib cage pushed through the pale skin. Harry coughed weakly, and his body was still.

Rising up behind the soldier, Gene wrapped his forearm around the scrawny neck. The AK-47 dropped to the ground. Strengthening his grip on the soldier's neck, Gene looked down at the VC's face. The brown eyes blinked open and filled with tears.

"Just a boy," Gene said, and he released his death grip. Pulling the scalping knife from the sheath, Gene held the boy by the neck and sliced the blade across his cheek. "Show that to your VC comrades," Gene said in Vietnamese, and he released his grip. The boy tripped, regained his balance, and raced down the trail, disappearing in the jungle.

Gene stood over Harry for a moment. There was a loud flapping noise, and a gray buzzard, followed by a second, swooped down and alighted in the bamboo. Gene sheathed the scalping knife and walked into the dark shadows.

Slouched in the elephant grass, the boy-soldier waited. When only familiar bird sounds came from the jungle, he limped into the clearing. Walking cautiously, eyes darting in all directions, he approached the body propped against the bamboo. The protruding knives reflected rays of silver light that momentarily blinded him.

"Jungle Ghost," he whispered, and he reached for the white ivory handle. With a great effort, he pulled the knife out of the earth. Harry's wrist plopped into the pool of urine and blood. Fighting nausea, the boy-soldier gripped the second knife. Beady eyes glowing red, the buzzards hovered motionless in the bamboo.

Lieutenant Chase took a drink and stared at the ocean. The buoy in the distance cast a dim glow; a second tanker sailed across the horizon of moonlight and shadow. A black cat crept down the boardwalk, leaped to the sand, and disappeared. Eating French fries, Conner and Matt walked to the porch.

"You guys are out late," Gene said.

"We ushered Cindy and Alice to their house," Conner explained. A moist wind blew from the ocean. Gene coughed and motioned to Matt.

"Come here, Matt." Gene grabbed Matt's arm, sniffed his sweatshirt, and made a face. "Now I know why there are so many cats around. You smell like dead fish."

"I don't smell nothing," Conner said smartly. "And no one else did either. The boardwalk was packed. We had a great time. Well, I did, anyway. Matt looked seasick when he came back from the beach."

"You two should wash and go straight to bed. And don't stay up all night bullshitting like you do at the house."

"We don't bullshit, Dad. We discuss important things." Conner nudged Matt in the shoulder; French fries spilled onto the boardwalk.

"Sure, you do," Gene said. "Good night."

"Good night," they both said. Conner opened the screen door, and they went inside.

"That's what I miss the most," Lieutenant Chase said, getting to his feet.

"What do you miss, Lieutenant?"

"Simple family talk. I miss Beth and the boys, especially in the evening." Quiet for a moment, Lieutenant Chase stared past the boardwalk at the line of breakers rolling toward the beach. "Thanks for telling me about Harry. I'll sleep better tonight." Chase managed a smile and entered the house.

There were three rooms on the second floor of the beach house. Conner and Matt were in the middle bedroom. Lying on the top mattress of the bunk bed, his body wet with perspiration, Matt was wide awake. Below him, Conner had his hands folded behind his head. The ceiling fan hummed, rolling waves of heat across his body.

"Matt, it's so hot in here, I can't sleep."

"Conner, I have a bigger problem than the heat."

"What's your problem?"

"I can't talk about it because you'll laugh."

"What's the problem, Matt? I promise not to laugh."

"Okay, then." Matt hesitated. He took a deep breath and studied the blades of the ceiling fan. "I don't know what to do about Alice."

"You don't have to do anything about her, Matt. She thinks you're great."

"Not anymore. Not after tonight."

"Why? What'd you do? Did you go too far? Did you grab her tits?"

"No, I didn't grab any body parts. We were alone on the beach. Alice liked the teddy bear, and everything was cool. Then we moved closer, and I think I got scared. It was like I was in a nightmare. Nothing seemed to work."

"What didn't work?"

"Mostly my lips. I don't know how to kiss."

"Everyone knows how to kiss, Matt. You just put your lips together."

"I did that, Conner. But Alice started going wild with her tongue."

"The tongue's a good thing, Matt. It works with the lips. It gets you excited."

"I didn't feel any excitement," Matt admitted gloomily. "I didn't know what to do with her tongue moving around like that. My mouth filled up fast with a sweet juice. I almost choked, but it tasted good."

"Choked!" Conner laughed, but noticed the hurt expression on Matt's face. "Sorry."

"Then quit laughing and talk some sense to me. What can I do?"

"Well, Matt. All I can say is just do it back."

"Do it back!"

"Yes. Whatever she does, do it back to her. When she's done in your mouth, push your tongue into her mouth and move it around." Conner covered his lips to hide a smile.

"You make it sound easy."

"Maybe not at first, but it gets easier the more you do it."

"If it's so easy, why was I scared?" Matt asked. "Is that what you do with Cindy?"

"Sometimes."

"What do you mean, sometimes?"

"It's hard to explain. Cindy wants to do all these things. Sometimes I won't do them because I worry about what might happen. It's mostly about Mom and Dad."

"That's crazy, Conner."

"No, it's not. My parents weren't ready. They had me when they were young. They weren't even married. Then Dad went to Vietnam. All those years I didn't have a dad. I missed him. When he came home, he argued with Mom all the time. Now Mom's gone, and Dad's on the porch drunk every night. He never uses my name. He calls me soldier. It's like I'm part of his military unit, not his family. Jeez, I wish Mom was home. Sometimes I want to run away and live with her."

"You can't, Conner. I couldn't handle being alone again. Promise not to run away."

"I promise."

"Thanks," Matt said. "There's something else bothering me, Conner. My bed won't stop moving."

"Yeah, I heard you up there. You shouldn't jack off in bed. Go in the bathroom."

"I'm not jacking off." Matt leaned over the side and looked at Conner. "I'm serious. The whole damn bed's moving. I feel like I'm still on the Rainbow."

"It's natural to feel that way. Dad says your body adjusts to the rocking motion of the boat, and it takes a while for it to readjust to land."

"What about this?" Matt asked. He swung his legs over the side of the bunk and jumped to the floor. Lifting his T-shirt, Matt pointed at the dark bruise below his ribs. "It feels like someone kicked me in the stomach."

"I've got one of those, too," Conner said, sliding up his T-shirt, exposing the bruise. "When you're fighting a monster fish, the end of the rod digs into your stomach."

"You've got a little mark. My whole side's black and blue."

"You're all skin and bones, Matt. You need some muscle on your body. Maybe you should start working out."

"Maybe I should," Matt said, and he jumped to the upper bunk, landing heavily on the mattress. Moments later, he complained loudly, "The bed's still moving."

"This will help," Conner said. "Whoopee!" he shouted, kicking the upper springs, knocking Matt in the air. They both began laughing. In the adjoining room, Gene pounded the wall with his fist; the boys quieted simultaneously. Outside the window, seagulls alighted on the boardwalk and squawked noisily over the scattered pieces of French fries.

Chapter Twenty-Three

The low howl of a wolf pierced the evening sky. Dan Boonie opened his eyes. The strap from the helmet dangled in front of him, impairing his vision. When Dan reached for the strap, his muscles convulsed. Spasms ripped the length of his body. His leg burned. Dan gritted his teeth and lay motionless. In the desolate silence, minutes passed slowly. The sun dropped low in the sky and cast an icy, waxen glow over the mountain. Shivering, Dan slid off his helmet. It rolled down the mountainside, hit a rock, and shattered.

Dan sat up and tugged at his leg. There were bright flashes of silver and red. When the pain subsided, Dan saw a twist in his leg and how a fragment of bone protruded from a rip in his jeans. The glow of the setting sun disappeared; the sky turned gray and then dark. Extending his arm, Dan began pulling himself over rocks and tree branches. His body inched slowly upward. The night air turned colder, numbing his leg, congealing the blood around the exposed bone.

After two hours, Dan stopped. He heard the sound of engines and looked at the distant outline of the road. Headlights sliced through the darkness, and a car raced by. Spinning red-and-blue lights, a second car followed close on the bumper. Its siren momentarily blasted the silence.

"Luther and Max," Dan whispered. "And the police!" He thought about Lisa; tears rolled down his face. Dan pushed off forcibly. His body moved upward again. His muscles hardened. Rolling awkwardly on his side, he cracked his leg against a rock and lost consciousness.

Hours later, Dan opened his eyes to the sound of engines. Two cars careened down the side of the mountain. The revolving red-and-blue lights of the police car filled the night sky. Tires crunched dirt and stone; loose gravel rolled from the berm, hitting Dan in the shoulders and head. A few yards from the edge of the road, his heart beating wildly, Dan rested for a long time.

Moving out of the shadows, a wolf crossed the road and paced back and forth. When the night wind carried the scent of blood, the wolf lowered its head, sniffing the air. Trembling from the cold, Dan looked up and saw the wolf's silhouette; the glaring red eyes expanded and moved closer. There was a sharp snarling noise. A paw descended and dug giant claws into Dan's outstretched hand.

Working in the church, Andrew and Joyce heard the barking dog. When the noise grew louder, they walked in the darkness to Boonie's house. Straining at the leash, the Irish wolfhound paced, its deep chest expanding, its muscular neck arched high in their direction. The porch lights turned on, and Joseph and Grace Boonie walked through the door.

"Ruggs just started with the racket," Grace said, stroking the dog's head. "Dan's usually home to feed him by now. Something's wrong. I called Green Hollow. They said Dan left at noon. We were just about to go look for him."

"Joyce and I will go, too," Andrew volunteered.

"Thanks," Joseph said. "We'll take the road to the camp, and you can check the mountain. Dan likes to scout for deer up there."

Andrew and Joyce hurried back to the house. Andrew grabbed a spotlight and drove the truck back to the Boonies, who were just pulling out of the driveway. Barking loudly, Ruggs strained at the lease. Andrew turned the truck around, and just as he accelerated,

Ruggs broke the leash, raced across the yard, and jumped in the back of the truck.

"We have company," Andrew said to his wife. Ruggs slid the length of the truck bed, and his head pushed through the open window. Driving across the Barree bridge, Andrew stomped on the gas pedal.

With Joyce shining the spotlight, Andrew went through the intersection to Green Hollow Pike. They searched miles of empty road. Approaching the steep grade of the mountain, Andrew braked suddenly. Joyce directed the light on a dark form at the side of the road. Ruggs barked; his ears pricked, and he jumped out of the truck. Caught in the glare of the spotlight, the wolf turned just as Ruggs lunged. Ruggs clamped down on the wolf's throat, and the impact sent them both over the side of the cliff.

"Ruggs," Dan whispered weakly as the bodies of the dog and the wolf tumbled past.

Andrew slid the truck to a stop, and he and Joyce ran to the edge of the road. Joyce flashed the spotlight on the rocks and Dan's body. She cringed when she saw the twisted knee and the stark whiteness of the bone protruding from the jeans. Dan's eyes were open; his body was shaking against the rock surface.

"I'll call the ambulance," Joyce said, and she ran back to the truck.

Andrew bent down. When he removed his jacket and slid it over Dan, he saw Dan's lips move. Sliding next to the boy, Andrew listened intently. The words were jumbled, interrupted by long pauses. Joyce returned and put her hand on Andrew's shoulder.

"The ambulance is coming. And I called Joseph and Grace. They'll be here soon."

"Dan told me there's a girl named Lisa at Muddy Run Camp. She's in bad trouble. I'm going there now." Andrew looked at his wife, who was kneeling next to Dan. "Can you ride back with Joseph and Grace?"

"Yes, of course."

"I'll meet you at the hospital," Andrew said. He rushed to the truck and was pulling out when he saw car lights racing up the mountain. Through his rearview mirror, he saw the car brake to a stop; Grace Boonie opened the door and ran to the side of the road.

At three o'clock Sunday morning, Andrew drove around the pond, parked in front of the cabin, and stepped out of the truck. There was no wind, and dark clouds covered the moon. Frogs and crickets filled the darkness with noise. Taking his flashlight, Andrew looked at the empty porch, the stack of firewood piled on the steps, and the sign "Muddy Run Camp" hanging from the roof.

Climbing the steps, Andrew turned the doorknob, which rattled loosely. He walked to the window and swung the light from the fireplace to the sofa to the cushioned chairs. Mosquitoes and small moths began to fly in and out of the beam of light. Swiping at them, he steadied the light on the row of beer cans on the table.

Someone's been partying, he thought.

Returning to the steps, Andrew picked up a log and smashed the end into the door, shattering the lock. Andrew stepped inside the cabin and turned on the lights. He searched the kitchen and living room, and jumped the steps to check the bedrooms on the second floor. Returning to the living room, he slumped down on the sofa. The trophy mount on the wall caught his gaze. A policeman's cap was hanging from the antlers. Andrew walked over, picked it out of the cobwebs, and read the label.

"Officer Oliver Wright." Andrew shook his head when he read the words under the name. "With Love and Pride, Mom."

As Andrew stuffed the cap into his coat pocket, he heard a scraping sound coming from the wall. The large rug that covered the entire wall had a pack of wolves running through snow and dark forest. Jaws open and spewing foam, the wolves were on the heels of a large buck, its antlers stretching to the top corner of the rug. Andrew heard the scraping sound again. Moving closer, he lifted the rug and saw the door.

Andrew pushed the door open and stepped inside the room. The girl's body was in the corner. Her mouth was taped, and her hands and legs were bound with rope. While Andrew was untying the knots, he noticed the bruises on her legs and thighs. The girl made a groaning noise.

"This might hurt a little," Andrew said, and he ripped the tape from her mouth. Her eyes gleamed with moisture, but she remained quiet. "You're Lisa?"

"Yes," she said, wiping at the tears. "It was the guard from Green Hollow, wasn't it? Dan sent you."

"Yes."

"I knew he would." Lisa got to her feet, and Andrew helped her to the main room.

"We have to report this to the police."

"We can't do that," Lisa said.

"A policeman was here, wasn't he?"

"Yes. His name is Oliver. And the other two men are guards at Green Hollow. Their names are Luther and Max."

"Max is Oliver's older brother. I know them both. When they were boys, they came to my church." Andrew's face hardened. He grabbed the blanket from the sofa and placed it over Lisa's shoulders.

"Thank you," she said. "I don't know what to do now. I have no place to go."

"You can stay at our house. My wife's a nurse. She'll look after you."

They went outside and got into the truck. The full moon reflected a perfect circle in the pond. Three deer were on the bank, their heads lifting at the sound of the engine. As Andrew drove the truck past the pond, the deer bolted into the woods.

Early Sunday morning, Luther stopped the car at the Green Hollow guard station. Sitting next to him, Max was snoring. The glass window slid open; Earl James had a big smile on his face.

"Good morning, cuz. I got the call to report to work. Thanks for hirin' me again."

"I didn't hire you, Earl. And when you're on duty like now, call me Mr. Cicconi."

"Sure thing, cuz. I mean, Mr. Cicconi." Earl scratched the stubble on his chin. "Did you hear about Dan Boonie? They found his body this morning."

"When's the funeral?" Luther asked, nudging Max awake.

"Oh, Dan's not dead. His leg's busted up, that's all. They took him to J. C. Blair Hospital." Earl coughed loudly, stretched his head out the window, and spit on the ground. "He's not comin' back, is he? That boy stole my job the first time. I'm kind of worried he might steal it again."

"I wouldn't worry none about that," Luther said encouragingly.

"That's good news for me and the family." Earl did a complacent thumbs-up and slid the window shut.

"Son of a bitch." Max scowled. "What's it gonna take to get rid of that boy?"

"Right now I'm thinking it's gonna take a trip to the Brick Yard."

"I hear ya," Max said. "I'm looking forward to that. And the sooner the better."

Chapter Twenty-Four

A hazy mist covered Wildwood beach Sunday morning. Drinking his second cup of coffee, Gene watched shadowy figures walking in and out of the fog that was low over the boardwalk. A couple on a two-seated bicycle pedaled past the house. The wooden planks rumbled noisily. Rising with a bright glow, the sun burned through the fog. Tiny waves broke lines of bubbles in the sand; seagulls stood motionless in the foam. Pushing open the screen door, Lieutenant Chase stepped onto the porch.

"The boys have the jeep loaded," Chase said. "You were right about those two. I don't know what problems they were solving, but they talked all night."

"Probably discussing their girlfriends." Gene placed the cup on the table and walked with Chase to the street. Opening the door to the jeep, he turned to the lieutenant. "Thanks for putting up with us."

"It was no trouble. I'm glad you visited. I'm glad we had the chance to talk." They shook hands, and Gene got into the jeep. As Gene drove away, the boys waved at the lieutenant. When Gene reached the drawbridge, red lights flashed, and he braked in front of the descending wooden bar. Within seconds, the middle section of the bridge began to elevate. There was the sound of a horn from the channel.

"The Rainbow!" Conner yelled. He pulled Matt out of the jeep, and they ran to the railing. Cutting a foaming V-line of waves through the middle of the channel, the Rainbow approached the bridge. Robby stood at the bow; the boys waved and shouted his name. He whistled and waved back. The cabin door opened, and a woman, clutching a blue pillow, pushed a wheelchair onto the deck. The veteran in the wheelchair sat tall and straight.

"Sergeant Rawlings!" Conner shouted. Both boys were jumping up and down and hanging over the railing. The sergeant looked up; a big smile spread across his face. He waved his hand, and his wife also waved at the boys. The Rainbow passed under the bridge. The horn sounded again; the bridge began to vibrate, and the center section lowered with a loud grinding sound. Conner and Matt ran back to the jeep. The bar lifted, and Gene led the line of traffic onto the bridge.

"Dad?"

"What?"

"On the boat I asked Sergeant Rawlings how he injured his legs."

"What'd he tell you?" Matt asked excitedly.

"Why do you keep bothering people?" Gene interrupted. "It's none of your business what happened to his legs. You're both too damn curious." Gene threw change into the basket at the tollbooth and turned the jeep north on the Garden State Parkway.

"You're right, Dad. It wasn't any of our business."

"What caused it, Conner? Was he in a big battle? Did he kill any Communists?"

"Nothing like that, Matt. He was only a week in Da Nang, wherever that is. A supply truck backed into him and crushed his legs. At the hospital when the doctor told him he would never walk again, he said he wanted to kill himself."

"Damn," Matt said. "That's terrible."

"That's why you don't need to know everything," Gene said in a brusque tone, and he pulled into the passing lane.

"Dad?"

"What?"

"I'll never ask about Wally again."

The sun's glare flashed off the windshield. Gene remained quiet. Driving fifteen miles per hour over the speed limit, he raced by a truck. Blinking bright lights, horn blasting sporadically, a red Corvette sped to his bumper. Putting on the turn signal, Gene moved to the inside lane, and the Corvette roared past them.

Hours later as they approached the King of Prussia exit on the Schuylkill Expressway, Conner and Matt complained about being hungry. Gene pulled into Kentucky Fried Chicken and picked up a container of drinks and a bucket of legs and wings. He turned on Route 13, drove through Valley Forge National Park, and stopped at General von Steuben's huge black statue. Conner grabbed the bucket, Matt grabbed the drinks, and they walked to a bench overlooking the Grand Parade Ground. The boys were devouring the chicken and gulping down Mountain Dew when Gene sat down on the bench. There were large cumulous clouds in the blue sky.

"This tastes great, Dad." Pulling out a greasy drumstick, Conner pointed at the herd of deer grazing on the edge of the parade ground. "I wish I had my gun."

"The deer are protected here, soldier," Gene said. He looked at Matt, who dropped a chicken wing back into the bucket. "What's wrong, Matt? Aren't you hungry?"

"I feel guilty. We're sitting on this bench stuffing our faces with chicken."

"So?" Conner said, biting into a drumstick.

"In 1777, soldiers starved to death right here, Conner. I read about one of them in the book, *The Chicken Thief Soldier*. He stole a chicken to stay alive. The farmer killed him."

"That's crazy. A farmer wouldn't kill one of our soldiers. You're making this up."

"I'm not making anything up." He pointed to the blue-uniformed man standing in front of General von Steuben. "Go ask that park ranger about the Chicken Thief Soldier.

"Okay," Conner said. He walked over and politely addressed the man, who shrugged his shoulders. Conner returned and sat down on the bench.

"I was right. The ranger never heard of the Chicken Thief Soldier"

"He's probably just been transferred here and doesn't know anything."

"He said the park rangers know the important history."

"The Chicken Thief Soldier was important. I think he's more important than von Steuben or Lafayette. Come over here. I'll show you his marker." Matt led Conner and Gene to a large tree. Overhanging branches cast dark shadows on the ground. Matt pointed to a squared gray stone partially covered by grass.

"This is the Chicken Thief Soldier Memorial. No one knows the soldier's name. He was starving, went to a local farm, and was killed stealing a chicken." Matt noticed something white sticking out of the ground next to the marker. Bending down, he scraped the grass and picked it up.

"What'd you find?" Conner asked.

"A bone." Matt cleared off the dirt, studied it, and then shaking his head, he replaced it in the ground. "It's clear how the US government works. The influential generals get the big monuments. The common soldier gets a flat unmarked stone no one can find."

"That's not right," Conner said. "Sergeant Rawlings was injured in the war. There's no memorial for him. And none for you, Dad."

"Don't worry about me, soldier. I have my memorial."

"Can we go see it?"

"No, it's too far away."

"Where is it?"

"On the Ho Chi Minh Trail," Gene answered, and he walked toward the jeep.

It was midafternoon when Gene pulled into the driveway. Barking loudly, SenSay ran across the yard and jumped all over Matt. Matt filled SenSay's bowl with fresh water and joined Conner and Gene in the kitchen.

"Mr. Brooks," Matt said. "Last week, I found some old home movies at the mansion. Can we watch them tonight? I have the projector and everything."

"Sure."

"I'll call Cindy and Alice," Conner said. "They can come over. We can stay up late."

"Not too late, soldier. You have school tomorrow." Gene looked at the smug expression on Conner's face. "Oh, wait. Monday's a teacher in-service day, isn't it?"

"Yep," Conner said. "We're having a picnic on Blood Mountain."

"I think that mountain is the wrong place for a picnic."

"Why, Dad?"

"Because people disappear up there, that's why." Starting down the steps, Gene hesitated and looked at Matt. "Are your home movies better than *The Dukes of Hazzard*?"

"I don't know," Matt said. "I hope so."

"Me, too," Gene said. "You get everything ready for tonight. I'm going to the Huntingdon jail to see Pete Rogers." Gene walked across the yard to the jeep.

Driving over the speed limit, squealing tires on the multiple curves along the Petersburg Pike, Gene reached the Huntingdon County Prison in twenty minutes. He noticed one empty space in the parking area and braked in front of a large blue sign, "Reserved for Sheriff." The FritoLay van was next to the jeep. Gene walked to the back and opened the door. Except for a few crushed bags of potato chips, the van was empty. When he closed the door, the bold lettering under the Penn State Nittany lion caught his attention.

1968
Undefeated
11–0

"1968," Gene whispered, scraping his hand over the logo. Turning away, Gene went to the main entrance and hit the recessed button next to the door.

"What?" a voice squawked.

"I'm here to see Pete Rogers."

"Show me some ID, Mr. Brooks"

Gene slammed his Pennsylvania driver's license into the lens and was buzzed inside. Sitting at the desk, Oliver Wright was a middle-aged high-school dropout who had worked three years on his GED. He had a big head and a big mouth, which he was filling with potato chips. There was an empty bag of Lay's Sour Cream & Onion on the desk. Crunching at the chips, his mouth opened.

"You can't do that, Mr. Brooks. I mean it. You can't park in the sheriff's spot."

"Don't tell me what I can or can't do, Deputy Wright."

"I warned you. I'm just doing my job like I'm paid to."

"Is that part of your job, eating evidence from the van?"

"What evidence?" Oliver asked. "Oh, these?" He pushed the empty bag into the trash can. "I was gettin' hungry, that's all."

"Do you happen to live near Burnt Cabins?"

"Yeah, what's it to you?"

"Burnt Cabins was built over the ruins of a village called Dumb-Fifty."

"I don't know nothin' 'bout that history stuff."

"You don't know much about anything, do you?"

"I know my job as a deputy."

"Then do it. I'm here to see Pete."

"Hello!" Oliver said, looking amused. "You already told me that.

Go through that door and sit down and wait. And you'd best be careful."

"Careful of what?"

"The sheriff says Pete's dangerous. He rapes little girls and kills 'em."

"That's pure bullshit!"

Oliver coughed, and cracked pieces of chips dropped from his mouth. He hit the button; the lock on the door made a buzzing noise. Gene entered the small room and sat in a chair next to a thick glass window. Looking through the glass, he saw a folding chair, a table, and a microphone attached to a stand. The door slammed open, and Pete was shoved inside. Wearing an oversized orange uniform, Pete sat down and clicked on the microphone.

"Hi, Gene. Thanks for coming."

"Hi, yourself," Gene said, noticing the stubble and dark lines on Pete's face. "You look terrible. Is it that bad in here?"

"Sheriff Parks says I'm a child molester and keeps me locked up tight. The cell stinks. They won't let the kids visit."

"How's Sarah doing?"

"She's taking it worse than I am. She can't believe this is happening."

"None of us can. Don't worry. It'll be over soon. You'll be out on bail."

"The judge won't set any bail. He says the sheriff's got all that evidence they found in the van."

"I parked next to your van. I noticed the 11–0 Penn State sticker."

"1968 was a long time ago, Gene. Why think about that now?"

"Because—" Gene began. He stopped speaking when he heard a low humming sound. "They've got this room bugged?"

"Probably," Pete said.

"You bastard, Oliver!" Gene shouted.

"Your time's up in there!" Oliver announced loudly. A guard rushed into the room, grabbed Pete by the arm, and pulled him out of the room.

There was a long buzzing sound, and the door clicked open. Striding past Oliver's desk, Gene exited the building just as Sheriff Parks was getting out of his patrol car. The sheriff pulled the rim of the Stetson calvary low over his forehead and hurried across the street.

"Why the hell you parking in my reserved spot?" he shouted.

"It was empty when I got here. You run a nice office, Rosco. Do you always supply your employees with confiscated chips and pretzels?"

"That's none of your business, Gene. What are you doing here?"

"I came to see Pete."

"Why would anyone want to visit a child molester?"

"Pete's not guilty of anything."

"He's guilty. Pete will be in prison so long you won't recognize him when he comes out. And I'll spread the word. Our hard-core convicts know how to treat perverts."

"Why are you such a Dumb-Fuck?"

"*I'm* a dumb-fuck!" Parks said. "Wake up, Gene. Your friend's in jail. Your wife left you. You're a loser now. And you were a loser in high school. I can't believe we were on the same team together."

"That's it, isn't it?"

"What?"

"Basketball! You're still pissed off about basketball. The final game."

"I don't even know why Coach Port had you on the floor. You were no good. You averaged 1.8 points a game."

"Do you remember everyone's average?"

"No, just the highest and the lowest. Mine was 27.8 points per game. I led the league in scoring. In the league championship game, you were supposed to pass the ball to me."

"You had two guys on you. I threw it to Pete. He was open."

"I could score on two guys. I was doing it all year. So you pass the ball to your friend. Great decision! Pete misses, and we lose the championship."

"You still got your scholarship to Delaware," Gene said. "I wasn't surprised when they threw you out after one year."

"At least I made something of my life. Look at what you do for a living!"

"I'm good at what I do."

"You're a janitor! Who couldn't be a janitor?" Sheriff Parks laughed.

"Cleaning up's important work, Rosco. If people like you did your job, cleanups wouldn't be necessary."

"What the hell are you talking about?"

"You'd better hope you never find out," Gene cautioned. Getting into the jeep, he started the engine and backed out of the sheriff's parking spot.

It was dark when Gene reached the house. As he walked into the living room, he saw Cindy, Alice, and Matt on the sofa. Matt was holding an old shoe box. A white sheet was tacked to the wall, and the eight-millimeter projector was on a small table in the middle of the room. Gene sat next to the table and turned the switch. A dull square of light appeared on the sheet. As he slowly rotated the focus knob, the square brightened. Conner came from the kitchen and gave cans of Mountain Dew to Cindy and Alice. Matt opened the shoe box, took out a plastic reel, and gave it to Gene.

"Why this one?" Gene asked, threading the end of the film on the projector.

"It has 1956 on the label. I was born that year."

"I like baby movies," Alice said.

Baby movies, Conner thought. After turning off the ceiling light, he sat beside Cindy and looked at Matt in the shadows. Matt's eyes were open wide, and when the projector clicked into motion, they glistened in the light.

"I don't think this is a good idea," Conner whispered to Cindy. A series of numbers flashed on the sheet, and then the sheet filled with color. The sofa and cushioned chairs were dark green. Hanging low from the ceiling, the huge chandelier sparkled with light. Set in an ornate golden frame, the painting of Gainsborough's Blue Boy hung on the wall. Plumed hat at his side, the boy stood straight and tall, his feet firmly planted on a hillside of tree shadows and soft rock colors.

"The boy in the picture looks like you, Matt," Alice commented.

Not responding, Matt sat very still. He watched pensively as the camera angled toward the red-carpeted staircase. The person holding the camera began climbing the stairs. The image bounced up and down, sometimes showing red carpet, sometimes crystal chandelier, and sometimes the wooden banister. The image leveled at the top step and focused on a door.

"That's my room," Matt whispered above the ticking noise of the projector.

The camera moved closer, and a small hand, a woman's hand, pushed the door open. Inside the bedroom, the walls, the ceiling, and the carpet were blue. The camera moved through the door. There was a temporary loss of image when it swept across the bright light of an open window. The camera steadied and settled on a large pirate ship painted on the wall. Captain Hook was on deck brandishing a silver sword. He had an oversized head topped by a wide red hat with a white feathered plume. The ocean cracked frothing waves against the side of the ship. A crocodile with a gaping mouth waited in the water at the end of the gangplank. Alice laughed.

"The crocodile ate the captain's hand and his clock," she remarked. "Now whenever Hook hears a ticking sound, he panics. Hook's real funny."

"I don't think he's funny," Matt mumbled. "I hate Captain Hook. I hate the way he watches me."

The camera was placed stationary on a table. It focused on the rocker crib in the center of the room. The crib had a fancy laced hood over the top; the figures of Peter Pan, Wendy Darling, and Tinker Bell were painted on the side.

There was the sound of footsteps, and a woman wearing a yellow dress moved across the room. Her face was soft yet gleaming in the light. Captain Hook stared ominously in the background. The woman placed her hands around her waist, which was rounded and full in her pregnancy. When she smiled, Matt got up from the sofa, inched closer to the wall, and dropped to his knees in front of the sheet. His chest heaved.

"What's wrong?" Alice asked.

"I never saw my mom until now," Matt said, taking deep breaths.

The woman began to rock the cradle. There was a radiant glow on her face, and she laughed. It was a joyous sound that drifted lightly across the room. Breathing heavily, tears streaming down his face, Matt rose clumsily, painfully to his feet. His shadow shrouded the images on the sheet. The room was quiet except for the lingering sound of laughter and the steady ticking noise from the projector.

"Mr. Henry said I killed my mom," Matt whispered. He wavered for a moment. Then turning quickly, he rushed out the door. Matt stumbled down the steps, and arms swinging at his side, he ran across the yard. Barking loudly, SenSay chased after him.

Conner, Gene, and the girls burst through the screen door. They watched Matt stop at the river and collapse on the grassy bank. SenSay's barking turned to a whimper; the dog began licking Matt's face. Alice rushed across the road and sat next to them. Moonlight flashed waves of light over the glittering surface of the river.

"My mom's beautiful, isn't she?" Matt asked softly.

"Yes," Alice said, holding him tightly.

"I never knew. Until tonight, I never knew how much I loved her." Clouds moved over the moon, and the current in the river turned black. At the house, Cindy shut off the projector; Conner ripped the sheet from the wall. Gene opened the refrigerator, grabbed an Iron City, and sat on the hammock.

It was ten o'clock when Conner and Cindy went down the steps to the bicycles and called for Matt. After a few minutes, with SenSay following, Matt and Alice walked to the yard. Alice hugged Matt, and getting on her bicycle, she pedaled down the road with Conner and Cindy. Matt climbed the porch steps.

"Mr. Brooks, I want to drop Mr. Henry's glass eye in the Shadows of Death. I'm ready to go down the rapids"

"I've given this a lot of thought, Matt. Even for experts, the rapids are deadly. It's too dangerous for a kid."

"I'm not a kid. If you won't help, I'll go down the rapids myself."

"You should go to bed, Matt. You'll feel better in the morning."

Matt looked at Mr. Brooks for a moment. Then he opened the screen door and entered the house. Listening to the sound of Matt's footsteps, heavy and scraping on the floor, Gene jumped up from the hammock and shouted through the screen door.

"Matt, wait a minute!" He hesitated and lowered his voice. "Tomorrow I'll get the canoes ready. You can go down the rapids in the evening."

"Thanks, Mr. Brooks," Matt said, and he climbed the steps to his room.

The low howl of a wolf sounded from across the river. SenSay ran to the railing and began to bark. Picking up the dog, Gene carried him into the house. When Gene put him down, SenSay scampered up the steps to the bedroom. Gene took the shotgun from the rack and returned to the porch. Sitting on the hammock, the shotgun balanced across his lap, he swung back and forth in a slow arch.

Chapter Twenty-Five

Early Monday morning, Andrew replaced the receiver in the phone, unlocked the desk drawer, and took out a Colt .38. Opening the cylinder, he put in six rounds of ammunition. Joyce came through the door and saw him tuck the revolver under his belt.

"I never liked the idea of a gun in a church. Why did Gene give it to you?"

"For protection."

"Why are you taking it out now?"

"Dan just called. He told me he needed a gun."

"For what?"

"He didn't say."

"You don't know the reason, and you're still giving Dan a gun?"

"After what's he's been through, I'd give him a cannon."

"You're sounding more and more like your brother."

"Maybe I am. And that might be a good thing," Andrew said. "How's Lisa?"

"She seems okay, but she won't talk about what happened at Muddy Run. I tried to get her to call home, but she wouldn't. She's really worried about Ira. Can't you do anything?"

"I *am* doing something," Andrew said. "I'm taking this gun to Dan." Grabbing his jacket, he kissed his wife and left the church.

Twenty minutes later, the gun heavy under his belt, Andrew walked cautiously down the hall, around a group of nurses, and into the room. Dan's forearm was bandaged; the cast on his left leg was elevated. Andrew approached the bed and slid the Colt under the sheet.

"You're sure you need this?"

"I'm sure. Is it true what Dad said about Ruggs, that he made it home okay?"

"It's true, Dan. That's some dog you have. I took him a steak."

"Thanks," Dan said, a large smile on his face. "I can just see Ruggs eating a steak."

"What about you? Do you need anything else, like a knife or grenade?"

"No," Dan said, laughing. Then he grimaced at the pain.

"Sorry." Andrew straightened the sheet over the Colt. "Lisa wanted to come in and thank you, but Joyce said she should get some rest. And you'll need to rest, too. We can't figure out how you managed to crawl up that mountain with a fractured leg."

"I was worried about Lisa. She was worse off. I couldn't quit."

There was noise at the door, and Joseph and Grace Boonie walked into the room. Dan slid the revolver deeper under the sheet. After talking with the Boonies for a few minutes, Andrew left the hospital.

The sound of *Another Brick in the Wall* blasting from the window, Cain gunned the truck down the dirt road. Reaching the end of Polecat Hollow, he saw Becky on the porch and screeched the truck to a stop. She ran across the yard. Abel got out and opened the door, and Becky jumped into the middle seat.

"Why are you in such a hurry?" Cain asked, swinging the truck around.

"Wayne's been watching me. He doesn't like me going out with you."

"That little shit can't do nothing."

"I know. He's really annoying," Becky said. The truck raced away. Dust rolled over the side of the hood. "It's great there being no school today. Where are we going?"

"Redemption Mountain," Cain said. "You're in for the time of your life." The truck hit a deep hole and bounced in the air. Taking one hand off the wheel, Cain put it around her shoulder. "Don't worry none, Becky. You're safe with me."

Wayne heard the engine noise, ran to the porch, and saw the truck pulling away. Becky was in the front seat bumping shoulders with Cain and Abel. Throwing on his jacket, Wayne jumped down the steps and ran to the barn. He pulled out his bicycle and began pedaling furiously down the road.

After Cindy and Alice packed a bag with venison sandwiches and fresh apples, Conner and Matt loaded the food and a large blanket on the bicycles. Alice looked at the rope wrapped around Matt's handlebars.

"What's the rope for?"

"I need it," Matt said, and he pushed off on the bicycle. The air was cool and fresh, and the sky was a deep blue. It was eleven o'clock when they reached Blood Mountain. Alice looked at the steep path and turned to Matt.

"Why can't we eat at the river? Climbing the mountain is hard work."

"We don't have to climb no mountain," Matt said. "Wait right here." He got on his bicycle and pedaled to the shed. Removing the key from under the rock, he unlocked the door, pulled out the red four-wheeler, and drove back to Conner and the girls.

"Everyone get on. I'll chauffeur you up the mountain."

"Matt, where did you get the wheels?" Conner asked.

"From a friend. He said I could use it anytime."

"What are all those dark spots?" Alice asked.

"A bad paint job."

"Have you ever driven it?" Conner inquired, a suspicious look on his face.

"Sure," Matt lied. "Lots of times."

After they attached the food, blanket, and rope, they squeezed onto the seat and side carriers. Matt drove slowly, but at a steep grade, he accelerated and the four-wheeler bounced high in the air. The girls began screaming and laughing. Alice held onto Matt with both hands. At the summit, Matt raced the vehicle around the boulders, skirted the cone-shaped ant mounds, and parked in the shade of the large pine tree. While the girls began unpacking the food, Matt grabbed the rope, and he and Conner walked to the edge of the cliff.

There was no wind. The vultures were perched high on the tree branches, their heads drooping and lifeless. The Shadows of Death was a foggy mist below. Matt looked at the rock ledges and stunted trees jutting out of the mountainside.

"Do you think it's true what your dad said about Matthew?"

"About him killing all those Indians?"

"No. About watching his sister, Beatrice, falling to her death. About the memorial he made for her."

"I don't know how much of that is true."

"There's only one way to find out," Matt said, tying the rope around his waist. "I'm going to see for myself."

"Matt, you're crazy."

"I know," he said, and he gave the end of the rope to Conner. "Please hold on tightly."

"It's not long enough."

"I only need to get to the first tree."

"Hey!" Alice shouted. "What are you two doing?"

"Tell Alice not to worry," Matt said to Conner, and dropping onto his stomach, he lowered his feet over the edge of the cliff.

"Hey!" Alice shouter louder, and she ran toward the cliff. Matt quickly slipped over the side. Two vultures dropped from the tree, and wings spread wide, they drifted downward.

With the rope pinching his stomach, Matt dug his fingers into the rock surface. After a few minutes of descent, his feet hit against the tree. Sitting down, straddling the trunk with his legs, he untied the rope and gave it a tug. When he looked up, he saw three faces staring at him. Matt waved his hand and maneuvered his legs over the side of the tree. As he slid his body through the branches, he was completely covered by gray shadows.

Luther raced the car down Green Hollow Pike. When he swerved around a pothole, Max grabbed his ribs and made a face.

"Can you slow down a little? My ribs still hurt. Thinking about that kid makes me madder than hell."

"Be patient. Dan's as good as dead." Luther turned onto the Petersburg Pike. Cresting a hill, he saw a red truck in the middle of the road. Luther hit the horn, and when the truck raced by, he looked at the three laughing faces in the front seat.

"Damn kids," he said. "Why ain't they in school?"

"Probably another holiday. They've got more holidays than we ever dreamed of," Max complained. Ten minutes later, a boy on a bicycle sped toward them. Max grabbed his ribs again; Luther slowed going past the bicycle. It was noon when he pulled into J.C. Blair.

Alone in the hospital room, staring at the TV mounted on the wall, Dan Boonie watched the Channel Ten sports reporter walk to the statue of the Nittany lion. The reporter first talked about the record crowd of 84,587 fans at Beaver Stadium on Saturday. Then he talked about Penn State's 21–7 loss to Nebraska. His tone turned belligerent when he commented on Penn State's seven turnovers and how the offense had only 33 total rushing yards to Nebraska's 287.

Dan hit the button on the remote, shutting off the TV. He leaned back on the pillow just as Luther and Max walked into the room. Luther stared at the bed and the elevated plaster cast and laughed. Max closed the door and stood there holding his ribs.

"How're you doing, Boonie?" Luther asked. "You look like you're in some pain."

"It's not so bad," Dan said. Sliding his hand under the sheet, he gripped the Colt .38.

"I've learned through trial and error that pain is good." Luther smiled and took a step toward the bed. "It helps get the message across."

"That's far enough," Dan warned. As he aimed the revolver, the sheet lifted in the air.

"Well, look at this, would ya? Gettin' a hard-on, are you, Boonie? I didn't think you'd be that glad to see us." Luther took a step closer to the bed.

Watching the smirk on Luther's face, Dan fired the gun. The explosion of noise blasted through the room. The bullet hit the wall, and chunks of plaster fell on the floor. Luther tripped backward, bouncing against Max.

"I think you'd better leave," Dan said, lowering the gun slightly.

Max swung the door open, and holding his ribs, he ran out of the room. A startled expression on his face, Luther turned and hustled after him. Within seconds, a nurse came running through the door. She glanced at the cracked plaster and the hole in the wall.

"Are you all right?" she asked.

"My ears are ringing, and there's a burning sensation in my leg. But I actually feel pretty good. I have to call Mr. Brooks. Can you dial his number for me?"

"Sure," the nurse said. She hit the buttons and gave him the phone. When Dan heard Andrew's voice, he asked him to come for the gun.

"You get some rest," the nurse said, taking the phone. "I'll cover that hole."

When Andrew arrived at J. C. Blair Hospital, he rushed to Dan's room. After taking the gun and putting it under his belt, he listened to Dan's story. Dan had a smile on his face when he pointed to the strips of surgical tape on the wall. There were loud voices in the hall, and dressed in his blue uniform, Deputy Oliver Wright burst through the door.

"What's going on in here? I received a report of gunshots."

"I know who called in the report," Andrew said. "It was your brother, Max."

"Who cares who it was, Pastor Brooks? Or should I say, Mr. Brooks, since you lost your church. For your information, there's a jail sentence for anyone who shoots a gun in a hospital. And I'm thinking it's the boy here who done the shooting."

"Is that what you're thinking?" Andrew asked. He looked at the big mouth, shifty eyes, and black hair plastered flat with cream.

"You're out of uniform, aren't you, Oliver? You're missing your cap."

"I left the station in a hurry. My cap's on my desk."

"Are you sure about that, Oliver? Are you sure you didn't leave it at Muddy Run Camp!" The veins on Andrew's neck doubled in size and began to pulsate. A dark, ominous expression spread over his face. He spoke in a dour tone. "I know what you did there."

With a slow, calculated movement, Andrew placed his hand inside his jacket, slid his palm over the metal surface of the Colt .38, and positioned his finger on the trigger. Beads of perspiration coalesced on his forehead. There was a clicking sound, and a voice squeaked over the intercom.

"Dr. Haskins, report to the ER."

"What?" Andrew asked nervously. He glared at Oliver's bloated face. There was a long moment of silence. Then Andrew jerked his hand out of his jacket.

"What's the matter with you?" Oliver blurted. "What you got hidden?"

"Is this yours?" Andrew asked. Ripping the policeman's cap out of his pocket, he shoved it into Oliver's face.

"Hello! I already told you my cap's at the office."

"Does your cap have your name in it?"

"Yeah, it does. Mom was all happy when I got the job. She sewed it there herself."

"I found it at Muddy Run." Fisting the cap in his hand, he pushed Oliver in the chest. "Get the hell out of this room, Oliver, before—"

"What are you doing?" Oliver interrupted. "You can't be shoving a police officer,"

"You, a police officer!" Andrew laughed. Stepping quickly, Andrew swung his fist into Oliver's face. Oliver hit the floor, stumbled to his feet, and raced out the door. Dan had a smile on his face.

"Wow. I never thought I'd see a pastor punch a police officer, Mr. Brooks."

"Neither did I." Perspiration rolled down Andrew's face; his hand was trembling.

"What's wrong, Mr. Brooks? You look worried."

"I am worried, Dan. I'm becoming more and more like my brother. I had this urge—I mean a really strong urge—to take the gun and shoot Oliver. I think it's what Gene would have done."

"But he was in the war. He killed to defend himself."

"Once, trying to explain about that, Gene said something I didn't understand. He said we were all soldiers, and sooner or later, war would come to us. I think I understand what he meant." Andrew was quiet for a moment. "When are your parents returning?"

"Later this afternoon."

"Someone should be with you at all times." Andrew took the remote and sat in the chair. "You relax. I'll watch TV till they get here." He turned on the TV, and without seeing any of the images, Andrew began clicking through the channels.

Matt's two feet were jammed inside a narrow ledge. Spread-eagle against the cliff, his face hard against the cold rock surface, he inched his way downward. Looking through the clouds of gray mist rising from the rapids, Matt saw the pine tree jutting out of the wall. The gnarled roots of the tree partially covered the entrance to a cave.

Matt lowered himself to the entrance and swept his hand through the moist layer of cobwebs crisscrossing the mouth of the cave. A gigantic black spider appeared and scurried across his hand and up the side of the cliff. Matt hesitated a moment. Then he bent low and crawled into the cave. Peering through the dim patterns of light, he saw the jagged cross and the name carved into the wall.

"Beatrice," he read, but his eyes focused on the white figure in the deep recesses of the cave. The skeleton was in a sitting position, its back against the wall. Large vacant eye sockets stared at Matt. Hanging from a rawhide cord on the neck, a green arrowhead was twisted inside the rib cage.

There was a roar of noise from the rapids, and dark clouds boiled around the cave entrance. Matt felt a sudden chill. Gasping deep breaths of air, he watched the shadows swirl through the cramped space and penetrate the rib cage. Matt leaned closer, and with a trembling hand, he lifted the rawhide cord. Being very meticulous, Matt wiped the arrowhead on his sleeve until the green stone glistened. Then Matt slid the cord around his neck, never taking his eyes off the skeleton head.

"I know who you are," Matt said in a resolute voice. Leaning against the soft matting of roots and cobwebs, Matt breathed easily. Moisture formed on his forehead.

The roaring noise from the rapids subsided; shouts from above echoed down the side of the mountain. Matt heard his name again and again. He got to his feet and began to climb the rock cliff. When he reached the tree where the rope was hanging, he saw Alice next to Cindy and Conner. Alice was jumping up and down. As soon as he tied the rope around his waist, the three of them pulled him up fast, his arms and knees scraping against the stone.

Matt slid over the edge and got to his feet; Alice hugged him. Not saying a word, she and Cindy returned to the tree. Matt untied the rope from his waist. Looking over the cliff, he saw how the blue water emptied out of the big pool and crashed against the protruding rocks below. Currents of warm mist rolled up the side of the mountain.

"Dad says you're going down the rapids this evening. I think it's a crazy thing to do, Matt. But I'll be there if you need me."

"I always figured that."

"Lunch is ready!" Cindy shouted from the pine tree. Conner and Matt rushed over and sat down. Apples and sandwiches were in the center of the blanket; red-and-black ants crawled at the corners.

As he pedaled down the dirt road bordering the Juniata River, the mountain casting dark shadows across his face, Wayne noticed light reflecting off a glass surface. Getting closer, he saw the red truck parked in a grove of trees. Wayne dropped the bicycle and looked at the steep shale slide on the side of the mountain. Directly above it, the entrance to the cave was dark.

Wayne started up the mountain. When his feet lost traction on the loose rock, he began to crawl. Reaching the entrance, he stood and coughed at a rancid odor. Wayne walked into a wide tunnel; the odor became stronger, burning his nostrils and throat.

A series of lanterns lit the tunnel. Covering his nose, Wayne followed the lanterns to a wide cavern. Scented candles dotted the walls; violets were scattered on the stone floor. Taking tentative steps, Wayne saw a human form chiseled into the stone wall. The head and body were empty spaces, but the arms and legs were filled with decaying flesh.

His heart racing, Wayne noticed two tunnel-like openings, one on each side of the cavern. He walked cautiously to the first and slid inside. There was a metal cage in the center of the room. Moving closer, Wayne saw a white rabbit. After opening the cage, he grabbed the rabbit by the ears and shoved it inside his jacket.

Wayne exited and went to the second tunnel. As he stepped inside, he heard noise and stopped in the darkness. Balancing a pole on their shoulders, Cain and Abel walked into the main cavern. Swaying back and forth, the body of a wolf was trussed to the pole.

Moving quickly down the tunnel, Wayne entered a circular alcove lit by a single candle. He heard a muffled noise, and looking in the shadows, he saw Becky. Her mouth was taped, and her hands and legs were bound. There was blood on her clothes. Wayne undid the ropes, and when he pulled the tape away, Becky made a whimpering noise and hugged him. Loud voices echoed down the tunnel.

"It's Cain and Abel," Wayne said. "Is there another way out?"

"Over there." Becky pointed to an opening in the wall. She entered quickly, and Wayne followed. There was a scrambling noise behind him; Abel burst into the alcove.

"You farm-fuck!" he shouted. Abel dove and grabbed Wayne's foot.

Wayne kicked, making solid contact with Abel's face, and his leg broke free. Moving faster, he caught up to Becky. The tunnel narrowed, and Wayne turned his body sideways against the rock. Making squealing noises, the rabbit scratched frantically, its paws digging into his chest. Becky led Wayne into a dark open area. Hearing a distinct rattling sound, Wayne stopped and reached for the box of matches.

"Don't move," he told Becky, and he lit a match. Through the flickering light, he saw snakes of all sizes on the floor of the den. The match trembled in his hand, and he pulled Becky closer. Behind them, angry voices echoed from the darkness.

"I see light ahead!" Abel shouted from the tunnel. "Shit! It's too tight. I can't get through. Cain, you go first."

"We're twins!" Cain shouted back. "We're the same fuckin' size!"

"They can't reach us," Wayne said. Glancing through the shadows, he saw a hole in the stone wall. There was a snake in front of it. When the snake made a soft rattling noise, Wayne tossed the burning match at its head. The rattling noise increased; the flame went out, and there was total darkness.

"Be very still," Wayne said to Becky. He lit another match. In the bright flash, he saw the rattlesnake slither toward them. Reaching striking distance, the snake coiled gracefully. Its eyes reflected a thin vertical flame; the forked tongue flicked. Wayne felt small feet scratch at the opening in his jacket. Pink-and-white silky ears appeared, and the rabbit jumped. In a blur of motion, the rattlesnake caught the furry body in midair. Instantly the jaws opened, releasing the rabbit.

Wayne lit another match and stared at the rabbit. Hind legs paralyzed, the rabbit twitched erratically. The snakes advanced toward the flurry of motion. As the rattling noise increased, Wayne and Becky pressed their bodies tightly against the wall and crawled into the hole. They walked and crawled through a series of tunnels that slanted upward. The last match flared brightly and went out; Wayne's fingers were black and raw. He held onto Becky, and hands sliding along the wall, they moved through the darkness. There was a dim glow of light ahead. When they squeezed their bodies through the narrow fissure and stepped into sunlight, Wayne saw the spectacular silver outline in the blue sky.

"The Flaming Cross," he muttered. Birds sang from the bushes, and a cool breeze blew over the mountain. Wayne and Becky walked quietly down the path. Nearing the central plaza, they heard a loud, angry voice.

"Hey!" the Reverend Towers shouted angrily from the door of the church. He rushed down the steps, stopping in front of them. "The church is closed. You're trespassing." Then, looking at their torn clothes and Wayne's blackened hand, he spoke in a comforting tone. "Are you all right?"

"I was lost," Becky said. "Can you take us home?"

"Sure." The Reverend Towers led them to his car, and they got inside. Matt noticed the "NRA Cross & Assault Gun" insignia on the side window. As the reverend drove down Commandment Road, there was the sound of squealing tires, and the red truck approached them. Wayne glared at Cain and Abel sitting in the front seat. Abel had the swollen imprint of a shoe on the right side of his face. Wayne managed to smile. The reverend slowed, waved, and blew the horn when the truck raced by.

"You're students at Twin River. Do you know my sons, Cain and Abel?"

"We know them," Wayne admitted. "But we're not friends."

"Oh," the Reverend Towers said. "Of course not. You're younger. They're in a higher class that you. They're both fine boys. They orchestrate the music for Sunday mass. Do you mind if I play something now?" The reverend hit the button on the cassette player. The four speakers clicked simultaneously; music filled the confines of the car.

> Going forth with weeping, sowing for the Master.
> Through the loss sustained our spirit often grieves;
> When our weeping's over, He will bid us welcome;
> We shall come rejoicing, bringing in the sheaves.

"My wife's favorite hymn," the Reverend Towers stated with pride.

Wayne stared out the windshield. Listening to the refrain, *We shall come rejoicing, bringing in the sheaves*, he pointed at the intersection, and the reverend turned into Polecat Hollow. When they reached the house, Becky saw her dad standing on the porch. She banged the car door open and rushed up the steps and hugged him.

Chapter Twenty-Six

At the end of the in-service day, Twin River High School was eerily quiet. Gene walked up the steps to the second floor. Unlocking the door to Charlie Hesston's room, he stepped inside and switched on the lights. There were six rows of student desks. The side blackboards were spotless; the middle blackboard had the day's assignment:

> Ordeal at Valley Forge
> Discuss the following points in your essay:
> 1. George Washington suffers defeat at Brandywine
> 2. Continental Congress flees to Lancaster
> 3. General Howe occupies Philadelphia
> 4. Horrendous suffering and loss of life at Valley Forge
> 5. The Chicken Thief Soldier is killed at a local farm
> 6. Baron von Steuben trains Colonial Army

Gene went to Hesston's desk and pulled out the wide middle drawer. It was cluttered with rubber bands, thumbtacks, a plastic ruler, and some pennies. The bottom drawer on the side was locked. Gene opened it with his master key, and moving some notebooks aside, he saw a bundle in the corner. Unfolding the cloth, Gene picked up the Smith & Wesson handgun. Just as he clicked open the cylinder, the speaker above the blackboard clicked on, and the principal's voice filled the room.

"Mr. Brooks, please report to the office."

Gene hesitated. The last dismissal bell rang, shattering the stillness of the room. In the din of noise, Gene looked at the rotating cylinder of the .38 special. The shrill ringing ended abruptly. Gene lingered at the desk for a few moments. Then he replaced the gun and locked the drawer. Descending the staircase, he entered the principal's office.

"Great in-service day, Mr. Port. I watched half of the staff drive out after lunch." Gene shrugged his shoulders. "Why did you call me?"

"What have you heard about Pete? I've known him since grade school. His arrest makes no sense at all."

"I saw Pete yesterday. He's not looking too good. It would help if you—"

"I'll go there tonight. Then I'll get the wife, and we'll visit Sarah and the kids."

"Pete would appreciate that. He's got no friends in the jail. Sheriff Parks has pronounced him guilty."

"It's hard to understand the sheriff. You guys played on the same team."

"It never was a team."

"You're right, Gene. Parks was the star. No one else mattered." Mr. Port grabbed some memos, stacked them in a pile, and looked at Gene. "Mr. Henry's been gone almost a week now. How's Matt handling it?"

"Matt's doing fine. He's going on a canoe trip in a few minutes."

"Great," the principal said. "It'll relax him. Keep his mind off his dad. The river's beautiful at this time of year." He nodded to Gene, and Gene left the office. Stopping in the maintenance room, Gene grabbed a bag of M&M's from the desk drawer.

His Winchester strapped over his shoulder, Conner waited with Cindy on the riverbank. Two green canoes slanted sideways in the sand. A short distance away, Matt and Alice were arguing. Alice held a yellow teddy bear at her side. In the background, the Shadows of Death created shifting plumes of mist that obscured the rocky crags of Blood Mountain; vultures circled the pine trees at the summit.

Gene walked down the trail carrying paddles, orange life vests, and a Twin River football helmet with the image of Chief One-Eye painted on the side. Gene gave two of the life vests to Conner. Still talking loudly, Matt and Alice walked to the canoes. Approaching Conner, Matt immediately noticed the Winchester.

"What's the gun for?"

"I don't know. Dad told me to bring it."

"Why, Mr. Brooks?"

"Put this on," Gene said, ignoring the question. He slid the football helmet over Matt's head and clicked the snap shut.

"It's tight."

"That's because you have a big head. And wear this, too." Gene handed Matt the life vest. Matt slid it over his shoulders and tied the front laces.

"I look like an idiot," Matt said. "Anything else?"

"Take this," Gene said, and he placed a whistle on a strap around Matt's neck.

"Why do I need a whistle?"

"I have one, too. It's how we communicate. When the rapids smash the canoe into little pieces, your body will wash up somewhere downriver. If you're not dead, blow the whistle so we can find you."

"Great. Where are my snorkel and goggles?"

"It's not funny," Alice said. "Please don't do this."

"Don't worry. I'll be fine."

"Sure, you'll be fine," Gene said. "Your paddle's in the canoe. Wait here a few minutes, Matt. We're going to the island. When we're in position, I'll blow the whistle. Then you can start your journey. Do you understand?"

"Yes, I understand."

"Don't move until you hear the whistle," Gene cautioned, and he slid the canoe into the water. Matt reached out for Alice, pulled her close, and hugged her.

"Why did you bring Mr. Teddy?"

"For good luck," Alice said. Matt glanced at Conner.

"I still don't understand why you need a gun."

"Me neither," Conner said, getting into the canoe with Cindy and Alice. Gene pushed them off, jumped in the back, and began to paddle toward the island. Avoiding the pull of the rapids, he guided the canoe to the slow channel. After a few minutes, Gene beached the canoe in a sandy cove.

"You three go to the positions that I showed you. Be ready for anything."

"I'll be ready." Conner walked through the pine trees to the center of the island. He selected the largest boulder on the bank and climbed to the top. Clouds of mist splashing over his body, he slid the Winchester off his shoulder and sat there facing the raging current.

Alice and Cindy went to the tip of the island. Alice waded out; the current tugged at her body. Holding her hand over her eyes, she saw the white water that boiled over the huge rocks. Then she heard the shrill blast of the whistle.

"Finally," Matt said. He grabbed the paddle and pushed off in the canoe. The water in the pool was placid. A cool wind blew; ripples lapped against the side of the canoe. Reaching into his pocket, Matt pulled out the glass eye and held it tightly in his fist.

The roar of the rapids grew louder. For a brief moment, Matt saw the deep channel to the right of the island, and then he was caught in the current. Propelled downward, the canoe hit a massive wave. Matt was drenched. Water whipped over his body and blasted through the opening in the helmet, stinging his eyes and face.

The canoe entered the Shadows of Death, slammed against a rock, and was catapulted high in the air. Lifted from his seat, Matt dropped the paddle and grabbed the side of the canoe. Crashing down in a turbulence of white water, the canoe straightened and was caught by the next wave. Momentarily, Matt saw blue sky. Then he watched as dark vulture shapes glided downward. Matt unclenched his fist.

"You son of a bitch!" Matt shouted, and he threw the eye into the Shadows.

The canoe was momentarily still, tilting precariously on the breaking wave. Then the wave broke violently and capsized the canoe, tossing Matt into the river. Matt sank through glittering shafts of sunlight. The weight of the helmet spun him deeper in the current. In a frantic motion, he removed the helmet. Immediately, Matt became buoyant and floated upward. Just as his body broke the surface, a vulture swooped down. Razor-sharp talons tore through the life vest. Wings flogging the air, the vulture extended a curved beak toward Matt's face.

Matt screamed and lifted his fist out of the current. There was a booming sound, and the vulture's head exploded in clumps of blood and tissue. The body dropped heavily on Matt's chest. Gliding out of the Shadows, a second vulture picked up the mutilated form. As the vulture rose through the mist, its stomach burst open, and it spiraled downward.

The current whipped Matt's body over a ridge of rocks into a deep pool. He attempted to swim, but the undertow sucked him deeper. Glancing up, Matt saw the dead vultures, their red feathered wings undulating gracefully on the surface of the pool.

Matt's head began to pulsate; he heard an ominous ticking sound and kicked furiously. His leg hit pliant objects. When he kicked again, his ankle scraped against a labyrinth of broken branches. Wired to the branches, ghostly skeletal shapes swayed back and forth. Turning his foot, Matt twisted it deep through the bones of a rib cage. It stuck there. Eyes opening wide, he saw there were no legs on the skeleton.

Son of a bitch! Big Calvin got me, Matt reasoned; water filled his throat.

Alice watched as the canoe lifted high off the wave and tossed Matt into the boiling water. Two gunshots made hollow, popping sounds above the roar of the rapids. When the capsized canoe approached, she lunged and grabbed the side. Alice turned it over, straightened it, and pushed it toward the bank. Tears forming in her eyes, she stared at the stretch of rapids and the rocks, which sprayed white water in the air. Trailing a line of bloated intestines, a vulture drifted past her.

Losing strength, his hands rising listlessly over his head, Matt was suspended vertically in the swirling depths of the pool. Inexplicably, a glistening orb, an eye that blinked red, appeared in the Shadows and spun mockingly toward his head. His heart pounding, his mind racing, Matt stomped his foot through the rib cage, splintering the circle of bones.

Freed from Big Calvin's grasp, Matt was swept away by the current. A gray darkness enveloped him. An oscillating thunder filled his ears; the weight of the water crushed his chest. Slicing from the light above, hands grabbed him and lifted him out of the water. Matt coughed for air. Breathing deeply and wiping at his eyes, he saw Alice. She cried his name and held him steady against the current.

"I'm all right," he said, struggling to stand. Alice helped him wade to the island. Clutching the Winchester, Conner sprinted down the rocky shore to meet them.

"You're a damn good shot, soldier!" Matt complimented him, and he gave Conner a hug. The air was cool; Matt's body was trembling. Conner pulled off his Twin River sweatshirt.

"Take this, Matt."

"I can't stop shaking." After he put on the sweatshirt, Matt rushed over to Gene and shook his hand. "Thanks, Mr. Brooks."

"You're welcome." Taking the bag of M&Ms from his pocket, Gene gave it to Matt. "Here, you've earned these."

"I sure did." Matt ripped off the top, lifted the bag, and poured the M&M's into his mouth. Some of them bounced off his nose and landed on the rocks. Matt laughed, ran over to Alice, and took her by the hand.

"We have to go downriver," he said, leading Alice to the canoe.

"You're crazy, Matt!" Conner exclaimed. "You came close to losing your life."

"My life's just beginning." Matt moved the orange vests and Mr. Teddy out of the way and helped Alice into the canoe. Then he pushed the canoe to deep water and jumped inside. "Can you pick us up in Huntingdon?" he asked as an afterthought.

"We'll be at the bridge," Gene said, a smile on his face.

"Don't encourage him, Dad. He's nuts. You don't think he's crazy?"

"No, he's not crazy. Matt's experiencing something he's never felt before. He's experiencing how great it is to live without fear."

"Fear of what?"

"Mr. Henry."

"But Mr. Henry's on vacation!"

"I know that."

The cracked football helmet with Chief One-Eye's image drifted against the bank. A gray mist from the Shadows of Death enveloped the island; vultures circled lazily over Blood Mountain. Intermittent blasts from the whistle echoed up the river.

"I still say he's nuts."

The whistle trumpeted again, and after a moment, except for the frog sounds, the river turned quiet. Conner, Cindy, and Gene walked across the island, got into their canoe, and began to paddle to the school.

Low on the horizon, the lingering rays of the setting sun cast a burgundy glow the length of the river. The canoe hit a stretch of deep water; the slow current turned the canoe sideways. Lowering the paddle, Matt removed the strap from around his neck and threw it into the river. "I don't need a whistle anymore." He moved closer to Alice.

"Matt, back at the rapids when the canoe overturned and you went under, I was so scared, I couldn't stop crying." Alice leaned forward and kissed Matt vigorously on the lips.

"But..." Matt began to resist and then remembered Conner's words. *Whatever she does with the tongue, just do it back to her.* Maneuvering his tongue forward, Matt tasted the warmth and sweetness in her mouth. Pressing his body against hers, he felt her breasts rising and lowering. The moisture under his sweatshirt turned warm, then hot. Alice broke off the kiss and spoke in a soft voice.

"I'm embarrassed to say this, Matt. Something's growing in your swimming trunks."

"I don't think I can do anything about that," Matt admitted. "I'm sorry."

"Don't be sorry."

"Okay. I won't be sorry," Matt said. "I'll be happy, real happy." Matt positioned the life vests under Alice. After he placed Mr. Teddy under her head, he dropped heavily against her. Large, puffy clouds drifted across the crimson-tinted sky. The clouds cast warm shadows over the river and the canoe, which rocked low in the water.

"I taste something sweet, like chocolate," Alice said.

"Me, too," Matt said.

It was dark when the canoe reached Huntingdon. Lights from the bridge illuminated the river. Gene was waiting at the jeep; Conner and Cindy were on the bank when the canoe scraped to a stop. Conner grabbed Alice by the hand and pulled her onto dry land.

"I'm starving," Alice said.

"I'm ravenous," Matt said. "Totally ravenous!" He helped secure the canoe to the roof of the jeep. When everyone was inside, Gene drove to KFC. At the counter, when Matt ordered extra chicken, Conner nudged him in the shoulder.

"Matt, you didn't kill any of these chickens. You can't use your waiver here."

"You're right, Conner, but I feel this sudden urge to eat meat. Maybe I don't want to be a vegetarian anymore."

"If you keep following these crazy urges, you won't be Matt Henry anymore."

"I know who I am, Conner. I'll always be Matthew Henry." He slid into the booth next to Alice. When their number was called, Matt jumped up and rushed to the counter.

Chapter Twenty-Seven

On Tuesday, Jeffery finished eating lunch at the Pump House. He was on the staircase when he heard the phone. Unlocking the door, he entered his apartment, picked up the phone, and recognized Nathaniel's authoritative voice.

"Jeffery, I need you at the cabin. Xanadu is relocating to Willow Mountain. You've been there, right?"

"Yes, I got the complete tour. What do you want me to do?"

"We're ditching the FritoLay van. I want you to drive it to the Brick Yard. Max will meet you there at three o'clock."

"Where's Luther? Isn't that his job?"

"Luther's home sick," Nathaniel said after a slight pause. "Just deliver the van to the Brick Yard. Do you understand?"

"Yes," Jeffery said, and he hung up.

Entering the school cafeteria, walking past Mr. Hesston, who was stroking his beard, Matt noticed the two kids at the end of the table. Walking over, he sat directly across from Lilly Cicconi and scrutinized the bruises under her scarf. When Matt tried to talk to her, both Lilly and Jack left the table. Charlie Hesston glared at Matt. Sporting a big smile, Conner came over and sat down.

"Mr. Hesston is giving you the evil eye."

"He gives that evil eye to all the students. I don't trust him."

"Why?"

"He acts like Moses. Except that Moses brought down the commandant, "Thou shalt not kill," from Mt. Sinai. Mr. Hesston with all his NRA pronouncements promotes the opposite. He promotes killing." Matt turned toward Conner. "Why are you so happy?"

"I just finished making plans with Cindy. We're taking a canoe trip today."

"That's great." Matt laughed. "Who's picking you up in Huntingdon?"

"We're not going that far. We're just going to the bridge below the school."

"That's not even ten minutes."

"I know. I don't need much time." Conner winked, slapped Matt's hand, and walked to the exit, circumventing Mr. Hesston's imposing figure at the door.

"Mr. Brooks, I wanted to talk to you about Lilly and Jack." Matt said, entering the custodian's office at the end of the day. Gene looked up from his desk.

"The Cicconi kids?"

"Yes, I've been watching them. They're nervous all the time. Today Lilly was wearing a scarf at lunch, but I could see dark marks on her neck. And Jack's always wearing long sleeves. It's how I used to cover my bruises. I'm sure someone's hurting them." Matt walked to the edge of the desk. "I want to help Lilly and Jack like you helped me. I want to go after whoever's hurting them."

"I don't think so, Matt. I agreed to teach you how to hunt animals, not people."

"But you hunt people, Mr. Brooks. Mr. Henry was doing bad things to me. You stopped him. We need to do the same for Lilly and Jack."

"You have no idea what you're talking about. No idea at all." Gene sat quietly for a moment. Staring at Matt, Gene shook his head. "I saw Captain Hook on your bedroom wall. Why did you scratch out his eyes?"

"He watched what Mr. Henry did. He didn't help me."

"But Captain Hook wasn't real."

"I don't care, Mr. Brooks. I'm real. I want to help people." There was a moment of silence. Matt's gaze didn't waver. Gene let out a low sigh.

"Mr. Cicconi works at Green Hollow Correctional Camp. Have you ever met him?"

"I've never met him."

"Then how can you be sure?"

"When I look into Lilly's face and Jack's face, I just know. We can go to their house. We can see for ourselves."

"Then we'll go there now," Gene said, standing up. "They live near the Brick Yard. I'll talk with Ann Cicconi, and you can talk to Lilly and Jack. We'll find out if the kids are being hurt. Is that what you want?"

"Yes, Mr. Brooks." Matt followed Gene outside to the jeep. As Gene left the parking lot, a gray car drove by them and stopped at the side of the building.

"Who's that?" Matt asked.

"Sheriff Parks," Gene answered. "He's preventing the next school massacre."

Gene turned the jeep onto Route 305. When he slowed down at the one-lane bridge, he saw Conner and Cindy wading out of the river. Gene blew the horn. After pulling to the side of the road, he and Matt ran to the steep bank.

After school, Conner and Cindy had pedaled their bicycles to Conner's house. Cindy waited in the canoe while Conner ran inside the house. He picked up the cassette player and some cushions and hurried to the river.

"What's the cassette player for?"

"Mood music." Conner smiled. "I found something very romantic." He dropped the cushions and cassette player into the canoe and pushed off. The current propelled the canoe downriver. A look of anticipation on his face, Conner hit the play button on the cassette.

> I joined the navy to see the world
> But nowhere could I find
> A girl as sweet as Cindy,
> The girl I left behind.

Delighted at the expression of joy he saw on Cindy's face, Conner spread the cushions evenly. The canoe drifted into a stretch of calm water. In the shadows downriver, one large rock protruded from the water. Far below the rock, the bridge was a dark silhouette. Birds sang from the trees; the canoe rocked back and forth.

"This is so perfect," Conner said. "It's like being on a water bed." Conner took off his shirt and began to unzip his jeans. The soft melody of *Cindy* drifted over the water.

"I love this song," Cindy said, removing her blouse. She stretched comfortably on the cushions, her head resting on the wooden crossbar.

"I love *Cindy* more than you," Conner said, lowering his jeans and shorts. "I love Cindy more than you could ever imagine." Conner leaned over her. His head resting between her breasts, he breathed the sweet scent of her body. The canoe tilted; a stream of water flowed over the side. Conner quickly shifted his weight, balancing the canoe. The waves made a lapping sound; the rocking motion bounced her breasts lightly against his face.

"This is great," Conner said. "This is unbelievably great." Humming along with the music, Conner lowered his body over hers. He trembled with the swelling buildup of fluid; his chest heaved. The canoe settled deep in the water and began to move faster.

> Cindy, oh, Cindy,
> Cindy, don't let me down.

Write me a letter soon,
And I'll be homeward bound

Abruptly, there was a harsh grating sound. The canoe slid smoothly onto the moss-covered rock and rolled onto its side. Emitting a loud scream, Cindy grabbed onto Conner, and they both fell into the river. Conner watched the cassette player sink in a stream of bubbles and disappear in the dark depths.

Conner helped Cindy to the surface. The canoe and cushions drifted toward the bridge. Struggling in the current, Conner pulled on his jeans. When Cindy was dressed, they began swimming toward the canoe. Minutes later, splashing in the shadows under the bridge, they pushed the canoe onto the sand.

"Are you all right?" Conner asked. Wiping water from her face, Cindy nodded her head. A horn sounded; Conner saw the orange jeep. He grabbed Cindy's hand, and they rushed up the bank to the road.

"What happened?" Gene asked as they walked to the jeep. Conner opened the door for Cindy.

"Our canoe hit a rock and overturned."

"Conner, there's only one damn rock in this whole section of river! What were you two doing out there?"

"We were just drifting in the current enjoying the music. Then the canoe hit the big rock and overturned."

"It could happen to anyone," Matt said quickly in a sympathetic voice. "The important thing is that you're both safe."

"Get those blankets in the back and cover yourselves before you catch a cold," Gene advised. He got in the front seat, put the jeep in gear, and pulled onto the road.

"Where are we going, Dad?"

"To the Cicconi house. We won't be long."

Matt turned in his seat and mouthed the words slowly, *Did you do it?* Shrugging his shoulders, Conner projected a bleak expression; Matt turned his gaze back to the road.

Jeffery reached the cabin at two fifteen. He went to the kitchen and opened a can of dog food. There was a trace of smoke in the air. Looking at the table, he saw two empty Heineken cans and a cigarette butt in the ashtray. The puppies began barking. Jeffery descended the steps to the basement, grabbed a bag of dog food, and while he was feeding the puppies, he saw the red VCR light. Jeffery walked to the workstation, turned on the TV, and hit the VCR play button. The Michael Jackson lyrics, *Do what you want to do. There ain't no rules* blasted through the speakers.

My great movie debut, Jeffery thought, his eyes focused on the TV screen:

Wearing the blue bathrobe, Jeffery picked up Skippy and Tippy. The puppies were yelping and licking his face. Jeffery was delighted. Then the scene changed to the Shangri-la Room. Brenda lay on the bed. Jeffery entered the room, and opening the bathrobe, he approached the bed. Her face glowing in the light, Brenda sat up, covered her face with her hands, and began to cry.

"I'll come back and burn this," Jeffery vowed angrily, and he hit the rewind button. He put the puppies in the cage, grabbed the keys, and walked to the FritoLay van.

Jeffery was in the van for only a few seconds when he noticed the odor. He rolled down the window, but as he drove, the odor became stronger. When Jeffery reached the turnoff to the Brick Yard, he stopped and jumped out. Opening the back door, he saw the stuffed garbage bags. The odor was stifling.

"What the hell!" he exclaimed, and grabbing the plastic, he ripped it open. A cloud of putrid air burst from the bag.

Covering his nose, Jeffery glimpsed the thawing, blood-smeared face. He tripped backward and fell in the dirt. Coughing and getting quickly to his feet, Jeffery ran through the woods. Nearing the Brick

Yard, he heard voices and knelt behind some brush. A car was parked near the water; Max was standing at the wooden platform. He was talking and gesturing with his hands. A loud cough sounded from the shadows.

"Luther," Jeffery whispered. Jumping to his feet, Jeffery ran back to the van. He got in the front seat, slammed the door shut, and smashed his foot on the gas. As he raced away, clouds of dust rose in the air.

Jeffery slowed at the Route 305 intersection. An orange jeep was at the stop sign. When Jeffery drove by, he saw blanketed figures in the backseat and a man and a boy in the front. The man glared at Jeffery through the windshield.

The noise of the slamming door echoed over the Brick Yard. Two ducks splashed out of the water and circled squawking above the platform. Inhaling deeply, Luther blew a cloud of smoke in the air and looked at the ducks.

"What set the birds off, Max?"

"There was a gunshot or something."

"Jeffery?"

"I doubt it. He's a lover and a wimp, not a gunman. It's getting close to three o'clock. How long should we wait for him?"

"I don't know. It's Jeffery's final scene. Nathaniel said to give him plenty of time." Luther struck a match, lighting another cigarette.

Hands glued to the steering wheel, Gene stared at the orange-and-black van. Conner shrugged his shoulders.

"What are you looking at, Dad?"

"The FritoLay van," Gene said. "There's something wrong. It was at the police station Sunday night." Watching the van turn in the intersection, Gene noticed the Nittany lion pasted on the back door. When he saw "Undefeated 1969," he smacked his hand on the dash. A slow-moving truck and then a station wagon went by; the FritoLay van disappeared.

"It's not Pete's van," Gene said, and he spun the jeep through the intersection. "There's been a change in plans, Matt. We're going after the van." Gene raced the jeep down the empty road. For the next ten minutes, he turned into numerous lanes and circled the cabins. They entered a heavily forested area. Conner pulled the blanket tightly around Cindy.

"Dad, it's getting cold back here. Can we go home?"

"Quit all the complaining, soldier," Gene said in an irritated voice. The sun dropped low in the sky; a burst of sunlight blinded Gene. Covering his eyes, he drove by a logging road with an open security bar. A silver car raced down the logging road and turned sharply. Gene got a glance at the driver and spun the jeep around.

"You'll never catch him, Mr. Brooks," Matt advised. "He's got a Porsche."

"Right now I'm more interested in the van." Gene drove past the security bar and accelerated down the road. When he spotted the open gate and the FritoLay van in front of the cabin, he stopped behind a row of trees.

"Wait here." Gene shut off the engine and stepped out of the jeep.

"What about me?" Matt asked. "I want to come with you."

"Stay close, then," Gene said. Matt rushed to catch up, and walking shoulder-to-shoulder down the middle of road, they went through the open gate. The glare from the spotlight covered the van and the porch. Smelling the stench from the van, Matt coughed.

"That's worse than the chum on the Rainbow. What is it, Mr. Brooks?"

"Someone's dead."

"How do you know?"

"It was a common smell in Vietnam." Gene climbed the porch steps and pushed the door open, and he and Matt went inside the cabin. As they walked across the living room, Gene heard the barking downstairs. They went through the open door and down the steps.

Yelping loudly, their tongues swinging back and forth, the puppies were in a cage in the corner. Matt started toward them.

"Don't bother the dogs," Gene advised. He noticed the red VCR light at the workstation. "Let's watch one of their movies. I need to be sure we go after the right person."

A cloud covered the moon; dark shadows fell over the jeep. There was a chill in the air. Pulling the blanket tighter, Conner moved closer to Cindy and loosened his jeans. When their bodies touched, he felt the warm smoothness of her skin.

"What are you doing?"

"What we had planned to do in the canoe," Conner answered. Waves of heat spiraled upward, reddening his face. Conner lowered his jeans and began to hum in her ear, *Cindy, oh, Cindy, Cindy, don't let me down.*

"Conner, your dad might come back at any time."

"I don't care," he whispered, nibbling on her ear.

"Neither do I," she admitted, and she began to remove her blouse. "You're all wet."

"I know," Conner informed her.

The cloud drifted away; moonlight streamed in through the windows. Breathing deeply, Conner leaned heavily into Cindy. He let out a gasp when their bodies came together. An owl hooted from the pine tree. The springs of the jeep made a squeaking noise, and then the Confederate flag on the roof began to sway erratically.

Standing in front of the workstation, Gene hit the play button on the VCR. The shrill sound of music echoed in the background, *Do what you want to do. There ain't no rules.* The monitor blinked on; Gene's face hardened in the light.

"What's wrong, Mr. Brooks?"

"I hate that voice."

"It's Michael Jackson. He's the most popular singer in the world."

"I hate that voice," Gene repeated.

Two puppies flashed on the screen. A young man wearing a blue bathrobe walked toward the cage. The puppies jumped on him. Picking them up, the man called them "Skippy" and "Tippy," and they yelped and licked his face. The screen turned to black. Then exotic yellow-and-red colors flashed on the screen. The camera focused on the nude girl lying on the bed.

"It's Brenda," Matt whispered. Tears streamed down Brenda's face. The young man entered the room and removed the blue bathrobe. The camera zoomed in on the clear features of his face.

"That's the driver of the van. And also the Porsche," Gene said, shutting off the monitor. "Did you get a good look at his face?"

"Yes, Mr. Brooks."

"Remember it, Matt. You won't see it again."

"Why?"

"It's the face of a dead man."

"Mr. Brooks, I want to be there. I want to be on Blood Mountain when—" The door slammed upstairs, and there was the sound of voices. Gene grabbed Matt by the arm and led him outside.

"It's the kidnappers, Matt. Let's get back to the jeep." Using the trees as cover, Gene and Matt ran along the fence and through the open gate. Matt reached the jeep first and saw the windows were covered with steam.

"Wake up in there!" Matt rapped his knuckles on the glass. There was hurried movement inside.

"What's taking so long?" Gene mumbled. He opened the front door, grabbed the revolver behind the seat, and shoved it under his belt. Conner finished buttoning his jeans and covered Cindy with the blanket. Gene pulled the set of keys from his pocket and handed them to Conner.

"I need you to go to the state police barracks on Route 22."

"Jeez, Dad, I've only driven the jeep a few times."

"Don't say Jeez all the time. Just be tough, soldier." He held the door open and waited while Conner got in the front seat. "You have to hurry. Don't stop for anyone. Tell the sergeant that the missing girls are here. And tell him the kidnapper's FritoLay van is here with a dead body in it. That means Pete Rogers is innocent. Can you remember that?"

"Sure, Dad," Conner said, starting the engine. Matt backed away from the jeep.

"I'm going with you, Mr. Brooks."

"No, it's too dangerous. Just get into the jeep." Glaring at Matt, Gene waited. When Matt got inside, Gene closed the door and walked into the shadows. Wiping the windshield clean of moisture, Conner drove forward, swerved around a line of bushes, and bumped the jeep onto the road. Matt sat nervously, and then glancing at Conner, he swung the door open.

"Stop! I'm going with your dad!" As Conner braked, Matt jumped out and began running toward the cabin.

"Matt!" Conner called. Cindy climbed in the front seat. Conner watched Matt disappear around the bend. Then shaking his head, he slammed his foot on the gas.

"I did see someone sneaking around," Max said, standing at the window. "And he was too big to be Jeffery."

"It could be anyone. Maybe someone hoping to get the reward money. Let's lure him to the basement." Luther shut off the light, and he and Max started down the steps. Luther went straight to the Shangri-la Room, picked up Brenda, and carried her to the Nymph Room. After locking her inside with Sally, he ushered Max to the Shangri-la room and turned on the strobe light.

"You always wanted to get in Brenda's bed. Well, here's your chance." Luther walked to the bed and lifted the sheet. "Get under there."

"You want me to pretend to be Brenda!" Max exclaimed.

"Your body's small enough. Just tuck in your knees." Luther

nudged Max into the bed. "And turn your back to the door. Show this stranger your nice little ass." Luther laughed and walked to the entertainment center. After popping in a cassette, he hit the play button on the VCR. Sensual music filled the room; a nude couple appeared on the screen. Luther took out his blackjack, walked behind the door, and took a position against the wall.

The spotlight lit up the cabin. Kneeling at the window, Gene checked every corner of the room. Then he walked inside and down the steps to the basement. The puppies sat quietly in the cage; a flickering light flashed from the Shangri-la Room.

Moving cautiously, Gene approached the red door. He heard soft music and a woman's groaning voice. Peering into the room, he glanced at the nude couple on the screen. The strobe light brightened and flashed color over the bed. Gene studied the odd shape of the figure under the sheet.

"You dumb-fuck," he muttered. Raising his gun, he aimed at the center of the sheet. Skippy barked, and when Gene turned, he was struck on the head. There was a blinding flash, and he fell to the floor.

Chapter Twenty-Eight

"Slow down!" Cindy pleaded, holding onto the dash with both hands. The jeep roared down the straight stretch of road in front of Twin River High School.

"I can't slow down," Conner said. "Dad ordered me to hurry." As Conner accelerated past the parking lot, an unmarked gray car sped out from the corner of the building. Reaching through the window, Sheriff Parks stuck the revolving red light onto the roof. He hit the siren; Cindy turned at the noise.

"You'll have to stop, Conner. It's the sheriff."

"Parks is the last person I'd stop for." Conner raced past the Main Street Cafe and headed for the bridge. The gray car was directly behind him. When Conner bounced the jeep onto the bridge, bright lights approached from the other end. Hitting the brake, Conner lost control, and the jeep crashed into the steel railing. Releasing the wheel, Conner grabbed Cindy, who was completely covered by the blanket.

"Are you all right?"

"I think so," Cindy said.

"You stupid shit!" Sheriff Parks shouted, jerking open the door. He grabbed Conner around the neck and pulled him out of the jeep. Strengthening his choke hold, he lifted Conner off his feet.

"Let him go!" Cindy screamed.

Conner struggled to breathe. Swinging wildly, he hit the sheriff on the side of the head. The sheriff's cavalry felt cowboy hat flew over the railing, splashed into the river, and disappeared under the bridge.

"Resisting arrest!" Sheriff Parks slapped Conner in the mouth, splitting his lip. "I've been wantin' to do this for a long time!" The sheriff swung his fist into Conner's forehead. Conner collapsed against the side of the jeep.

"No!" Cindy cried, jumping onto the pavement. The approaching car slowed to a stop in front of the wrecked jeep. Caught in the bright beam of light, Sheriff Parks dragged Conner to his vehicle and threw him in the backseat. He turned toward Cindy.

"You're an accomplice. You're coming with me!" Cindy didn't move. The car door opened, and the driver stepped outside. He was a big, broad-shouldered man.

"Mr. Evans," Cindy said, recognizing her neighbor. "Can you take me home?"

"Sure," he answered. "Is she free to go, Sheriff, or do you want to slap her around, too?" When Parks didn't answer, Mr. Evans walked Cindy to his car. He opened the door for her, and sliding into the driver's seat, he backed the car off the bridge. The sheriff turned on the radio and called Dively's Garage.

"I said right now! Tow that damn jeep off the bridge right now! No, I won't be waiting here. I got me a criminal to process." Sheriff Parks looked at Conner in the backseat. "You're just like your fuckin' dad!"

The sheriff turned the car around and drove to the end of the bridge. Lights on and engines running, five vehicles were backed up to the intersection. Ignoring them, the sheriff spun the tires and raced the gray car down the road.

The spotlight cast a bright glow over the cabin. Matt covered his nose at the stench from the FritoLay van. Climbing the porch steps, Matt ducked under the half-open window. He heard voices and the sound of beer cans snapping open. Then the phone rang.

One of the men picked up the receiver and talked in a muffled voice. Matt heard the words, "No, we haven't seen Jeffery. But we've got that crazy school janitor tied up in the basement." There was a moment of silence, and the man hung up the phone.

"Nathaniel will be here soon."

"What's he gonna do?"

"He was pissed. He said he would handle the problem."

Matt descended the porch steps and crept around the cabin to the basement. Pushing open the door, he saw Mr. Brooks bound on the floor next to the dog cage. Matt went to the workstation and picked up heavy scissors. Leaning over Mr. Brooks, he cut through the rope; one of the puppies made a low growling noise.

"Please don't bark," Matt whispered; the puppy wagged its tail. Matt grabbed Mr. Brooks by the shoulders and pulled him across the floor. Maneuvering the body through the door, Matt dragged him across the open ground to the trees.

"I'm not going home yet," Cindy said to Mr. Evans. "Can you take me to the state police barracks?"

"Is it about the accident?"

"No, Mr. Evans. It's about the kidnappings at Twin River."

"Those poor girls," Mr. Evans said, accelerating.

The area around the Pennsylvania State Police Barracks was brightly lit. Mr. Evans drove past a row of patrol cars and parked at the main entrance. Getting out quickly, he and Cindy walked through the swinging doors. The duty officer sat behind a glass window. Cindy approached the window, tapped on the glass, and asked to see Sergeant Smith. Looking at the damp hair drooping over her face and the blanket dragging on the floor, the officer hesitated.

"He's busy now. Can I help you?"

"I need to talk to Sergeant Smith about the kidnapped girls."

The officer jumped to his feet and disappeared behind a closed door. Returning quickly, he ushered Cindy to a corner office. Sergeant Smith looked up from his desk and pointed to an empty chair. Cindy sat down, and speaking in a high-pitched but controlled voice, she explained everything that had happened.

"You say Gene Brooks found the kidnapped girls at this cabin, and there's a dead person in a FritoLay van?" Cindy nodded; the sergeant stared at her. "You and Conner know the location of this cabin?"

"Yes."

"Then let's get Conner right now."

After picking up the phone and ordering Trooper Owens to meet him at the entrance, Sergeant Smith took Cindy to the waiting room. He thanked Mr. Evans, who left the building. Trooper Owens entered the room and escorted Cindy to the patrol car. Sergeant Smith instructed the duty officer to notify the local ambulance service and the ER nurses at J. C. Blair Hospital to assemble at the Petersburg Fire Department parking lot. Then Sergeant Smith rushed to the patrol car and fastened his seat belt.

"No time to waste," he said to Trooper Owens.

"Got it." With red lights spinning and siren blaring, Trooper Owens cleared all traffic from both lanes on Route 22. Barely slowing down, he raced through three red lights and two stop signs. It took him six minutes to reach the sheriff's office. Seeing the vacant space, Trooper Owens parked in front of the "Reserved for Sheriff" sign.

"Wait here," Sergeant Del said to Cindy, and he and Owens got out of the car. With a glance at the FritoLay van, Del walked to the entrance and pressed the button, and the door buzzed open. Holding a bag of potato chips in his hand, Deputy Oliver rose to his feet.

"Sheriff Parks just left the building."

"I came for Conner Brooks."

"Conner ain't goin' nowhere. The sheriff even said no visitors. You can bet the boy will be locked up in a cell for a long time. Conner done something really stupid. He knocked that two-hundred-dollar cowboy hat into the river. Sheriff Parks ordered me to fish it out first thing in the morning. But no way is that my job as chief deputy."

"The hell with the sheriff's hat. Conner knows where the missing girls are."

"He was shoutin' something 'bout that. But he's a liar."

"Get him up here immediately!" Sergeant Del ordered, slamming his fist on the desk. "If I don't see Conner Brooks in three seconds, I'm going to arrest you for impeding an investigation. And if anything happens to those two girls, you're the one who'll be in a cell."

"There's no cause to be threatening me like that. We're all on the same side of the law, ya know." Dropping the bag of chips, his face turning red, Deputy Oliver grabbed the phone. "Steve, bring that boy Conner Brooks up here right now." Oliver chewed on his lip and pulled his cap, which was crushed on both sides, low over his eyes. The door opened; Conner was pushed into the room. There was a gash on his forehead, and his lip was cut.

"You cowardly bastard!" Sergeant Smith bellowed.

"Sheriff Parks … he done that," Oliver stammered. "I never touched the boy."

"We'll settle this later," Sergeant Smith said, and he took Conner by the arm. "Let's find your dad." At the door, he turned and glared at Oliver. "Take my advice, Deputy. Get release forms for Pete Rogers. He's not guilty of anything."

Ten minutes later when Sheriff Parks entered the office, Oliver told him about Sergeant Smith taking Conner, about the kidnapped girls at the cabin, and about the sergeant's instructions to release Pete. The sheriff swore and rushed out of the office. As the car pulled away, Chief Deputy Oliver reached for the phone.

Gene heard voices from the cabin and opened his eyes. Grimacing, he struggled to a sitting position. Matt rushed over and helped him to his feet.

"Are you all right, Mr. Brooks?"

"Now I am," Gene said, breathing slowly. "What are you doing here?"

"I couldn't leave you. I came back."

"Good thing you did. You didn't see my gun anywhere, did you?"

"No, but I saw two men in the cabin. They're waiting for Nathaniel. I think he's the boss. He's coming here to take care of the problem."

"I guess I'm the problem," Gene stated, getting to his feet. A horn sounded through the night air; headlights flashed along the side of the cabin. "That must be Nathaniel. Let's get deeper in these woods," Gene advised, and they began walking through the brush.

Loud voices shouted from the cabin; the basement door burst open, and the bright glow from a flashlight swept through the trees. Watching the light move closer, Gene pulled Matt behind a large bush. Then a phone began ringing. The flashlight stopped and pointed harmlessly to the night sky. Footsteps pounded back to the cabin; the door slammed shut.

Rushing to the table, Nathaniel grabbed the phone. Max paced back and forth; Luther lit a cigarette. Nathaniel slammed the phone down.

"It was Oliver. The state police are on their way. We've got to leave."

"We should take care of that janitor first," Max cautioned.

"We don't have time to fool with him."

"What about Sally and Brenda?"

"Are you deaf? I said we don't have time." Nathaniel rushed to the door. "Get your car and follow me. We'll take the back way to State College." When Nathaniel heard the siren in the distance, he hurried to the BMW, started the engine, and raced the car through the gate. After driving only a short distance, he turned at an unmarked intersection. Wheels spinning dust in the air, Luther and Max were on his bumper.

———————

"The kidnappers got out of here fast, Matt," Gene said, climbing the steps to the cabin. "Let's see if they left anything."

"Okay, Mr. Brooks." Matt followed Gene into the cabin. Walking around the room, peering under furniture, he saw round objects under the sofa. Matt picked up two tokens and gave them to Gene.

"Pump House," Gene read.

"What's that?"

"A popular student bar outside State College." Gene pocketed the tokens.

"Will the kidnapper be at the Pump House?"

"Are you kidding, Matt? He gets free drinks there." The siren grew louder; Gene and Matt walked to the porch. The stench from the FritoLay van permeated the night air; Matt held his nose.

"Mr. Brooks, how did you know this was the kidnapper's van?"

"This is the van I saw the morning of Sally's kidnapping. It has a 11--0, 1969 Penn State sticker on the door. Pete's van had an identical 11–0 sticker, except the year was 1968. There were two different vans."

Sirens blasting and red lights spinning through the darkness, a line of patrol cars, a fire truck, and an ambulance slowed and parked in a tight half circle around the cabin. Gene and Matt walked down the steps to the lead patrol car. Slamming the door, Sergeant Del Smith shouted orders. Officers began stretching yellow tape around the area. Moving quickly, Trooper Owens led a group of men and two nurses into the cabin. Sergeant Smith pulled Gene aside.

"Your son had some problems with the sheriff," Del said, motioning to the patrol car. The back door opened, and Cindy and Conner stepped out. Gene saw the bruises.

"What happened?"

"Sheriff Parks hit him!" Cindy shouted.

A lone siren pierced the night air. The sheriff's car barreled through the gate and slid to a stop next to the ambulance. Sheriff Parks cut the engine. With the noise of the siren lingering, Gene ripped the door open and pulled Sheriff Parks from the seat. Standing him vertically against the side of the car, he smashed his fist into the wide-eyed, blubbering face. The sheriff's body hit the ground. The toes of his white alligator boots pointed straight in the air.

"Dad, I'm fine," Conner said, rushing over. He stared at the crumpled body for a few moments. When he looked up, he had a worried expression on his face. "I'm sorry, Dad. I kind of had an accident with the jeep. I heard the sheriff call Dively's Garage. Don't worry, Dad. It only has a few dents."

"Just a few dents," Gene said, managing a smile. Looking past Conner, he watched the kidnapped girls and two nurses walk through the cabin door. There was barking from the side of the house, and Trooper Owens appeared with the puppies on leashes. Skippy and Tippy pulled in opposite directions.

"Can I take care of the puppies?" Gene asked, reaching for the leashes.

"Sure," the trooper said, and he gave the puppies to Gene.

"I think we should get you and the kids out of here," Del suggested politely, and he ushered Gene to an empty patrol car. Matt, Cindy, and Conner took the puppies to the backseat. Sergeant Del opened the door for Gene. "Trooper Owens will take you home. I'll get your statements later. And concerning the problem of Sheriff Parks, I didn't see nothing." Del laughed, shutting the door. "As far as I'm concerned, the sheriff walked into a tree."

"Thanks, Del," Gene said. The car pulled away. Following Gene's directions, the trooper drove to Cindy's house in Barree. On the porch, Cindy hugged Conner and smiled.

"I'm sorry the canoe overturned. I'm sorry you got beat up. But I had a great time tonight."

"I had the best time ever," Conner said enthusiastically. We'll go canoeing again. I'm free all week." Cindy's parents appeared, and glancing at the police vehicle, they pulled her through the door.

Conner returned to the car. The trooper drove to Gene's house. Conner stepped outside, but Gene didn't move.

"Matt and I will pick up the jeep. We'll be back soon."

Hesitating a moment, Conner nodded and walked to the porch. Gene leaned back; the bruise on his head began to throb. It was a short drive to Diveley's Garage. Gene thanked the trooper, Matt gathered up the puppies, and they walked to the dented jeep. Gene spoke with rancor in his voice.

"We're going to the Pump House."

"I figured that." Matt smiled; his eyes gleamed. "What will we do with the kidnapper?"

"You already know that answer, Matt."

"You're right. I *do* know," Matt said, a note of excitement in his voice.

Chapter Twenty-Nine

At the Pump House, Jeffery left the apartment, unlocked the Porsche, and dropped his suitcase inside. As he walked to the entrance, he saw three vehicles in the parking lot. Two cars were parked up front, and an orange jeep was far back in the corner. Jeffery stared at it for a moment. Then he hurried inside the Pump House and placed a token on the bar. Josh brought over a rum and Coke.

"Thanks," Jeffery said, taking a drink. "It's my last token."

"I remember when that rich fella gave you those," Josh said. "He was here asking questions about you."

"What'd you tell him?"

"I haven't seen you. I got the impression he would keep looking."

"I think you're right," Jeffery said, handing Josh an envelope. "Here's five hundred. I'm checking out of the apartment. I need to find a better job in another town." Finishing the drink, he left a five-dollar bill on the bar and walked to the door.

The night air was brisk. Jeffery was only a few steps into the parking lot when he stopped in his tracks. Tied to the door handle of the Porsche, Tippy and Skippy began barking and straining at their leashes. Jeffery ran to them.

"What are you two doing here?" Jeffery picked them up. The puppies yelped and licked at his neck and chin with pink sloppy tongues. Then a shadow appeared from the side, and a heavy object thudded against his head. Jeffery collapsed in total darkness.

A fire burned at the summit of Blood Mountain. Lashed to the tree, his mouth taped shut, his face smeared with blood, Jeffery wore only boxer shorts. Lines of black-and-red ants exited the coned mounds at his feet. Gene and Matt walked from the shadows. Gene carried the Arkansas Toothpick. The Roman death hammer was tucked under Matt's belt.

"You wanted to be a hunter, Matt—a real soldier. Are you ready to prove it?"

"Yes." Matt pulled out the death hammer. It was heavier than he remembered. His arm trembled with the weight.

"Before I gagged him, he said his name was Jeffery. Well, Jeffery's the worst kind of person, Matt. He kidnapped Brenda and Sally. He did bad things to them and put it on video. Jeffery doesn't deserve to live."

The fire crackled brightly. It cast flickering shadows over Jeffery's body. Jeffery's face and neck muscles bulged as he strained to move his lips; bubbles appeared around the edges of the tape. Taking deep breaths, Matt tried to steady the hammer.

"But I didn't see him do anything bad to the girls."

"We watched the video together. You saw him in Brenda's room, didn't you?"

"Yes."

"What do you think the son of a bitch was planning?"

"I didn't see him do anything bad," Matt whispered again.

Jeffery's watery eyes were open wide. Blood flowed down the side of his face and dripped off his chin, forming dark wet circles on his boxer shorts. Matt gasped when he saw the line of ants moving up Jeffery's leg, moving under the folds of the shorts. He became nauseous. His grip on the death hammer loosened.

"I didn't think it would be like this."

"Don't make this difficult," Gene said in a calm voice. "Let's get started here. I'll show you how easy it is." Gene raised the Toothpick and stepped arm's length from Jeffery. In a swift motion, he sliced the blade in a diagonal line the length of the abdominal muscles. Blood streamed from the wound. Jeffery strained violently against the ropes, and his body arched forward. His face turning ghostly white, he began to bite at the tape.

"Don't be fooled, Matt. The wicked and the damned all cry and pretend they're innocent. But this is Blood Mountain. There is only retribution here. It's time to use your hammer."

Matt stood perfectly still. The fire crackled; flames reached high in the air. In the light, Matt watched the blood ooze from the thin cut on the abdomen. Jeffery's body shivered; his chest heaved. Matt found it difficult to breathe. Tears filled his eyes; Matt wiped at them with his hand. Stepping next to him, Gene stared at him incredulously.

"This isn't the time for crying, Matt. You're a soldier now. You're not turning chicken shit, are you?"

"Don't call me that," Matt muttered. He lowered his head and stared at the ground. Ants were crawling over his shoes. He scraped at them and shuffled away from the tree. Gene watched him closely.

"You don't even look like a soldier," Gene said in an exasperated voice. He ripped Matt's T-shirt, exposing the bony rib cage and pale flesh. Gripping Matt's arm tightly, Gene swiped his hand across Jeffery's abdomen. Turning, he vigorously rubbed his bloody fingers into Matt's face, mouth, and chest.

"Do your job, soldier," Gene ordered.

Matt gagged at the silvery taste. A gust of wind blew from the cliffs; shadows rose from the abyss. Incongruously, the shirtless, flabby figure of Mr. Henry materialized. Mr. Henry pinned Matt to the bed and tore away his pajamas. When Mr. Henry crushed him with his weight, Matt again smelled the stench of whiskey and sweat. Eyes disfigured, Captain Hook stood motionless behind Mr. Henry. The shadows darkened, and the grinning god of death, Dis Pater, stepped forward.

His face turning grim, Matt lifted the Roman hammer. Focusing on a pale spot of flesh next to Jeffery's eye, Matt swung the hammer with incredible force. As the hammer descended, Matt felt sudden, sharp pressure on the side of his head. The hammer slipped from his hand; Matt fell to the ground.

Matt woke up in the bedroom and stared at the ceiling for a long time. When he finally sat up, he saw Conner in a deep sleep. Removing the torn, bloodied T-shirt, Matt slid a Twin River sweatshirt over his head. Then he went downstairs, picked up a flashlight, and ran outside. Getting on his bicycle, Matt pedaled furiously down the road.

Out of breath, his chest heaving, Matt reached the utility shed, grabbed the key from under the rock, and opened the door. He pushed the four-wheeler outside and got on, and with a roar of noise, the vehicle kicked into motion. Leaning over the handlebars, Matt raced the four-wheeler. After a few minutes, he made the sharp turn onto Blood Mountain.

At the summit, Matt stopped in front of the fire. Glowing coals illuminated the wet smear of blood that streaked up the side of the tree. Matt's heart began to pound. He walked to the tree and pulled himself through the lower branches. Pausing at times to catch his breath, Matt climbed from branch to branch. His Twin River sweatshirt was soaked with perspiration when he reached the platform. The towering cross on the mountain glowed with a bright intensity. Exhausted, Matt sat down and buried his head in his arms. Ants crawled on the platform; an owl screeched.

Moments later Matt got to his feet and began to climb. As he approached the top, his legs began to tremble, and his heart beat faster. Taking a deep breath, he lifted his head and stared at the long thick branches piercing the sky. The higher branches gleamed white with skeletons; the nearer branches were empty.

Matt hesitated; then turning, he descended slowly. When he

reached the platform, he collapsed on his back. A calming wind blew, and the sky offered a panorama of stars. The lines of the Big Dipper were clear and lucent. Matt watched the stars; their pulsating brightness brought tears to his eyes.

Tippy and Skippy barked and chased each other. Sitting on the sofa in the basement of Holy Waters Church, Gene Brooks was laughing at *The Dukes of Hazzard*. With the air horn playing "Dixie," Luke and Bo Duke raced the Dodge Charger down the dirt road. Lights blazing and siren blasting, the sheriff's Plymouth Fury was trailing in a cloud of dust.

"Damn Rosco," Gene said. Holding a steaming cup of coffee, Joyce walked into the room and sat on the sofa.

"You sure you don't want a cup?" she asked.

"I'm sure," Gene said. "It's really late. Where's my brother?"

"Dan Boonie had a bad motorcycle accident. For some reason, Andrew's staying nights with him at the hospital." Joyce sipped at the coffee.

"How's Jeffery doing?"

"There was a lot of blood," she said. "But the wound wasn't deep. He won't even need stitches. I put in some clamps and bandaged everything. He'll be fine."

"He'll have a scar?"

"Oh, yeah, Gene. But he's a hunk. A scar on his body will only make him more attractive. What is he, a movie star or something?"

"He was on his way to stardom."

"Where do you find these people?"

"I don't know," Gene said. There were footsteps at the door. As Jeffery walked into the room, Skippy and Tippy ran to him. Jeffery reached down and petted them.

"Behave, Tippy and Skippy," he said. After buttoning his shirt, Jeffery sat on the La-Z-Boy. His hair was damp from the shower;

his face had a clear glow. Leaning back, he began to rock slowly, his eyes focusing on Joyce.

"Thanks for fixing me up."

"It's my job. How do you feel?"

"I never felt better. I can't believe I'm still alive."

"You're lucky," Gene said, getting off the sofa and scooping up the puppies. "Let's go to the Pump House and get that Porsche before someone steals it."

Jeffery stood, and after thanking Joyce again, he followed Gene to the door. Gene dropped Tippy and Skippy in the backseat. Driving through Barree, he glanced at Jeffery and was met with a hard stare.

"What's the matter, Jeffery?"

"You. You're so calm now, but back at the mountain, you had the face of a killer. It was the worst face I've ever seen. Even worse than that chainsaw killer in Texas."

"Thanks, that's quite a compliment."

"I mean it. You intended to kill me, didn't you?"

"Yes, Jeffery. When I saw the video of you and Brenda … right then I made up my mind to kill you."

"Why didn't you?"

"It's complicated, Jeffery. I don't think you'll understand."

"Please tell me, Mr. Brooks."

"It's mostly what you did at the cabin, Jeffery. When I saw how much you cared about the puppies and how much they cared about you … that's when I changed my mind. That's when I figured you had some good in you."

"That was it?!" Jeffery shouted in disbelief.

"What can I say, Jeffery. I trusted the dogs." Skippy and Tippy jumped and barked in the backseat. Gene looked at Jeffery's face in the mirror. "I knew you wouldn't understand."

"Maybe I do understand." Jeffery managed to smile. He turned around and hugged the puppies, who were yelping and licking his face. "Skippy and Tippy, I love you." Jeffery released the dogs and sat back in the seat. "And what about the boy? He turned crazy and was swinging that hammer. I was scared. I blacked out. What happened to him?"

"The boy's name is Matt. I dropped him off at the house."

"I hope Matt's okay." Jeffery stared out the window. "This has been the worst night of my life. I was … like … losing my mind the whole time I was tied to the tree. I tried to talk, but I couldn't. I wanted to tell you I didn't do anything to the girls."

"On the video, Brenda was naked on the bed."

"I know. I was so damn dumb to agree to do the videos. But I ran out of that room before anything happened. When you cut me loose from the tree and I could think clearly, I realized I had broken all kinds of laws." Jeffery was quiet for a moment. He lowered his head. "Are you going to turn me in?"

"No, you're a free man, Jeffery. But you need to be careful. The girls can identify you. You should get out of this area."

"I was planning to leave last night." The puppies began to bark, and Jeffery turned around. He picked them up and dropped them in his lap. When they quieted, he stared at Gene. "Can we do something before I leave?"

"What?"

"Nathaniel has another cabin. I know where it is."

After listening to his every word, Gene spun the jeep around and headed toward Spruce Creek. Following Jeffery's directions, he drove to the end of a recently cleared road on Willow Mountain and stopped next to a chain-link fence. One spotlight lit up the empty parking area. Getting out of the jeep, Gene studied the cabin.

"It looks identical to the place at Hare Valley."

"Nathaniel uses the same contractor. I think they're cousins."

"I'm going in, Jeffery. You wait here with the puppies." Leaving the jeep, Gene forced open the security gate. Then he hurried to the cabin, climbed the steps, and kicked in the door. After turning on the lights, Gene picked up the telephone. He dialed the sergeant's number, and when Del answered, Gene gave him directions to the cabin.

"We'll be there in thirty minutes. Wait for us."

"I can't wait." Gene hung up and went downstairs to the basement. There was music coming from both the Nymph Room and the Shangri-la Room. Gene grabbed a hammer and knocked off the doorknob to the Nymph Room. The girl sitting on the bed screamed when he entered. Tears ran down her face.

"Don't be afraid. I'm here to help you. What's your name?"

"Denise," she answered. "Who are you?"

"I'm a friend, Denise. Get dressed. You're going home."

Gene broke open the door of the Shangri-la Room. When he entered, he saw a girl cowering under the sheets. The video camera clicked; Gene threw the hammer and knocked it off the wall. Denise rushed into the room. Gene waited outside while she helped the girl get dressed. After a short time, they came to the hall and followed Gene upstairs.

"The state police will be here soon," Gene said. "The phone's on the table. You can call home. You can tell your parents you're safe."

"Thank you," Denise said, and she ran to the phone. After waiting until he heard Denise talking to her mother, Gene left the cabin and walked to the jeep. The puppies began barking. Gene started the motor and drove down the road.

"Are the girls all right?" Jeffery asked.

"Yes, I've never seen happier faces. I'm so damn glad I didn't kill you, Jeffery."

"Thanks," Jeffery said. "Thanks a hell of a lot."

"I believed you were guilty. I was wrong. I swear it won't happen again."

"What do you mean, Mr. Brooks?"

"I'm done with it," Gene answered emphatically. The sirens were a distant sound at first. Soon, flashing red lights appeared on the winding road. Slowing down, Gene turned off the lights and drove the car behind some trees. "Jeffery, we'll get your car, and you can disappear with Tippy and Skippy. Does that sound all right to you?"

"It sounds great," Jeffery said.

With sirens blasting and red lights spinning, two patrol cars raced by. Gene waited and pulled back onto the road. He was halfway down Willow Mountain when an ambulance suddenly appeared. Gene drove slowly by the speeding vehicle. When he reached the bottom of Willow Mountain, he turned the jeep toward State College.

Driving past the front entrance of the Pump House, Gene saw a glow of light from a car across the street. Gene turned the corner at the end of the block, went down the alley, and stopped the jeep in the corner of the parking lot. The Pump House was in shadow; moonlight reflected off the Porsche. Jeffery pushed open the door.

"I'll get the car."

"Wait a minute. Someone's watching us from across the street. He lit a cigarette."

"It has to be Luther. He's always smoking. What should I do?"

Before Gene could answer, Tippy jumped out of the jeep and raced across the asphalt. Skippy moved to follow him, but Jeffery grabbed his collar and jerked him back inside. When Tippy reached the Porsche, he barked and shoved his head under the passenger door. His body low to the cement, Tippy snarled and bit into something.

The noise of the explosion was deafening. A blinding heat wave swept across the parking lot, blasting into the side of the jeep. Fire and black clouds of smoke rose in the air. Skippy was yelping; Jeffery held him tightly against his chest. Starting the engine, Gene left the parking lot and drove through the blinking red lights and deserted streets of State College. Jeffery had his head lowered; his face was moist with tears.

"It's all my fault."

"It's no one's fault. The dog saved your life. Probably saved mine, too." Gene turned the jeep onto Route 26 and began the climb up

Pine Grove Mountain. "You can stay at the house tonight. Then I'll take you to the train station in the morning. Where do you want to go —Pittsburgh or Philadelphia?"

"Philadelphia," Jeffery said. He petted Skippy. "I've got no place to keep him. Can you take care of Skippy until I get settled?"

"Sure."

"Thanks. I think Skippy likes you."

Gene accelerated down the empty road. When he parked the jeep in the yard, he saw the front door was open. Jeffery grabbed Skippy, and he and Gene entered the house. Gene pointed to the sofa. Jeffery removed his shoes and collapsed on the cushions. Wagging his tail, Skippy jumped up next to him, resting his head and paws on Jeffery's chest. After Gene covered them with a blanket, he climbed the stairs and looked into the boys' bedroom. Conner was asleep; Matt's bed was empty.

"Where the hell are you?" Gene asked. He descended the stairs to the kitchen, grabbed the Roman hammer and a can of lighter fluid off the table, and went to the porch. With two strong swings of the hammer, he knocked out the wall supports. After rolling up the hammock, he strode to the riverbank. Gene dropped the hammock in the sand, dosed it with fluid, and tossed a lighted match on the bundle. Smoke and sparks shot high in the air. Gene stepped back.

"I'm done with it," he whispered. The fire was a fierce, expanding flame. Within seconds, the fire dimmed, leaving smoldering strands of fiber in the sand. Wading into the river, Gene scooped handfuls of water on the red embers. A cool breeze blew. The sky was clear. Deep in the heavens, the North Star and the Big Dipper glowed in the night sky.

Chapter Thirty

At ten in the morning, Gene drove Jeffery to the train station. Two college girls were waiting on the platform. A big smile on his face, Jeffery walked over and talked to them, paying particular attention to a blond wearing designer sunglasses. With its horn blasting through the station, the Amtrak train arrived and screeched to a stop. Doors opened, and the conductor appeared. Jeffery rushed over and shook Gene's hand.

"Thanks for everything," he said, and he jumped onto the steps. When the train left the station, Jeffery pounded on the window and waved. Gene smiled and waved back, noticing the blond girl sitting there, her arm around Jeffery's shoulder.

Crazy kid, Gene thought as the train disappeared down the track. Crossing the street to Mark's Corner Store, Gene bought two packages of M&M's. Then he drove to Twin River. When the bell rang to change classes, he climbed the steps to the second floor. The hall was empty; Matt was sitting in front of the display case.

"Why aren't you in class?"

"My shop project's done. Mr. Gates is grading it now."

"Can we go outside and talk where it's quiet?"

"It's quiet here," Matt said.

"Not for long," Gene said, noticing Charlie Hesston glaring at them through the open door. Matt saw him, also. He got up and followed Gene to the river. They sat on the wooden steps. Sparrows darted up and down the bank and skimmed the surface of the river. Gene reached into his pocket and gave a package of M&M's to Matt.

"Thanks," Matt said, tearing open the package.

"I looked into your room last night. You weren't there."

"When I woke up, I went to Blood Mountain. I wanted to see what happened to Jeffery. I wanted to see if you put his body on the branch like you said you would. I was surprised. Jeffery wasn't there."

"I released Jeffery after you left. He's on his way to Philadelphia now."

"Last night on the mountain, I was more confused than ever in my life. Did you want me to kill him?"

"No. I tried to make it so terrible that you wouldn't think about killing him. When I cut Jeffery and smeared his blood over your face, I was sure it would make you sick. I was wrong. You swung the hammer with such force it would have crushed Jeffery's skull."

"That's when you stopped me?"

"Yes, I stopped you."

"Last night was confusing. I don't remember everything that happened. I saw Mr. Henry in the Shadows. I wanted to kill him. Maybe I wanted to kill Jeffery, too."

"You had me fooled. I was wrong about Jeffery. I was wrong about you."

"It's not your fault, Mr. Brooks. I hide my inner thoughts very well." Matt looked at the river. The rapids boiled dark clouds up the side of Blood Mountain; the Shadows of Death covered the pine trees on the island with a fine mist. Matt stared at Gene. "I returned to the mountain and climbed the tree." Matt reached inside the bag and took some M&M's. "It was strange. When I saw the branches were empty, I cried."

"Because you knew Jeffery was alive?"

"No, I cried because you didn't kill him. All sinners deserve to die, Mr. Brooks."

"You could kill a helpless man?" There was a splashing sound from the river. At the bank, a heron stood motionless, thin legs sticking out of the water, a fish flapping crosswise in its beak. "You have so little regard for human life?"

"It's what I read in Genesis, Mr. Brooks. God said, "man's heart is evil from his youth." God was so angry that he destroyed all of mankind in the great flood. God could have done it instantly, but He made it painfully slow, Mr. Brooks. Forty days and forty nights—why did it take so long?"

"I don't know. I never thought about it."

"I'm sure it was because of man's wickedness. Man deserves to suffer."

"That's what you want to do with people like Mr. Henry?"

"Not the suffering part, Mr. Brooks. I will dispatch them with god's hammer."

"It's wrong to dispatch people, as you call it."

"Will you try to stop me . . . again?" Matt hesitated, staring at Gene.

"It would be a waste of time to follow you around, Matt. You're the only one who can control that anger you feel, that desire for vengeance. But I know one thing, Matt. You have an advantage that I never had."

"What advantage?"

"Your demeanor," Gene answered. "When people look at you, they see the innocence of a lamb. No one would think you were capable of killing."

"Maybe God meant it that way," Matt said, his oval eyes opening wide. "It's the lamb, not the lion, who takes away sin from the world."

There was noise on the road behind them. Gene turned and saw the black-and-white state police car pull to the curb. Sergeant Delaware Smith got out and walked toward them. Gene stood up, and they shook hands. The sheriff noticed the boy.

"Hi, Matthew. Any word from your father?"

"He called and said he was having a great time at some mountain resort." Throwing a handful of M&M's into his mouth, Matt stared casually at the river.

"Del, what happened at the cabin last night?" Gene asked.

"We found two girls. One girl was from Tyrone, and the other was from Clarion. The girls said nothing was done to them. They're at the hospital with their parents."

"Do you know anything about the body in the van?"

"Nothing yet. The body had no identification. At first, I was worried. I thought it might be …" Studying the boy's face, Del hesitated. Matt shuffled his feet back and forth and spoke in a cheerful voice.

"It couldn't have been Mr. Henry."

"That's right," Del agreed. "He's vacationing on some mountain. I guess he's the lucky one." After shaking hands, Sergeant Del got into his car and drove across the parking lot. The late bell rang, and finishing his M&M's, Matt took off running toward the door. There was movement in the corner of the parking lot. Gene watched a hooded figure sneak between the row of cars and dart through the emergency exit.

Chapter Thirty-One

Matt jumped the steps to the second floor and rushed into the wood shop class just as the late bell ended. Mr. Gates had placed note cards under each student project. There were birdhouses, mailboxes, gun cabinets, book cabinets, and an oversized wooden NRA bald eagle grasping an assault rifle in its claws. Matt's model Colt .45 was one of the smaller projects. A big smile formed on his face when he saw the A+ on the note card.

"Mr. Gates," Matt called, picking up the Colt and rushing to his desk. "Can I show it to Mr. Brooks?"

"Sure." Mr. Gates scribbled the time on the hall pass and handed the paper to Matt.

"Thanks," Matt said, and he left the room. Matt was walking down the hall when he saw Cain and Abel enter the restroom. Abel hesitated at the door, turned, and gave Matt the finger. Walking by slowly, Matt raised the Colt .45.

"Right between the eyes, you piece of shit." Matt sneered and made a popping noise with his lips. "You smell real bad. You need to go inside and wipe your face."

"I'll rip off your face," Abel growled. He lunged, but Matt sidestepped around him. Matt fired off another shot and jumped down the steps to the first floor.

Wearing a black hooded sweatshirt, Wayne leaned against the side of the toilet stall. There was a small cassette player tied to a cord around his neck. He gripped the Victory Model tightly in his hand. Wayne heard the door open and listened as Cain entered and went into the first stall. The toilet lid smacking hard against the bowl, jeans scraping against the floor, Cain sat down with a loud farting noise. Abel entered the restroom, stopped in front of the urinal, and lowered the zipper on his jeans. Clicking the button on the cassette player, Wayne turned up the volume; the voice of Kenny Rogers filled the restroom.

> Everyone considered him the coward of the county …
> But something always told me they were reading Tommy wrong.

"Who the hell's playing that shit?" Abel mumbled. He zipped his jeans and began kicking the doors. When Abel reached the last stall and pushed the door open, Wayne cracked him in the forehead with the Victory Model. Abel collapsed. Wayne quickly put a strip of tape around Abel's mouth and eyes and then taped his hands.

> Promise me, son, not to do the things I've done.
> Walk away from trouble if you can.

"Abel, what the hell's going on with that country shit?" Cain stood, flushed the toilet, and stepped out of the stall; Wayne clubbed him above the ear. Cain's glasses spun away and ricocheted to the bottom of the sink. Dropping heavily, Cain landed next to Abel. Wayne turned down the music and taped Cain's eyes, mouth, and hands. The twins made grunting sounds; Wayne leaned over them.

"I have a gun," he said. "Give me a reason, and I'll shoot you bastards right here." Wayne tapped the barrel against Cain's forehead. "Get to your feet."

Breathing heavily, the twins struggled to stand. After picking up the glasses and sliding them over the tape on Cain's eyes, Wayne nudged Cain and Abel toward the door. They moved clumsily, their bodies bumping into the sink, against the urinal. Wayne pushed the door open, and they stepped outside. Walking down the empty hall, Conner Brooks stopped in his tracks.

"What the hell!" he exclaimed.

Down the hall from Conner, Charlie Hesston heard the music and glanced through the half-open door. He saw the bloodied pastor's sons and the boy holding the gun. Kenny Rogers sang mournfully from the cassette player.

> Twenty years of crawlin' was bottled up inside him.
> He wasn't holdin' nothin' back; he let 'em have it all.

"This is fuckin' unreal," Mr. Hesston gasped. Without warning, the boy fired the gun twice; Cain and Abel collapsed. Shouting at his students to get on the floor, Mr. Hesston scrambled to his desk. He unlocked the drawer and grabbed the .38 Special.

Gene Brooks was in the principal's office when he heard the loud cracks. He saw Mr. Port stand and rush to the intercom. Shouting at a high pitch, the principal's voice blasted through Twin River High School.

"This is a Code Three emergency. All faculty are to lock their doors. No one is permitted in the hall." Dropping the microphone, which rattled on the desk, Mr. Port called JC Blair Hospital, the state police barracks, and the sheriff's office.

Matt was on the stairway when the shots went off. Grasping the Colt .45, he jumped the steps. The principal's announcement exploded over the speakers as Matt reached the second floor. He saw everything in one quick glance. Conner stood perfectly still in the middle of the hall. Wayne hovered over the bodies of Cain and Abel. Matt heard a clicking sound; Mr. Hesston raised his gun.

Beads of perspiration dripped down Mr. Hesston's face. Eyes squinting, he stared at the boy at the restroom door. When he saw Wayne turn toward him, Mr. Hesston aimed and fired. Wayne's body fell inside the restroom; his tennis shoes, grimy with dirt, protruded into the hall. There was movement on the staircase, and Mr. Hesston saw another boy with a gun. Oval eyes opening wide, the boy lifted his hands in the air.

"You dumb bastard!" Mr. Hesston exclaimed, firing quickly. His shoulder and back muscles turning rigid, he laughed nervously when the boy's body collapsed down the stairs.

"No!" Conner shouted, and he charged at Mr. Hesston. Wiping perspiration from his eyes and pivoting at the noise, Mr. Hesston saw a dark body closing in on him; he fired at point-blank range. But the body kept coming and crashed into his face and chest.

Gene Brooks was vaulting up the staircase when he saw Matt's body sprawled on the steps. Grabbing Matt's shoulders, he propped him against the wall. Matt's eyes opened wide and vapid.

"Can you hear me, Matt?"

"Yes," Matt responded tentatively.

"Stay here. Don't move an inch no matter what." Gene released his grip on Matt, and jumping to the top of the steps, he saw Mr. Hesston level the gun at Conner and pull the trigger. The explosion of noise filled the hall. Gene dove at Mr. Hesston and hit him at the same time as Conner. As Mr. Hesston fell to the floor, Gene grabbed hold of Conner.

"Don't worry, son. You'll be fine."

Charlie Hesston swore and lifted the .38 Special. Gene punched him in the face; Mr. Hesston's head cracked on the floor. It was quiet for a brief second. Then Mr. Hesston made an incomprehensible wailing noise.

"Shut the fuck up!" Gene bellowed. Kneeling, he crushed his fist into Hesston's throat. Blood gushed from Mr. Hesston's mouth and flowed the length of his beard. Gene took Hesston's gun and shoved it under his belt.

Groaning loudly, their right kneecaps shattered, Cain and Abel squirmed on the floor. The pool of blood around their feet expanded slowly. The door to the restroom creaked noisily. His face pallid, his eyes darting left and right, Wayne stood and rubbed his hand across the front of his sweatshirt. Mr. Brooks walked toward him; *Coward of the County* echoed down the empty hall.

"Just relax, Wayne," Gene instructed. Clicking off the cassette, he carefully took the gun, led Wayne across the hall, and positioned him next to Conner.

"Step back," Gene told them. When they were out of the way, he aimed Wayne's Victory Model and fired a shot into the wall near the staircase. Wiping the gun clean, he bent down and pressed it into Hesston's hand.

"Dad, what are you doing?" Conner asked.

"Don't worry about it, son. You did great." He put his hands on Conner's shoulders. "How do you feel?"

"Fine, I guess."

"I have to get Wayne out of the building. The police will be here soon. Can you tell them you saw Mr. Hesston shoot Cain and Abel and shoot at Matt on the staircase? Most important, tell them that when the gun went off, you saw me run for the exit. I know it's not true. But tell them that's what happened. Can you do that?"

"Sure, if that's what you want."

"Don't say a word to Sheriff Parks. Just talk to Sergeant Del." Gene Brooks grabbed Conner and hugged him. He felt Conner's heart pounding against his rib cage. "I'm proud of you, son. I'll see you tonight on Blood Mountain."

"But Matt was shot!"

"Matt's okay," Gene said. "You bring him tonight. And bring Wayne, too." Gene released Conner, and he and Wayne hurried to the emergency exit. Ducking between the cars in the parking lot, he ran Wayne to the jeep and pushed him into the backseat. Sirens blasting loudly, two police cars and an ambulance turned into the school. Gene started the jeep and drove around the opposite end of the building.

"You can come up front now," Gene said, pulling the jeep onto Route 305. He waited for Wayne to crawl over the seat. "Did anyone see you in the building?"

"No, I wore the hood the whole time."

"You had everything planned, didn't you?"

"Yes, down to the last detail."

"I enjoyed your music selection, Wayne. Why Kenny Rogers?"

"I like the way he sings. I kept the music loud to disguise the gunshots. Maybe I'll go to jail for shooting Cain and Abel. I don't care."

"You won't go to jail, Wayne. No one saw you in the building." Gene drove the jeep down the hill into Alexandria. When he turned and crossed over the bridge, the waters of the Juniata River sparkled in the sunlight. Looking through the windshield, his face pale in the light, Wayne spoke in a worried voice.

"Mr. Hesston witnessed everything. He'll tell the police what happened."

"I hit him pretty hard. When he wakes up, I don't think he'll remember anything. And if he does, he won't be able to talk about it for a long time."

"That's why you smashed his vocal cords?"

"No, Wayne. When I saw Hesston shoot at my son, I wanted to kill him."

"But you didn't."

"No, I didn't." Gene sat quietly. Seeing an ambulance and the sheriff's car, he pulled the jeep to the side. Swerving and knocking a mailbox in the air, the sheriff's car passed the ambulance. Gene waited and pulled the jeep onto the road. A TV 10 Action News van approached. Wayne stared at the van, his hands moving nervously on his jeans.

"There's something I don't understand, Mr. Brooks. Mr. Hesston shot me. The bullet knocked me through the restroom door. Why ain't I back in the hall dead?"

"Can we talk about that later?"

"Sure, Mr. Brooks."

Gene reached the intersection at Water Street and turned onto the narrow, winding road that led through Polecat Hollow. After a few minutes, he stopped at the Wilson house. Wayne opened the door, stepped to the ground, and stared through the open window.

"Mr. Brooks, I need to tell you something."

"What is it, Wayne?"

"Do you know what a rattlesnake does right after it strikes?"

"It releases the prey immediately."

"Do you know why?"

"The snake's very clever. It stays out of danger and waits for the victim to die. I'm a little confused, Wayne. Why are you asking me about rattlesnakes?"

"It's what I was thinking when I shot Cain and Abel in the knees."

"You wanted the twins to die—to die slowly and painfully?"

"Yes," Wayne said. "It wasn't about me so much. They hurt Becky." Wayne turned and looked at the house. The doors were closed, and the shades were drawn. Still looking at the house, Wayne spoke in a quiet voice. "Becky's pregnant."

"I'm sorry to hear that."

"She's really scared. She wants to have an abortion."

"Please don't let her do that."

"Why? She hates what's inside her. She hates Cain."

"She has reason to hate Cain, but the baby's innocent. Do you understand that?"

"I think I do. I'll tell Becky what you said."

"Tell her Conner and I will help. And my brother, Andrew, and his wife, Joyce, will help, also."

"I'll tell her everything you said. See you, Mr. Brooks. And thanks." Wayne walked to the house. The curtain on the upstairs window moved; Becky was standing there. Gene watched her for a moment. Then he turned the jeep around and drove down Polecat Hollow.

Lucy Brooks stood at the checkout counter at the Shady Maple Gift Shop. On the TV opposite the counter, the picture of Twin River High School flashed on the screen. A customer carrying a glass figurine of a unicorn came to the cash register. When Lucy saw the police cars and ambulance in the school parking lot, she rushed past the customer, knocking the figurine out of her hands. The unicorn hit the floor and shattered into pieces.

Sitting comfortably on a stool at the Screwballs Sports Bar & Grill in King of Prussia, Jeffery watched the large TV. The orange Dodge Charger created clouds of dust as it raced down the empty country road. There were dried-up cornfields, a barn, and a collapsed silo. Hidden behind the silo, Sheriff Rosco Coltrane pulled the rope that lifted a crudely painted sign, "Hospital Zone 15 M.P.H." Rosco's face was grim and determined as he turned on the siren and raced after the Charger.

"Hospital Zone." Jeffery laughed. Glancing at the mirror below the TV, Jeffery saw a woman in a blue dress walk into the room. He immediately began to scrutinize the trim curves on the body, the rounded breasts, the smile forming on her face. She paused for a moment, looked at the scattering of empty seats, and began to walk slowly to the bar.

"Sweet." Jeffery smiled.

Suddenly, *The Dukes of Hazzard* was interrupted by a TV 3 News Flash. Taking his eyes off the woman and glancing at the screen, Jeffery saw the picture of the school building and the flashing lights of the emergency vehicles in the parking lot. The caption under the picture, "Massacre at Twin River High School," was in bold black letters. Jeffery threw a ten-dollar bill on the bar, and circumventing the woman in the blue dress, who had paused directly in his path, he ran to the parking lot.

JJ Jackson sat in his high-rise office on Broad Street in Philadelphia. An associate came into the room and showed him the news report from Huntingdon County.

"Twin River is near that Mennonite school in Belleville. Isn't that where you killed that bastard Leroy?"

"Yes," JJ answered. "I have friends at Twin River. I've got to get up there."

JJ exited the parking garage, entered the Schuylkill Expressway on South Street, and raced wildly through the traffic. Horn blowing loudly, he was approaching the Conshohocken exit when a state police siren sounded. The pursuit and loud altercation that followed caused a two-mile traffic backup.

The setting sun cast a brilliant glow over Wildwood. Inside the beach house, Lieutenant Chase Butler watched the Twin River news report on TV. His eyes lingering on the word *Massacre*, he picked up the phone, called information, and was connected to the Huntingdon Police Station.

"This is Chief Deputy Oliver Wright," a voice answered.

"I'm Lieutenant Chase Butler. My nephew attends Twin River. Can you tell me what happened there?"

"I'm always glad to cooperate with a fellow officer of the law. It was a real dirty massacre. I'm sorry to say it was even worse than the one at that Mennonite school. Some students, maybe five or six, were shot. I just talked to the sheriff. He said the janitor had something to do with it."

"The school janitor, Gene Brooks?"

"Yes," Wright answered. "Mr. Brooks was seen running out of the building. He's some kind of Vietnam psycho."

"You should be real careful how you handle Vietnam veterans."

"Hello!" Oliver blurted. "I'm guessing you've had trouble with those bastards, too?"

"Every day," Chase said. Slamming the phone down, the lieutenant went to the bathroom. He showered and then shaved with a deluxe Dovo Shavette straight razor. When he finished drying his face, Chase walked to the bedroom. Rummaging through the dresser, he pulled out a black Special Forces T-shirt that had the white skull and Green Beret logo on the front. "De Oppresso Liber" was written in strikingly bold letters under the logo. Chase slid the T-shirt over his head.

The lieutenant exited the house and walked down the center of the boardwalk. After ten minutes, he approached a group of boisterous college students wearing Delta Upsilon shirts. Without breaking pace, Chase walked between them, bumping shoulders with a muscular, solid figure.

"Hey, asshole," the man barked, grabbing Chase by the arm. "You've got a real problem. You need someone to teach you how to walk!"

Chase pivoted smoothly, and without saying a word, he smashed his open palm powerfully into the man's chin. Lifted off his feet, the man tripped backward, flipped over the railing, and landed facedown in the sand. The man's fraternity friends backed away; Chase started down the boardwalk again.

At Morey's Pier, Lieutenant Chase walked down the steps to the beach. Shouts and laughter from the water park and brightly colored Ferris wheel drifted across the sand. Farther down the beach, a boy tossed a tennis ball into the water. Barking loudly, a black Lab jumped into the surf and retrieved it.

Chase walked to the breaking waves. Removing his Special Forces shirt, he folded it neatly on the sand. Then he waded into the surf. When the water reached his waist, Chase began to swim. He sliced through the water with long, smooth strokes that took him past the end of the pier. After fifteen minutes, Chase slowed. Suspended in the water, his legs were heavy in the undertow. Chase lifted them and rolled onto his back.

There was no wind; the night sky was clear. The North Star shone brightly overhead. The horizon was aglow from the lights of Wildwood. Reaching into the side pocket of his shorts, Chase pulled out the Dovo Shavette razor. Flying low over the water, a lone seagull cried out with a piercing noise

Breathing lightly, Chase slid the blade across his wrist. As blood spurted into the ocean, Chase closed his eyes and spread both arms over the water. Buoyant, his body rose and dipped with the rolling motion of the waves. Thin red globules expanded in the water, creating a glistening sheen that washed over him. A line of glowing phosphorus settled in the deep, jagged scar that crossed his forehead.

The seagull returned and hovered over the mysterious glow. Its wings were black shadows that swooped low over the floating object. The lieutenant's eyelids flicked open; glassy pupils gazed upward. The seagull flew off with a piercing scream.

Chase looked at the clear night sky. The constellations touched the ocean and glimmered with a dazzling brilliance. Chase took a deep breath. His chest heaved, and a slight moaning sound escaped his lips. The edges of the North Star blurred; Lieutenant Chase Butler closed his eyes to the swirling darkness.

Chapter Thirty-Two

The setting sun and the glow from a burning fire lit up the summit of Blood Mountain. Leaning a chainsaw against the pine tree, Gene Brooks threw a branch on the fire and sat down. He heard noise on the trail, and the three boys joined him around the fire. Speaking in an excited voice, Conner stared at Gene through the crackling flames.

"It was all crazy, Dad. I talked mostly with Sergeant Del. When Sheriff Parks came over, I didn't say a word. He shouted at me that you were guilty of leaving the scene of a crime." Conner shook his head and laughed.

"What's so funny?"

"The sheriff … the way his eye was swollen shut."

"I wanted to laugh, too, but I didn't," Matt said. The sheriff took my Billy the Kid Colt .45 and put it into a plastic evidence bag."

"How are Cain and Abel?" Gene asked.

"I guess they're okay," Conner said. "Aunt Joyce put tourniquets on their legs. She was about done when Mr. Stedman came running down the hall pointing a gun at everyone. He fell in the blood and hurt his wrist. He never did come back."

"They should retire that man," Gene commented sourly.

"Dad, Sergeant Del said officers were coming to the house. Did you talk to them?"

"Two patrol cars came over," Gene said. "I was on the porch when the officers ran up the steps. They seemed really disappointed with me. They figured a Vietnam vet with all that war experience shouldn't have run away."

"That's just what I told them, Dad. I didn't like saying it, but I said you panicked and ran like hell."

"Good work. What about Mr. Hesston?"

"Mr. Hesston was crazy," Conner answered. "He tried to kill us all."

"I put my hands in the air, and the crazy son of a bitch shot me." Leaning forward, Matt stuck a finger in the middle of his chest. "I was hit right here. I was dead and rolled down the steps. Then Mr. Brooks appeared out of nowhere, started talking to me, and I was alive again."

"Dad, the police drew a circle around the hole in the wall. Sergeant Del said Mr. Hesston was a lousy shot. But you made that hole. And you put Wayne's gun in his hand to make it look like Mr. Hesston shot Cain and Abel."

"Yes."

"But I don't understand," Matt said, his eyes squinting, deep furrows forming on his brow. "I saw the gun pointing right at me. I was shot for sure."

"I was running at Mr. Hesston when he shot me. Why didn't the bullets hit us?"

"Conner, they weren't real bullets," Gene explained. "During the in-service day, I searched Hesston's room and found the gun. I replaced the bullets with blanks."

"But I was sure," Matt stammered.

"It was just the loud noise and tons of adrenaline running through your body."

"Loud noise and adrenaline," Matt repeated, shaking his head. He glanced at the chainsaw on the ground next to the pine tree. Ants crawled up the handle. "Mr. Brooks, why did you bring the chainsaw up here?"

"I planned to cut down that tree. I had this crazy idea that it would make me feel better. But the tree ..."

"It's way too big, Dad."

"I found that out the hard way. It doesn't matter. I have no reason to come to Blood Mountain anymore. I'm spending more time at home. I'm starting a new life."

"What do you mean, a new life?" Matt asked incredulously. "I think your life's just fine the way it is. Look what you did today. You saved us all."

"Things worked out well today. But like I said, I plan to spend more time at home. Here, Conner." Gene reached under his belt and pulled out Hesston's .38 Special. "We don't want anyone examining this. Can you throw it into the rapids?"

"Sure," Conner said, taking the gun. He and Wayne went to the edge of the cliff. Matt stayed behind.

"That's real clever, Mr. Brooks, pretending to lose interest in the tree." Matt spoke in a sincere, respectful tone. "When do you plan on doing it?"

"Doing what?"

"Finding the man who hit you at the cabin. And maybe finding the owner who runs the video business." Matt stared at Gene. "And we still have to help Lilly and Jack!"

"I wasn't pretending, Matt. I'm done with it."

"You can't quit," Matt argued in a loud voice. "There's no one else to help. You're the best!"

"Listen to me, Matt. Get it through your thick skull. It's over. Keeping the family together is more important than being judge and jury for all of Hartslog Valley."

"One, two, three!" Conner shouted. He threw the .38 Special spinning into the Shadows, and he and Wayne walked back. As he approached the tree, Conner saw Matt's tightly closed lips and how his hands were knotted into fists.

"What's the matter?"

"Nothing," Gene answered. "Now that everything's settled, let's get off this mountain. You guys put out the fire."

Matt stood silently. Conner and Wayne threw dirt on the dying embers. A thick cloud of mist rose from the Shadows of Death. The moisture settled over the ashes; thin lines of smoke spiraled upward. When the pit was completely black, Gene walked to the trail. Conner was directly behind him, and the other boys followed. Stepping closer to Gene, Conner tapped him on the shoulder.

"Dad?" Conner hesitated. Gene slowed his pace.

"What?" he asked, staring into Conner's face.

"At the school after all the shooting, you didn't call me *soldier*. You called me *son* for the first time ever."

"I did, didn't I? Isn't that remarkable?"

"I think it's great, Dad."

"So do I," Gene agreed quickly. A smile on his face, Gene picked up the pace again. Conner and Wayne were laughing and joking behind him. Dropping farther back, Matt walked quietly in the shadows. At the base of Blood Mountain, moonlight reflected a sparkling glow off the flowing waters of the Juniata River. On Redemption Mountain across the river, the Flaming Cross blazed high and bright in the darkness.

After dropping Wayne off at Polecat Hollow, Gene drove down River Road. When he neared the house, he saw two cars parked in the lane. In the glare of the jeep's headlights, Skippy and SenSay were barking and chasing a tall figure in the middle of the road. Holding onto Skippy, Jeffery laughed and waved. There was the soft music of *Lucille*, and a familiar figure waved from the porch. Gene stopped the jeep; Conner jumped up in his seat.

"It's Mom!" Conner shouted, leaping out of the jeep. Gene shut off the motor and watched his son hurdle the steps into Lucy's outstretched arms.

"You took a fine time to return, Lucille," Gene whispered. Seeing his family safe on the porch, seeing the happiness on their faces, Gene lowered his head and wept. A cool breeze blew from the river; the North Star glittered in the night sky.

Matt stepped out of the jeep and started walking across the yard. When Jeffery saw him, he approached slowly and reached out his hand. Matt hesitated. Seconds passed. Lowering his head, Matt slid his hand under his shirt and traced his fingers over the green arrowhead. It was warm to the touch. Then looking up, his oval eyes beaming innocence, Matt grabbed Jeffery's hand and shook it enthusiastically. Skippy and SenSay filled the yard with their barking; the sounds of *Lucille* drifted through the air.

Andrew Brooks drove to the one-lane bridge outside Barree, saw the approaching headlights, and pulled to the side. The vehicle bumped across the bridge, and bright lights swept across the windshield. As the car went by, Andrew saw Green Hollow Correctional Camp written on the door.

"You can get up now," he said. There was movement in the backseat, and Lisa's face appeared in the rearview mirror.

"Where are we going, Mr. Brooks.?"

"My brother's house." Andrew drove across the bridge. "I'll tell him the whole story. I'll tell him about Luther and Max. He'll know what to do. He'll help us."

"How can he help us? Is he a judge or something?"

"He's a janitor," Andrew said, laughing at the look on Lisa's face. Driving slowly, he approached the house. Dogs were barking and chasing two figures in the middle of the road. Andrew saw Conner and Lucy on the porch; he saw Gene walking across the yard.

"Don't worry, Lisa," Andrew said. "It's just a family reunion." He parked the car behind the jeep and turned off the lights.

Chapter Thirty-Three

HO CHI MINH TRAIL, LAOS

1980

Captain Comrade Wan Sook was thirty-four years old. He finished buttoning his government uniform and looked at his reflection in the mirror. His skin was cracked and sunburned; there was a thin scar on his cheek.

Twenty-two years ago the Pathet Lao conscripted Wan Sook and six other boys from the village to work on the Ho Chi Minh Trail. Because he knew the area and was a good tracker, Wan Sook often patrolled with the white *farang* soldier. They had many successful trips. Whenever the *farang* added a *souvenir militaire* to his hemp belt, Wan Sook was appalled and would walk away. Then Comrade Chi came from Hanoi and ordered them to kill the Jungle Ghost. The *farang* was excited, and they smoked and drank and toasted the People's Army of Vietnam.

Two weeks after the celebration Wan Sook returned to camp as the lone survivor. The doctor bandaged his wound, and he was interrogated. On the second day, Comrade Chi handed the silver knives to Wan Sook and saluted him. There was a ceremony, and Wan Sook was promoted. Staring into the mirror, he smiled proudly.

Next to the mirror, the two silver knives were chained securely to the wall. Nodding his head, Wan Sook remembered the great struggle with the Jungle Ghost. He remembered the wound he received and how he escaped in the jungle. He remembered the courage he felt when he journeyed back to the clearing.

The blond hair of the *farang* soldier was a dark crimson. Wan Sook managed a brief smile when he saw the *souvenir militaire* stuffed in the *farang's* mouth. Red and white ivory handles perfectly vertical, two knives impaled the *farang* to the ground. Wan Sook stood motionless for a long time before he removed the knives.

"That day in the jungle when I fought the Jungle Ghost ..." Wan Sook muttered to himself. He slid his fingers tenderly the length of the scar. "On that day I took his weapons and I became a *phuyai*."

It was hot and muggy when Wan Sook walked to the porch. Balanced on the side of the mountain, his house was one of three. The other two were missing roofs and sections of wall. During the last monsoon season, the water and mud flowing down the side of the mountain had created deep gullies between the houses. There were no trees or any other signs of vegetation as far as Wan Sook could see.

Wan Sook got on his bicycle and pedaled down the path. After twenty minutes, he reached Route 6. There was a rickety food stand at the intersection, and Wan Sook bought a plastic bag of tea. Drinking the tea, he watched the line of trucks. Piled high with logs, they rumbled toward the Vietnamese border.

Captain Comrade Wan Sook finished his tea and continued down the road. More trucks raced past him. When he reached the immigration building, an old cement outpost the French had abandoned thirty years ago, Wan Sook was covered with dust.

There was a backup of eleven trucks at the building. Pushing his bicycle past the trucks, Captain Comrade Wan Sook listened to the complaints of the Vietnamese and Chinese drivers. Some made rude gestures. Taking his time, scraping the dust off his uniform, Wan Sook climbed the steps and unlocked the door. Going inside, he threw open the windows and latched them into place. Two more immigration police arrived. One of them sat at a desk and began stamping the stacks of government papers. The horns blared loudly from the trucks; the man looked up from his papers and glanced at Wan Sook.

"We believed things would be better after we were victorious. But now …"

"But now," Wan Sook continued in a bitter voice, "our comrades take the trees and destroy our forests. The monsoons wash away the rich soil. Nothing grows here."

Going outside, Wan Sook released the wooden barrier and swung the pole across the road. The truck engines burst into noise. The drivers moved across the speed bump, switched gears, and sped toward the three-story Vietnamese immigration building on the other side of the border. Comrade Captain Wan Sook watched them approach the newly painted, air-conditioned building. After money was exchanged and invoices were checked, the trucks turned north toward China.

"The last tree," Lee Chen said. Glancing upward, he strained to see through the thick canopy of branches. "And it's the biggest damn tree I have ever seen."

Black stumps and empty bomb craters dotted the mountainside. Sitting in the bulldozer with the motor under him cranking loudly, Lee Chen cursed silently. It was eleven o'clock, and already the Laotian laborers were leaving their implements in the dirt and walking to the makeshift shelter.

The midday sun scorched the barren landscape. The only noise came from the bulldozer and the blaring radio at the shelter. While a few Laotian workers were drinking, most of them were prone on grass mats. With beads of sweat pouring down his face, Lee Chen looked at the massive tree.

"Aie ha" he swore loudly. Taking a gulp of home-brewed *lao lao* from a green bottle, he kicked the bulldozer into gear. Iron plates spinning, the vehicle jerked forward and slammed into the trunk. The tree tilted; Lee Chen stomped on the pedal. As the blade sliced deeper into the bark, the tree trembled; dry branches broke loose and fell to the ground.

"Die!" Lee Chen shouted. "Die, tree-ghost. Die!" Lee Chen shrieked and nervously reached for the green bottle. The roar of the engine blasted the mountainside; the tree slanted downward. Lee Chen smiled and drank.

Walking slowly, burying the tip of his bowed crutch in the dust, a Buddhist priest stopped at the workers' shelter. He watched intently as the massive tree held firm and then began to straighten. Its motor grinding loudly, the bulldozer was pushed backward.

"Aie ha!" Lee Chen swore again and shifted gears. The bulldozer rammed into the trunk. The tree quaked violently. A branch hit the door of the bulldozer; a larger branch hit the windshield, splintering the glass. From the highest branch, a white object twisted free and ricocheted downward.

Lee Chen froze; the bleached skeletal head spun through the cracked glass and landed on the seat. Large blackened eye sockets glared at him. Squealing, Lee Chen kicked the door open and stumbled outside. A rib cage hit him in the face; Lee Chen took off running, tripped, and fell. A fierce moaning emanated from the inner recesses of the tree. The dozing workers jumped to their feet and pursued Lee Chen. Cowering, covering their ears, they collapsed next to him.

Emitting smoke and fire, the bulldozer surged forward and slammed against the massive trunk. The tree shook; outer branches quaked in the scorching sun. The weathered bindings unraveled; bones of variant lengths spun downward, hit the ground, and rattled to the bottom of the craters. The grinding motor belched black clouds of exhaust that shrouded the tree. When the dry wind blew, ghostly shadows drifted through the branches and soared upward before disappearing in the hazy blue sky.

A series of shrill cracks echoed across the desolate landscape; the myriad roots split. Dirt and wood fragments exploding in the air, the tree crashed to the earth. The bulldozer made a clunking noise and was quiet. In the eerie silence, a cloud of debris settled over the craters, covering the bones with dust and splintered wood fragments. The workers got to their feet and stumbled over the burial ground in disbelief. His feet wobbly, Lee Chen retrieved the green bottle from his pocket, lifted it to his mouth, and gulped the remaining *lao lao*.

Alone at the abandoned shelter, his orange robe tattered but resplendent, Pradit stood motionless and stared unblinking at the newly formed mounds of dirt. "Jungle Ghost," he whispered in a solemn voice. As the glare of the midday sun burned into his eyes, he lowered his head and wept.